D1082481

THE DULE TREE

THE SULLIVAN GRAY SERIES

H.P. BAYNE

BAYNE
INDEPENDENT
PUBLISHING

1

Dez Braddock hadn't seen it coming, the blow to the back of the head which sent him plummeting into darkness.

He awoke to pitch black and deafening silence, the ringing in his ears doing its best to fill the void.

His still-dazed brain began to keep time with his heart, thoughts spinning faster and faster. He tried to skirt past the one that nagged at him, the one telling him the throbbing injury to the base of his skull had caused so much damage he had lost the ability to see or hear.

Panic caused him to squirm, the sound of his own movement reaching his ears and pulling an unexpected laugh from his throat. It was enough to clear his brain, to get him reaching for his mobile phone within the chest pocket of his jacket. Steeling his nerves with a deep breath, he closed his eyes and moved the handset toward his face, hoping to make out the display once he'd clicked the home button. On the way up, his arm collided with something hard. He felt around with his free hand. Between the hard surface and his palm was a layer of slick fabric, like satin; its feel took him back to the touch of his wife's negligee, the one she'd worn on those nights that promised great things.

Now he sought comfort where he could find it, praying to a

God he no longer believed in as he manoeuvred the phone into a spot near his face, clicked the home button and slivered open one eye.

A second rush of relief hit as he took in the blessed sight of the display, a photo of the lake at sunset his daughter had programmed in the last time he'd seen her. The time read 10:24 p.m. Barely any time had passed since he'd started pursuing Raynor, since he'd first entered this ....

Cemetery.

The relief passed as quickly as it had come, his mind turning to his current predicament, to whatever it was he'd managed to step into this time. He could practically hear Eva's voice in his head, her tone reflecting her position as both wife and cop: "Damn it, Dez, you've got a brain. Learn to use it."

Too late to avoid the mess he was in, he hoped he could use his brain to find a way out. Thumbing in the phone's password, he was rewarded with a second photo his daughter Kayleigh had put onto his home screen. Naturally, it was one of herself. The seven-year-old smiled impishly from behind the apps she'd also installed, most of them ones he'd never learned to use. One was useful right now and he tapped the small square featuring a flashlight.

And immediately wished he hadn't.

The space around him lit up, nearly blinding him at first, the steady beam illuminating white satin. As his eyes adjusted, they took in the full horror of his situation, his heart back to pounding as he pushed against the surface above, finding it unmoving, himself sealed inside.

Not until this moment was he able to shift past the pain at the base of his skull, past the fear, to realize the discomfort the rest of him was in, wedged tight between two immovable objects, knees and shoulders pressed hard against the walls of his prison, head resting against something firm yet moveable. He knew what it was without looking, fought against the urge to turn his head. But he was unable to resist a look down toward his feet, bathed in the light from the flash and the pale satin. His heart pounded against his ribs. He saw not one pair of feet but two, the corpse's newly shined shoes resting against his own scuffed boots.

He resisted the urge to scream, a noise that sounded like a choked sob making its way from his throat instead. Kayleigh smiled on his phone's home screen, still smiling at him, dark ponytail defying gravity as she bounced on the trampoline he'd bought her for her last birthday. And he couldn't look anymore, couldn't face the possibility he wouldn't see her again.

Going into his contacts lists, he located Eva's number, hit the phone icon and waited.

Nothing.

He could see now there was no reception here, the tiny message at the top of the screen reading "No Service." He tried again anyway, waited until the phone stopped the call of its own accord.

Fighting the rising panic, he next tried to text Eva, not caring as his fingers fumbled over the on-screen keys, creating words no one would understand. She would know. If he could just get a message through to her, Eva would know.

He waited again, long enough to receive the message the delivery had failed.

With nothing left to do now but panic, he slipped deeply into it, hands pushing hard on the lid of the casket just inches from his face. Ramming his shoulder against it, as his hands made no impact. He shoved once, twice, three times. Reality trickled in with the sound and smell of soil sprinkling down the side of his tiny prison. The coffin wasn't locked or strapped shut.

It was buried.

He was underground, far enough down to render his mobile phone useless, trapped inside this small box, his only companion a dead man.

He knew what he should be doing with no air coming in. If he avoided further panicking, he likely had no more than twenty minutes of oxygen remaining. He had to do everything he could to conserve it, to allow Eva time to find him. He tried to ignore the reality she couldn't have any idea where he was; even if she realized something was wrong, she'd never get here in time.

No one would, even if he managed to buy himself every second he could. They had been alone in the cemetery, he and Raynor.

No one was coming.

He released the scream he'd been holding onto, the sound deafening in the enclosure, drowning out the satin-muffled pounding of his hands.

He had no idea how long it went on, his terror stealing precious seconds of air, replacing oxygen with poison. He'd passed being light-headed, was edging back into what he knew would soon be unconsciousness. He welcomed it, relished the idea of it, arms too tired now to strike as he sank into the space beside and above the emaciated body, his head finding as comfortable a spot as he could alongside the corpse's substantial nose. His breathing slowed as his eyelids fluttered shut, the sound of his pulse dull in his ears, muffled and yet persistent.

It must have been the lack of air playing with his brain that had him hearing what seemed to be two pulses now, his own and another coming oddly from above. The one beyond was a pace quicker, less even and yet no less constant, no less willing to give up on its life-sustaining rhythm.

It was going to have to give up. He certainly was.

His thoughts turned to his daughter, and he considered how Eva was going to have to break the news to her, the little girl he doted on, the little girl he didn't deserve. Would never deserve. There was no taking back the past, after all.

And yet, here he was, hearing the past in his head, the voice of his baby brother, forever five, echoing across time and space.

"Hold on, Dez. It isn't time. Please hold on. It isn't your time."

They were not the words of a five-year-old, and yet there was no mistaking the source. He heard Aiden's name on his lips, breathed it out like a prayer, the whisper of the word reverberating in his brain long after the sound had died in his ears.

"Dez, hold on. Sully's coming. Just hold on for Kayleigh. Sully's coming."

His brain caught on the name Sully, wondering what it meant that the little boy had uttered the name of Dez's foster brother, whose own grave had been added to this same cemetery two years ago. But the question fell away as he settled into the feeling of the long-lost voice, Aiden's presence, so palpable, so close he felt as if the child might be a solid presence lying there beside him.

He drifted again, his brother's voice no longer enough to draw him back. As the darkness folded around his body, enveloping him in warm nothingness, he felt both lifted up and dragged down.

A sound like thunder broke through, replacing the encroaching void with something substantial and firm, something that left no doubt it was part of the mortal world.

He initially fought to remain in that warm, dark place, where Aiden wasn't confined to videotape and memory. Hands—he knew they were hands—tugged on his shoulders, urged him into consciousness, pulled him from the brink. They swept aside the fog from his muddled brain as he made the unwilling trek into consciousness and the horrors he knew he would find there.

But it wasn't a satin-lined prison and a deceased cellmate he saw greeting him; it was a lean, hooded figure crouched on top of the casket, hands holding Dez up to sitting. Above the hooded figure, just visible in the light of the moon cresting the edge of the grave, the shape of a large dog peered down at him. The sound of canine panting mixed with the nighttime noise of crickets and a breeze rattling the branches of the cemetery trees.

He considered for a moment he might have gone farther down than he'd thought. "Is that a hellhound?" he asked, voice a croak.

"What?" The hushed voice from the hooded figure was not

what he'd expected from Death, masculine but not deep, human rather than demonic.

More than that, it sounded familiar.

"This isn't hell?"

The reply came in the form of an almost whispered, "That's a matter of perspective."

The hooded male helped Dez crawl out of the casket and it was somewhere between there and standing on solid ground that his senses fully returned, bringing with them a rush of emotion and nausea. He fell to his knees and vomited violently to the side of the grave, a hand against a pile of displaced dirt all that kept him from falling face-first into the mess.

He heard movement around him, the closing of the coffin lid, the shifting of fabric and earth as the hooded male pulled himself out of the grave, the pelting of stone and soil back onto the casket.

"Wait," Dez managed around a couple of heaving breaths. "My phone. I need my phone. I have to—"

A hand landed briefly on his shoulder, long enough to draw his attention to the smartphone on the ground near him, flash side down, just a couple feet from the large black dog. Ignoring the animal for now, Dez grabbed his handset, hit the home button and was rewarded with a glimpse of that lake. A few more clicks had him looking down at the smiling face of his little girl.

He couldn't resist the giddy laugh. "I'm not dead?"

"No."

Dez struggled to his feet, considered he should be helping his saviour re-bury the dead guy. He shut off the flashlight, dropped his phone into his pocket and moved to help, but was stopped by a hand on his arm. Straightening, he was surprised to find he had a good five or six inches on the other male. He'd expected his rescuer to be gargantuan in proportion rather than six feet and lean bordering on skinny. The guy swam in his clothes, a pair of baggy cargo pants and a dark hooded sweatshirt tucked beneath an army jacket, both clearly a few sizes too big. The hood, which Dez had initially mistaken for a cloak or a robe, was still up, forming a halo for the strands of long hair concealing the man's face in shadow.

"I've got this," the guy muttered, the near-whisper again striking Dez as one he'd heard before. "Get out of here."

"I can help."

"I don't need any."

Dez helped anyway, kicking dirt into the grave for the time it took to rebury the casket. They worked in silence, both huffing with exertion and exhaustion. Dez expected some sort of conversation at the end, was shocked when the other male simply whistled for his dog to come and started away from the grave, away from Dez.

He reached out, grabbing hold of the guy's arm, and was instantly met by a light warning growl from the dog. He released the man, but did what he could to hold him with a question. "Did you get a look at the guy who put me down there, enough to provide a statement to police?"

The man didn't turn to face him as he provided a one-word answer. "No."

Damn. "What's your name?"

The man's head turned slightly, the moonlight catching just a hint of his profile. "Does it matter?"

"You saved my life. Yeah, it matters."

There was no reply, leaving Dez to fill the void.

"I'm Desmond Braddock .... I don't know you, do I?"

"Goodbye, Desmond." The male took a step to leave, and Dez was unable to stop himself from grabbing ahold of him again. This time, he jerked him a little too hard, causing him to spin, the hood to fall away and the shaggy veil of pale brown hair to shift. The dog barked, but Dez's attention was locked onto the face of the young man rather than the potentially dangerous animal at his side.

"Oh my God," Dez whispered as the light of the moon and scattering of cemetery lamps revealed hints of the other man's face, concealed behind the remaining curtain of hair and unkempt beard. It was the eyes—the slightly more visible right one, anyway—that revealed the truth, that and the finely shaped nose and cheekbones. Two years had passed since he'd set eyes on him, but a decade and a half had made him an expert on Sullivan "Sully" Gray.

Sully put up what fight he could but was deftly taken to the ground by Dez, whose mental exhaustion had cleared with the return of both precious oxygen and his brother. Another low growl emanated from the dog, but it didn't attack like Dez had anticipated, despite the fact its master was struggling futilely next to the resealed grave, pinned beneath the weight of the larger male. After a minute or so of useless fighting, Sully went more or less limp in his brother's grasp.

Dez used the defeat to sweep the remaining hair from the younger man's face, needing absolute certainty before allowing himself to give in fully to the joy and confusion of the inexplicable reunion.

"Sully?"

"Yeah, Dez, it's me. Let me up."

The sound of the voice, spoken now at normal volume and tone, was the final proof he needed. Dez jumped up and staggered backward as if attempting to escape another corpse.

"I was there when the cave collapsed. They told us no one could have gotten out. We held a funeral for you, damn near spitting distance from here."

Sully rose to his feet, eyes pinned to Dez's as he kept his own expression guarded. "I know. I was there."

"Where?"

Sully angled his chin toward the treed edge of the cemetery, visible just beyond the far row of lamps that lit the bordering driving paths. "In the trees."

"Watching?"

Sully nodded. "Hardest thing I ever had to do."

"Hardest thing *you've* ever …." Dez let the parroted statement go midway, the rage rising unexpectedly and channeling itself into his fists. He barely saw it coming himself as he unleashed his fury in one solid punch, laying his brother out on the ground.

Sully lay there a moment before balancing himself on one elbow, cupping his jaw in his free hand and testing it cautiously before quirking up one side of his mouth in a smile. "Still pulling your punches for me, bro."

The raised eyebrow and warm smile were pure Sully, had Dez extending a hand and hauling his brother up in one fluid move-ment. He didn't let go until the smaller man was encased in a hug tight enough to restrict breathing. Dez ignored the fact he could feel Sully's ribs even through the jacket, and the smell that suggested the guy hadn't managed a shower in at least two weeks. Right now, all that mattered was his brother—a man who had shared everything with him but blood—was back.

At long last, he held Sully at arm's length, casting an appraising eye over him. "You look like hell, kiddo."

Sully chuckled, the sound ending in a lingering grin. "Damn good to see you, Dez."

He pulled away and turned, and Dez realized Sully didn't mean to stay. "Where are you going?"

"Away."

"You're going to have to do better than that."

Sully turned partway, enough to meet his brother's eye. "I can't."

"Listen, man, judging by the look, feel and smell of you, I'm going to take an educated guess and say you don't have anywhere to go. You can come home with me, all right? Maybe then you can fill me in on what the hell you've been doing the past two years."

"Dez, I can't. It's not safe."

"Hey. It's me. You always said there was no one you trusted more to have your back."

"I didn't mean it's not safe for me. I meant it's not safe for you."

Dez took a step forward, worried this was going to come

down to another battle. He wasn't prepared to let Sully go. Not now, not until he had some answers, not until he knew his brother was safe. "Let me decide what's best for me. You look exhausted, you're clearly not eating properly and you're as weak as a kitten. You barely gave me a fight a minute ago. Never mind the fact you need a shower and a change of clothes like right now."

"Dez—"

"Don't. Don't even say it. I'm not taking no for an answer. If you wanna go toe to toe with me on this, I'm good to go, man. But I promise you, you'll be leaving this cemetery unconscious and over my shoulder. I'd rather we walk out together."

Sully was quiet and Dez could see his brother studying him, looking for signs of a bluff. But he was far from bluffing and it took Sully little time to understand.

Thankfully, for both of them, he chose option two.

2

THE DULL ACHE at the base of Dez's skull proved a steady reminder he had suffered a head injury.

So as the city moved past the window of his SUV, he caught himself stealing sideways glances at his passenger to assure himself he hadn't hallucinated Sully's return.

His brother had yet to disappear, was still sitting there, face turned toward his window as he watched the night-lit city sweeping past. Things had changed since Dez last saw Sully. Kimotan Rapids—better known to residents as KR—had never quite recovered from the devastating flood four years back, leading to a loss of businesses and homes and a swath of once-productive citizens on the unemployment lines. While that seemed to result in better-than-average business for the city's drinking establishments, not all had fared as well.

Sully noticed what Dez expected he might.

"The Black Fox is gone?"

Dez looked to the boarded-up front that once provided entry to the pub Sully had helped manage on behalf of its owner, Dez's uncle Lowell.

"Yeah. Not long after Betty died and you ...." He paused, considering his words, uncertain now how best to phrase it.

"After you left. People used to joke the pub couldn't survive without the two of you."

Sully's answer was spoken through a smile. "I don't know whether to be touched or troubled by that."

Dez bristled. "I said *people* used to joke. Not me. I haven't exactly been in the laughing mood for the past couple of years."

"I didn't mean it like that. I'm sorry, D. I really am."

He'd kept his eyes on the road, but the sound of Sully's response suggested he'd turned to face him, smile gone.

The mix of emotions he'd experienced upon reuniting with Sully returned full-force, and Dez bit his tongue to keep from saying something he'd regret. Blessedly, Sully allowed him the conversational space, focusing a moment on scratching at his dog's head as it protruded between them from the back seat.

The questions were there, and plenty of them, poking around inside begging for release. He debated exactly how he felt, how he should feel, about Sully's sudden return from the dead. There was anger, the sting of betrayal by someone who had once sought his advice on every key decision, someone who knew him and his pain-stricken past well enough to realize what his leaving in that way would do.

But mixed up in the simmering anger was an equally intense sense of gleeful relief, a feeling of the clouds parting after two steady years of rain. Sully was family; Dez didn't deny he'd cast Sully into the void left by Aiden, plugging up the brother-shaped hole in his heart as much as grief and time would allow.

Sully said nothing. But the silence broke when Dez took a left onto Endlin Road, setting a course that would take them into the older section of the downtown core, the part the respectable public avoided by night.

"Where are we going?"

God, they had a lot to talk about. "I told you. Home."

"What happened to the place in Gladstone?"

"It's still there. So is Eva. I've got a lovely little dive on Twenty-fifth."

"Hold on. So you and Eva …?"

"Split up over a year ago. I left her with the house and every-thing in it. Just 'cuz she and I are done doesn't mean I want Kayleigh to suffer for it."

"Jesus. I'm sorry, man. Is Kayleigh with Eva full-time then?"

"I visit, take her out on weekends. Obviously, I don't bring her back to my place."

"And that's enough for you? Your world revolves around that kid."

"I know, all right? Which is why I'm not fighting Eva on this. Kayleigh deserves the best and I can't give it to her right now. I'm man enough to know that."

"That sucks, D."

"Don't I know it."

"How is she? Kayleigh, I mean?"

"She's good. You know kids, they're resilient. Misses her Uncle Sully though. I'll take you to see her this weekend. Better let me ease them into it first, though. They're going to be on the floor, seeing you."

"Dez, no one can know about me, all right? I can't stay."

"Like hell."

"I can't, man. I can't stay."

Dez's hands gripped the wheel a little tighter. "If you think you're going anywhere until you've given me some answers, you're in for an unpleasant surprise."

Sully sighed, the sound as old as their relationship, a tell he hadn't forgotten there was no point arguing.

"I'll tell you what I can," he said. "What do you want to know?"

"We've got a hell of a lot of ground to cover, you and me, so let's start easy. How'd you know I was in trouble tonight? Did you see Raynor put me down there?'"

"Raynor? Forbes Raynor?"

"I take it that's a no."

"I saw someone running from the cemetery, but I didn't think it was him. Why? What kind of beef does he have with you that you think he'd try to kill you?"

"Uh-uh. You first. How'd you know I needed help?"

Sully went back to staring out the window. "How do you think?"

The answer sent a chill down Dez's spine. He knew what Sully could do. Any doubts he might have once harboured had washed away years ago by the conviction with which Sully had always described the things he witnessed. It was impossible to explain away the extent of the silent terror in the child's eyes and, with time and experience, the muted but continued alarm that turned Sully's face into a pale, wide-eyed stone. Dez had taken his cues from his brother, finding plenty to fear in what, for him, was an unseen world. And while Sully's fear of the dead had abated for the most part as he moved into adulthood, Dez's was still very much present and accounted for.

Sully wasn't looking at Dez, but apparently sensed his brother's widened eyes on him nonetheless. "Watch the road."

"I thought you stopped seeing them."

"I did for a while, but they came back once I was out of Lockwood. I wasn't sure I wanted to tell you."

"Why not?"

"Seriously? This stuff always scared the hell out of you."

"Hey, man, I can deal with it, okay?"

"So it doesn't bother you there's a dead woman sitting in your backseat right now?"

Dez's eyes flew to his rear view mirror but just as quickly returned to the road as he realized he didn't actually want to see for himself. "Jesus! What?"

"See? You still can't handle it. Anyway, I was kidding. All that's back there is Pax."

Dez smacked Sully on the head, drawing a laugh from the younger man. "Damn it, Sull. You're a jerk, you know that?"

As Dez's heart rate coasted back to some version of normal, it occurred to him he had no choice but to wade back into the world of the dead.

"So the cemetery tonight. Who was it you saw?"

Sully fell back into silence, this time putting Dez in the position of having to wait. Dez had known Sully a long time, since he was ten and Sully seven, the two of them raised as brothers from that point on. It didn't take any work for Dez to sense the turmoil radiating off Sully now.

Though he'd been waiting on an answer, he didn't expect the one that came, two softly spoken words nailing him like a fist in the gut.

"Your brother."

Dez's foot reacted of its own accord, slamming down on the brake and sending the dog's nose into the back of Sully's shoulder. The canine emitted an indignant yip as Dez threw the vehicle into park and turned to face his passenger.

"You saw Aiden?"

"He came to me, led me to you. That's how I knew you were down there, that you were in trouble."

"How do you know it was him?"

"I've seen his photo a million times, Dez. I grew up surrounded by them, and you carry one in your wallet everywhere you go."

Dez's thoughts revolved at breakneck speed, rolling over each other as he grasped the full meaning of what Sully had told him. In the end, it all came down to one thing.

"But you …. Sull, you only see them if they've been murdered."

Sully dipped his head. "If they've died before their time." The correction was weak.

But Dez's memory had not faded, his recollection of Sully's ability as sharp as it had been in the days immediately after he'd first learned of it.

"No. You said you only see them if someone killed them."

"Dez—"

"Are you telling me someone killed Aiden?"

Sully finally met his brother's eye, and the emotion held there —straddling a line between worry and sympathy—told Dez how wild he must appear right now. He'd made efforts to bury his grief, but the grave had been a shallow one, the emotions it held easily disinterred with any mention of Aiden's name. Dez knew he'd been shaped by the childhood tragedy, appreciated the loyalty he held for the people he loved and the need to keep them safe had been born of that summer day when they'd found Aiden's tiny body caught up in the reeds that bordered the Kettle-Arm.

He had yet to receive full answer to his last question and, while he wasn't sure he really wanted one, he knew he needed one.

"Sully?"

"I don't know that, okay?"

"Can't you ask him?"

"You know it doesn't work like that with me. I can't hear them, and there's no way I can just demand answers. They appear to me when they want to, not the other way around."

"If someone hurt him, I have to know. I *have* to know, man. If something bad happened to him, I need to get justice for him. Mom needs that. I need that."

"I don't know if I can help. He didn't say anything to me."

The panic took a backseat as memory returned—the voice that had spoken to him less than an hour ago. "But he said something to me."

This time it was Sully's voice holding surprise. "What?"

"When I was down there, and the air was running low, I started thinking how easy it would be to just let go, just go to sleep and not wake up. Then I heard Aiden's voice. He told me to hold on, that you were coming. It felt so real, like he was right there."

Sully smiled. "That's because he was."

Building heat in Dez's eyes had him turning away from Sully, facing the windshield where the yet-unshed tears could be kept as private as possible. Sully said nothing more, allowing Dez the moment to recompose himself, to force the tears away through a focus on the mechanical as he put the SUV back into drive and pulled onto the roadway.

"We aren't finished with this, Sull."

Sully went back to staring out the window. "I know."

DEZ PULLED into a parking spot off the back alley behind the Golden Hand Pawn, pulling the keys from the ignition and waiting until Sully and his dog had joined him on the cracked pavement before locking the vehicle. Flipping through his keys until he found the right one, Dez led the way through a security door and up a narrow flight of stairs to the top floor of the two-storey brick.

"You live above a pawn shop?"

"After paying child support, I don't exactly have enough left over to buy myself a condo in the Regal Towers. Don't worry, it's a dump but it's got everything a guy needs."

"It's a palace next to some of the places I've laid my head."

Dez spared him a glance before stopping at a door, one of four suites on the upper floor, this one facing the street. Ordinarily, a street view would beat overlooking an alley, but the difference was negligible in this part of town.

His bachelor suite, neither large nor comfortable enough for anyone besides himself, provided ample reason not to entertain company. With little room to play with, furniture was sparse, the largest consisting of a pull-out sofa and a kitchen table. The unit itself hadn't been redecorated since the 1970s, with the faded orange carpet, the olive green fridge and stove, and the rust-hued kitchen floor peeling in more places than just the borders.The one concession was a fresh coat of paint, and Dez had no desire to improve on the place in any other way. Utilitarian rather than homey, the apartment was somewhere most people would stay a month while looking for something better.

Not in Dez's case, though, no boxes or suitcases left unpacked and everything in its place with military precision. Having determined this was all he could afford on his savings were he to allow financial space for supporting Kayleigh and his drinking habit, Dez had put up a few photos of his family and made the place as much of a home as it would allow.

"Nice place," Sully said.

Dez snorted. "You've always been a crap liar, Sull."

The dog whined, drawing their attention to him.

"I don't suppose you have anything to feed Pax, huh?" Sully asked. "He hasn't eaten since this morning."

"I'm sure I can find something for him. You too, for that matter."

"He's fine with whatever I'm eating. I don't usually have a lot to spend most days, either."

Dez crossed to the fridge and rummaged through the contents. "I can do up some grilled cheese. I've got to do a grocery run pretty quick."

"Don't do it on my account. I'll stay the night but I've got to head out first thing."

"Bullshit, you're heading out."

"I am. I have to."

Dez turned and faced him, convinced his expression showed every ounce of the big brother he'd become to Sully all those years back. Dez had fallen into the role quickly and naturally, bestowing on Sully the same verbal and visual expressions he'd once reserved for Aiden. He knew the one he was wearing now shouted, "Over my dead body."

And despite the time that had passed, Sully moved immediately back into his old role. Dez knew the lack of argument meant Sully's brain was searching silently for the words that would change his brother's mind.

There were none existing in the English language, and Dez

stifled any attempt his brother might make by pointing him toward the cramped bathroom.

"Not that much I own is going to fit your tiny ass, but I'll see what I have," Dez said. "We can find you something better at the secondhand place down the road tomorrow. That stuff you're wearing should be burned."

Sully smiled. "That's really kind of the point when you're trying to stay invisible on the streets."

He closed the door before Dez could ask any additional questions. There would be time for those soon enough.

WHEN SULLY RE-EMERGED, with damp hair hanging in strings around the shoulders of a baggy T-shirt, and a pair of drawstring pyjama pants rolled up at the cuffs, a plate of grilled cheese waited at the table next to an expectant Dez. Pax had a couple sandwiches of his own, and the dog was lying contentedly at Dez's feet, allowing the man to rub his ears.

Sully raised his eyebrows. "He likes you."

"Why wouldn't he?"

"Pax is pretty choosy in his company. He's not much of a people dog."

"Well, I haven't been much of a people person lately, so I guess he and I have an understanding." Dez scanned Sully's body now, drowning as it was in his clothes. "Damn, Sull, how much weight have you lost?"

"No idea. A bit, I guess."

"Well, you can start working on that with these sandwiches while you fill me in."

Sully sat down and picked up half a grilled cheese, talking around the bite. "So what do you want to know?"

"Gee, I don't know. How about where the hell you've been for the last two years? Why you decided to fake your own death and leave me out of the loop? And you can tell me how I sort out what happened to Aiden."

"We could be up all night with all that."

"Or we could go to bed now and deal with it in the morning."

"Dez ...."

"Never mind. I'm not arguing the point. Let's start with what the hell you were thinking, letting me believe you were dead. How could you put me through that?"

"I hated doing it, Dez. I really did. But it was better than the alternative."

"You mean the one where I wouldn't have spent months drinking myself to sleep at night? That alternative?"

"I thought you'd be okay, man. You had Eva and Kayleigh and your mom. You had your career."

"So you figured, what, I'd just wake up the day after the funeral and magically be all right? That I'd just forget about you and get on with things like nothing ever happened? You're my family, Sull. Burying you, it was like .... It was like Aiden all over again. Only it was worse, because I was there when it happened. I saw it. I felt it. Hell, I relived it every single night for months after. It nailed me, man. And I've lost everything because of it."

Sully's tanned cheeks paled a shade. "What do you mean you've lost everything?"

Dez didn't spare the details, hitting Sully with full truth. "I fell apart. I hit the bottle hard, and everything else took a backseat. My job was the first thing to go. I narrowly avoided losing it for helping you escape, but I got canned after Raynor caught me at a bar during shift and confronted me. I narrowly missed being hammered with a criminal assault charge over that episode. My marriage tanked not long after. For damn near a full year, Eva tried to see me through it, but I was too far gone. She finally hit the breaking point and kicked me out, said she wasn't going to let Kayleigh know me like that. I didn't argue. I knew she was right. I was a crap husband and a crap father. I wasn't good to anyone anymore, not like that. So, you want to tell me again how you playing dead was supposed to be okay for me?"

Sully's mouth had dropped open slightly and he shut it, looking down at his knees in a way that allowed Dez to see the guilt as easily as if the younger man had voiced it. And as angry as Dez had felt a moment ago, it faded fast as his own guilt took its place. There were things he knew about Sully, things he'd learned over the years, and it had made him plenty protective of his foster brother and continually vigilant about his physical and psychological well-being. When the two of them were kids, Dez had blackened the eye of a kid who'd put that expression on Sully's face, so even now, years on, he couldn't handle being the one to put it there.

His chair creaked under him as he sat forward, closing a hand over Sully's forearm. "Hey, Sull. Forget it. I'm talking out of my ass. I'm sure you had your reasons."

"I thought it would keep you safe. I didn't mean to …."

"Keep me safe from what, Sull?"

"From exactly the sort of thing that happened tonight."

"That had nothing to do with you."

"So what then? Why would someone do that to you?"

"You know Raynor."

"Sure. He's a jerk, but he was never homicidal."

"He's gone off the rails recently, man. I guess we all have. Let's get back to you. What's going on?"

"Nothing's changed. There are people who want me, people who won't stop if they know I'm alive. I thought maybe they'd gotten to you tonight."

"People from Lockwood, you mean?"

Dez saw the flinch, the muscles in Sully's face jumping involuntarily under the name as if it had come with a physical impact. Dez chastised himself inwardly and gave Sully's arm a little shake to draw him back.

"Hey, you're not going back there, all right? You didn't belong there and you still don't."

"Not everyone believes that."

"They don't know you. Hey, Lockwood probably does some good work for the people who need it, but—"

"There's nothing good about that place. It's hell. The things they did …."

"You don't have to remind me. I know it was hell for you. That's why I got you out. You didn't have to fake your own death to escape it, man. I would have protected you, still will."

"If the rest of the world thinks I'm crazy, it's going to take more than you to convince them otherwise."

Sully had yet to meet Dez's eyes, but Dez was convinced his overly intuitive brother had to know he was being carefully scrutinized. Sully had left Lockwood Psychiatric Hospital on a pass in Dez's care to attend the two-months'-delayed burial service for their father. He'd been due back the next day but Dez, having spent the time observing his brother, took matters into his own hands. He'd gathered just enough information about Sully's experience at the institution to ensure staff would have to crawl over his dead body to get his brother back.

Instead, two weeks later, it was Sully's dead body he'd been standing over. Or so he'd thought.

Sully had gone to extremes to fully escape the place, but his physical salvation clearly hadn't equated to mental freedom as Dez watched the thoughts play out over his face, his memory taking him unwillingly back through the rooms and corridors of Lockwood.

Or maybe there was something else, something Dez had yet to learn.

He broke into Sully's thoughts carefully, quietly. "There's more to it, isn't there? This was never just about you going to extremes to hide from a mental health warrant and the likelihood of going back to that place. There's something you haven't told me."

Sully at last lifted his eyes to Dez's. "I'm really tired, Dez. Can we do this tomorrow?"

"Does that mean you'll stick around without me having to resort to force?"

Sully smiled. "Yeah. For now. You've got a right to some truth here."

"Tell me one thing. These people looking for you, the ones you said weren't going to stop. We are talking about Lockwood, right?"

"If I had all the answers, I could probably find a way to stop running."

Dez gave his arm a solid pat and released him. "Then we're going to find those answers."

3

For a few hours, it was like coming home.

There had been many nights in the past two years—more if he counted the hellish months he'd spent at Lockwood—Sully had managed sleep only by conjuring up memories of his years growing up in the Braddock house, imagining he could hear Dez's snoring nearby.

As he awoke in a darkened room to the sound of his brother's noisy breaths, Sully had to remind himself of the reality of the moment, to wait until his brain fully cleared of sleep. Only then could he grasp that Dez was a solid form next to him and not merely a conjured image standing guard against the loneliness in which he'd been forced to dwell.

He could barely make Dez out in the darkness, a large, black shape outlined in the orange glow filtering in through the window from the streetlight outside. But there was no mistaking the sound or the feeling.

Sully had never known a home until the Braddocks had taken him in, and it had been the hardest thing to give up. He hadn't intended this reunion, had planned on staying away forever if need be. But the tiny vision of Aiden with panic in his eyes and a radiating pain based in the present and not the past, had brought

Sully running straight back to his old life. Now, here he was, all but trapped between his brother and the wall, between the life he wished he could have and the one to which he needed to return.

There would be no way to explain it to Dez, none he would accept anyway. He had promised to stay until morning, to provide Dez with the explanation he wanted, needed and deserved, despite the difficult situation it would create. Because the longer he stayed, and the more he shared, the smaller his chances of getting out. Settling back into any vestige of his old life would make it increasingly difficult to leave it behind once again.

At this point, he knew his best means of escape were either to leave now while Dez was in the midst of deep sleep or wait until tomorrow night and hope the truths laid at Dez's feet wouldn't be enough to keep him awake and prevent Sully's leaving.

Then the decision was made for him.

He felt her before he saw her, a feeling almost as familiar to him as Dez's presence. She stood just this side of the window, but though she should have been backlit by the streetlights, she was fully visible as if bathed in a glow from within.

Her image had once terrified him, the blood soaking the side of her pale, teenaged face and caked in dyed-purple hair around a wound near her left temple. And it hadn't been lost on him that each time he saw her, something bad was sure to follow. He'd formerly blamed her for the traumas of his earlier years. But age and wisdom had helped him see the truth; she was simply a harbinger foretelling the imminent approach of something terrible, allowing him—once he learned to listen to her wordless warnings—to take steps to avoid the fall.

So after years of sporadically encountering the nameless ghost he knew only as the Purple Girl, Sully was left in no doubt as to what he needed to do.

He had to leave. Now.

Sully fell back on years of experience and sleepless study to take him, with stealthy, practiced movements, out of his spot next to the wall, had him up and out with more ease than he suspected most could have managed. He'd been careful to study the floors last night, had paid careful attention to the creak at the juncture of kitchen and living area, and so avoided that spot as he stripped off the loaned pyjamas and exchanged them for his own street-scented clothing.

A wave of guilt crashed over Sully as he studied the shadowed form of Dez, still sleeping hard. Judging by the dark circles under his eyes last night, the guy hadn't managed a proper sleep in quite some time, and there was little doubt Dez's current state of comfortable slumber was thanks in large part to Sully's return.

Sully struggled to ignore the inevitable turmoil morning would bring for his brother as he placed the borrowed PJs onto the dresser. He turned, forcing his gaze past Dez's face to Pax's, signalling to the dog with a hand flattened toward the floor.

Pax heeded the silent command, lifting slowly to his feet and staying low as he padded across the floor to Sully's side.

The Purple Girl was by the door now, eyes directing him where voice could not, and he followed as she passed through the wall. Sully opened the door wide enough to allow Pax to slip into the hall before him.

The hinges caught as he sought to accommodate his own exit, creaking noisily until he stilled the door in his grip. His breath hitched as Dez, mere feet away, released his own and rolled over on the pullout. Sully studied his brother's form long enough to realize he was no longer watching for signs of waking, but rather memorizing this scene, one he expected would both shelter and curse him in times to come.

At last, Dez once again still and peaceful in unknowing sleep, Sully slipped into the hall and eased the door shut behind him.

SULLY's earliest memory of the Purple Girl dated back to the year before he started school, and he wouldn't be surprised if she predated even that, if she'd been a part of his life even before he had the capacity to recall. She'd been a terrifying presence to him back then, pallor and blood and a set of huge, kohl-rimmed eyes staring at him with such intensity, he was convinced she could see rather than simply hear his heart thumping against his chest wall.

As the first ghost he'd encountered, her silence had been nearly as frightening as her appearance, leaving him cowering beneath his covers while his brain spun with unasked and unanswered questions. And, although his fear had dwindled with age and better understanding, he had yet to learn what she wanted from him.

Except, if he were to guess, erring on the side of hope and experience, she wanted him to live and to stay safe.

Looking back, the turning point had come during his stay at a foster home in McCoy Falls, a small community downstream from Kimotan Rapids. He'd lived there nearly a year, his last placement before he'd been blessed with the Braddocks.

That foster home had been a nightmare, Mr. Blake a man slow to show compassion and patience but plenty quick with a belt, while his horny teenage son practiced his skills on the girls the family took in. Only Mrs. Blake was decent, although Sully had never fully forgiven her tendency to turn a blind eye to her loved ones' sins.

So Sully had felt remarkably little on the night of the fire.

To this day, he had no idea what had woken him, but he recalled snapping his eyes open to the sight of the Purple Girl hovering over him. The intense expression of dread on her face had probably rivalled his own.

He smelled smoke, saw it seeping beneath his closed bedroom door. Sully woke Brennan in the next bed, the only other foster kid staying there at the time, and began to tug the sluggish teenager toward the door.

The Purple Girl blocked his path, materializing so suddenly he fell down on his backside. The room was filling with smoke, so Sully, regaining his feet, dared to take another step toward the door. But she wouldn't budge, and he sure as hell wasn't about to try to move through her.

He took the only other path he could, towing a panicked Brennan toward the window.

The two boys took shelter beneath an elm tree in a park across the road as fire crews fought the blaze. Sully watched as Mr. Blake stepped through the front door, untouched by flame, and stared down at his own smoke-blackened corpse, pulled from the living room by firefighters. Sully averted his eyes, hoping Mr. Blake would not notice him, would not realize Sully saw something no one else could. Thankfully, Mr. Blake was too busy watching his house burn, staring down in disbelief at his own body and running back and forth like a madman as he yelled wordlessly at crews to save his wife and son. But the men couldn't hear him and, regardless, there was nothing they could do, no way they could attempt to re-enter that inferno.

Sully heard later they'd found the other two Blakes inside the next day, once the scene had cooled enough to do a full search. By then, Sully and Brennan had been thoroughly questioned as suspects, seven-year-old Sully reduced to tears by a particularly enthusiastic interrogator until then-Staff Sergeant Flynn Braddock came down to the interview rooms and put a stop to it.

They later charged a teenager with the arson, a disturbed girl who claimed to have suffered abuse at the hands of both Blake males. Sully never learned what had happened to her, although he'd heard rumblings she spent some time at Lockwood.

Looking back on it now, what really stuck with him wasn't the arsonist, or even the charred body of Mr. Blake or his frantic, confused ghost. It was the presence of the Purple Girl, and the suspicion that had she not blocked their path to the door, Sully and Brennan would have joined the Blakes.

So even now, Sully suspected she was trying to protect him as she led him further and further from Dez's, leaving Sully to question what danger she foresaw that he didn't.

Which spawned a new question, one that had him turning and

running back across Endlin Road, back toward Twenty-Fifth: if she was trying to draw him from danger, where did that leave Dez?

Sully sprinted down Twenty-Fifth with Pax at his heels, the two of them narrowly avoiding a collision with a delivery van as they dashed across an intersecting street. The Purple Girl wasn't giving up, positioning herself in his path at virtually every turn, providing an obstacle he was forced to duck around as he worked to close the gap she'd placed between him and his brother.

No movement was visible at Dez's building once he arrived, out of breath with a panting dog and a frantic dead girl next to him. Sully was about to head to the back door and the buzzer system he recalled seeing last night when his brain kicked in above his pounding heart. Would he really be doing Dez any favours by returning now? Sully knew Dez, knew if he were in immediate danger, he would be putting up one hell of a fight, one Sully would hear from the street—and a man who towered over most people and packed some incredibly solid muscle on that imposing frame would give anyone a run for their money.

Sully hung back, deciding the better option was to keep a watch on the place, make sure no visitors to the building triggered his instincts. If any suggestion pointed to Dez might becoming a further target, Sully would go in and provide what help he could.

Patting his leg as an indication for Pax to follow, Sully jogged across Twenty-Fifth, having spotted an alley he thought would provide enough shadow and cover to keep him out of sight, both to Dez and to anyone who might come calling.

There, he hunkered between a dumpster and a stack of discarded boxes, and waited.

WHEN THEY'D BEEN KIDS, Sully had often sought refuge with Dez from the horrific memories of his past and the often-terrifying visitors only he could see. Dez had willingly allowed the trembling, wild-eyed kid to climb into bed with him, had spent many a night talking and telling stories until the shaking gave way to sleep, so that when morning came, it wasn't unusual for Dez's mom to find the two of them sleeping peacefully side by side.

Despite the time that had passed and the fact they didn't fit so easily into a double-sized pullout as they once would have, Dez had found comfort in the familiar. He'd slept more soundly than he had in years without the aid of alcohol to rock him into oblivion.

But every silver lining held onto a cloud, and this one covered a sky that had temporarily cleared with Sully's return.

Dez had slept on the outside edge of the pullout, having tugged his late grandmother's patchwork quilt over and around himself, one foot free and braced against the floor to prevent an accidental fall. Though he'd left a space on his other side for a second person, he discovered upon waking there was no longer anyone there to fill it, barely a dent in the pillow where a head should have been.

Dez fought dizziness as he sat up too fast, a reminder of the blow to his head. He blinked hard twice, willing his sight to still so he could better scope his surroundings.

But the quick visual sweep of his apartment contained no answers, at least not the ones he wanted. He felt the peace of last night straining away beneath the cold douse of water this morning had brought.

Sully was gone.

4

He gave it an hour, hope fading as the minutes ticked toward seven with no sign of Sully or Pax.

Dez used part of the time to scour the small suite for clues—a note, missing items, anything to reveal where Sully had gone and, more importantly, whether he was planning on coming back.

He found the pyjama pants and the T-shirt he'd lent Sully atop his dresser, the grubby clothes the younger man had arrived in no longer anywhere to be seen.

Dez clicked on his small television, seeking escape in a meaningless reality program until he found he could no longer avoid the one his own life had become.

Sully wasn't coming back.

Dez had been eighteen and fresh out of high school when he'd followed in his father's footsteps, securing a place on the KR Police Department.

With many young candidates turned away due to a lack of life experience or relevant education, Dez had been all too aware of the judgmental looks and hushed conversation, the belief he'd only managed it because his father was deputy police chief. Dez had known from the start he'd have to work twice as hard, be twice as good out there, to prove otherwise.

But policing came naturally to him, his instincts honed through years of listening to his father's stories, his hands and mind steady with strength and practice, his sense of humour and warmth commending him both to colleagues and to the people they encountered each day.

Within months, he'd found himself enveloped within the fold that policing both engendered and required, and had settled into a career that felt as natural to him as home.

Losing his job had felt like an amputation of a major limb, one he'd spent months trying to learn to live without before it occurred to him one broken night he might never get there.

Now with Sully gone, Dez fell back on ingrained instinct and training, launching a search for anyone who might have had occasion to witness something of a man who, come right down to it, didn't even really exist.

He began where answers seemed most likely, with his neighbour across the hall. Very little slipped past Miss Crichton, an elderly spinster who had lived in her tiny suite since the builders had laid the brick and installed the plumbing. She made it a habit to never sleep past sunrise—or so she'd told Dez shortly after he moved in—and he'd had more than enough sleepless nights to know the truth of it, having been awake to hear her open her door at the crack of dawn to retrieve her newspaper.

As always, Miss Crichton was pleased to see him, although he suspected she would be just as happy with a visit from a salesman for the sake of some company.

"Come in, Desmond, come in." Her oversized glasses made her eager eyes even rounder.

He smiled politely, though he felt desperate enough at the moment to resort to rudeness should the need arise. "I'd love to, ma'am but—"

"Emily, please," she said. They went through this every time, she insisting on being called by her first name, Dez feeling awkward using anything but a respectful title when addressing an octogenarian.

"Of course, I'm sorry. It's just I'm not able to visit right now. I'm looking for someone, and it's really important I find him. Maybe you saw a young man who stayed with me last night?"

Miss Crichton smiled in such a way that had Dez thinking he'd better explain, and quickly. "He's my brother."

"Oh! I didn't know you had a brother. Of course, I don't know much about your family, really. I've only met your mother twice and never anyone else."

Dez found his smile wavering. "Listen, the thing is I haven't seen my brother in a couple years, and when I woke up this morning, he was gone. No note or explanation or anything. I'm trying to figure out when he left and where he might have gone."

"I didn't see anyone leave, I'm afraid."

"Did you hear anything?"

"No, and I've been awake since five. He must have gone out before then, or I'm sure I would have noticed. One can hear a pin drop in the hall with these creaky old floors."

The early hour explained how Sully had managed to crawl over him without disturbing him. Dez tended not to wake easily in the middle of the night on those occasions when he was actually managing a decent sleep. Of course, Sully would know that.

"Thanks, Miss Crichton, I'm—"

"Emily, please."

"Right. Listen, I'm going to head out and look for him. You've still got my cellphone number?"

"Right by my phone, dear. But I'm sure there's nothing to worry about."

"That may be true, but if you happen to see him come back, could you please give me a call anyway? He's twenty-four years old, six feet tall and thin with long, light brown hair and a beard. He'll probably be wearing something that seems pretty grubby, but don't let that bother you. He's a really great guy. Oh, and he'll have a big, black dog with him."

"He knows this is a no-pet building, doesn't he?"

"His dog's really quiet. If you weren't staring right at him, you wouldn't even know he was there."

"I would."

Dez smiled. "You didn't know he was here last night."

Miss Crichton frowned. "I went to bed early with a terrible headache. Don't get me wrong, Desmond. I think you're a wonderful young man and a very considerate neighbour, but I really wish you wouldn't allow animals in the building. There are rules, you know."

"It was only going to be one night and I hadn't seen my brother in a long time. I didn't want to miss out on spending time with him because his dog couldn't stay."

He was playing on her sympathies and, judging by the kindly smile spreading across her face, he guessed he'd done a sound job.

"Of course, when you put it like that. Don't worry. Our little secret. Now, don't worry, I'm sure your brother will turn up. And if I see him before you do, I'll be sure to let you know."

"Thanks, ma'am," he said, giving her the little salute that always made her giggle before turning and heading for the stairs.

"Emily, please," she called after him.

DURING HIS YEARS with the police, Dez had spent plenty of time in the part of KR he was now unfortunate enough to call home. He'd made contacts on the streets, people he could tap for information when need be. During the past two years, he'd tended more toward calling on them for a drink at whichever bar was closest, convincing himself he didn't have a true drinking problem if he wasn't tossing it back alone.

Anyway, truth lived in the adage "misery loves company," and

Dez's new barroom buddies certainly made for some miserable company. But they were company nonetheless, and giddy moments played out in the midst of the long drunken evenings when he found escape with them, listening to stories that made his problems seem like molehills next to mountains.

One thing about those people: they knew this part of town, some of them calling the streets home during the summer months, before the bitter cold of winter drove them behind whatever doors they could find.

Back in the old days, this part of KR had been a place for business and family, had seen new buildings popping up well into the 1960s. Named for the neighbourhood in which it sat, Riverview Park had been designed with families in mind, a place for picnics, carnivals and fishing. But repeated flooding—and the big one four years ago—had led to a turnover in the Riverview neighbourhood. The park, too, had changed hands. The benches and bushes had become makeshift beds, the public toilets were office space for drug pushers and prostitutes, and the handful of sculptures had been not-so-tastefully redesigned by vandals and graffiti artists.

But to a cop—or, in Dez's case, a former cop—it was also the first place to look for those with answers.

It took all of two minutes to locate Bulldog. Born William "Billy" Bird, he'd earned his nickname through his short and stout appearance, jowls tugged ever lower with gravity and age, and a tendency to growl with the onset of severe intoxication. When he was sober, though, he was all smiles, stories and back slaps and, thankfully, that was the Bulldog Dez found this morning.

"Copper, how the hell are ya?" Bulldog asked, pumping Dez's hand in one of his shoulder-dislocating handshakes.

"I'm good, thanks. How many times do I have to tell you to stop calling me Copper? I got canned from the force a year ago."

"I don't call you Copper because of that. It's your hair. Or would you rather I call you Carrots?"

"I'll stick with the original, thanks."

"Didn't see ya last night. Figures. You said next round was on you. Where'd you end up, anyways?"

That was a story Dez wasn't much in the mood to tell, and so he settled on the abridged version. "I ran into an old friend."

"Really? What kind of friend?" He was grinning and winking so hard any good mother would warn him his face might stick that way.

"Not that kind of friend. It's a guy."

Bulldog shrugged. "Who's judgin'?"

Dez rolled his eyes, and spoke quietly, hoping to engender the same hushed tone in Bulldog's response. "Sully, you goof. I'm talking about Sully."

"Sully who?"

"Bulldog. Sully. My brother."

Bulldog's jowls dropped as his mouth popped open, jaw moving without sound. It took a moment for the words to come. "Jesus Christ."

"Listen, man, I need you to—"

"Are you drunk, Copper? You don't smell drunk."

"I'm stone sober, Bulldog. Now shut up and—"

"Then you're obviously on some other magical substance, or you've just lost whatever was left of your friggin' mind. Sully Gray is dead."

Dez had given it plenty of thought on the way over, had initially thought only to provide Bulldog with Sully's physical description and ask the man to check around for anyone who might have seen someone matching it. But he'd thought better of it. Bulldog knew Sully, knew him well and genuinely liked him, for years guarding his secret about seeing the dead. And there was the other reason for honesty; Bulldog was lousy at selling bullshit to Dez but a pro at smelling it. Any attempt by Dez to lie to the man—someone he considered a friend—would result in nothing but hurt and hard feelings.

"I'm on the level here, Bulldog. But I need you to keep this on the D-L, all right? No one can know. No one."

"You're serious."

"You think I'd be anything but serious about Sully? I thought he was dead until last night."

Bulldog regarded him, his eyes locked onto Dez's with squirm-inducing intensity. Dez refused to break eye contact, needing his friend—Sully's friend—to see the truth.

Dez knew Bulldog had gotten there when his face lit up, the expression of a twelve-year-old unwrapping a new BB gun on Christmas morning. "Holy hell. Shit, man, that's amazing!"

"No one can know, Bulldog. I mean it. If anyone finds out, his life is over. You hear me?"

Bulldog wiped the grin away long enough to fix Dez with an indignant glare. "Listen, Copper, I love that kid. He was decent to me—hell, to everybody. He was one of the only bar guys I ever knew who didn't look at me funny or kick my ass out on the street. Even gave me somewhere to sleep a few times in winter when I was so drunk off my ass I probably would've frozen to death tryin'a make it to the Sally Ann. If no one's supposed to know about him, then no one's gonna know it from me, all right?"

There was no sign of a lie in Bulldog's earnest face, leaving Dez with only the very real concern for what might happen once the guy was too drunk to know better.

"This isn't going to come out when you're pissed, though, is it?" Dez asked. "Face it, you're not exactly known for discretion after you've had a few."

"Come on. Most people who don't know better think I'm full of shit when I'm sober. When I'm drunk they think I'm a bloody loon."

Dez smiled. "That's 'cuz you are."

"Yeah, yeah. So, what's going on? Why's he been playing dead?"

"I don't have a lot of answers, Bulldog. That's the problem. He was with me last night and this morning he was gone. All I really know for sure is he's on the run, and he's in trouble. I want to help him, but I need to find him first."

"So you want me to keep an eye out for him, huh? Can do, my friend."

"You won't know what to look for."

"Are you kidding me? I spent almost as much time with him as you did those last few years. Anyway, he hasn't exactly got one of those faces that blends into a crowd. Pretty Boy turned plenty of heads."

"His hair's grown a lot, past his shoulders, and I think he keeps it over his face most of the time to hide his features. He's also got a full beard, likely for the same reason. And he's skinnier than he was and is dressing a lot grubbier. He was wearing black cargo pants and an oversized sweatshirt with the hood up. He had a dark green army jacket over that. Oh, and he's got a big, black dog with him. Sound like anyone you've seen?"

Bulldog appeared to mull it over. "No. No one like that. I think I'd have noticed, especially with the dog and all. Well, and the fact people with their faces concealed freak me out a bit. It's the eyes, you know? Gotta see the eyes. Only way to really know they aren't makin' to stick a knife in your gut."

Somewhere behind Dez, a dog barked twice, the sound closer to attack than warning. In this neighbourhood, the noise wasn't exactly unusual, meaning Bulldog's rationale made plenty of sense. Around here, more than just dogs could put bite before growl. "But you'll keep an eye out for him, right?"

"Course I will. And, before you ask, yes, I still have your cell number."

"The personal one, not the work one. Someone else will have my old work phone by now."

"Hey, let's not forget, I was your best snitch before I was your best buddy. I always called your personal cell."

True. "Thanks, man. If you can maybe put the word out I'm looking for someone with that description without mentioning any names, I'd really appreciate it. I don't have much, but I'll pay you whatever I can."

"Will do. And you don't gotta pay me. I owe the kid. If I can help you to help him, I'm good."

Dez smiled, allowing his gratitude to show before turning to make his way out of the park.

Bulldog called out his name, drawing Dez to a pause.

"What are you gonna do now, Copper?"

He turned long enough to meet his eye. "I don't know."

Leaving Bulldog behind, he hiked back toward Endlin Road.

5

Concealed between cardboard and steel, Sully nearly missed when Dez emerged from the apartment entrance next to the Golden Hand.

Even with the distance, he couldn't mistake the tension tightening Dez's jaw and creasing his brow as he looked up and down the street, eyes searching but not seeing. Sully instantly felt the same clawing guilt that had devoured him when he'd attended his own funeral and he'd watched Eva attempt to wrap her much larger husband in arms not quite up to the mammoth task. Sully had left before the service ended, unable to bear the pain he'd caused.

Back, now, in that same agonizing place, he felt Dez's panic as if it were his own.

Dez's gaze headed toward the alley, and Sully sank back against brick. He sensed rather than witnessed Dez retreating inside, and Sully knew his brother would head out the back to get his SUV, enabling him to cover more ground in his search.

Sully trailed the SUV at a distance, watched as it pulled over a few blocks east, next to Riverview Park. Dez emerged, hands in the pockets of his hooded jacket as he stalked down into the green space. Sully continued forward, trying to keep his brother in his sights. There were blind spots in the park: thick and untrimmed sections of brush, a couple of tunnels, and structures once used for entertainment and maintenance—plenty of places for a potential assailant to hide. Although Sully suspected last night's attack on Dez was, in some yet-unexplained way, about himself, he hadn't managed a good look at the person responsible and had no way of knowing whether Dez's rescue had been witnessed. And there was still a possibility his brother had been the target all along, and that the Purple Girl—visible on the park's borders ahead, that same expression of abject panic colouring her features—was simply trying to keep Sully from becoming collateral damage.

It didn't matter. If anything happened to Dez, Sully would happily go with him.

Sully gained the park's edge, picking Dez out easily against the others present; his brother dwarfed everyone within sight, and the early morning sun made a flaming beacon of his hair. The Purple Girl hovered next to Dez, but Sully—uncertain about her intentions and his next move—hung back, pressing past a line of lilac bushes and into the small grove of trees beyond.

Dez approached a man Sully recognized as Billy "Bulldog" Bird. Sully's resulting grin quickly disappeared with the sudden return of the Purple Girl at his side, arm extended and index finger pointed toward the road. Following the direction of her hand, he spotted an unmarked, white delivery van illegally parked, facing the opposing lane of traffic. If he was to guess, the same van had nearly hit him earlier this morning.

Sully could see no one behind the wheel, although there was a possibility someone was slumped back against the seat, positioned so he wouldn't make them out from here.

Sully returned his gaze to his ghostly companion. "I'm sorry. I don't know what you're trying to tell me."

Her response was another motion, a turn of her body and the extension of the arm in the opposite direction. Back toward Dez.

Beside him, Pax growled, eyes fixed on something in the trees that Sully couldn't see.

The dread rushed him hard as he realized the driver of that van, still hidden from sight, might well be the one who had tried to kill Dez. If so, was he waiting here now, possibly set up in the trees, lining up a shot?

Sully stood, pushing back through the lilacs, the Purple Girl be damned. If it meant protecting his brother, Sully would happily put himself in front of a bullet, would give up everything if it meant saving the person who had saved him.

He'd barely taken two steps forward, had just opened his mouth to yell when he was distracted by the sound of rushed movement behind him. He turned. It wasn't purple hair and blood-painted white skin he saw.

Two people faced him, one well-built and one slight, faces covered by balaclavas. Sully knew his strengths, knew his current condition meant fighting wasn't one of them, so he turned from them, intending to run for Dez.

Pax barked twice. Just twice. There was no accompanying human shriek of pain, leaving Sully in little doubt as to what that meant. Torn between checking on Pax and escape, Sully realized too late the decision was not his to make. A hand went over his mouth while more vicelike fingers seized him. He was dragged, off-balance, back into the trees, taking him past the prone form of his dog in the tall grass along the trees' edge. Regaining purchase as they stopped moving, he brought a heel down on the foot of his nearest attacker. While a pained grunt and the release of one arm resulted, his success was short-lived as a fist collided twice with his skull. Stunned, Sully was wrestled to the ground and held there on his belly by the larger of his assailants while the second temporarily vanished, reappearing only long enough for Sully to see the syringe.

The sight of it sent him plummeting into the past, where Dr. Gerhardt peered down at him with eyes as lifeless as death, where Sully knew he'd awaken to a cold blue room and a bed from which there was no escape. And yet, held within that flash-back remained a tenuous grasp on his current reality, the fact Dez was standing within screaming distance, were Sully able to do so.

But he could not pull away from the hand that prevented his calling out. Nor could he fight the lightheadedness as he struggled to breathe through his partially obstructed nostrils. The panic and the need to get breath, to try to get help, to escape from that approaching syringe lent Sully temporary strength and he struggled against his attackers. But he had barely budged the man sitting on top of him when he felt the all-too familiar jab in his hip, the dull heat of liquid chemical flowing into him, a rubbing hand dispersing the sedative.

Because, within seconds, he knew that's what it was. His vision swam as the tension in his body eased beneath the weight of the man and the predicament, his brain fogging over with an enemy sleep.

She was the last thing he saw, wide, horrified eyes holding unshed tears beneath a long, violet halo.

———

DEZ DROVE the streets and alleys of the old city centre a while, on the hunt for a needle in a haystack.

He was thankful for the existence of Pax, as it seemed to him it would be a hell of a lot easier to spot a large, black hound than it would be to pick a particular human out of the crowd in a city populated by close to 850,000 people. Particularly when Sully's sloppy street wear formed the equivalent of a uniform amongst those in the Riverview neighbourhood.

Dez lost track of time, eyes riveted to the sidewalks either side of the road, the alleyways, the storefronts and empty lots. He scanned the faces and figures of everyone in view, searching both for Sully and for anyone he recognized who might have a clue he didn't.

When he at last looked down to the dashboard clock, no luck after what felt like half a day's worth of searching, it read 9:13

a.m. Dez pulled over, put his SUV into park and lowered his head into a hand, massaging his temples between fingers and thumb. His head reeled under the realization it was only mid-morning, that he hadn't actually been out here all that long.

And yet he'd scoured every street, every alleyway, had trolled past every park at the risk of being thought some sort of pervert. He'd talked to three street people he recognized from his years on the force, all individuals with a detailed knowledge of the comings and goings of those in their world. No one had seen anyone resembling Sully and, perhaps more strangely, none had seen a large, black dog.

Somewhere in the back of his head remained a niggling, foolish hope: perhaps Sully had stepped out to take Pax for a walk or a leak, or had developed such an affinity with the outdoors that he couldn't bear sleeping in an actual bed. Illogical and improbable, it was enough to send Dez back in the direction of home. If nothing else, he needed to check. He would also have to force down some breakfast so he could continue sorting through this mess if Sully wasn't there.

He put the vehicle back into drive and pulled into traffic, setting a course for the his apartment.

DEZ TRUDGED UP THE STAIRS, hands buried in the pockets of his hooded jacket, barely looking up as he approached his apartment door.

He had his key in the lock when a door opened across the hall. Dez's eyes moved heavenward as he fought to keep from voicing a groan. *God, not now.*

"Hello, Desmond."

"Hello, ma'am."

"Emily, please. And I wonder if I might trouble you a moment."

"Actually, I'm just in the middle of—"

"It's about your brother."

The magic words. They turned Dez in place and took him the few steps across the hall to Miss Crichton's open suite door.

"Well, more specifically"—she edged the door open a little more to allow Dez a better view into her apartment— "what I'd assume is his dog."

Dez stepped up to the gap Miss Crichton had created and felt his stomach drop. It was indeed Pax. No denying it, not the way the dog had perked up his ears and was now tail-thumping earnestly against the floor. But if anything was more unsettling about Pax being here without Sully, it was the way he wobbled and nearly fell as he rose to greet Dez.

"How'd he end up here?" Dez asked as he pushed through the door and moved to examine Pax, holding him up as well as he could against his leg.

"I found him outside, at the rear door. He seemed to want in badly, and appeared so unwell, I simply didn't have the heart to leave him out there. It was all I could do to coax him away from your suite, though. If I didn't know better, I'd say he was looking for you."

"And my brother? Did you see him? Did you see anyone around the dog?"

"No, I'm sorry. Just him, the poor fellow. I gave him a piece of chicken, boneless of course. I hope that's okay."

"It's fine, thanks. And you're sure, you're absolutely sure, you didn't see anyone? You looked?"

"Oh, yes. I could see how concerned you were this morning. I can't imagine why this fellow would have made his way back here all on his own, especially in this state. I hate to suggest it, but you might want to check with the hospitals."

That seemed like a good idea to Dez, albeit a less-than-palatable one. "I'll do that. Thank you for taking care of Pax."

"Is that his name? It's Latin for peace, you know."

Dez hadn't really thought about that, but it made sense. If

Sully had no one else the past two years, no doubt peace was exactly what the dog had provided, at least in some measure.

"Thanks again, ma'am."

"Emily, please. And I'm thinking you might want to take him by a vet, just to make sure. He seems a little dizzy and sluggish. I'd be worried about a head injury given his symptoms."

"I'll look after him. Thanks."

Dez stepped away from Pax and patted the side of his leg, watching as the dog took a few tentative steps toward him. Pax held his ground and followed Dez from the apartment, tail wagging wildly as if, despite his predicament, he had just found some reason to hope.

But Dez's own hopes had been dashed, and were crushed further still when a glance inside his apartment revealed no sign of his brother.

He turned back to Pax, meeting watchful brown eyes which appeared to question him, inquiring about the next step. And Dez knew, his guts rolling with the realization, he had no answer.

6

IF THERE WAS one thing Dez knew, it was he didn't have money to pay a vet.

There would be a cost for the exam, for X-rays if a head injury was suspected, the likelihood of housing Pax at a clinic while he was monitored and additional tests were run. And treatments themselves wouldn't be cheap; Dez expected even the basics would run into the triple or even quadruple digits once everything was said and done.

He didn't know any vets, no one who would run tests at a massive discount or who owed him any kind of favour. But he did know a doctor—of a kind.

Granted, Dr. Kindra Abraham was more used to dealing with the sort of patients who didn't bark or bite or, for that matter, complain. But right now, he'd take what he could get.

With Dez propping him up, Pax managed the stairs down to the parking lot. Dez had hoped the fresh air would help revive him; he wanted to take a walk around the neighbourhood, where a miracle could happen in the form of the dog leading him to a clue or, with any luck, to Sully himself. But walking any great distance did not appear to be a possibility at the moment, not for this dog whose belly was dragging ever nearer the ground with each step. If Pax was going to help find their mutual loved one, he'd need to be in a better state to do that first.

Mind made up, Dez picked Pax up and lugged the large canine to his SUV, placing him with no small amount of difficulty into the backseat where he covered him with a blanket from the hatch. With his furry passenger as comfortable as possible, Dez drove off in the direction of the KR morgue.

PAX, sitting up and watching the passing city, appeared to have perked up by the time Dez reached the large brownstone. He even managed to hold himself largely upright as Dez led the way into the building's rear door, waving at Larry the commissionaire on the way in.

"I'm not sure the doctor will appreciate a dog in her autopsy suite," Larry said.

Dez paused long enough to bestow a friendly and hopefully off-putting smile on the retired postal worker. "Don't worry. If any of the patients start sneezing, I'll take him right out."

Dez pushed through the doors and headed down a pair of hallways, past two large rooms lined with refrigerated compartments housing the bodies awaiting dissection by Kindra and her staff. Four autopsy suites were just beyond those rooms, and in one of these he spotted the pathologist he was looking for.

At fifty-two, Kindra Abraham—Lowell Braddock's wife—was still an attractive woman, even covered as she was by a gown, mask and surgical cap. A window offered viewing from the hall, enabling police to have families identify deceased loved ones. Dez rapped at the glass and watched as the older woman glanced up from her work.

Dez was no fan of autopsies, and he quickly averted his eyes as Kindra stepped away from the corpse on the table, exposing the inner workings she'd just been digging into. She was alone in the suite, the lack of a police presence suggesting this one was not a suspicious death—a fact that made him feel better about causing this distraction.

Kindra peeled off her gloves, paper gown and cap, rolling them up and tossing them into a waste bin on the way out.

She greeted him with a smile and a warm hug. "Desmond. It's wonderful to see you. I can't remember the last time we talked."

"Mom's birthday in February," he said.

"Has it been that long? How have you been?" It was a loaded question, one that didn't have an answer that wouldn't end in pity and a good, stiff drink later.

"I've been getting by," he said instead, hoping it was passable as truth. "How are you?"

"I'm fine," she said. "So is your uncle Lowell. He'd love to see you, you know. He misses you. Ever since your dad died, well …. It's been very hard for him. He and Flynn were so close."

"Yeah, I know."

Kindra was evaluating him, her eyes narrowed, lips turned up in a small smile. "You still haven't forgiven him, have you?"

They'd never had this conversation, the idea of it almost as uncomfortable as the act itself. He bought himself a moment by playing dumb. "For what?"

"You know what. He's the one who insisted on Sullivan's committal to Lockwood. You didn't want that."

"Sully didn't belong there."

"He needed help, Desmond. You remember what he was like then, don't you? He tried to kill himself twice."

"I'm not denying he needed help. Lockwood wasn't the kind of help he needed."

"He needed someone with him around the clock to ensure he didn't harm himself. You had a young family of your own to provide for. He was too much for your mom to manage, especially since it was so soon after your dad. And Lowell and I work long hours. Short of keeping him tied up somewhere, Lockwood was the only option. You know that."

He didn't know that. Not anymore. Lockwood had done nothing but make things worse for Sully, and Dez had felt the committal a betrayal by the only real family Sully had ever known.

"I know Uncle Lowell was trying to do right by Sully. But I don't think any of us really knew how bad things were at Lockwood."

"Are you so sure it was that bad? All you have to go by is Sullivan's word."

That was as far as Kindra was going to take him on this topic. "His word was good enough for me. Look, I'm sorry I haven't been around much. The past couple of years have been pretty rough."

"I can certainly understand that. No need to apologize. Just please think about forgiving Lowell. He meant well. He really did." Her eyes went to the dog at Dez's side, and he was relieved to find an end to that conversation. "And who's this?"

She reached out to pet Pax's head, but the dog uttered a low growl, causing her to draw her hand back.

"Pax, no," Dez said. Then, as if the dog could understand, "She's my aunt. She's fine."

Dez returned his attention to Kindra. "Sorry. Pax isn't really a people dog. And I'm worried he might have a head injury."

"Did he hit it on something?"

"No idea," Dez said. "He went out this morning and I couldn't find him for a few hours. When I finally did, he was pretty wobbly and dopey."

"Did you take him to a vet?"

"I can't really afford one right now."

Kindra's smile was a knowing one. "So you thought maybe I could take a look."

"I know it's not exactly your area of expertise."

"Not even remotely."

"I'm sorry. I just didn't know what else to do."

Kindra was still smiling at him, albeit with more sympathy now than amusement. "All right, fine—as long as he keeps his teeth to himself."

THANKFULLY, the X-ray didn't reveal anything of note, no obvious signs of head injury. And, Dez noted with no small amount of relief, the longer they stayed here, the more alert Pax became until he no longer needed help to keep his legs.

With no other immediate prognosis, Kindra took a blood sample while Dez hovered, ensuring Pax didn't leave the pathologist with a need to seek treatment herself.

"I'll send this off to the lab over at LOBRA, ask them to check it ASAP," she said.

"They won't mind?"

"It's my husband's company. I'm pretty sure they'll be happy to accommodate my request."

"Good point."

"So, I'm curious. How did you end up with a dog? You didn't have him the last time I saw you."

Dez chose his words carefully. "A friend of mine had to move, and he couldn't take him, so I've kind of adopted him, I guess."

"Well, he's a little rough around the edges, but he seems nice enough once you get to know him."

Dez looked down at Pax, sitting quietly on his haunches next to him. While the dog had made no other threatening moves toward Kindra, he was still regarding her with an unnerving intensity Dez could only describe as suspicion. Dez guessed Pax hadn't often had occasion to be poked and prodded by a vet, let alone a forensic pathologist, and he wasn't likely to go too willingly back to either should the future require it.

"Yeah, he's a pretty good dog."

"I remember you wanted one when you were small."

"Yeah, I did. But Aiden ...."

Kindra finished up where Dez had trailed off. "Was allergic. I remember."

Dez caught himself staring at his feet to avoid his aunt's eye. "I used to resent him for that."

"You were eight years old."

"Doesn't change anything. If I hadn't been so pissed at Aiden, he'd probably still be alive."

"Why would you say something like that?"

"I was barely speaking to him the week he died. But you know little brothers. He refused to stop buzzing around me, wanting to play. I suggested hide and seek. Aiden was overjoyed, took off like Christmas morning. And I ...."

The pause hung in the air, while he tried to swallow the lump in his throat. After an uncomfortable amount of time, he provided what Kindra was obviously waiting on.

"I never went to look for him. I let him stay out there. And I knew the river was down there, that he'd always been fascinated by it. I should have been there with him. If I had been, if I'd just been the big brother I should have been ...."

This time, there was nothing more to add, nothing more he wanted to say.

"Desmond, your brother's death was not your fault. Do you understand me? You were just a young kid. At some point, you're going to have to stop blaming yourself."

Dez tried to smile but couldn't quite get there. "I've spent almost two decades perfecting it. Why stop now?"

Kindra's answering smile was as humourless and tight as Dez imagined his own must have been, the sight of her pity pulling his gaze back down to his feet. He drew in a long breath and released it slowly. While he'd never erase thoughts of Aiden—and wouldn't want to if he could—he had learned how to function around them if he worked hard enough. It took a moment, but when he looked back up at his aunt, it was with a smile that was closer to genuine.

"I'm sorry. I didn't mean to lay this on you. It's been a tough morning."

"I'm happy to help if I can. And for heaven's sake, you never need to apologize to me, all right? You're like a son to me. You can talk to me about anything. You know that, right?"

"I know. Thanks. I appreciate you taking the time to look at Pax. I know it's not a normal daily task for you."

Kindra chuckled. "You got that right, kid. But it's no problem. Anyway, it was lovely visiting with you."

"You too. I suppose I should let you get back to work."

Kindra looked over her shoulder to where the open hall door revealed the autopsy suite in question. "Well, it's not like Mrs. Wilson is going anywhere. But you're right. I probably should get back. I'll send Pax's blood work and ask them to put a rush on it. I read in the paper there have been a few dog poisonings lately, so I think it's best to make sure everything here is okay."

"I'd appreciate that, thanks."

Kindra saw Dez to the door and hugged him. "It was so good to see you. Please stop by our place one evening."

"I'll do that." There were other things Dez wanted to say, not least of all a thank you for her support through the losses of Aiden, their dad and Sully. Kindra had been the rock neither Dez nor his mom had the capacity to be at the time, providing a shoulder to lean on and a listening ear for Mara Braddock as she tried to keep her head above water through those losses. That had freed Dez to go off and deal with his own grief as he saw fit, assured he was leaving his mother in hands more capable of comfort than his own. Kindra had been invaluable, and still was.

But there never seemed to be a right time or place to say it, so Dez kept the words to himself, hoping Kindra would know it all the same.

Instead, Dez patted his leg for Pax to come, and the dog

trotted after him as they made their way back down the hall to the rear entrance.

"Did you find what you were looking for?" Larry asked.

"Not yet," Dez said. "But I hope I'm getting closer."

DEZ DROVE the Riverview area again, this time watching for Sully-related tells from the dog, whose head was hanging out the two back windows in turn as Dez steered slowly up and down the streets.

But there was nothing besides the obvious canine curiosity, the joy at feeling the breeze on his face, that suggested Pax had noticed anything helpful. Dez opted to get out and walk it, hoping his brother's dog might lead him to something significant. Whatever had happened to Pax, it was unlikely he'd made it very far in the condition he'd been in, suggesting something had occurred within a few blocks of Dez's place.

Pax trotted ahead of him and Dez allowed it, hoping the dog had some idea where he was going. He appeared to be part shepherd by breed, certainly not a bloodhound with ingrained tracking ability but, given the circumstances, Dez would take what he could get.

Pax made his way east, taking the same route Dez had earlier when he'd gone looking for Bulldog. And, sure enough, Pax led him the few blocks to the park, his pace quickening so Dez had to shift to a light jog to keep up.

Pax kept to the grass near the sidewalk, his path more or less straight as he headed for a grove of trees bordered this side by lilac bushes.

There, on the street side of the trees, virtually within sight of the spot where Dez had met with Bulldog earlier, Pax stopped.

Dez watched as Pax's nose went into overdrive, his head lowered to the ground as he paced in circles around the immediate area.

"What is it, boy?" Dez asked as he squatted down next to the spot where Pax finally focused his attention. The unmown grass was flattened here in places but it was two parallel patches of bared earth, each a couple inches wide and a foot or so long, that drew Dez's attention. He'd been a cop long enough to have seen signs of a struggle before, and these looked to have been caused by a shoed foot dragging along the ground.

Pax had moved off a few feet, was back to sniffing the ground in one spot. Dez joined him, casting a hand carefully through the grass until it settled on something metallic.

Pushing the grass aside, he visually searched, wanting to see what it was before chancing further handling. A piece of red fluff came into view first.

"Oh, shit," Dez said, guts twisting as the tranquilizer dart suggested an answer to two plus two. It made sense, given Pax's previous symptoms; he'd been tranqued, but this new evidence gave Dez more to worry about, not less. Sully had obviously not tranquilized his own dog, and there were the drag marks to contend with. The scene came together in Dez's head in enough detail to leave him physically ill; evidence and instinct told him Sully had been taken.

His first thought was to call 9-1-1, get police on this immediately now that he had found some actual proof Sully hadn't just walked away from his old life a second time. He pulled his phone from his pocket and punched in the first two numbers before his senses kicked in, his finger hovering above the keypad as he thought through what he was doing.

Sully was, as far as the world was concerned, dead. Had been for a couple of years. He'd only revealed himself in what had been a life or death situation, had tried to leave before Dez recognized him, had told his brother he needed to remain hidden. Maybe it was all about Lockwood, maybe it wasn't. But Dez knew he couldn't chance blowing Sully's cover without knowing if he'd be further endangering his brother.

Leaving the dart where it lay for the moment, Dez opened the camera app on his phone, falling back on skills learned in policing as he snapped a few photos of the scene, focusing in particular on the dart and the drag marks. He'd have to play the role of lead investigator, forensic identification officer and patrol all in one, at least for now.

He had no choice.

7

THE OBVIOUS NEXT step was a return to Kindra.

"You say the dog led you to this?" she asked, holding the dart by the fluffy end. Ordinarily, it should have been in an exhibit bag, but Dez wasn't walking around with many of those on his person these days.

"In Riverview Park, yeah. I'm wondering if it's loaded with some sort of tranq. I'm thinking it might match up to whatever Pax had in his system."

"I can certainly take a swab and send it in. I already couriered over the bloodwork, and they said they will have an answer for us later in the day. If I get this sent over now, they should be able to compare it to the tox screen."

"I'd appreciate it, thanks."

Kindra peered at him through eyes narrowed in thought, and Dez waited for the inevitable question. "This isn't all about Pax, is it? There's something else bothering you."

Dez considered how best to answer without revealing a truth not his to tell. In the end, there wasn't anything he could say, so he settled for a mild lie; better that than further risk Sully's life until he had a handle on what he was dealing with.

His reasoning might have been noble, but that didn't stop the shame he felt creeping through him as he spoke the words.

"There's nothing else, Auntie K. Everything's fine."

EVERYTHING WAS FAR FROM FINE. In fact, the distance to fine was so great Dez couldn't have spotted it with the Hubble Space Telescope.

Not so long ago, he would have gone to Eva to talk this through, knowing he would have come away with both comfort and the start of a solution. Now, that was no longer an option.

He had been sitting in his vehicle, Pax eyeballing him mournfully from the backseat for the past twenty minutes. Dez knew he had to look pathetic as he sat there trying to think this through, searching for some plausible scenario in which the evidence he'd found was completely innocent or unrelated to Sully.

But rational thought had joined with intuition, providing a solid slap of cold reality whenever he ventured too far into a best-case scenario. Sully was in trouble. Given the dart and the drag marks, he was in big trouble.

Dez thought again about going to the police. If someone had taken Sully, it probably meant he no longer had any cover that needed protecting. And there was a chance if Dez didn't find his brother fast, he'd be burying him for real this time.

But his mind flashed back to the conversation in his apartment last night, to the hint from Sully there might be something, someone, more he was running from than just Lockwood. It would probably be easy enough to find out if someone from the institution had recognized Sully and executed the warrant. What wouldn't be so easy was figuring out a way to keep Sully concealed from other potential enemies if word got out he was alive. Lockwood was a lot of things, and not a lot of them were good in Dez's opinion. But if nothing else, it was private, keeping the names of its patients to itself. If Sully was back there, there was no reason anyone on the outside would ever find out.

Unfortunately, it wasn't likely anyone there would be willing to share that information with him. He'd nearly lost his job after he aided Sully's escape, and he expected the only reason he hadn't was because Sully had then died. No one felt right about sanctioning him too harshly after that, especially so soon after his dad's death.

But Dr. Roman Gerhardt at Lockwood hadn't been as forgiving. The chief psychiatrist had been at the front of the line demanding Dez's job and the filing of criminal charges. And he'd had plenty to say to the KRPD brass on the subject upon learning his wishes had not been granted.

Dez knew he needed help, if for no other reason than to check Lockwood for Sully. But that help couldn't be official.

Maybe Eva was an option, after all. She loved Sully too.

He gave her a call, learning she was working a swing shift that week. She agreed to let him come over to talk, the added benefit being the opportunity to see his daughter for a few minutes during her school lunch break. He left Pax in his SUV with a window cracked, not wanting to take the chance he would react to Kayleigh or Eva in the same way he had with Kindra earlier. Anyway, the introduction of a dog would divert Kayleigh's attention and, given what little time he got to spend with her these days, he wanted her all to himself.

He didn't want to think about the day when Kayleigh wouldn't come running up to him like she did now, eager for one of his up-off-the-floor hugs.

"How's my big girl?" he asked, setting his daughter down and holding her at arm's length for an inspection.

"Fine, Daddy."

"What happened to your hand?"

"Don't ask," Eva said, emerging from the kitchen. God, she looked good, messy dark bob tucked behind her ears, no makeup, workout clothes showing off tight muscle and curves. The only thing that could have made her more beautiful would have been the sight of their wedding ring on her left hand. But he knew better, knew it was tucked away safely in her jewelry box upstairs, hopefully waiting for the day when the past was forgotten and the future more promising.

But at present, this was where they were, and Dez knew he had to take some comfort in the fact they could still have a civil conversation and support each other when it was most important. He knew plenty of former couples who weren't so lucky.

He pried his eyes away from Eva, kneeling and taking Kayleigh's hand in his for a closer look. "Come on. What happened?"

"Tyler Buchanan called Mommy a bad name."

Dez sensed where this was going, fought like hell to contain both his anger at Kayleigh's smart-ass, racist schoolmate and pride in his daughter. "And what did you do?"

Eva stepped in. "I walked Kayleigh to school this morning, and Tyler called me something I'm not going to repeat, but referring to my Indigenous background. He hadn't meant for me to hear it, just Kayleigh."

"Asshole," Dez said.

Eva flashed him a dangerous look. "Dez, don't use that language."

Dez returned his attention to his daughter, eager to hear this out. "So let me guess. You punched that little bastard in the face."

"Dez!"

"Hard, Daddy," Kayleigh said. "I hurt my hand."

"Yeah, punching looks easier on TV than it is in real life, huh?"

Kayleigh nodded, her expression solemn.

"So what did Tyler do after?"

"He fell down and starting crying."

Dez struggled to keep the smile in check. "You just hit him the once, though, right? Not when he was down?"

"No, Daddy. I know that's bad."

"So is hitting," Eva said. "Kayleigh, people are going to say bad things sometimes. Violence isn't the answer. Now go finish your lunch in the kitchen. I need to talk to your dad for a minute."

Kayleigh trotted off, and Eva returned her attention to Dez. God, her eyes were brilliant when they sparked fire. Her hands fisted against her hips.

"Dez, you can't speak to her like that. It's not the way I want her dealing with problems. Now she has to write an essay and we have a parent-teacher meeting."

To Dez, meetings and assignments were a waste of time; the little turd had gotten what he deserved. He held his tongue, though, needing her fully onside.

He spent the rest of the lunch hour with Kayleigh and then cautiously introduced her and Eva to Pax, who took to them like long-lost pack mates. With Pax next to him, Dez walked Kayleigh to school, Eva warning them to behave themselves before they left.

Picking the Buchanan kid out of the crowd didn't take long, the beginnings of a shiner forming around his left eye. Dez restrained himself from complimenting his daughter on her arm, but took some immature pleasure in watching Tyler's eyes widen as they travelled up Dez's mountainous form to his glaring expression. Message sent and received.

Eva was waiting for him at home, eyebrow raised like she already had formed an opinion. "You didn't intimidate the kid, did you?"

"Hey, I just stood there. I didn't say a word."

"If he saw you, then you intimidated him."

"I can't help being this big."

"All right, what's up?"

Dez had been trying to figure out how best to broach the subject, and still wasn't certain he should be getting into it at all. But with little else to go on, Eva might be his only real shot at finding Sully.

"I don't really know how to say this. Something happened last night."

Eva, sitting next to him on the sofa, fixed him with a look that did nothing to conceal her dread. "God, Dez, what did you do this time?"

"Why do you automatically think I did something wrong?"

"Because that's what you do these days. You go out, you drink with your new loser friends, you get plastered and next thing I hear, some overly kind ex-colleagues of yours are lugging your ass home and tucking you into bed."

"Well, that didn't happen last night. I was attacked."

"What?"

"Raynor's ex was at the same pub I was at. I'd gone outside for a breather and saw her leave. Someone was tailing her down the street. I followed, figuring I could stop it if Raynor attacked her again."

"You don't even know he attacked her the first time. No one knows that, Dez. She refused to provide a statement."

"I know it was him. He's a scumbag."

"I'm inclined to agree, but you know as well as I do investigations are built on evidence, and there was never anything on that one. Anyway, what do you mean you were attacked? Were you hurt?"

Dez shook his head. "Just let me talk. Greta stuck to the street, and the guy detoured into Riverview Cemetery. I followed him in but lost sight of him in the dark. Out of nowhere, I got whacked on the back of the head. Next thing I know, I'm coming to in a coffin with a corpse under me."

"Jesus, Dez!" Eva's hand was on his head now, gently prodding at the lump that had formed there. A jolt of electricity ran through his body at the touch, negating the jab of pain. "Did you go get checked out? You could have a concussion."

"I'm fine. I get a bit dizzy occasionally, but not bad."

"Damn it, Dez. You've got a brain. Learn to use it."

Dez smiled. "That's exactly what I thought you'd say. Here's the thing. I wasn't just inside a coffin. It was buried, like six feet under. I couldn't get out and I was running out of air. I thought I was going to die."

"How *did* you get out?"

"That's the thing. Someone dug me out. It's the who that you're going to have some trouble with."

Eva pursed her lips. Dez hesitated, thinking through for a final time what he was about to do. Still, he could find no alternative.

"It was Sully, Eva."

"Sully who?"

"Sully. You know, *Sully* Sully."

Eva's gaze drilled into him, the same look he imagined she wore while interviewing lying suspects. "Sullivan Gray?"

Dez nodded slowly.

"Sully's dead. He was killed two years ago."

"I thought so too. But he's not dead, Eva. It was him."

"Dez, come on."

"It's true."

"You just told me you left a bar, were knocked unconscious and nearly suffocated inside an occupied coffin. You're talking a combination of intoxication—"

"I wasn't drunk."

Eva ignored him. "Possible concussion and extreme trauma-induced stress that's likely to cause PTSD."

"It wasn't just a few seconds seeing him, Eva. He spent last night at my place. We talked."

"Dez ...."

"I'm not making this up."

"Look, I get what you've been through the past couple of years, okay? I know losing Sully so soon after your dad threw you into a tailspin. I get it. I miss him too. But you're going to have to accept it if you're ever going to—"

"Eva, listen to me. Sully was there. He wasn't a figment of my imagination. He wasn't an alcohol-induced hallucination, and he wasn't the result of a brain injury. Hell, Pax is his dog."

"So you're trying to tell me what, exactly? Sully faked his own death and just magically turned up in the nick of time to dig you out of a grave?"

"It sounds crazy when you put it like that, but that's exactly what I'm telling you. Sully's alive. And he's in trouble."

"You're damn right he's in trouble if I find out you're on the level here. If he put us through that—if he put our daughter through that—I'll kill him myself."

"I don't think it was his choice. He's running from someone. Or he was until this morning." Dez filled Eva in on the day's events, including his finds in the park. "I've hit a roadblock. I don't know what else to do. I can't report this as a possible kidnapping as Sully doesn't technically exist anymore, and he insisted it has to stay that way. But I can't just not do anything. He's my brother. I need to help him."

"So what is it you want from me?"

"You still don't believe me, do you?"

"Dez, I'm sorry. I don't know what to believe anymore. Just tell me what you need."

"If the mental health warrant's been executed, Lockwood should be notifying the police of that, especially since his death was the subject of an investigation."

"I can check on that easily enough, although I would expect any warrants would have been nullified with his death."

"But since he's not dead, if they found that out, wouldn't that nullify the nullification?"

"Huh?"

"Never mind. Anyway, if it's not reported, I was hoping you could go over there and ask Gerhardt."

"Hold on. You want me to ask the head psychiatrist whether he's had a mental health warrant executed on a man who died two years ago? God, Dez, they'll be locking me up next."

"Well, I can't exactly ask him myself, now, can I?"

"No, you can't. He almost got you fired, and for good reason."

"For good reason? Eva, they were torturing Sully. I couldn't leave him there and I couldn't let them get their hooks into him again. You know I couldn't."

That much they could agree on, as he could tell by the small, humourless smile she gave him. "I know that. You're right. I'm sorry."

"So you'll ask?"

"I'll check whether there's anything new in the system on Sully. But Dez, that's as far as I can go. I can't ask the questions you want me to, not without some sort of evidence. You think Gerhardt's going to let that slide? He'll be on the phone to my sergeant in ten seconds flat. You say you need to keep Sully a secret. Asking questions like that is the best way to accomplish the exact opposite."

"So what am I supposed to do?"

"First thing is you let me take you to the hospital. You need to be checked for concussion. After that, you have to go to headquarters and report last night's attack."

"I can't provide a detailed statement to police given who got me out. And I sure as hell don't have time to spend half the day in an emergency room waiting on doctors and medical tests. I need to find my brother."

Eva crossed her arms and sat back on the couch. "How do you plan on finding someone who doesn't exist?"

Dez didn't have an answer. "I've been asking myself that all morning."

8

THE ROOM WAS LIT by a bare lightbulb, coated in a layer of dust and dangling on a frayed wire from the ceiling.

That was the first sight to greet Sully as he slivered his eyes open and struggled to reconnect his brain with his physical senses.

The second, of course, was *her*.

The Purple Girl stood at the end of the thin mattress upon which he was lying, her eyes fixed on his with tearless sorrow. If possible, she seemed even bloodier, her white nightgown dyed a deep red along one shoulder and down past her left breast, her arm beneath her capped sleeve shiny with the stuff. While he'd never known her to change in appearance with the lighting of a room, she seemed to him to be half in shadow so that he didn't know whether it was a result of the blood blackening swaths of her hair or something more.

Because it seemed to him as he watched her that she was fading, the white of her skin and the nightgown turning to grey in the dark. But the feeling of her, that palpable state of terror that seemed to make up the core of her presence, remained strong around him.

He didn't need the added dread. Though her image was unsettling to say the least, he had decided some time ago he would be better off emotionally with seeing rather than feeling her.

Keeping her in his peripheral vision, he took a moment to scan his surroundings as he pushed himself to sitting. His head throbbed and reeled with the effort and he recalled the injection he'd been given. The memory sent him into a panicked tailspin, had him up off the mattress fast. Too fast. He braced himself against a wall as he fought the wave of dizziness. He couldn't name the drug, but he could name the feeling, recalled it taking him down countless times as he sought escape or struggled to save himself from another of their experiments. Always he would awaken to the cold, blue room, the tension of the restraints and the knowledge of what was to come. And while he didn't believe he was truly mentally ill, not like some of the others, there were many times he knew they were trying hard to drive him there.

There were other drugs, in particular the one they gave him before each visit with Dez or anyone else in his family, the one that left him a zombie. It was like seeing his family through a dense fog, like being bound and gagged as they chattered on around him. He doubted they knew it, but their visits had kept him balanced on a tightrope of sanity when everything else around him was crumbling into that black chasm Gerhardt and his minions had dug out beneath him.

This wasn't that blue room, and he wasn't restrained, which he tried to take as some comfort. But it didn't explain what he was doing here, in this small, bare, windowless, cement-encased cell.

Little else was in the room besides the mattress and the bulb, merely a drain in the floor and a bucket in the corner, which, he presumed, was meant for use should the need arise. Other than that, the only other notable feature was a solid-looking wooden door across the room. He moved to it, and found there was no handle, no visible hinge structure. He had only to shove against the wood to verify there was no escape this way; the door was locked tight. It was clear it opened outward, the final confirmation for Sully this was indeed very much a prison.

He turned, finding the Purple Girl just this side of invisible.

"Where am I?" he asked, knowing he wouldn't receive an answer, wouldn't hear one even if she tried.

But right now she was all he had, this waif-like, blood-soaked teenager.

"Please. I need to know. Am I back there?"

If there had been one gift to having lived a life like his, it was his ability to play it cool, to keep a whirlpool of emotion hidden beneath a carefully constructed, albeit shaky, surface—one he allowed only a trusted few to see beneath. He'd become so skilled he could sometimes hide the full height of his emotion from even himself.

So the audible fear within his own desperate request unnerved even him.

She was barely visible now, but he could feel her pity and her pain. There came what he could only describe as a flash of energy, a charge in the air like that of a coming electrical storm, and suddenly she was there again, solid before him. And, for the first time since he'd begun seeing her all those years ago, he watched as her mouth opened in an effort to form a verbal reply.

He held his breath, waiting. But his anticipation was replaced with horror as from her mouth poured a torrent of blood. Thick and black, it rushed down her chin, flowed over her chest, painted the front of her nightgown straight to her bare toes.

He shut his eyes against the image, although he found it seared into his brain like a flash copy.

When he'd gathered up enough courage to wrench open his eyes, she was gone.

As terrifying as the sight of her had been, the idea of being alone in this place was far, far worse.

His eyes searched out the dark corners for any sign of her, anything to suggest she was still here somewhere.

There was nothing, no sign of her, not even a lingering impression of her fear. But he found he had more than enough of his own to fill the void she'd left.

Sully lowered himself onto the mattress, back against the cold wall, and waited.

As far as Dez could tell, he was out of obvious options—short of storming Lockwood and getting himself arrested for assaulting and threatening staff in a search for answers he knew they'd never willingly provide.

And while he wasn't above using brute force when necessary, he suspected that wouldn't help him in this case. He'd visited Sully often enough at Lockwood to remember the size of some of the orderlies and nurses. He knew he could get past a couple of them easily enough, but there was no way he'd manage all of them, particularly with them rushing him several at a time as they no doubt would. And he couldn't imagine any way to break into a place capable of being secured like Fort Knox. He knew there was a wing for the criminally insane and those deemed otherwise dangerous or a flight risk, and he expected Sully would have ended up there. The thought turned his stomach, but he'd need a lot more than muscle or even cunning to get himself in and Sully out.

He'd need a bloody miracle.

Somewhere along the way, Pax had wormed his way into the front passenger seat, and Dez reached over to scratch the dog under the chin as he drove back toward the city centre, its skyscrapers gleaming in the near-distance. The sun was out in full, the afternoon a perfect combination of warm and gently breezy—the kind of day he would once have spent chasing a giggling Kayleigh through the backyard.

It seemed wholly appropriate now, given his change in circumstances, he should instead visit the cemetery.

Dez steered his SUV down the gravelled pathways, searching for the place where he'd first encountered Sully last night. If he couldn't find a way to get to his brother in the present, he'd fall back on the investigative technique of piecing together as many of Sully's previous movements as he could in the hopes of finding something he could use. After all, Sully might not be back at Lockwood; if someone else had him, Dez would be wasting his time—and, quite possibly, Sully's life—by allowing himself to be blind to other possibilities.

The cemetery looked different by day, challenging him to recall his path last night. He parked near the chapel. After climbing out, he held his door open long enough to allow Pax to join him. They paced back and forth through the rows of newer graves until, at last, his eyes settled upon what he knew to be the right one. There was no mistaking it, the mess he and Sully had left in the dark, soil strewn over the grave's grassy edges and petals scattered here and there from destroyed flowers—the ones they hadn't completely buried in their rush—with half the site bordered by large paw prints.

The family of the "Lovingly Remembered" Mr. Edward Overton, aged eighty-two, would not be pleased.

Dez wasn't sure what he expected to find here, but all he'd really ended up with was disappointment. For his part, Pax was providing no help, sitting back on his haunches and looking up at Dez as if inquiring about the next move.

"I don't know, boy," Dez said. "I haven't got a clue. If you want to tell me where you two have been laying your heads, that might be a good start."

Pax opened his mouth but, as expected, no answer emerged, his tongue simply lolling out as he panted in the sunshine. Dez trained his sight on the inside of his eyelids as he shook his head. "Asking a dog for answers. I'm an idiot."

When he reopened his eyes, he discovered he wasn't the sole human occupant of the graveyard. In the distance, a few sections away, a woman stood, head bowed, hand gripping what could be a white flower.

Dez's mind flashed back two years, to a graveside service at which he'd choked his way through a eulogy he'd spent several painful nights writing while Eva massaged his shoulders and edited his grammar. He'd avoided the spot since, hating cemeteries as a rule, particularly hating this one for holding the graves of both his brothers and his father.

Now he found himself drawn back to the site of Sully's grave, the questions rewriting themselves in his brain as he neared, shifting from wondering whether the woman was there for Sully to why. Because, as he reached the edge of the section, there was no doubt she was there for him.

She turned to Dez as he approached, eyes wide with surprise and shiny with yet-unshed tears. Her honey-coloured hair was streaked with a grey that could be mistaken for highlights in the sun, and her features were youthful and pretty despite the scattering of fine lines that suggested she was close to forty.

Her smile did little more than turn up the corners of her mouth, coming nowhere near her eyes.

"I'm sorry," she said. "You startled me."

"Sorry about that." Dez looked from her to the grave, then back again. "How did you know Sully?"

Something behind the woman's eyes shuttered closed. Were this a suspect interview, Dez would take that as his cue to back off a touch, to revert to relatively suspect-safe and relationship-building subjects like hobbies, skills or the symbolism behind tattoos. But right now, with Sully missing, he didn't have the luxury of time.

He decided to offer her some information about himself in the hopes of some quid pro quo.

"He was my brother."

"Sullivan didn't have a brother."

Dez tried to conceal his surprise but knew, even without the benefit of a mirror, he was failing miserably. "How would you know that?"

The woman broke the connection with Dez long enough to kneel next to the headstone and lay the white rose along the base, avoiding the silk arrangement Dez's mother had likely placed there during her last visit. The woman rested a hand on the stone, her fingers lightly tracing the letters of Sully's first name.

Dez stood in the silence, his mind formulating the answer before she'd even given one, so that when she finally spoke, his shock was somewhat lessened.

But not by much.

"I'm his mother."

9

Pax had proven himself hard to predict, but judging from his low growls and rigid stance, he'd decided he didn't much care for his missing human's mother.

For his part, Dez hadn't yet made up his mind on whether he should side with Pax on that point. The woman had, after all, dumped Sully on someone's doorstep in the middle of the night, abandoning the infant and leaving him to the mercies of the weather, wandering animals and, potentially, predators of the human persuasion.

As far as Dez was aware, no one really knew the story of Sully's birth, the last name Gray simply given to him when the investigation failed to turn up any clue to his real identity. The infant Sully had come in a second- or-thirdhand bassinet with a piece of paper tucked in beneath him, block letters written in black marker: "Please call me Sullivan."

It was all Dez had ever learned, information gleaned from the police file he'd managed to sneak a peek at during his years with the KRPD.

Now, with the potential for answers at his fingertips, he had to hold back from jumping too far and too deep without first testing the waters. Policing had instilled in him a healthy dose of skepticism and, with everything that had transpired within recent hours, he had plenty to be suspicious about.

With Pax on one side and the woman on the other, Dez led them to a bench near the treed edge of the cemetery. Dez guessed it had to have been near here that Sully had stood two years ago, watching his own funeral. He tried to ignore the anger that bubbled up at the thought. Dez had a keen recollection of breaking down in Eva's arms after gingerly lowering Sully's empty urn into the cool, damp soil. The idea that Sully had been nearby, had seen their suffering and had done nothing to stop it, was infuriating. But Dez's anger was tempered through his awareness of Sully's continued fear of the possibility of returning to Lockwood. There was only so much fault Dez could find with his brother, particularly given the childhood he'd endured prior to finding a home with the Braddocks.

That traumatic childhood had been thanks in no small part to Sully's mother.

"Lucienne Dule," the woman said, extending a small, finely boned hand.

Dez shook, finding her grip firmer than anticipated. "Dez Braddock. Sully came to live with my family when he was seven."

"Did your parents adopt him?"

"In a way, I guess. He was a foster and the placement went well, so it became a permanent one."

"They were good to him?"

"They were good to everybody. And they loved him. Damn sight more than I can say about anyone else he'd been placed with to that point."

It was a low blow, he supposed. But she was, after all, the reason Sully had ended up in foster care in the first place, and he wasn't of a mind to hold back for her sake.

"What do you mean? Was he mistreated before?"

"That would be putting it mildly. I won't get into details, but it took a few years of counselling to get him more or less sorted out."

"But he was okay then?"

"Well, he had us. So, yeah, I guess he was."

Lucienne studied Dez, a small smile on her face as she looked to be piecing something together. "You don't have much use for me, do you?"

"I don't know you."

"And neither did Sullivan. Therein lies the point."

"Look, you've got to understand. I love Sully. In every way that matters, he's my brother. So, yeah, I'm pretty protective when it comes to him."

"You speak about him like he's still here."

Damn. Dez thought fast, came up with an answer in short order that seemed to make sense. "He still is to me, I guess. I've never been able to make a whole lot of sense of it, but I believe there's something beyond this life."

Lucienne inhaled, a signal she was about to say something else, but Dez jumped in. He had some questions he wanted answered first.

"He always wondered, you know, where he came from, why he was given up. I've had some questions of my own on that count."

"And you'd like me to answer them."

Dez said nothing more, allowing his silence to form his response.

Lucienne nodded slightly, a tight smile forming before she looked away, gaze returning to Sully's grave.

"I was young when I had him, just sixteen. Please understand, I didn't want to give him up. I was just a child myself, and my parents wouldn't support me. I was given an option, just one: do what they said was the right thing and give him up, or learn how to be an adult on my own with my son. Obviously, you know what decision I made. It's one I've regretted ever since."

"You left Sully on someone's doorstep."

"Not just someone. She was a social worker, a very nice lady named Denise Wilson. I didn't know her personally, but I knew of her. It was naïve of me, I suppose, but I really hoped she'd just fall in love with Sullivan and keep him."

"You really thought that would happen? No investigation?"

"I was sixteen. I didn't know anything back then."

"What about your parents? They didn't bother to set you straight?"

"I just told you they said they'd kick me out with my newborn child, no money, no job, no support. You think they cared whether I left my son on a doorstep? He wasn't even a human being to them. He was nothing but a major roadblock for all their plans for me."

"What about his father? Did he ever consider taking Sully?"

Lucienne uttered a low chuckle, free of humour. "What father? Listen, I was a teenage girl, and a pretty screwed up one at that. My parents were strict and I rebelled. I went through a phase where I slept around with what some people called the entire male half of the school population. Sullivan's father could be virtually anyone. And let me tell you, when it became clear I was pregnant, not one of those boys approached me to see if the baby might be his. I sure wouldn't have wanted someone that irresponsible or unfeeling in charge of my child."

"I hate to tell you this, but there were plenty of irresponsible, unfeeling people in charge of your child. At least until he was seven."

Lucienne looked away, her gaze flitting to the grave before moving off, her head turning just enough he couldn't tell what she was looking at. But the way her shoulders slumped told him his statement had hit home, and he found that more difficult to swallow than expected. After all, he'd had fifteen years with Sully, enough time to watch him find a safe place to put the pain from his past—at least until Lockwood. At this moment, Lucienne had nothing but Dez's words.

"I'm sorry," he said. "You're right. You were a kid. You were trying to do the right thing."

"It doesn't feel like the right thing."

"Look, Sully had a good life with us. We took care of him, made sure he found a way to be happy."

Lucienne looked back at him finally, a smile on her face belying the sheen of tears in her eyes. "I'm grateful to you. All of you. Thank you for that."

"There's no need. We got as much out of it as Sully did." Dez wasn't about to go further down that road with a complete stranger, so threw out another question before Lucienne could get her own in. "These plans your parents had for you. Did you get there?"

"I do well for myself, I suppose. I have a good job in IT that pays enough. But I've never stopped thinking about my son."

To the non-skeptical, Sully's birth mother turning up at just this moment, just as Dez was struggling to figure out how to find his brother, might have seemed little more than a monster coincidence. But Dez was plenty skeptical and, as a general rule, hated coincidence. "You been here before?"

"No."

"So why now? Why turn up at Sully's grave two years after his death?"

"I wasn't able to find him before."

"How'd you find him now?"

"I hired a private investigator," she said. "He was able to secure information for me about the last name Sullivan was given. I was happy he'd been able to keep his first name—it was my grandfather's name. Unfortunately, one of the first pieces of information that came up after learning his given last name was the obituary. It took me a while to screw up the courage to come here."

"Why not hire someone sooner, try to find him before now?"

"I thought about it. Thought about it a lot. But I always came back to the same place. I'd given him up, and I wasn't sure I had the right to search for happiness and forgiveness through him, or to interfere in whatever life he'd made for himself. And, perhaps most importantly, I wasn't sure he'd actually want to see me. I didn't know what I'd do if I met him and he told me he wanted nothing to do with me."

"Sully's not like that. He's one of the best people I've ever known. I don't know how he does it, but he's not one to stay angry. He doesn't forget, mind you, but most of the time, he forgives."

"You're referring to him in the present tense again."

Double damn. "I guess I am. Hard to get away from."

"You don't need to explain to me," Lucienne said. "I believe very strongly there's something beyond this flesh and blood world too."

Dez didn't say anything; at this point, he figured he'd better focus on getting his head screwed on straight before reopening his big mouth. Lucienne stepped into the silence.

"Do you believe some people have a greater knowledge of a world beyond this one?"

"What do you mean?"

"You said before you believe there's something beyond this life. Do you also believe there are people who can see into the other side?"

Dez stalled, trying to think through how best to answer. Of course, the answer was yes. But Sully had told precious few people about what he could do, and for good reason. Dr. Gerhardt had diagnosed him as a paranoid schizophrenic suffering from episodes of psychosis and hallucinations. And Sully had spent much of his young life enduring the effects of being different merely because of his personal history and his shy, sensitive nature; the last thing he'd needed was for that other huge difference to become common knowledge.

Even so, there was no denying the truth of what Sully could do. Dez had become a believer, albeit a reluctant one, early on.

"Yeah, I guess I do."

"Sullivan was one of them, wasn't he?"

Crap. "Look, Ms. Dule, I'm not trying to—"

Lucienne cut him off with a hand on his. "I'm sorry. I didn't mean to upset you or put you on the spot. Let me explain—and I believe I can because I think you know. I think Sullivan was able to, and I think he would have told you. What he didn't know, what he couldn't have known, was he got it from me. I've always been able to see and speak with the dead."

This time, Dez turned to Sully's grave, as if he would find some clarity there. This conversation was fast going in a direction that had him regretting ever approaching this woman.

"I'm not meaning to make you uncomfortable," Lucienne said. "You don't have to tell me about Sullivan. I can see you're telling the truth about being protective of him, and I appreciate it very much. But I need you to know I share his ability."

"Why? It's none of my business."

"It is your business. It's your business because you love him."

"What's that got to do with you telling me you see ghosts?"

"Because I have never stopped seeing them. But I have never seen *him*. And the reason I think I have never seen him is because I don't believe there's anything there for me to see. Dez, my son is alive. And I think you suspect that too. Maybe …."

She paused, all but forcing his eyes back to hers before she continued. "Maybe you don't just suspect. Maybe you *know*."

What he knew or didn't know was nothing he was prepared to share, not with people close to him and certainly not with a stranger. Not without learning more about this woman, not without assuring himself she could be trusted with Sully. "I don't know what it is you can see exactly, but I know what I saw. I stood right here two years ago, and I buried my brother."

"Are you so sure you did?"

"What's that supposed to mean?"

"How did he die?"

Nothing in her tone suggested she harboured any of the heated anguish or cold dread he himself had felt when the cave had collapsed. She hadn't experienced it when Sully failed to respond to his desperate calls or when Dez had bloodied his hands, arms and knees trying to shift unmovable rock until a punch from Forbes Raynor had knocked panic down to despair. Even though Sully had, in fact, managed to escape, the agony of that experience was still fresh in his mind.

Without another word, he walked away from the woman, aware of Pax trotting along beside him.

"Wait," Lucienne called out. "Please."

He heard her following, felt her hand on his arm as Pax growled a warning at her. Dez laid a hand on the dog's head as he turned to face Lucienne.

"What did I say?" she asked.

"Just like that? Just like that, you want to know how he died, like it means nothing?"

"It doesn't mean anything because he's not dead."

"I was there, all right? It destroyed me. You want to know how he died? He was crushed to death under a pile of rock. He was inside a cave we found as kids, one I'd taken him to a couple weeks before the collapse, thinking he'd be safe there for a while, at least until I could find something better. A crew spent four full days shifting rock and searching where they could get to. At the end of it, they told us there was no way anyone was alive down there, no way anyone could have gotten out."

"Then they were wrong."

For his part, Dez had a few questions about that, too, but he'd deal with it down the road, once he'd found Sully. "Come on. No heat signatures were down there. No one and nothing alive. They were certain."

"You can't argue with a mother's intuition, or the fact I have other ways of knowing things. Now, please listen. I need your help."

"I've got stuff to take care of. Important stuff."

"More important than saving your brother?"

"What?"

"It's not just that he's alive. He's in danger. I know he is. Now, I know you're a police officer."

"I was a pol—Hold on. How'd you know?"

"The obituary. I ran internet searches on the people listed as family. I wanted to know as much as I could about the people who raised my son."

"But a few minutes ago, you acted like you'd never heard of me."

"I needed to be sure you were who you said you were. Like I said, my son is in danger and I'm afraid I might be, too. Dez, please, I need your help."

"Ms. Dule, I'm really—"

"Please, Dez. As his brother. I need you to help me find Sullivan. Before it's too late."

ARGUING WITH LUCIENNE WAS POINTLESS.

Dez hadn't decided whether to confide in the woman about Sully's sudden return, but he didn't question their shared desire to find him.

The real question was how to go about doing it.

Dez walked the woman to her car in the cemetery's parking area while Pax kept a short distance back, sniffing around a few trees and lifting his leg where he deemed necessary. Lucienne drove a white BMW X3, further proof she'd gone the distance fulfilling her parents' wishes.

"I'll look for Sully," he told her as she slid in behind the wheel. "Not because I believe you but because I'd hate myself forever if he needed me and I let him down."

The statement contained more truth than lie, so it rolled off Dez's tongue in a way that didn't make him feel like a guilty schoolboy.

"Thank you so much," she said. "Where do we start?"

"We?"

"Of course, we. He's my son."

"No offence, ma'am, but I think I'll be able to handle this on my own."

"That may be true, but I'm still going to help."

"Ms. Dule—"

"Please don't argue. I missed out on a whole life with Sullivan. I let him down in the worst way a mother can let down her child. You have to see I need to do this, for him and for me."

Dez knew all about letting people down, had spent much of his youth and his entire adult life shadowed by guilt and regret. And so he knew, loathe as he was to entertain company on this journey, he couldn't refuse her this opportunity to make things right.

"I'm going to need to speak to your P.I."

"Why?"

"Because he's somehow been able to connect dots we were never able to. I think it would be helpful."

In all honesty, in Dez's opinion, the only truly helpful move right now would be finding an invisibility spell to enable him to pass unseen through the halls of Lockwood until he found Sully. But, should the alternative prove true and his brother not be there, Dez knew he'd need all the information he could get his hands on. If Sully had been targeted, there was a reason, and it was something Dez couldn't get his head around given what little he currently knew. And if Sully was running from something other than Lockwood, there was a good chance it was connected to his past—a past some P.I. had apparently been able to unearth.

"I'll give him a call, see if he'll agree to meet with you."

"You're paying him. He'll meet with me if you say so."

"I've already paid him, actually. But I'll see if I can set something up, anyway."

Dez waited outside the car, watching as Lucienne dialled and held the phone to her ear, then repeated the process twice more.

"That's weird," she said after the third attempt. "He's not picking up. He always picks up."

"Maybe he's in the middle of something."

"Maybe."

"Why don't we just head over to his office? He's got an office, right?"

"Yeah. Yeah, we could try that."

"Let's take my vehicle," Dez said. "I have a feeling you won't be wanting to vacuum dog hair out of your car. Anyway, I shouldn't leave mine parked on the path over there."

He led the way to his SUV and held the back door for Pax to hop in before opening the front passenger side door. "Sorry about this," he said as he swept the dog's hair off the seat. "He sheds quite a bit and it's kind of all over the place."

Lucienne climbed in, hair and dried dog drool notwithstanding. "That's fine. I've got bigger problems."

Pax made a sound that was half-growl and half-bark.

"He doesn't like me, does he?" Lucienne said.

"It's not you," Dez said, although he wasn't sure that was altogether true. "He likes to ride shotgun."

Dez was circling the vehicle to get in himself when his phone rang. His heart gave an involuntary thump as he saw Eva's name and image on the call display, a photo taken in happier times. She was wearing one of those beaming smiles she used to show so often, one she reserved for the old Dez, a guy neither of them knew anymore. Those had been carefree times in their marriage, hopeful ones.

With any luck, he'd get back there, and to her.

"Eva?"

"Hey, I checked with Lockwood. Of course, they're not able to provide names, but I asked anyway whether there were any warrants executed or if they've had any recent admissions. The woman I spoke to said no to both."

"Who did you talk to?"

"No one in admin—for good reason. I don't want this coming back to bite me in the ass. So are you going to let this go now that you know Sully isn't there?"

"We don't know for sure."

"I just told you there were no new admissions."

"None they told you about."

"For God's sake, Dez."

"Listen ...." He turned his back to the truck, enabling him to speak privately without fear of Lucienne reading his lips or his expression. For added measures, he took a few steps away and spoke quietly. "I came back to the cemetery where I was attacked last night."

"Did you report that yet?"

"No."

"Go to the hospital?"

"No. Listen to me. While I was looking around the spot where I'd been buried, I saw a woman standing next to Sully's grave. She says she's Sully's mother."

"Damn it. Why didn't you go to the hospital?"

"Did you hear what I just said?"

"Yeah. Yeah, I heard you. That's kind of weird, isn't it?"

"Her turning up when all of this is going on? Yeah, damn right it's weird. I'm hoping you can run her name for me, see if anything comes up. Her name is Lucienne Dule. She says she was sixteen when she had Sully, so I figure that makes her about forty now. She's on the short side, blonde hair—"

"Dez, no. You know damn well I can't just run random searches on people."

"Eva—"

"No. I was investigated too after all that stuff went down with you helping Sully two years ago. I'm still working my ass off to convince people I didn't know what you were up to."

"You didn't."

"At first. I'm not an idiot, you know. Sully doesn't go back to Lockwood at the end of his pass and you come up with some cock-and-bull story that he got away from you. I know you— better than you know yourself."

Dez couldn't argue with that logic. "So you won't check her out for me?"

"No!"

"Okay, babe. Thanks anyway."

"Don't call me babe ... Snowman."

Eva disconnected the call, but left Dez dangling somewhere between disappointment and hope. She didn't sound eager to help him out with what could prove to be another awkward request, that much was clear. But she had looked into the Lockwood angle, and there was still a chance she would oblige him on his second query too.

Then there was the other thing. She hadn't called him Snowman in close to a year and a half, her use of the pet name having dwindled and finally died an untimely death during those months after Sully's funeral, when Dez had stopped taking comfort in his wife and gone looking for it in a bottle.

He'd missed the name almost as much as he missed her.

Dropping the phone back into his pocket, he pinched at the corners of his eyes to stem the threatening tears before returning to his vehicle.

WITH LUCIENNE ACTING as guide from the passenger seat, Dez drove them across the Kimotan River to the city's North Bank district.

The flood had created uninhabitable shells of many of the buildings on the riverbank—those that hadn't slid into the raging river—but plenty of work had been done in this district to tear down and start over. Dez suspected the quick rebuild had something to do with the fact this part of the city was within view of the glitzy city centre where KR's displaced wealthy had sought refuge in newly built condo towers and, just to the west, ill-advised river-facing estates. They didn't want their views tarnished by ruin, so efforts had been made to reestablish the North Bank as quickly as possible. That meant new middle-class homes and businesses fronted older parts of the neighbourhood, much of it remaining a classy throwback to the Victorian era when

KR was first established. The new builds reflected the old, providing a uniform look to the area that pleased the rich who peered at it from the windows of their skyscrapers.

To Dez, the falsely classical structures befitted a neighbourhood full of people yearning to be something they were not. Streets were filled with expensive brownstone row houses that cost far more than they were worth and San Francisco-esque Victorian mini-mansions that had their owners trapped in a debt they'd never escape. All so they could pretend for a few brief years—until the bank came calling with foreclosure notices—they, too, could have the comforts and luxuries so common on the South Bank.

Not everyone was so heedless about economics, though. Some of the Victorian homes had been subdivided into apartments, while others—such as the one Lucienne had him pulling up to— had been converted into office space.

"Nice digs for a P.I.," Dez said, trying to make out the signage on a brass plate next to the door. "What's his name?"

"Lachlan Fields."

Dez turned his gaze to his passenger. "Lachlan Fields?"

"Yes. Do you know him?"

"Yeah, I know him. Or I did. He retired from the KRPD last year. Amazing career, brilliant investigator. They say he almost singlehandedly solved the Co-ed Killer case while he was with Homicide."

"Co-ed Killer? I think I read about that. Some lunatic was running around strangling university students, wasn't he?"

"He killed two, was actively targeting a third when Fields caught up with him using a combination of psychological and geographic profiling and some good, old-fashioned police work. He's a legend to anyone with a badge."

"That makes sense," Lucienne said. "I went looking for the best, and everyone recommended him, said he could find the unfindable."

"I'm curious," Dez said. "If you've got him, why do you need me? I mean, I'm no dunce, but next to Fields I look like some half-witted wannabe. Why not just ask Fields to look for Sully?"

"Because Sullivan clearly went to a lot of trouble to have the world believe he's dead. The way I see it, the fewer people who know he isn't, the better—at least until we know more about it. You care about Sullivan, want the best for him. So you'll keep anything you find to yourself. As much as I like Mr. Fields, he's an outsider, an unknown. Right now, I just want people around I can trust."

Dez nodded. That seemed to make sense, at least as much as anything did at the moment.

Dez cracked the window for Pax and was following Lucienne toward the building when the dog barked behind them.

"Bloody hell," Dez said, turning to find Pax's eyes fixed on the front of the Victorian as he continued to voice whatever was troubling him. "I'd better bring him with us. I'm getting the impression he hates being left out of the loop."

"I'm not sure it's a pet-friendly building."

"It is today." Dez reached the vehicle and opened the door, allowing Pax to spill out onto the sidewalk. Unfortunately, that wasn't the end of the matter; the dog took off toward the building's front door. Lucienne stepped aside to avoid being run down. Once at the double doors, Pax stood on his back legs, placing his front paws against the oval glass panes as he continued to bark.

"Pax!" Dez said as he rushed up and pulled the dog off the door. "Down. Down! Holy hell, what's up with you?"

Pax looked up at him, a protracted whine breaking off into a bark.

"Okay, okay, relax. Jeez." While Pax wasn't leashed, he had a collar at least, enabling Dez to hold the animal back as he opened the door and stepped into the entrance hall.

A man popped his head out of one of the offices, eyebrows lowered, a practiced set of frown lines suggesting he didn't spend a whole lot of time smiling. "This is a no-pets building."

"Then you're in luck," Dez said. "He's not a pet. He's my service dog."

"What kind of service?"

"Mainly domestic," Dez said. "He's good at bringing me stuff, but he sucks at housecleaning."

The man glared and slammed his door shut. Dez grinned, but Lucienne was all business.

"He's on the second floor," she said, stepping around Dez and the dog as she led the way up a carpeted wooden staircase. Pax tugged at his leash, wanting to venture past the stairs toward what looked to be a rear entrance, but Dez kept him in check, and the two of them brought up the rear as they stepped onto the second-floor landing. Three separate offices were up here, all of which Dez guessed were once bedrooms. One of them, according to the brass plate on the solid-looking oak door, belonged to Lachlan Fields.

Lucienne rapped quietly with delicate knuckles, then waited a moment. There was no answer. She knocked again, louder this time. Still nothing.

"Must be out," Dez said. "Might be on a job. That would explain why he wasn't picking up your calls earlier."

"Maybe."

Dez looked around at the other doors. "Maybe someone in these other offices can tell us when he went out."

"No good," Lucienne said. "There's no one in those offices. They're still for rent."

Dez looked closer, noticed the plates had yet to be engraved.

"Could you just try the door?" Lucienne said.

"Why don't you try the door?"

"I'm scared."

"Of what?"

Lucienne shook her head, her eyes closing tight and her lips clamping together so hard they virtually disappeared.

Dez felt the blood drain from his face as it hit him. Pax's barking. Lucienne's anxiety. The inability to reach the detective.

Dez put a hand out on the wall to steady himself as his head spun with his heart, now pounding inside his chest. "You see him, don't you?"

She neither opened her eyes nor parted her lips. Her simple nod was answer enough.

"Ah, shit," Dez said. "Okay, just—Bloody hell …. So if you're seeing him, he's dead already, right?"

Another nod.

Dez had seen dead bodies before, of course, had seen far more than his share on the job. The likelihood of finding Lachlan Fields dead didn't trouble him; in all honesty, the guy was kind of an asshole. It was the idea the entire process was being monitored by the man's ghost. Dez could handle "dead." "Undead" was what he had the problem with.

But there was no getting around it. He couldn't just call this in as a death without confirming it first, no way to realistically explain how he knew without having actually entered the room. And he couldn't, in good conscience, allow Lucienne to go first, uncertain exactly what they were going to find on the other side of that door.

"Okay, just …. just stand over by the stairs. I'll check it out."

Blowing out a breath and keeping one hand on Pax's collar, Dez gripped the brass handle through the cotton fabric of his T-shirt. The knob turned in his grasp, clicking through as the unlocked door opened for him.

He eased it open just a crack at first, keeping his eyes squinted as if that would make what he found inside easier to manage. He'd never seen a ghost himself, but he knew enough about them from Sully. The idea of seeing two versions of Lachlan Fields—one lying on the floor or slumped in a chair and the other standing in front of him—was more than he would know what to do with.

But there was nothing.

He pushed the door, opening the gap until he hit resistance. Then he saw the mess. Papers, files and various desk supplies covered the floor. His gaze landed on a pair of legs sticking out from behind the far side of a large oak desk.

And the blood. The blood was everywhere.

He was unable to see a second version of Lachlan Fields, and he took some comfort in that as he slipped into the room.

"Stay in the hall," he told Lucienne, then turned to close the door, effectively keeping both her and Pax in the hall and out of what looked like a significant crime scene.

Watching the floor to avoid stepping in potential evidence he might otherwise accidentally step in, Dez circled the desk, intending to check on the man. Sure, Lucienne said she'd seen his ghost, but Dez knew he had to make sure.

It was Lachlan Fields, all right, a large gash to his head oozing blood, one of the man's own awards—a golf trophy by the looks of it—lying nearby as the likely murder weapon. To make matters worse, a letter opener protruded from Lachlan's chest, more blood seeping from that wound.

Dez looked closer. The man was lying on his back, providing a good view of the blood stain spreading across the front of his rumpled button-down. And Dez recalled something he'd heard early on in his career.

The dead don't bleed.

11

UTTERING A QUIET CURSE, Dez closed the rest of the distance between himself and the older man, squatting to check for a pulse.

Lachlan gasped. A bloody hand reached out, caught Dez's wrist and held on like a vice.

Dez fell back on his ass with a sound similar to the one Lachlan had just made, and worked to twist his wrist out of the older man's grip. When that didn't immediately work, and not wanting to injure the man further, Dez settled for talking to him as he pulled out his phone with his free hand and used his thumb to dial 9-1-1.

"It's Dez Braddock, sir. I'm getting some help for you. Just hold on. Help's coming."

The man released him and sank back into unconsciousness as Dez spoke to the operator, speaking over Pax's sudden barking in the hall to provide an address and the man's identity—a surefire way to get police here quickly. Lachlan Fields may be retired, but Dez was certain this would nonetheless be treated as something akin to an officer down.

Sure enough, it took just over a minute for the first unit to arrive, patrol officers taking over first aid duties from Dez. By the time he made his way back into the hall to take charge of Pax, an

EMS team and four more units—two patrol and two plainclothes —were arriving.

Unfortunately, one of the plainclothes members was Sergeant Forbes Raynor.

Forbes had managed to secure himself a place on the Major Crimes unit, along with the accompanying promotion to sergeant, a couple years before Dez's departure from the KRPD. But where Lachlan's healthy sense of self-worth had been well-earned, Forbes's ego—at least in Dez's view—had little to back it, his promotion the likely result of connections within the PD brass and the business community at large. Forbes's father, Charles "Bad Luck Chuck" Raynor, was the city's longtime mayor and so sat at the head of the Board of Police Commissioners when his son had been angling for the promotion. While conflict of interest legislation meant Bad Luck Chuck was unable to interfere in his son's affairs, Dez had little doubt the older man's position nonetheless had some considerable impact on Forbes's moving up the ladder.

Forbes wasn't a slightly built man by any means, making his treatment of his wife Greta all the more deplorable in Dez's mind. Though he came in several inches below Dez's considerable stature, Forbes carried himself as if he were the largest man in any room, broad shoulders back, head held high and back ramrod straight while holding his heavily muscled arms away from his body to create additional space around himself. While he worked hard to project steely self-confidence, Dez knew better, recognized the man's innate awareness he would never fully measure up to someone of Lachlan Fields's status.

But in struggling to build himself up, Forbes had inadvertently torn himself down too, alienating anyone who might have otherwise called him a friend.

Dez remembered a conversation he'd had once with Sully at the Black Fox during one of his brother's breaks. Dez had barely managed to escape a group of his drunken cop buddies as they cajoled and hung onto his arm, yammering slurred words into his ear. Dez and Sully had temporarily retreated to a quiet back table,

Dez waving off another attempt from three friends at drawing him over for a round of shooters, when he noticed Forbes glaring at him from a nearby bar stool.

Back in those days, Dez had been a different person, liking being liked and dwelling far too deeply on those rare instances when he wasn't. Sully had read Dez's silence without needing to ask, and had answered the unasked question by falling back on that unsettling ability he had to see far beyond what a person chose to reveal.

"He's jealous," he'd said. "You're constantly surrounded by people who want to hang out with you. He just sits at the bar by himself, watching everyone else."

"Yeah," Dez said. "It's downright creepy. It's like he's hoping to catch someone at something he can use against them later."

Sully had smiled at that and sat forward. "Did you think that about me when I was a kid?"

"That was different. You were never like him."

"Are you sure about that? You don't really know him."

"I know *you*. You're a good guy. He's ...."

Sully finished Dez's statement in his own way. "What I could have become if I hadn't ended up with Mom and Dad and you. Bitter, isolated and lonely."

Dez guessed that conversation went back two or three years, before he'd lost his dad and Sully was involuntarily committed to Lockwood. Plenty had changed since then, none of it for the better, so it seemed fitting Forbes Raynor remained the sole constant.

"I should have known you'd be in the middle of this," Forbes said now, looking Dez up and down. His gaze was both appraising and condescending. Dez knew Forbes was examining him for evidence of involvement in the attack, but he had the distinct impression he was also putting him on notice he disapproved of his very existence.

Then again, after last night, Dez had what he figured was good reason for a counter-appraisal. For now, he kept his suspicions to himself. Throwing out accusations without proof, particularly when the likely perpetrator was a police officer, would be a dumb move.

"I'm not," Dez said. "I just got here and found him like this."

"Right."

"Hey, go ahead and ask the guy downstairs. He saw me come in not five minutes ago. I think it's pretty obvious Lachlan has been on the floor a fair bit longer than that."

"I'll leave that to Ident to confirm, thanks."

Forbes's partner Sgt. Clark Davies entered the conversation, having taken a moment to check on the victim, now in the hands of an advanced care paramedic. "Leave him alone, Forbes. You know damn well Dez didn't do this."

Clark turned his attention to Dez. "Did you notice anyone leaving the building as you were coming in?"

Dez shook his head in the negative. "Nothing, man. Sorry. And like I said, I'm guessing Lachlan was attacked some time prior to me getting here. Some of the blood around him was already looking tacky when I got to him."

Clark nodded. Forbes harrumphed.

"What were you here about?" Clark asked, the question giving Dez pause.

"It's kind of weird, but I ran into this woman at the cemetery today while I was visiting my family there. She was upset and said something about having hired Lachlan to look into a matter for her but was having trouble reaching him by phone. I agreed to come down here with her to check it out. This is what I found."

"And this woman," Forbes said, making a show of looking around. "Where is she exactly?"

That was a good question. "I don't know. She was here a minute ago. She's got to be around somewhere."

Clark flipped to a new page in his notebook. "We're going to need a name and a description."

Dez thought fast, uncertain how much he wanted to reveal. It wasn't that he owed Lucienne anything, but there was more to this than her well-being. He didn't want this woman in the hands of police, given her belief Sully was alive. If someone inside the department managed to gain her trust, and she responded by turning to police in her search for her son, that would easily blow whatever cover Sully had created for himself and throw him into harm's way.

Then again, it was likely Lachlan kept records of his clients, meaning any attempt by Dez to deceive would do nothing but cast himself in a bad light. Should his own investigations reveal Sully had been taken by someone other than those at Lockwood, Dez expected he'd need the police with, not against, him.

Even so ….

"She used the first name Lucienne. I didn't ask her last name."

Forbes sneered. "Really?"

Dez returned his attention to Clark. "She was concerned about Lachlan, so that became my priority pretty quick. We didn't exactly have time to chat on the ride over as she was directing me here. I've never been to Lachlan's office before, and I had no idea how to find it."

"Fair enough," Clark said. "You have a description for me?"

"About five-four or five-five, between one-ten and one-twenty pounds, I'd say. She was blonde, about forty years old, but she has features that make her look younger. She was wearing a knee-length gray skirt and a white button-down shirt. I didn't notice much for jewellery but I think she had on some sort of silver necklace."

Clark snagged a passing patrol officer and had Dez repeat the description. Having sent the constable to conduct a quick search of the immediate area for the woman, Clark returned to Dez.

"I'm going to need you to provide a detailed statement."

"Yeah, sure. You need me to come in?"

"Nah," Clark said. "I'll go grab the forms out of the car. Just find yourself a spot somewhere and write something out for me. If we need more later, I'll give you a call."

By the time Dez finished with his statement, Lucienne still hadn't reappeared. Patrol officers turned up nothing more about her save the word of the man downstairs who recalled her coming in with "the big jerk and his dog."

Clark was busy briefing the forensic identification unit, which had recently arrived, leaving Dez to hand in his statement to Forbes. Naturally, the older man wasn't prepared to just leave well enough alone, which suited Dez fine. After all, he had a bone of his own to pick.

"You might be buddy-buddy with Clark, but I'm onto you," Forbes said. "Don't think I don't know the kind of company you've been keeping these days. Only a matter of time before you cross the line in a way that has everyone seeing you the way I do."

Dez chose to ignore the comment, focusing on his real concern. "Silver Sam's. You know it?"

"The pub in Riverview? Yeah, I'm familiar. Why?"

"Were you there last night?"

Dez watched Forbes for what he expected would be a lie, but didn't immediately see anything but confusion. "Why?"

"Just answer the question."

"No. I wasn't. Why?"

"Just wondered. Greta was there, is all."

Dez saw the big, red wall go up behind Forbes's eyes, anger barely contained. "You trying to start something here, Braddock?"

Forbes's tone was that blend of quiet and dangerous, the warning as clear as a rattlesnake's tail shake. But while Dez wasn't typically one to go spoiling for a fight, he wasn't about to back down from one either—particularly when he had a purpose in mind.

"Someone followed her last night," he said.

"Who?"

"I'm thinking you know exactly who."

Forbes lowered his chin, allowing him to glare up at Dez in a way that resembled an angry pit bull. Only there was more to his rage now, more than just Dez in its sights. "It wasn't me, you bastard. Did you follow?"

"Of course I did. That's when everything went to hell. I lost sight of them near the Riverview Cemetery. Next thing I know, I'm being attacked."

"What about Greta? What happened to her?"

This wasn't what Dez had been expecting, Forbes doing a more-than-adequate impression of a man in the dark—and a concerned one at that.

"So it wasn't you last night, in the cemetery?"

"I was nowhere near there. What happened to Greta?"

The answer to that question didn't make Dez feel a whole lot better, not to think it and not to say it. While he had few reservations under normal circumstances about upsetting Forbes Raynor, there were some lines he refused to cross. The biggest was messing with a guy's mind when it came to his family.

"I don't know."

———

DEZ HAD BEEN entertaining suspicions his attack last night had something to do with Sully. Now Forbes's believable denial left him in little doubt.

Had the whole thing been an attempt to draw Sully out? If so, it had clearly been done by someone with an inside line on Sully's abilities, given it had been the ghost of a dead five-year-old who had led Sully there in the first place.

That left Dez with the question of what his attacker had expected should Sully not have received the message. Any longer and there was no denying Dez would have needed a pine box or an urn of his own.

Which brought up some other concerns: If the purpose was to lure Sully out to grab him, why not just act on it last night while he was preoccupied in the cemetery? Was it possible the person who'd buried him alive had allowed Sully the opportunity to rescue Dez, thus sparing the culprit the guilt of murder? Dez allowed the hopeful notion only as long as it took him to look back down at his hands, coated in a sticky, dry layer of another man's blood. There was no evidence, of course, Lachlan's attempted murder was connected to Sully or his birth mother, but that would have made it a coincidence of monstrous proportions.

Dez guessed the real answer was Pax, Sully's would-be kidnapper could have been caught unawares by the existence of the large hound. That would have left the man searching for something with which to knock out or kill the dog first, and would explain the evidence Dez had observed and gathered earlier today. That likely meant the man had followed them back to Dez's building and kept watch there, following Sully in the morning and making a move as soon as it became practicable.

Dez had spent the day wavering between anger at Sully and deep worry, and found himself in that uncomfortable in-between again as he waited in his SUV to see whether Lucienne might return. He had questions for her too, such as how she'd seen the ghost of a man who wasn't dead. Sure, Sully had once had a similar experience, but it didn't erase Dez's doubts now.

With only Pax to hear, Dez voiced his frustration anyway: "Damn it, Sull." If only his brother had given him the chance to protect him, maybe this situation would have turned out differently. Maybe.

But then again, his life was filled to the rafters with people he'd let down, so maybe not.

———

With no way of knowing how long he'd been there, trapped in the small cell, Sully struggled to keep his mounting anxiety in check as he listened for the sound of someone approaching from the other side of the door.

Time passed, enough that Sully gave up trying to decide how

much. Morning could have passed to evening, or one day could have given way to the next for all he knew. Most of his thoughts were lost to the dread of seeing Dr. Gerhardt come through that door.

Once in a while, he would reach out mentally, trying to pick up on the Purple Girl, always without luck.

Sully guessed she must have given up on him when he'd repeatedly failed to heed her warnings. Lord knew she'd provided him with more than enough to have prevented this had he listened.

Instead, here he was, trapped in the exact situation he'd been trying so hard to avoid.

His stomach, which had been jumping around as if looking for its own escape, made a rumbling noise, reminding him he hadn't eaten since Dez's. But hungry though he was, Sully doubted his insides would accept food, not until he'd been able to decipher the precise nature of the danger he was in. There were priorities to contend with, after all, and food trailed miles behind the idea of his recapture by Gerhardt and his staff.

As if responding to his silent questions, light footsteps sounded outside the door. Then the sound of a key turning in the lock.

Sully scrambled to his feet, moving to place himself behind the door where his captors wouldn't immediately see him. He'd had plenty of time to think through a plan of attack. It might not be a very good plan; more than likely it was a terrible one. But he anticipated going up against several large orderlies—he'd go with whatever he had.

He listened to the sound of the lock clicking open.

The handle being turned.

The grate of steel on steel as the door was forced free of a sticking jamb.

The door began to open.

Sully pulled in a long, quiet breath. And he waited.

12

Sully had less than a second to size up the man who came through the door.

Enough time to realize he was in trouble.

While the man wasn't as big as Dez—a feat all but impossible —he still had an inch or two on Sully. And worse, unlike Sully, it looked like this guy had put away plenty of decent meals in the past couple years. While the man wasn't obese, Sully put the difference in their weight at somewhere between fifty and seventy pounds—more than enough to convince him he had a real fight on his hands.

And that wasn't even factoring in the possibility of someone else hovering behind this guy, out of Sully's view.

He didn't wait to observe the man further, seizing this one chance before the man noticed anything amiss in the semi-dark room.

Backing it with every ounce of strength, determination and will to live he possessed, Sully sprang from behind the door, slamming the full weight of his body into the other male.

He was rewarded with a grunt, the larger man staggering under the impact. But, Sully noted, not enough to push him out of his escape route.

Sully had never been highly skilled in a fight, but he was plenty agile. He managed to get in a second body blow, using his still-low position to drive his shoulder into the man's gut.

Though the man didn't shift as much as Sully had hoped, it sounded like the wind had been forced from his lungs, and Sully made a break for the small gap the move had created.

It wasn't enough.

Sully knew what it was to take a hit, had had plenty of opportunity in his pre-Braddock days to normalize the pain and fear that came with abuse. While he'd never been particularly good at dishing it out, he was more than capable of taking it and working through it.

Unfortunately, it seemed this guy had been taught the same lessons. He recovered fast, managing to grab Sully before he could get through the door. Sully felt himself spinning, then saw the wall coming at his face. He managed to turn his head in time to prevent a broken nose, but the impact left his right ear ringing and rattled his brain enough that he would have collapsed had the man not been pressed up against him, holding him in place.

It took a few seconds for the world to right itself, and he became aware the man was speaking to him, the voice deep and scratchy as if battling laryngitis.

"Stop fighting. I don't want to hurt you."

Sully gave up. His arms were wrenched behind his back, the wall and the large man providing a more-than-adequate rock and hard place. He let his breath out in a defeated sigh that continued through his question. "What do you want?"

The man didn't answer immediately; he seemed to be thinking. "If I let you go, you're not going to try anything, right? I don't want to have to tie you up, but I will if you make me."

Being trapped in this cell with no way out was bad enough. But he'd been in more than one room while strapped down, leaving him completely defenceless when Gerhardt and his henchmen had come at him. He might not be able to put up much of a fight in his current situation, might stand no real chance of escape, but at least if he stayed unbound, he stayed sane. Sully was relatively certain he could have coped with some of the things that had happened at Lockwood had he not been restrained at the time; it was the helplessness far more than the discomfort or pain that had left him with recurring nightmares and periodic flashbacks and panic attacks.

"Okay," Sully said. "Okay."

His voice sounded defeated even to his own ears, and it proved enough to secure his physical release from between the man and the wall. Sully turned to face his captor, the two of them taking several steps toward their intended targets—the man moving to block the door while Sully placed some distance between them.

There wasn't much light to go by, granted, but as Sully took his first good look at the man, he was struck by something familiar, a memory resting just out of reach inside his brain.

"I know you," Sully said. "Don't I?"

The man nodded slowly. "The fire at the Blakes'. McCoy Falls."

Sully stared at the man as the pieces snapped into place, the recognition making sense—even if there was little about this man that resembled any longer the boy he'd once been.

"Brennan?"

"You saved my life back then. You remember?"

It was Sully's turn to nod. There was no forgetting.

God knew he'd tried.

"Why did you bring me here? What did you do to my dog?"

"The dog will be fine," Brennan said. "Just a tranq. As to why you're here, we'll get to that. Right now, I just need you to tell me."

Sully waited for Brennan to further explain the request but, after a few seconds of waiting him out, Sully realized nothing more was forthcoming. "Tell you what?"

"How you knew. You never told me. After that night, after the police took us away, I never saw you again. So how did you know?"

"About the fire? I smelled smoke, I guess."

Brennan backhanded the wall with a fist. Sully jumped, took an involuntary step back, no longer so certain the larger man cared whether he hurt him or not.

"Bullshit," Brennan said. The word sounded like a slap. "Don't lie to me. How did you know?"

There was no good answer for that. The truth would in itself sound like a lie, and Sully had told precious few people about what he could see. The nature of Brennan's mood change, not to mention his role in Sully's kidnapping, strongly suggested the man was unhinged, and Sully didn't want to push him over the edge he was already teetering on.

"Answer me!"

"I don't know what you want me to say."

"I want the truth. It wasn't the smoke, it wasn't the flames. It sure as hell wasn't the Blakes, because they didn't even know what hit them."

"I didn't set the fire, if that's what you're wondering."

"I know you didn't," Brennan said, his voice quieter again. "That's not what I was getting at."

Sully had no idea what he'd said or done to bring about the change of emotion, which was too bad because that meant he had no idea how to replicate it. He didn't answer immediately, his brain doing a quick run-through of various scenarios, how they might play out. The best option seemed to be easing Brennan into it slowly, to avoid disturbing him any more than the words themselves would do naturally. He thought he'd come up with a good way to start when Brennan solved the problem for him.

"You know things," Brennan said. "Things other people don't. Things they don't want to know."

Sully waited Brennan out, hoping he wasn't done supplying his own answer.

"You saw a girl that night," Brennan said.

"The girl who set the fire?"

"The girl who wouldn't let us go through the bedroom door. She had purple hair."

The words were as startling as Brennan's earlier mood change. Sully responded without thinking. "You saw her, too?"

"I thought you knew that. You couldn't tell I was shitting myself?"

"I thought you were scared of the fire. You didn't say anything about her."

"I did."

"No, you didn't. I'd remember."

Brennan looked to be considering that, as if sending his mind back to that time and place. It didn't appear to be a pleasant trip, a fleeting grimace crossing his face before his eyes returned their focus to Sully. "You didn't say anything either."

"I don't say much to anyone about that sort of thing."

"So she's not the only one you've seen?"

If only, Sully thought. Out loud he answered, "No. There have been others."

"A lot?"

"Enough."

Brennan regarded him again, sizing him up within some yet-unknown test. Sully wasn't sure he wanted to know, so opted to continue the conversation. "What about you? Do you see others?"

Sully caught the flash of fear in Brennan's eyes before the larger man looked away, focusing on a spot on the wall to the left of Sully. Brennan's voice was soft, almost too low to hear, when it came. "All the time."

Sully glanced quickly around the room, finding it empty save the two of them. "Even now?"

To his surprise, Brennan nodded in the affirmative. "There's a man standing between us, leaning against the wall. He's dressed like people you'd see in those old black and white movies. I think he used to live here." Brennan paused, corrected himself. "Still does, I guess."

His eyes snapped back to Sully. "Don't you see him?"

"No, I don't. I can only see certain ones. From what I can tell, they're all victims of homicide."

Brennan's eyes, fixated on Sully, widened slightly. "People who were murdered?"

"I think, anyway. I'm not sure all the time. I've never really gotten a handle on it.'

"That's not what I heard about you," Brennan said.

"What are you talking about?"

"I heard you're pretty strong with this stuff, that you don't let it get to you. Let them get to you."

Sully uttered a low, humourless chuckle. "Well, you heard wrong. I don't know what the hell I'm doing. I don't know how to control it, how to communicate. I don't really know anything. I'd like to be able to help, but I don't know how."

Brennan's silence spoke volumes as his lips parted around gritted teeth, eyebrows lowering to accentuate the deep creases already permanent in his flesh. A long exhale of breath whistled through Brennan's teeth, and he began to shake.

In two quick strides, Brennan was on Sully, fisting the front of his hoodie and shoving him hard into the wall.

Something inhuman looked out of Brennan's eyes, something desperate and almost demonic. And Sully was faced with the chilling realization Brennan—this Brennan—was capable of killing him.

Mr. Blake had once attacked Sully, hands tightening around his throat, fingers squeezing while Sully stared into a face bearing the same expression Brennan wore now. Sully had ended it by kicking Mr. Blake in the groin. Had he not, he was convinced he would have joined the Purple Girl—hovering back then in the corner of the room, eyes closed and glowing with what seemed to be a building heat.

She was back now, again in the corner, eyes closing.

"Brennan," Sully said. "I'm sorry. I don't know what I did to upset you."

Brennan's breaths came fast through clenched teeth and flared nostrils, fists pressing into Sully as if trying to force him through the wall. It hurt, but Sully refused to reveal the pain to Brennan. Pain and fear were weakness, and he was convinced weakness—both the existence and the perception of it—was his enemy here.

Brennan's fists balled into the material of Sully's jacket, squeezed harder and harder. Squeezed like Mr. Blake had that afternoon.

The Purple Girl was glowing now, her core alight with yet-contained fire.

"Brennan ...."

Brennan gave Sully one last hard slam into the wall and released him. But the rage was still there.

He released it in a scream of pent-up fury. "What the hell good are you to me then?"

Fists clenched white, Brennan spun and stalked to the door, slamming it shut as he left the room. Sully waited until he heard the key in the lock before allowing himself to sink back onto the mattress.

He looked up at the blood-soaked teenager standing in the corner, finding her large eyes fixed on him. The fire was gone, exhaustion left in its place, a sense that she'd taken the beating he'd just avoided.

And, just like before, she faded and disappeared.

This time he didn't call out for her to stay.

This time he knew he didn't have to.

13

Dᴇᴢ ɢᴀᴠᴇ it half an hour but Lucienne didn't return.

He supposed it should have come as little surprise, crawling as the area was with cops. If someone unknown were after her, no doubt the last thing she'd want was to be embroiled in an attempted murder investigation.

Sitting in the late-afternoon warmth and silence of his SUV, Dez had entertained the possibility Lucienne might be Lachlan's assailant. He'd given up on the theory almost as soon as it had formed, considering the woman's small stature and—most crucially—the severity of Lachlan's injuries. Tough bastard though he was, Lachlan couldn't have been lying there all that long. Dez had seen plenty of serious wounds in his career, enough to know there wouldn't have been much left of Lachlan to save if Dez and Lucienne hadn't turned up when they did. While Dez hadn't timed it, he guessed Lucienne had been with him for close to an hour—far longer than Lachlan could have survived without help.

The more he considered it, the more Dez decided the attack lent credence to the woman's story. If someone had taken Sully and was also after his mother, it was possible they'd gone after

Lachlan looking for her. He'd have contact information for her, after all, would either know where she was or how to find her.

Dez's internet search on Lucienne Dule had come up empty. Near as he could tell, the woman didn't have a social media account or any other kind of online profile, at least not under the name she'd given him. There wasn't a single photo or reference he could locate tracing back to the woman he'd met in the cemetery. He recalled her saying she worked in IT—which seemed the perfect profession to enable someone living in fear to vanish off the grid. If there was something mother and son had in common, it looked to be their ability to both see and become ghosts.

Having given up on Lucienne, Dez headed back in the direction of his apartment, stomach rumbling and Pax likely in need of a good meal.

He had just crossed the river when his phone rang. He grinned as he saw Eva's face on his call display, and he pulled over to answer.

"Hey, Evie."

"Dez, what the hell? I just heard you're the one who found Lachlan."

"Word travels fast."

"It does around here, especially where you're concerned."

"What does that mean exactly?"

He was on the defensive, and her heavy sigh told him she knew it.

"It means people know you've had a rough go of it the past couple of years and they still give a damn about the big goofball they used to work with. Now stop being so damn touchy and tell me something. You reported you were with a woman when you found Lachlan. Do you mean Lucienne Dule?"

"Where are you right now?"

"Don't worry," she said. "I'm alone in my car. Listen, I checked her out—or tried to. There's nothing much about her in the system, save one incident: a suicide attempt when she was fourteen, when she tried to jump off the Forks Bridge. There was a full complement of officers called to that one, including a crisis negotiator. Eventually, they talked her down. She was complaining the spirits wouldn't leave her alone. The file ended with her committal to Lockwood."

"Huh. She didn't say anything about that."

"What did she say exactly?"

"All she said was that she sees ghosts, like Sully does. She definitely didn't say anything about Lockwood."

"I can't say I'm surprised. What were the two of you doing at Lachlan's office?"

"She said she hired him to find Sully."

"Why now, after all this time?"

"She said she believes he's in danger. Rightly so, apparently."

"Dez, be careful. It sounds like there's a good possibility this woman isn't stable. I think you need to consider she might be the one who hurt Lachlan."

"I thought about that," Dez said. "But the way I figure it, I had to have been with her when all that went down. She was already standing in the cemetery when I saw her, and we talked there for about twenty minutes. Another twenty for sure passed before we got down to Lachlan's office. I wasn't watching the time. The whole thing could have been less than forty minutes. No way he was lying there that long, not with those injuries."

"And she was with you the whole time?"

"I never took my eyes off her."

"They're still going to want to talk to her, given she was probably his most recent client."

"Or maybe he was working on something else, or had done, that pissed someone off enough to come after him."

"Believe me, they're looking into that. I've been told to be on the lookout for several cheating spouses and workers' comp fraudsters Lachlan outed in the past few months. I'm headed over to help pick one of them up now."

"Be careful, okay?"

"Always am. Listen, you be careful, too. Until you know more about Lucienne, I'd watch how much you share with her."

"Oh, believe me, I'm all over that. Listen, Eva, there's a file on Sully from when he was abandoned. I'm wondering if you could—"

"Goddammit, Dez. No, I'm not getting you that file. I looked into Lucienne only because I was worried about your safety. I am not putting my career on the line by removing a police file and handing it over to a civilian. I'm sorry, but that's more than I can do."

"Yeah, okay. You're right. I get it."

"Don't try to guilt me, Dez. You know it doesn't work."

Actually, he knew it did work, but he felt guilt all his own for having made the attempt. She was right. What he was asking was punishable by permanent dismissal and there was no way he'd be able to live with himself if that happened to her because of him.

"I'm not trying to guilt you. You're right. It was stupid to ask. I'll find another way."

"What other way?"

Dez smiled. "Way I figure it, I saved Lachlan's life. If I know anything about him, he wouldn't take on a client without researching the hell out of them first. Anyway, he managed to connect Lucienne to Sully when no one else ever had. I'm hoping I can convince him to tell me."

"If he lives."

"That bad, huh?"

"He's in emergency surgery, I hear. I'll keep you posted."

"I'd appreciate that. I'd like to be able to talk to him as soon as he wakes up. And, yeah, I know there's an 'if' there."

"What makes you think he'll talk to you? I don't know if it's covered by any real confidentiality clause, but I'm guessing private investigators aren't supposed to be sharing info about their clients with random people who come calling—even random people who've saved their lives."

"I'm not just any random person, though. I've more or less taken over Lachlan's job with Lucienne."

"Just don't take on everything that's come with it. I'd rather you don't end up in the hospital bed next to Lachlan's."

"Me too," Dez said. "The guy's an asshole."

***

WHILE DEZ FELT he was making no real progress in finding Sully, Lucienne wasn't proving nearly as elusive.

He was letting himself and Pax in the back door of his building when the dog's quiet growl told Dez to check his surroundings. Lucienne emerged from somewhere and was moving cautiously down the alley toward him, eyes fixed on Pax.

"Pax, it's okay," Dez said. Then to Lucienne, "Where'd you get to?"

Reaching him, she shook her head. "Not here. Inside."

Dez led the way up the narrow back stairs, forced to stop just this side of his suite door as the one to Emily Crichton's opened.

"Any luck?" she asked, spectacle-magnified eyes darting between Dez and his latest houseguest.

"Nothing, Miss Crichton."

"Desmond ...."

"Sorry. Emily."

Miss Crichton beamed and nodded approvingly, before fixing her gaze on Lucienne and extending a small hand knotted with age and arthritis. "Emily Crichton."

Lucienne gripped the other woman's hand. "Victoria Ward."

Dez turned back to his door, fidgeting with the lock to prevent his being dragged into the lie.

"It seems Desmond is having all sorts of visitors lately," Miss Crichton said. The words were followed by a giggle, but it was clear the woman was fishing for information.

Luckily, Lucienne had picked up on the same cue and spared

Dez the necessity and guilt of contributing to the tall tale. "I'm an old friend from his policing days," she said.

"I'm glad to hear it," Miss Crichton said. "He was quite upset earlier. And if there's anything I can do, please let me know. I'd like to help if I can."

"Thanks, ma'am," Dez said over his shoulder. "I appreciate that."

He ducked inside his apartment before she could correct him on his use of name for her, holding the door for Lucienne and Pax. Miss Crichton looked as though she wanted to join them but Dez, knowing Lucienne was unlikely to come clean with him with someone else in the room, closed the door with an apologetic smile at his neighbour. Besides, there were some things—namely Sully's earlier presence here—he wasn't quite ready to share with Lucienne, not until he'd had more of his questions answered.

Once inside, he recalled he was still short on groceries. Opening first the fridge and then the cupboards, he found a couple unopened cans of meat stew, which were quite possibly past their best-before dates, leaving him hoping for the best as he dropped the contents into a large bowl and, from there, into the microwave.

Dez hadn't yet made up the pullout, so waved Lucienne toward one of two kitchen chairs.

"Sorry for the state of the place," he said. "I'm usually neater than this. It's been that kind of day."

"What was your neighbour talking about?" Lucienne asked. "Why do you need help?"

Dez kept his eyes focused on rinsing out the cans to avoid being caught in a half-truth. "It's a long story, and we've got more important things to worry about right now. What's with the false name?"

"Until I know what's going on and who I can trust, Lucienne Dule doesn't exist."

Dez set the cans upside down in his drying rack, opting to lean back against his counter rather than join Lucienne at the table. "I can assure you, Emily Crichton is plenty trustworthy."

"Are you sure about that?"

"I know her." He crossed his arms as he regarded Lucienne. "A damn sight better than I know you, actually. Why'd you take off earlier? Why not stick around and talk to investigators? You're acting like you've got something to hide."

"I do. Myself. Listen, Dez, I know I sound paranoid but I think you would be too under the circumstances. It appears someone is after both me and my son, and it's evident they mean business. Look at what happened to Mr. Fields."

"We don't really know what happened to him," Dez said. "He pissed off a lot of people while he was a cop, and no doubt he's pissed off plenty more as a P.I. His being attacked isn't necessarily about you or Sully."

"Pretty big coincidence, isn't it?"

"Could be, yeah. We won't know until Lachlan wakes up and starts talking."

"So he'll be okay?"

"Too soon to say. Speaking of, you said you saw his ghost, but he wasn't actually dead."

"But he was close to death. You've probably heard about near-death experiences? I'd imagine that's why I was able to see him."

Dez wasn't completely satisfied, but it didn't seem like a debate worth having. "Look, given what's happened, I'm not about to argue with you on whether you go around using a fake name with the world at large. But I really think you need to talk to the police about Lachlan, and you need to do it as Lucienne Dule."

"I can't. Why can't you understand that? Once I become involved in a police investigation, I'm out there in the open. My name, address and phone number get written on a file some-where, and that becomes available to everyone who touches this case. I've gone to great pains to avoid sharing that information with anyone."

"Even Lachlan?"

"Of course. I paid him in cash, asked that he keep things quiet. As far as I know, he didn't keep any paperwork of our dealings."

"I hate to tell you, but it's going to be pretty obvious what he was looking into once investigators start checking. His name will be connected to searches, whether it be his internet history or whatever digging he was doing with various agencies or people connected to you or Sully."

"That's right. *His* name will be connected. But mine won't. Please, Dez, I can't be involved. I just can't."

The microwave beeped the completion of its task, but Dez had other things to deal with first. He studied the woman a moment before lowering himself into the other chair, the one he'd sat on last night as he talked to his brother. The brother whose fear of Lockwood had been so palpable the very mention of it had sparked a flashback. This woman had once had her own experience with the place, likely providing her with plenty of reason of her own to be afraid.

He approached the upcoming interrogation gently, as one might when dealing with a fragile witness to a terrible crime.

"I did a little digging after you took off," he said. "I know you spent some time at Lockwood."

She didn't speak right away, but the variety of expressions that flitted across her face, one after the other—shock, anger, dread— said plenty all on their own.

"I covered for you with the police," he said. "I needed to know I was doing the right thing, lying to them. For all I know, you were the one who attacked Lachlan."

Lucienne's brows crawled up her forehead, drawing her eyes wide. "What?"

"I've seen weirder. Besides that, my loyalty is to my brother first, not to you. I need to know I'm not putting him in danger, drawing him out for you—if, of course, you're right and he's still out there somewhere. You couldn't have expected anything less of me. The reason you came to me was because you know I'll go all in to protect him."

She appeared to be giving it some thought, and he held her eye as she went about it, determined he'd catch her if she started putting together another fakery like the one she'd sold Miss Crichton. When at last she opened her mouth, there was nothing in words or expression but acceptance and slight defeat.

"I understand," she said. "I wish you hadn't checked into me, but I understand."

"So, Lockwood. How long were you there?"

"The longest two years of my life. I wasn't really trying to kill myself on the bridge that day, you know."

"What were you trying to do?"

She looked at him as one might a child who hadn't been paying attention. "Exist," she said. "I was fourteen years old, living with parents who cared more about what I should become than who I was. I didn't have any real friends, and the thing that set me apart from everyone else, that made me special, was something I could never share. I told a good friend once that I could see the dead. She never spoke to me again. So I kind of became a ghost myself, just blending unnoticed into the background. I guess the bridge was my way of making people see me."

She stopped and when she didn't immediately continue with the explanation, Dez decided on some gentle prodding. "But that wasn't all it did, was it?"

Lucienne shook her head, and Dez saw in her eyes the same haunted expression he'd witnessed only recently on the face of his brother. "My parents already thought I was strange. They knew about my ghosts. They knew but they didn't believe. What they did believe was that I was crazy, and the bridge became their excuse to send me away, to have someone fix their disturbed daughter. But the doctors there, they didn't fix anything. I wasn't mentally ill, after all.

"But I was smart. I got good at playing their game. I stopped fighting them. I pretended I didn't see. After about two years there, they declared me fit to be returned to my parents. I dreaded the idea of going back to Lockwood so I kept on playing the game. I became the perfect daughter, I pulled up my grades, I learned to cook. But behind their backs, I was more screwed up than ever. That's how I ended up getting pregnant. And I guess that's why I didn't fight them as hard as I should have when they told me I had to give him up. It wasn't all about their plans for me and their lack of support and funds if I went against them. It was the knowledge they could drop me back into that hellhole any time they wanted. If I went against them any more than I already had, I would have been thrown back in Lockwood, and Sullivan would have ended up raised by strangers anyway. At least this way, I got to choose where he went, who he went to—or at least that's what I told myself. I know now how wrong I was."

"Let me ask you something. I'm not trying to upset you, but I need you to tell me. Do you think there's any possibility it's someone over at Lockwood—Gerhardt, for instance—who's looking for you? If Sully is alive, could it be they're trying to get ahold of him again? Or maybe that they already have?"

"I guess it's possible," she said. "You think he could be there right now?"

He echoed her words. "I guess it's possible. He escaped, after all. What about you? What reason would they have to want you back there?"

She broke eye contact, scanning the tabletop as if looking for answers in the woodgrain and crumbs. Unfortunately, the table provided as much help as anyone might have anticipated, and Lucienne came up with the same answer Dez already had.

But, in her case, the words stopped short of ringing true.

"I wish I knew."

14

DEZ DIDN'T QUESTION Lucienne further for the time being, giving them both a small break as they and Pax ate the stew that served as supper.

But, while Dez had chosen to remain silent for now, he had plenty going on in his brain as he regarded the woman. Lucienne Dule was hiding something. Though he didn't believe she was directly responsible for what had happened to Lachlan, he resolved to speak to the man as soon as possible. Dez was pretty good at smelling a lie; Lachlan was the human equivalent of a bloodhound, his nose so finely tuned that cops used to joke he could detect a fib being uttered in the next room to another investigator.

While he saw the value in keeping Sully's biological mother under his watch until this was sorted, he was really looking forward to her heading home for the night. He needed some space, some room to think, an opportunity to piece together the world that had been blown apart by the recent bombshells.

She interrupted the silence by clearing her throat. "I hate to ask, but I don't feel safe returning home tonight. I wonder if you might let me stay here."

His heart dropped as she poked at the food in front of her.

Never one to turn away a woman in distress, he couldn't do much other than to grant his reluctant consent. And, in this case, there was the added element; this woman in distress was also Sully's birth mother.

"You can have the pullout," he said. "I think I've got a clean sheet in the closet next to the bathroom. Sorry, but I'm a little short on other bedding."

"This will be just fine, thanks."

The apartment felt very full, the sensation he got whenever he had anyone over who wasn't family. While he wasn't an introvert, he liked his space, so decided he'd have to go looking for it elsewhere for a little while.

Bulldog was the perfect excuse.

"Listen, I've got to go check on a contact," he said. "The guy was going to be keeping an ear to the ground for me, listening for anything about Sully."

"I didn't know you'd been asking around."

Dez realized his conversation with Bulldog had taken place before he'd met Lucienne, so thought fast. "I made some phone calls after you wandered away from Lachlan's office. Thought I'd better get some balls in the air on this."

Lucienne frowned. "I really wanted this kept as quiet as possible. You knew that."

"It will be kept quiet. My contact's a trustworthy guy. Silent as the grave."

That bit of BS had Lucienne's frown turning upside down, though Dez read it as one of those knowing smiles rather than one denoting relief. "In my experience, the grave is far from silent," she said.

Dez gave the room a quick scan, hoping she wouldn't notice. If there was anyone else here besides the two of them and Pax, he couldn't see it. Of course, he'd never be able to anyway. "Right. Well .... I'll just be a while."

"Maybe I should come with you."

"No," Dez said, the reply coming too quickly. He toned it

down as he provided an explanation. "My contact gets skittish around other people. Why don't you put the TV on for a bit, try and get your mind off things? I'll give you my phone number, and you can give me yours. If anything comes up, give me a call."

"What if someone comes while you're out?"

"I'm not expecting someone. Just don't answer the door."

"That's not what I meant."

Dez felt an eyebrow creep up. "Oh. Well, no one knows you're here, do they? If it's true someone went after Lachlan to try to find you, there's no reason to think they'd know to look for you here. Right?"

"Unless we were followed."

"I wasn't followed," Dez said. "And given the circumstances, I'm sure you were paying attention when you made your way here. Do you think someone tailed you?"

"No. You're right, I was watching for that."

"So, you're fine. Just try to relax for a bit if you can. Don't go anywhere." He considered telling her she could go across the hall to Miss Crichton's, but he didn't want the older woman dragged into this. He'd never forgive himself if he put her in danger, particularly since she didn't seem the type to have ever faced it in her life.

"I'll call or send a text before I come back so I don't startle you," he said, jotting down his number and accepting the one she provided in return. "Call if you need something."

THE EVENING WAS WARM AND, still light outside thanks to the sun's extended summer hours, Dez opted to walk rather than drive to the park.

He and Pax were barely a block from home when his phone rang, and he allowed a sigh and an eye roll, wondering what his unwanted guest needed so soon.

But a check of his call display revealed not Lucienne's number

—programmed into his phone for safekeeping prior to his leaving the building—but his Aunt Kindra's.

"Desmond, I meant to call earlier, but I was busy finishing a report on my post-mortem from today. I heard back from the lab on Pax's blood work and the dart you found. The two match up. I'll spare you the big words but a drug called azaperone was found in both samples sent. I'm told it's often used in vet medicine in lower doses to reduce aggression, but it can be used for anesthesia in larger doses, which seems to be what was present here. They also found a second drug called zolazepam, which can be used in combination with azaperone for anesthetic purposes in vet med. Zolazepam, in particular, is water-soluble so has a fast onset. I'm thinking that makes it ideal for a tranq."

Dez moved to lean up against a building while he took that in. He'd been expecting it, of course, but this sealed it, robbing him of any hope he might have been carrying. If Pax had gone down quick, no way Sully would have left him willingly. In Dez's mind, there was only one reason to have tranquilized Pax, and that was to get him out of the way to prevent his natural instinct to protect his human.

"The good news is there should be no long-term effects," Kindra said. "Even so, as the dosage looked to be rather high, given the amount still in his blood when you brought him in, it's best you keep an eye on him. And if there are any further problems, I'd consider breaking down and taking him to an actual vet."

Still a little numb from the news, Dez nodded before it dawned on him his aunt wouldn't see, meaning a verbal response was necessary. "Thanks, Auntie K. This might seem like a strange question, but what sort of effects might the drugs have on a human?"

"Why? Did you poke yourself with the dart or something?"

"No, I'm okay. Just wondering." It was weak and he knew it.

So did she. "What aren't you telling me here?"

Dez looked down the street in the direction of the park. He

could just make out a few trees from here, their branches left to grow wild until they covered streetlights and signs. For not the first time that day, Dez's mind drifted through the scene that must have played out near there, and he considered the unthinkable—that Sully might have been taken while Dez was mere feet away, talking to Bulldog.

"I told you I was looking after Pax for a friend," he said. "I haven't heard from him and I'm worried something might have happened to him."

"Did you contact the police?"

"Not yet."

"Maybe you should. High doses of azaperone can cause respiratory depression in humans. If you have any concern your friend might have used or been administered the same drug, I would certainly notify police and have them begin a search. While I don't think what I saw in Pax would be enough to cause any real concern if administered to a human, it's impossible to say anything concretely without having someone here to test. Does your friend have a history of mental health or addictions issues?"

Dez was grateful this was a phone conversation rather than a face-to-face. "I don't think so, but I don't really know him all that well."

"Is there a possibility he administered the drug to his dog on his own, maybe to test dosage? It's been known to be used as an antipsychotic, which is why I'd asked about the mental health issues."

"Anything's possible I guess. I'm going to go have another look around for him. I appreciate your help, Auntie K."

"Anytime, kiddo. Take care of yourself. And come see us soon. I mean it."

"I will. Thanks again."

Dez disconnected, looking down at Pax as he dropped the phone into his pocket next to his apartment keys. "I wish I could see what you saw, buddy. At least then, I'd have some idea where to go from here."

As it was, the only place he knew to go was forward, his path taking him into the park.

Pax, he observed, became nervous as soon as he clamped eyes on the place, returning to circle the spot where Dez had found the dart and the drag marks earlier. Dez's heart sank as he was forced to return to the location, but he allowed Pax a few minutes before turning and pushing him from the bluff of trees. Staying there would do them no good. But, with any luck, finding Bulldog would.

There was a spot near the river, where the flood had washed away the grassy slope and left behind a tall bank, providing a perfect spot for those looking to escape the immediate view of authorities or the complaining public. Using the piles of dead wood the flood had left behind, park-dwellers found plenty of kindling to stoke the fires that kept them warm in the makeshift camp on the chillier nights—at least until winter came and chased them into overcrowded shelters or abandoned homes across the river in The Forks.

It was too early for a fire but, as evening settled in, Dez figured the riverbank camp was as good a place to look for Bulldog as any.

Pax was growling up a storm as he hovered at Dez's side, proving himself something of a machete clearing a path for them through the men and women who had made the place a temporary residence.

Someone had dragged a beaten up, legless sofa down here and that's where Dez found Bulldog. The stout man lay kicked back on it, looking for all the world like a guy having a blissful, after-work nap. Dez leaned over, was relieved when he didn't pick up on any odour of alcohol. And while Bulldog wasn't one to turn down a joint when offered, he stayed away from hard drugs as a rule, so Dez didn't have any qualms about dropping into the free spot beside the man and shaking him awake.

"The hell?" Bulldog grumbled as he awoke.

"Hey, Bulldog."

"Copper. I was having a very nice dream. That model from the shampoo ad. You know the one I mean."

Dez grinned. "You're still hung up on her? That ad's something like five years old. They haven't run it in years."

"Hey, I don't have a TV, and it can have all the air time it wants inside my head. What time is it anyway?"

"About seven in the evening."

"Great. Let's go get a drink somewhere, huh?"

"I can't tonight, man."

"You've never turned down a drink, Copper. What's wrong? You sick or something?"

"You know what's wrong. Unless you've forgotten already."

Bulldog stared at him, and Dez saw the moment memory clicked back into place. "Damn. Right. Sorry."

"Sorry, as in you didn't check around?" Dez asked.

"Sorry, as in I didn't find diddly squat. No one saw anything that I can find out. It's like our boy is one of those ghosts he chases."

Bulldog didn't add to the statement, and Dez didn't make any more of an effort, the two simply sitting and watching the river flow in front of them. Beyond that, across the wide expanse of water, lay The Forks, a large island so named as it forced the Kimotan to separate and rejoin downstream. If Riverview Park had been left to grow wild, The Forks had become the Amazon rainforest, trees and other vegetation having taken over until the shells of grand houses had all but disappeared behind them. Some of the largest and most elegant homes had been located there, along with a range of boutique businesses and a well-designed shopping centre that drew people from all over KR. But the flood had overrun most of the island, washing away many riverfront homes entirely and leaving the ground beneath numerous others unstable. Most homes and businesses had been so badly water-damaged they would have required full rebuilds to stabilize rotting walls. The mall, too, was destroyed, its entire north wing having collapsed into the river.

In the end, The Forks was deemed a write-off. It was a no-man's land now, overrun by the most troubled of KR's population. Street gangs were born and bred there, drug addicts bought, sold and died there, violent criminals prowled the heaving and cracked streets for potential victims there. Even police didn't go to The Forks anymore, the place more or less sealed off from the rest of the city thanks to the no-longer safe Forks Bridge. In the early days, there had been routine talk of calling in the Army to clean the place up, many former residents unable to bear the thought of their homes being used as gang strongholds or crack houses. But, in the end, The Forks had been left to the wolves, a carcass for them to pick clean as the rest of the city turned its attention to other projects.

Dez often found his attention straying to the old island, wondering what answers the place held to the city's unsolved crimes and missing persons files. As it stood, he doubted anyone would ever find out.

But, for now, he had answers of his own that needed finding.

"Have you ever heard of a woman named Lucienne Dule?" he asked his friend.

"Can't say as I have," Bulldog said. "Who's that?"

"She says she's Sully's birth mother."

Bulldog grunted, the sound suggesting either acknowledgment or disapproval. It was impossible to say which. "So what's she after then?"

"She thinks he's still alive and she's trying to find him."

"Coincidentally, so are you."

"Yeah, but it's the why I'm not so sure about. She knows about him seeing the dead, too, says she has the same ability."

"But you don't believe her."

"I don't know what I believe. I haven't seen anything to suggest she isn't legit. Her story seems to fit. She didn't tell me the full truth at the start, but I could understand why once I found out more about her."

"So you don't doubt who she is, you just have your doubts you can trust her with Sully."

Dez shrugged. "I don't know. I don't want to see him get hurt, I guess."

"First you gotta see him, period."

"Yeah," Dez said. "You're right. First things first."

"Want me to ask around about her?"

"From what I can gather, she was never street. Quite the opposite actually. I doubt anyone will know much about her."

"Never hurts to ask. I mean, you brought her up for a reason, right?"

"I guess. Sure, ask around. But don't lose track of Sully, okay? I need your eyes and ears on that full-time."

"Hey, like I told ya, he's my boy too. I'll keep my ear to the ground."

Dez nodded. "Thanks, man."

"Yeah. So tell me something. Why you so scared of ghosts anyway?"

As it happened, Dez had had an entire lifetime to think through that one. "I prefer threats I can see, I guess. And I like problems I can fix."

15

IT FELT LIKE NIGHTTIME.

But with nothing but a dim lightbulb in a windowless room to go by, it was always nighttime.

Sully had managed what felt like a short nap. He was still tired, exhausted even, the stress of the day taking its toll as he lay on the bare mattress, staring at the cobwebs in the corner above his head. It was just visible in the shadows, the web large enough that fine, pale threads of it escaped the darkness, connecting the short distance to the wall. Sully thought he could make out the spider sitting in the midst of it, but it was difficult to tell without getting up for a closer look. For all he knew, that tiny black dot could have been a fly trapped there, helplessly waiting for the spider's return.

With nothing else to do, Sully considered getting up to look. While he ordinarily didn't begrudge a spider a good meal, he had never before felt such an affinity for a fly. Because the longer he watched the web, the more convinced he became that's what he was looking at. He thought he could see the insect trembling as it tried to free itself, believed he could hear the frantic buzzing of its wings as it struggled.

Sully could only imagine the spider was there somewhere,

settled back in a dark section of web, watching the show, waiting for that perfect moment when entertainment gave way to hunger. Did spiders wait until their prey gave up, exhausted and welcoming death as a means to end the torment? Or did they move in earlier, enjoying the fight with a trapped insect for which there was no escape?

Sully had made up his mind to free the thing, had stood to reach the web, when the sound of a key in the lock changed his plans.

He stepped off the mattress, relocating to the stability of the cement floor where he at least stood something of a chance in a fight. Not much of a chance, granted, but something was better than nothing.

Brennan had learned his lesson, moving slower this time as he entered the room, using shoulder and leg in the door to avoid getting his head or neck crushed should Sully be waiting in his previous hiding spot. Brennan's head poked around the door next, eyes locking onto Sully across the room. Tension faded and relief took its place as Brennan stepped the rest of the way into the small cell, leaving the door open a crack.

Sully had thought through the earlier exchange and realized what the other man must want from him. Brennan knew his secret and, for some reason, believed Sully had the skills to control it. Sully suspected Brennan had been driven near to insanity—maybe beyond—by the things he could see. He was looking for ways to stop it, or at least hoping to find out how to stay on top of it. Either way, Sully had spent much of his life looking for the same answers before he'd finally accepted he was never going to find them. He'd made some tentative peace with it, was determined to do his best to maintain his side of the armistice. But Brennan, it seemed, was still in the midst of full-scale war, and had the emotional battle scars to prove it.

Sully wasn't sure the other man would be satisfied with a solution that required him to simply accept his lot in life and find a way to work within it. And giving the wrong advice, he knew, could prove devastating for both of them.

"Stay there," Brennan said, then motioned to the mattress. "Sit down."

"I'd rather stand."

The gathering tension on Brennan's face convinced Sully otherwise, and he lowered himself onto the mattress, back to the wall, keeping his eyes fixed on the other man. Once Sully was sitting, Brennan eased the door open further, leaned back into the hall and pulled a folding chair into the room, placing it so he could sit directly opposite Sully while maintaining a guard on the only escape route.

"Do you need anything?" he asked. "Food? Water?"

Sully hadn't thought much about food or water until now, his thoughts otherwise occupied. The words acted as a reminder, his brain suddenly recognizing the twinges in his belly and the dry mouth as something other than anxiety. "That would be good, yeah."

"We'll get you something."

Another reminder. "Who's 'we'? Who was with you earlier, in the park?"

He'd spoken loudly enough but Brennan carried on as if the questions hadn't been asked. "I know you're wondering why you're here. I would be, too, in your shoes."

Brennan paused, and Sully waited him out. The answer to this one was even more crucial than the "who," and would hopefully provide something he could work with. He thought he had a pretty good idea, of course, but it meant something more hearing it from Brennan. Anyway, the larger man was clearly unstable and, until Sully got a better handle on that, it was better to avoid any triggers for another violent outburst.

Brennan didn't look directly at Sully when he finally answered, choosing to focus on a spot just to Sully's left. No fear was in Brennan's eyes, so Sully guessed he wasn't looking at someone else, but rather *avoiding* looking at someone else. It was easier that way, confessing, making uncomfortable admissions without the eye contact.

"I remember, you know," Brennan said. "When we were kids, I mean. You were something like six or seven years younger than me, but it was like you were an old man in a kid's body. I could see you were scared of something, especially at night, but foster kids always were in that house, weren't we? You never said anything, so it took me until the night of the fire to really figure it out, that you could see what I did. Only you couldn't always, could you? You didn't see the old woman."

"What old woman?"

"The one who died in that house. She was crazy. She used to go around yelling at night. I think she was related to the Blakes somehow, probably a mother or grandmother. I used to sleep with cotton balls stuck in my ears to drown her out. But sometimes … sometimes she would come into our room at night. She'd lean over us, one at a time like, and she'd say some godawful things. 'The devil's going to take you.' 'Never too young to die.' 'No one will help you.' And her face. She was laughing when she said those things, but in a cold way. It was like some of those people at Lockwood, the way they'd sit there and—"

The name was a slap of icy water, drawing the question from Sully before he could stop himself. "You were at Lockwood?'

"So were you."

"When were you there? How long?"

"Too long. I spent more than ten years there. So long I lost track."

"God, man. Did it … did they help you somehow? Or did they …." He didn't finish the statement. If Brennan had shared his experience, he'd know what Sully meant.

Brennan's gaze dropped to his lap and he nodded slowly, providing the confirmation Sully didn't really need.

"I'm sorry, Brennan."

For the first time since initially entering the room, Brennan met his eye. "You too?"

"Yeah. And the empty unit? The blue room?"

"The one with no electricity or water? The one where no one else went? They took you there too, huh?"

"Yeah. Always at night, probably so no one else would know."

"Gerhardt?"

"And Hackman," Sully said. "And this other guy. I never saw his face or learned his name. He just stood there in a fright mask, never said a word."

"I remember Gerhardt and Hackman. I don't remember a third man."

"They used to drug me up pretty good before taking me there, to keep me quiet. It took me a while to realize the third man was real, and not a ghost or some sort of drug-induced hallucination. He wore this mask, a Halloween mask, this zombie thing with black mesh where the eyes were supposed to have been gouged out. I couldn't see any of his face at all."

"And you're sure he was real? He wasn't like the kind of people we see?"

"He was flesh and blood," Sully said. "He helped hold me down a couple times when things got really bad. Most of the time, no one laid a finger on me."

"But it didn't feel that way."

"No. It didn't."

"Did you ever figure out what the drug was, what they gave us?"

"They never said," Sully said. "I don't think they cared much about filling us in. It was some sort of mind opener, the stuff I'd experience. It was so real, but no one else seemed to be reacting to it. It was weird, like I was still alert in the room, but I was somewhere else too."

"Some*one* else."

Sully didn't answer, mind back in that room, body strapped to the table, the others watching him, coolly observing and taking notes as he screamed and writhed within the forced visions. Somehow—and he'd never found an explanation for this in his own mind—he'd become someone else, as if something had possessed him temporarily. And each time, he'd feel the pain and the panic of what he knew to be their deaths. He'd been beaten, raped, drowned, stabbed, shot and strangled—and no one had ever laid a physical hand on him. Sometimes it was more than the feeling of dying; sometimes he saw the face of his killer, hazy and largely unrecognizable, but very much present as it hovered mere inches from his own face. Save Lowell's, he'd never be able to sketch their features with any accuracy, but he'd known—at least in that heightened state of drug-induced awareness—that if he ever encountered any of those people, he would know it. Know *them*.

His awareness shifted from one dark room to another as Brennan's voice cut through the memory, Sully's captor, oddly enough, providing the lifeline he needed to escape an impending flashback.

"How many times did they do it to you?"

Sully had thought about that sometimes too, wondering. His time at Lockwood had been largely spent on one drug or another, making his ability to quantify days or events virtually non-existent.

"I don't know," he said. "It probably wasn't a lot, but it felt like it. I'm aware of at least eight different times, but nothing much about back then is clear, you know? What about you?"

Brennan's gaze had moved off again, only this time, it didn't seem to focus on anything.

His answer left Sully cold.

"Hundreds."

There was nothing Sully could say, nothing he dared verbalize. A range of emotions flitted across Brennan's face, none of them good, and Sully didn't want to cut in until he saw some sign of stability. That Brennan had become a minefield was no surprise, was perfectly understandable. But he was a minefield none-theless, and Sully knew better than to take a single step without having first been handed a map of the area.

Unfortunately, the Brennan who emerged was a different character from the one who had just been talking calmly to Sully. This Brennan brought to an end his trip inward by standing and hurling his chair against the wall.

Sully was back on his feet before the sound of metal on cement stopped echoing in his ears.

Brennan turned on him, teeth gritted, a vein in his forehead dangerously close to exploding. He raised one large arm, extending his index finger at Sully.

"Sit down!"

Sully stood next to the mattress, deciding whether it would be more dangerous to disobey or to place himself in a position in which he would be less able to react to a physical attack.

Brennan made the decision for him, crossing the room and shoving Sully back onto the mattress.

"I said, sit down!"

Brennan towered over Sully with fists clenched and breaths coming in hard and fast, his large form blocking the meagre light coming from the bulb and casting Sully in shadow.

Sully tilted his chin to seek out Brennan's eyes, but the uncontrolled rage there had him looking away quickly. Sully flashed back to a class in school that predated a field trip to Winteredge National Park. The teacher had provided instructions on what to do if they happened upon a large wild animal, and Sully remembered something about not looking it directly in the eye. The animal might take the eye contact as a challenge, she'd told them.

Whether or not that was true, Sully had no idea. But with no surefire way to get Brennan to back down, Sully was prepared to try anything.

He kept his eyes down, focusing them on Brennan's fists, balling and unballing, knuckles alternately white and red.

"Come on, Brennan," he said. "I'm not the enemy, here, okay? We've both been through the same thing."

The fists clenched tight and this time stayed that way, blood squeezed from knuckles, and Sully was left to wonder what he'd said to turn the conversation even further against him.

He didn't have long to think about it. He shrank back against the wall as Brennan leaned down, seizing large handfuls of Sully's hoodie. But just as suddenly as he'd moved in, Brennan released him and stepped away, head whipping around the room as if looking for something. He seemed to have found it in the chair, which he picked up and hammered against the wall. Once, twice, three times. Four, five, six.

Sully struggled against the instinct to run and stayed seated, Brennan's form still blocking the door. Instead, Sully watched the scene play out before him with mounting horror. The chair had broken now, screws forced from holes and welds releasing as Brennan continued to release his rage. The seat came loose, and the metal back danced wildly back and forth in its destruction, hanging on by only a few loosening welds.

The question formed in Sully's mind, kicking at him relentlessly: what would happen once there was nothing left of that chair, once there was nothing breakable in the room besides Sully?

The chair was in pieces when Brennan at last stopped. His chest heaved and, as Sully listened, he realized sobs were mingling with the gasps.

He hoped Brennan would leave, would refuse to be seen crying in front of another guy. He didn't, turning instead to his prisoner.

Sully released the breath he had been holding. Brennan's deadened face revealed he was as destroyed as the chair he'd demolished.

"I'm sorry," Brennan said, voice barely above a whisper. "It's not your fault. I'm sorry."

And Sully, despite everything, actually found some pity for the man. But for the Braddocks, but for Dez having ensured his escape from Lockwood, that broken man standing in front of him might be nothing more than an image glimpsed in a mirror.

"I don't know how to help you," Sully said. "But I'll try if you tell me how."

"That's just it," Brennan said. "I don't know how. I don't think anyone can."

Brennan picked up the pieces of the chair and left the room. Sully waited until he heard the key turn in the lock before allowing himself to lie back on the mattress, his entire body shaking now that the immediate danger had passed.

He raked trembling hands through his hair, combing it back from his face as he sought out something, anything to take his mind off what had just happened. His gaze found the spiderweb in the shadows. The black spot in the middle of the web was larger now, and the buzzing had stopped. But there was movement there.

Enough to tell Sully the fly's time of waiting and worrying was over.

16

DEZ SAT AT THE PARK, trying to psyche himself up to the idea of returning home—or, more specifically, to Lucienne—when his phone rang.

"Who's that?" Bulldog's voice was a little slurred, which was no surprise given the amount of alcohol he'd taken in so far tonight. A few guys had turned up with a bottle apiece and, as often happened around here, generosity won the day, with everyone taking turns swigging the alcohol straight. Kindness and love for one's fellow man would continue for a while, at least until the booze really took hold, and someone was deemed to have drunk more than his fair share. That's when the fighting would start and the police would be summoned.

Dez had taken a couple sips to be sociable but stopped after that. A good part of his drinking had been to do with depression over the loss of his loved ones and, later, boredom at finding himself with nothing productive to do. Sully's return last night had changed all of that—at least to a large extent—and he discovered he wasn't having much trouble resisting the urge to get plastered tonight.

So when his phone rang, Eva's face showing on the screen, he found he had nothing to feel guilty about.

"Eva," he told Bulldog, pushing himself off the legless couch with some difficulty.

"Don't say anything stupid," Bulldog advised as Dez moved away from the crowd to answer his phone.

"Where are you?" Eva asked, and Dez realized he hadn't moved quite far enough. "Are you at a bar?"

"No, not a bar," he said. "I promise."

"So where are you?"

"Riverview Park."

"By yourself?"

"No. Bulldog's here too."

"Hi, Eva!" Bulldog hollered from the couch, the effort causing him to topple over in a giggling heap.

"Dez, are you drunk?" Eva asked.

"No," he said. "I've had two swigs, just to be polite. That's all, I swear."

"So you're at the park hanging out with Bulldog's crew? Do you do this regularly?"

"I just needed to get out for a bit." He debated telling her about Lucienne, but decided it probably wasn't the best idea, telling his wife he had an attractive older woman at home in his bed.

"You know I hate it when you go there," Eva said.

"I'm not going to get drunk, okay? You have my word on that."

"I meant I don't like you being there, period. It's not safe. You know that."

He did know that. What he hadn't been so sure of was that she still cared, and he found himself smiling down into his phone. "I'm okay, Evie. I'm like a mountain troll compared to most of these guys."

"You know how that works, Dez. Some guys get a few drinks in them and think they're tougher than they are. They go looking for a challenge. How many times did you have to get into it with guys you busted on patrol because of your size?"

"Okay, point taken. I'll leave."

"Good. Anyway, I called you for a reason. I'm heading out your way to pick you up. Lachlan Fields made it through surgery. He's still pretty out of it on pain meds, but apparently was able to talk to investigators anyway. Thing is, he's holding back on them."

"About what?"

As soon as the question had left his mouth, he could almost hear her rolling her eyes. "If anyone knew that, I wouldn't be coming to get you now, would I? Lachlan's refusing to talk to anyone about what he was working on. Anyone, apparently, except you."

EVA ARRIVED WITHIN A FEW MINUTES, stopping at the sidewalk next to the park to allow Dez to drop into the passenger seat of her compact car.

It was a tight squeeze, his knees approaching his chest even with the seat pushed back as far as it would go, leaving less room for Pax to move freely in the backseat. Eva had bought the car after their separation, having insisted he take their SUV. Her car was small, but it was economical, and it wasn't like she and Kayleigh took up a whole lot of room between them.

"Where's Kayleigh?" Dez asked.

"I took her to your mom's. I didn't think she needed to be along to visit a man who was nearly bludgeoned and stabbed to death."

"Good call. So how is it you're the one phoning me about this? Why didn't someone from Major Crimes contact me directly?"

"Consider yourself lucky Forbes called me and not you. He didn't bother checking the old records for your personal cell number, so I said I'd get ahold of you and bring you down there."

"Right. Thanks."

"So what's the plan here, exactly? They're going to want to

know what Lachlan tells you. Not only that, but they'll want to know about Lucienne Dule."

"Well, they can add me to that list. I'd like to know about her too."

DEZ HAD BEEN HOPING for Sgt. Clark Davies. Naturally, what he got was Sgt. Forbes Raynor.

Forbes was waiting for them in the hallway outside the private room Lachlan had been moved into after surgery, a bored-looking uniformed officer posted next to the door on guard duty. Forbes didn't look happy about Dez's presence. But then, the uniform didn't look happy about Forbes.

"Do you know why you're here?" Forbes asked by way of greeting.

"Sure," Dez said. "Sperm meets egg, cells reproduce—"

"Dez," Eva muttered.

Forbes's eyes narrowed, lines showing at the outer edges and between his brows. While he was only in his late thirties, Forbes had established a fine set of frown lines and, in Dez's experience, the man took to exercising them regularly to keep them in peak form. "Don't be a smart ass. You know damn well what I'm asking."

"I'm as much in the dark as you are," Dez said. "Let me talk to the guy and get back to you, all right?"

"He won't tell us about the woman you mentioned. Says he can't discuss clients. I'd say he's obstructing an investigation."

Dez smirked. "You going to go to the chief and tell him Lachlan Fields is obstructing an investigation? He's the chief's golf buddy, never mind the fact he's the victim here."

"All true," Forbes said. "But you're neither of those things. If there's anything you haven't shared, you're in it deep when I find out."

The threat didn't have too many teeth for Dez, a man whose

home and work lives were already in tatters. At this point, a criminal obstruction charge would be nothing but gravy. "Whatever. Hang tight. I'll see what he wants."

Dez was surprised Lachlan had been placed in a private room on the surgical ward rather than ICU, particularly given the number of machines and tubes connected to him.

He looked small and pale, eyes closed, head and shoulders resting on a pair of stacked pillows, a chest tube running from one side of him with more tubes pumping fresh air into his nostrils. Machines beeped and hissed as they monitored things like blood pressure, heart rate, oxygen levels and who knew what else. Dez was reminded the only thing he hated more than morgues was hospitals.

He returned his attention to Lachlan's face, was startled to find the eyes open and fixed on him.

"You're obviously Desmond Braddock." Lachlan's voice was soft, weak. Nothing like the booming, confident pitch Dez had heard in the hallways around KRPD headquarters during the few years he'd had occasion to encounter the older man.

"Why 'obviously'?"

Lachlan gave a small smile. Even in his condition, it managed to look snide. "The size of you. Your hair. The fact you're the spitting image of your father. And, of course, the fact I've met you before."

"Only the one time," Dez said. "I wasn't sure you'd remember."

"Never forget a face. Your dad, by the way. Good man. Was sorry when he passed."

Dez nodded. "Thanks. Me too."

"They tell me you saved my life."

"I found you, if that counts."

"I don't remember much, but I have some vague recollection of seeing you there. Looked so much like Flynn, figured I was in good hands. You're wondering why I wanted to see you."

Dez didn't say anything, didn't need to. He gave Lachlan a

moment, watching as the man tried to shift and ended up grimacing with a groan.

"You need something?" Dez asked.

"They got me on the good stuff now," Lachlan said. "Couple days from now, not sure how happy I'll be."

That didn't really answer Dez's question, but he figured if anyone was capable of making a stink if he wanted something, it was Lachlan. So he gave the man the time to finish his careful adjusting.

"So about why you're here," Lachlan said once he'd achieved whatever passed for comfort in his condition. "There are things that can't be said to certain people."

Dez looked back, ensured the door was closed. Lachlan was already speaking far too quietly to be overheard, so Dez did his part and kept his voice down as well. "Police, you mean."

"You catch on quick, kid." The sarcasm was clear, but then everyone knew that was Lachlan's natural tone.

"Raynor's coming at me with obstruction threats."

"Raynor's a horse's ass," Lachlan said. "Wouldn't talk to that little turd if someone brought out the thumbscrews."

Dez grinned.

"Not alone in my opinion," Lachlan observed. "Anyway, like to see them come at me for obstruction. Would be fun."

"I have a feeling they're more likely to come after me than you."

"Leave them to me," Lachlan said. Then he was back to business. "You came to my office with a woman. Who?"

"Lucienne Dule."

"And you didn't share that with police."

"No. I told them I only knew her first name. I wasn't sure how much you'd share and I didn't want to look completely obstructionist. But I didn't think I should be giving her up either."

Lachlan nodded, the corners of his mouth turning up. "Good man. Where is she? Is she safe?"

"For the time being, anyway. She's at—"

Lachlan cut him off quickly. "Don't tell me. I don't want to know." He held up his left arm by way of explanation. "Morphine drip. God knows what'll come out of my mouth next. For that matter, we should make this quick. I'm liable to fall asleep in the middle of a sentence."

"Okay, so what's going on?"

"Ideally, we'd have this chat elsewhere. But it looks like I'll be staying awhile. Listen, I've done some digging into her past, searching for her son. I think I found him. Do you know what I'm talking about?"

"Sully."

"She filled you in."

"As much as she could, yeah."

"He was more or less raised by your parents."

"Yeah, he came to us when he was seven. He never knew anything about his birth parents. No one did, really."

"Doorstep drop. I know. He mean anything to you? You care about him?"

Dez suspected there was a test here he needed to pass. "He's my brother. I love him."

"He's not blood."

"In every way that counts, he's my family. How'd you piece it together anyway, connecting Sully to Lucienne?"

Lachlan scrutinized Dez before answering. Test passed. "I got ahold of the police file and Lucienne gave me the rest. I put two and two together."

"You have the police file?"

"Somewhere safe. I suspect that's what the masked man who attacked me was after."

That was a relief, Dez supposed. As usual, his poker face was way off.

"You suspected it was Lucienne who tried to do me in."

"I didn't think so," Dez said. "The way I figured things, she had to have been with me when you were attacked. But I wasn't sure, I guess. Truth is, I don't know much about her. I've only just met her."

Lachlan blinked up at him twice, then started to close his eyes.

Dez leaned in and grasped the man's arm. "Lachlan. Hey, Lachlan."

"Hmm?"

"Stay with me another minute here, okay? It's important."

"What's important?"

"You were telling me about Lucienne, the file. Is there a way I can look at it?"

"File … f … right. File. 1232 Landon Drive. 5901."

"You said 1232."

"5901. Got it? … Number 63."

"What's 63?"

"Just remember. Number 63."

Dez pulled out his phone to tap the numbers into his notes app, but Lachlan slapped his hand.

"Damn it, what?" Dez complained.

"Not where anyone will see. Write it down and burn it. Or better yet, remember. 1232, 5901, 63. That order."

Dez blinked his way through the numbers, committing them to memory—mainly because he was no longer in the habit of carrying a notepad and pen with him now that his policing days were over.

"Got it?" Lachlan asked.

"Yeah. Got it. Do I need a key?"

"Shit. My house, 1852 Cockburn. Degas."

"What?"

"Degas. Dear God, kid, don't you know anything?"

"The artist?"

"Bingo. Door code's 89179. Alarm is 9012. And go alone. No one else can know about this, any of it. Not yet."

"So why are you trusting me with this? It can't all be about me saving your life or who my dad was."

Lachlan drifted again, requiring another slight shake of the arm to bring him back around.

"Lachlan …. Why me?"

"You'll know what to do with it, and you'll do it quietly. Anyone else—even Lucienne—and people will get hurt. Sullivan's alive, Desmond. You need to keep him that way. He's the key."

"The key to what? … Lachlan?"

But Lachlan was out again and, this time, no amount of prodding or shaking helped.

Dez stared down at the man for what could have been one minute or five, trying to make sense of what he'd been told. He thought back to what Sully had said last night, hinting there were people looking for him who might not be connected to Lockwood. Lachlan knew Sully was alive; did he have any way of knowing he had been kidnapped? Would he have a theory, someplace else to start looking, someone to question?

But Lachlan wasn't budging from his drug-induced sleep and Dez knew he should count himself lucky he'd gotten as much lucid conversation out of him as he had.

With time ticking and a new path to follow, Dez decided he should track this lead rather than wait to see whether Lachlan would wake up. All he had to do was get past Forbes and hope to hell police weren't holding Lachlan's home as a scene.

Dez took a moment—Lachlan be damned—to punch the string of numbers into his phone's notes app. He was okay with numbers, but nowhere near that good.

Forbes was waiting just the other side of the door, a spider waiting to spring. "What did he have to say?"

"Not a whole lot that made sense," Dez said. "The guy's in and out constantly and, when he is in, he's still out. We just had a whole conversation about his shoes."

"He isn't wearing any."

"My point exactly. Look, if it's any help, he started to tell me something. Said it was a man who jumped him, but he said he was wearing a mask. Then he went off on a tangent about shoelaces, and that was it."

Dez glanced at Eva, but averted his gaze quickly. She was watching him quietly with arms crossed, a position she took only when feeling defensive, annoyed or sensed bullshit. Dez guessed, this time, it came down to Door Number Three.

"So you've basically got nothing, you're telling me," Forbes said.

"Basically. But I'd appreciate it if you'd let me know when he wakes up again. I think there's something else he was trying to say."

"If I find out you're bullshitting me, Braddock ...."

"Oh, one more thing. He really doesn't like you very much, Forbes. I think the term he used was 'little turd.' "

"Asshole."

"Him or me?"

"Dez," Eva warned, drawing his name out in a tone he knew meant business.

"Take your pick," Forbes said.

"You don't have to antagonize him, you know," Eva said once they'd walked away, heading to the hospital exit.

"I get precious few pleasures out of life anymore," Dez said. "Don't rob me of that."

"So now that it's just us, what did Lachlan want? And don't feed me the same line you laid on Forbes. We both know that's a load of bull."

Dez didn't answer right away, trying to determine the lesser of two evils: lie to his wife and face her wrath or break his promise to Lachlan and share info the P.I. believed could place Sully's life at risk.

Of course, Dez had already told Eva Sully was alive. And the fact remained he couldn't lie to her. It was a skill he'd never even tried to master. He'd never wanted to be that guy anyway, the kind who could lie to the people he loved.

But there were still too many unknowns, too many unanswered questions. Too much that could go wrong. And Dez wasn't sure he was willing to take some of the risks.

"I can't tell you that, Eva. He said I have to keep it between him and me, for Sully's sake."

"So he believes Sully's alive too?"

Damn. "No one can know that, okay? Please."

Eva took Dez's arm and pulled him—or pulled at him until he followed—partway down a quiet hallway where no one would overhear, her words hushed but urgent.

"So Sully's really alive?"

"What, I tell you that and I'm full of shit, but Lachlan says it and it's gospel?"

Eva had the good grace to look sheepish for a moment. But only for a moment. "You also have a really lousy history the past couple years, Dez. I don't know what to believe anymore where you're concerned."

Dez took a small step forward, a move that easily would have sent an opponent backward. He hadn't intended that in her case, and she wasn't one to back down anyway. It was why he'd fallen in love with her. "I may be a lot of things, Eva, but I have never lied to you."

She stared back up into his eyes, and he felt as much as saw the intensity of her gaze as she watched him, waiting for the break that might suggest he was being anything less than honest. An angry heat flared there, one that had Dez fighting the urge to kiss her right in the hallway of the hospital. They had the best sex when she was pissed at him about something, and it all started with that look she was giving him right now.

Naturally, she saw that too. "Get your mind out of the gutter, Dez."

"What?"

"You know what."

"So you don't want to?"

"What I want more right now is to know what the hell is going on."

Dez took a moment to revel in the "more" before moving on. She was right as usual, of course. Now wasn't the time. "I can't tell you much, mainly because I don't know much. I'm trying to find Sully, but I'm not making much progress. It's possible Lachlan's got some info I can use, but he was out before I could question him further. He gave me some numbers for stuff, at least one of which is an address. I need to get into his house for a key. Do you know if his place is under any sort of watch?"

"Not that I know of. I'm pretty sure investigators tossed it earlier, looking for any files or additional info he might not have at the office, but I don't know anything more about that."

"Can you drop me off at home so I can get my SUV?"

"You're heading to Lachlan's now?"

"I have to. If something Lachlan got his hands on holds the key to all this, I have to find it, get the ball rolling. I've got to find Sully."

"Okay, fine. But you're not doing this alone."

"I can't tell anyone else. No one can know he's alive."

"Well, I'm not anyone else. I love Sully too. If he really is alive, and he needs help, I'm in this. He's family. And then there's the whole problem of you. If you think I'm letting you walk into something dangerous with no backup, you're out of your mind."

Dez couldn't stop the grin, was pleased when he saw her fighting her own responding smile. Unlike him, she was more or less successful. "I'm not alone, you know," he said. "I've got Pax, and he's pretty decent backup from what I can tell."

"I'm thinking I'd rather know you've got a set of human eyes keeping a lookout. No offence to Pax. Anyway, hard to say. Dog his size, he's probably smashed through the window of my car and is running wild in the streets, eating people."

Dez's smile faded as he considered this further. As much as he loved the idea of having Eva at his side on this, he also knew things could get risky fast. The last thing he wanted was a situation that endangered both Kayleigh's parents in one go. "Evie, I appreciate what you're saying, but—"

"But nothing. Don't you worm around this, trying to protect me. I'm a cop, remember? I put myself in harm's way all the time, and you knew that when we met in training. Don't get all Big Man on me. I can handle myself."

"I know you can. It's just ...." He wanted to say it was because he loved her so much, because he'd lost so many people—at least twice due to his failure—and because he couldn't think of a worse fate, save one, than losing her.

But, as usual, he didn't have to.

She laid a hand on his chest, forcing him to meet her eye. It almost broke him, the emotion far too close to the surface. Her words proved the tipping point, had him swallowing against the lump in his throat and wiping at the tear that slipped free.

"I'm not going anywhere, Dez."

17

LACHLAN LIVED in a comfortable house in the city's North Bank neighbourhood, set far enough back from the river to make it affordable.

Dez recalled something about Lachlan having divorced during his career, but he'd been savvy enough to ensure a prenuptial was in place that meant he didn't lose his shirt in the proceedings. After all, there was very little doubt any split involving Lachlan was no one's fault but his own.

Having found the address, Dez was relieved to see no police units set up outside. To be safe, he asked Eva to take a quick drive down the back alley to check for patrol cars.

"Happy now?" she asked.

"I've got you going far enough off track here," he said. "Last thing I want is to make you an accomplice in breaking into a held scene."

Eva returned to the front of the house, parking next to a large tree Pax took to watering as soon as he emerged from the vehicle.

"Are you sure he should be coming in?" Eva asked. "Lachlan doesn't strike me as a pets kinda guy."

"That makes it even better then, doesn't it?"

"You know, he's not that bad," Eva said as the three of them walked up a set of stairs to the home's wraparound veranda.

"If you're comparing to Raynor, I guess you'd be right."

Dez stopped at the front door, keying in 89179. Thankfully, Lachlan seemed to have a head for numbers, the code holding true despite the morphine stupor. Once inside, an audible beeping drew Dez to a backlit alarm box, which took Lachlan's provided four-digit code.

"So what are we looking for?" Eva asked as Dez searched for a light switch.

"Degas, he said."

Eva peered at Dez out of the corner of her eye. "The artist? Are you sure he wasn't completely stoned when he said it?"

"I'm not sure of anything." Dez located a light switch and got his first good look inside. "Except we're screwed."

"What?"

Dez looked down at Eva. "You didn't by chance take an art history class at some point you never told me about, did you?"

Eva's eyes grew large as she took in what Dez had observed. Lachlan's house was like an art gallery, paintings taking up space on virtually every available wall surface. Some looked to be prints, while others, even to Dez's untrained eye, were clearly originals. And Lachlan had a broad taste in art, his collection ranging from realistic-looking portraits to surreal abstracts. Added to the problem were the sculptures, which sat on tables, shelves and mantles wherever space allowed. Dez remembered hearing DaVinci and his contemporaries had mastered both paintings and sculpture. Hopefully, Degas wasn't quite so well-rounded.

Eva had her phone out and a glance over her shoulder told Dez she was doing an internet search on the artist in question.

"He seems to have had a thing for dancers and women taking baths," Eva said. "And I hate to tell you this, but he dabbled in sculpture too."

"Damn."

Eva kept scrolling through pages until she found one showing the artist's work. "Okay, I'm thinking all we can do is go through here slow and look for anything that resembles these. Take my phone. I think I've got a pretty good handle on it."

"You always had a better eye for this stuff."

They split up, Dez moving to the study on the right while Eva went into what looked to be a formal sitting room on the left. The study contained a large oak desk, and it was clear the police had indeed been here, papers and files stacked on the surface a little haphazardly. No way Lachlan, obsessive compulsive as he was known to be, would leave anything in that manner, particularly in his own house. It appeared investigators had given some thought to the artwork, too, a couple of larger works a little off-kilter. Dez was grateful to see this room had fewer paintings—until he got a good look at Lachlan's monstrous book collection: two walls of floor-to-ceiling shelves, revealing numerous books on art. Lachlan hadn't specifically said the Degas he'd referenced was a physical piece, after all.

Dez blew out a breath, and reached down to pet Pax, sitting next to him with tongue out and eyes fixed on him. "You wanna take the bottom shelves, buddy?"

Pax sauntered away.

With no help to be had there, Dez went it alone, determining none of the handful of small paintings or sculptures were created by the man he wanted. He then turned his attention to the book-shelves, scanning the titles and hoping for the best.

It looked like investigators had entertained the same thought, the otherwise-organized shelves a little messier around the large books. Dez assumed searchers had been hoping to find a file or scattered papers concealed inside them. If there had been anything to find, it might be long gone, but Dez took some comfort in the fact Forbes was still in the dark. It was just possible something remained hidden, something police didn't spot or didn't recognize as significant. Whether Dez would see it and recognize it remained the question.

His breath caught as he spotted a large book on Degas's work. He pulled it out and flipped through the pages, but nothing fell out as he'd hoped. He continued the search, frustration mounting; Lachlan had his books organized by size rather than alphabet or artist. The larger books, like the one he'd just skimmed, sat on the lower shelves, with the smaller ones—biographies and the like—on the top. And Lachlan had taken it a step further, arranging his books to fit some sort of aesthetic only he would think to achieve. Where there weren't enough books of the same size to fill a shelf, he stacked others on either side to provide balance.

This meant, of course, no search would be simple; books on Degas could be anywhere on the shelves in front of him.

Directing his attention to the task by running a finger along the spines in a way that made him feel like a grade school student, Dez looked through the collection book by book and shelf by shelf, working his way upward. So far, he'd found three books about Degas, but none contained anything of note. Now up to the biographies, Dez followed the same process, locating one on the second-from-top shelf. This one was a small hardcover, still wrapped in its no-longer-glossy jacket cover. Dez flipped through it and, finding nothing, pulled the jacket away on one side.

There, on the outside back cover, just beneath the jacket, a key had been taped.

"WE NEED to get to 1232 Landon Drive," Dez said once the two of them were back in the car. He'd been careful to lock up before they left. Everyone knew Lachlan was anal about security, and leaving the place open to intruders was bound to be a life-changing mistake for Dez once the retired cop got through with him.

"You got some directions for me?" Eva asked as Dez keyed the address into the search bar on his phone and waited for something to pop up.

The results had him grinning, recognizing the whole thing as pure Lachlan. "Jed's Storage. East side of the city on the north side of the river. Edgewater Road is probably the easiest, and it's the other side of Lockwood."

"That's a long way out," Eva said. "I'd better call your mom and ask if Kayleigh can spend the night."

Dez had been enjoying this, investigating with Eva, spending time with her in a way he hadn't since their separation. But she was clearly torn, so he did what he could to lighten the load.

"Drop me at my place, and I'll pick up my vehicle. Go home. I've got this from here."

"No."

"Eva, seriously, I've got this."

"Got what? Lachlan was almost killed, and his office was torn apart. It doesn't look like they hit his house, but that's hardly surprising given about five people actually know where he lives."

"Listen, I appreciate you wanting to watch my back here. You have no idea how much. But I can look after myself, okay?"

"And I'm sure you said the same thing before you were buried alive last night, right?"

It was dark out, the only illumination coming from the glow of the streetlights outside. But it was enough for him to make out the worry on Eva's face.

"Dez, I don't know what we're in the middle of here, but it's not good. You were attacked and nearly killed. Sully's apparently alive but might not stay that way. Lachlan's been seriously assaulted and his office ransacked. Sorry, but I don't want you handling anything on your own right now, not until we get to the bottom of this."

"We don't know everything's connected. Not for sure."

"Pretty crazy coincidence if it's not, wouldn't you say?"

There was no point arguing. Eva had dug in deep, and Dez knew her well enough to know her mind would not be changed. In truth, her concern for his safety warmed him in a way he hadn't felt for some time. Convincing himself he didn't really matter was easy when he allowed himself to slip deeply into the depression and self-pity that had framed his world for the past couple of years. But once in a while, when he really listened to voices besides his own, he was reminded other people counted on his presence in the world.

"Drive," Dez said. "I'll call my mom."

DEZ AND EVA chatted most of the way, about Kayleigh mostly, but also about Eva's job and how things were going for her at home.

He'd not-so-subtly asked whether she'd tried dating, to which —to his immense relief—he'd received a resounding no. He noticed she didn't ask the same about him, but then realized the answer was blatantly obvious to anyone with a functioning brain. He was as hung up on her now as ever, perhaps more because he couldn't have her.

And she knew it. Why wouldn't she? She'd always been the smartest woman Dez had ever known.

As they approached the road to Lockwood, he stopped talking, felt his own silence as keenly as Eva must have.

Streetlights revealed the tall iron fence surrounding the expansive treed property. The intricate gate had the audacity to look graceful and welcoming rather than what it should have resembled in Dez's view: an electrified sliding gate of a super-max prison.

"You okay?" Eva asked.

The sound of her voice prevented a deeper slide into the dark, and he rewarded it with an answer. Such as it was. "Yeah."

"You sure?"

"He could be here now for all I know. He could be right here. And there's not a damn thing I can do."

"He might not be," Eva said. "We don't know anything yet. But I promise you, I will do everything I can to help you find him."

Eva was an experienced police officer and had worded her answer like one. Like Dez, she knew better than to make promises she might not be able to keep. As it stood, the one she'd given was good enough for the time being, her assurance he wasn't alone in this.

Dez didn't respond, didn't trust his voice to hold. Emotion sat close to the surface with him, often rendering him helpless in the moment.

If Dez's biggest perceived weakness was emotion, Eva had quickly become his greatest strength. She'd always provided him the power to rise above his own guilt, grief and anger. As she so often had in the past, she stepped into his silence.

"It's not your fault, you know," she said. "What happened to Sully." Her words offered redemption if only he could hold on to them.

Dez drew his lips together and stared out the passenger side window. They'd passed the Lockwood property, but a part of him had been dropped off at the gate. In his mind, he could see the inside of the building. The entryway where faux-friendly nursing staff greeted guests and newcomers while rough-and-ready order-lies hovered nearby, not half-hoping for some action. The sunroom that acted both as extra programming space and visiting area, providing family and friends with a false reality that enabled them to go home guilt-free.

"It's not your fault!" Eva's all-but-shouted words, cutting into memory and a silent car, were thunder, and yanked Dez back with such ferocity he physically jumped. "Whatever happened then, whatever is happening now, whatever happens in the future, it's not your fault. You hear me? You need to stop blaming yourself for everything. Hell, maybe you should be blaming your uncle."

"Part of me does," he said. "Part of me will hate him forever. But he thought he was doing the right thing, Eva. Sully was caught up in way more than he could handle, with Dad and Betty and the ghosts and everything. Forcing him into Lockwood was the wrong thing, but no one knew exactly how wrong back then.

What I did know was we'd already prevented two suicide attempts. There's an expression: three times lucky. I wasn't taking the chance, not with him. So I didn't fight it like I should have. I ran from it instead."

"I know. I remember. But I also remember you weren't far from tailspinning right behind him. You never were far behind him in anything. I sometimes felt like he was our kid, not your brother, the way you were with him. And I'm not faulting you. I loved you for that. I knew where it came from, why it was so important to you to keep your brother safe. We all have our child-hood crosses to bear. Yours was heavier than a lot of people's."

Exhaustion hit him, like he could just crawl into bed and sleep for a week. But there was far too much riding on him.

"If he's there, I can't let this go again, Eva. I won't. I don't care what it takes. I won't let him down again."

"If he's there, we'll find a way to get him out. Okay?" She saved him further, shining a light into the darkness with what he knew to be a joke. "If all else fails, we can all go on the run together, you, me, Kayleigh and Sully. I'm sure she'd love that. She used to want to be a gypsy, remember?"

"That was after the archeologist phase."

"Before archaeologist, after cowgirl."

"Right." Dez looked at Eva, watched the smile playing around her lips as she thought about their daughter, and he felt his own forming right alongside. "Thank you."

"For what?"

"Everything. Just being here. Kicking my ass. Pulling me out of the gutter time and again. I've never deserved you. I sure as hell never deserved Kayleigh."

Eva met his eye before returning attention to the road. The brief second was enough to reveal her amusement. "We both know you never deserved me. But Kayleigh's every inch her father's daughter."

"Sorry about that."

"Don't be. I'm not. The only problem with the two of you is

that you're too hard on yourselves over things it's not in your power to change."

"There are some things I can change."

"So when are you going to start?" Eva asked. "I'm getting tired of waiting for you, Snowman. We'll find Sully, all right? But since Sully proved the tipping point in your going off the rails two years ago, I need you to promise me you'll let him be your reason to get back on again."

"Eva, I love Sully, and getting him back will help me a lot with getting back on track. But you and Kayleigh are my reason. You always were. Don't you ever think otherwise."

Eva said nothing, and Dez smiled as he watched her swallow hard.

He hadn't expected the touch of her hand closing over his, a feeling both of forgotten warmth and of coming home. Afraid of bringing a premature end to this moment, of breaking whatever spell they were under, Dez didn't move.

Neither did she.

18

JED'S STORAGE wasn't far off Edgewater Road, marked by a beaming neon sign, a lit office and a locked compound containing several rows of large storage containers.

"Did you check their hours?" Eva asked as she pulled up to the office.

"No, but—" Dez pointed to a sign just under the main one, reading twenty-four hours, "—that looks promising."

"That's probably why Lachlan picked this one," Eva said. "He seems like the kind of guy who'd do most of his business in the wee hours."

Dez scanned the area and came up with something new to worry about. "Stay in the car and keep out of view. There's a camera above the gate over there, and no doubt there's one in the office too. Last thing I want is you getting made on this if someone comes at me for interfering in an investigation."

"Just play it cool. We aren't interfering in anything. We're just checking something out for a friend."

"Right," Dez said.

She answered his smile, but only just.

Dez headed inside where he found a young man behind a

counter tall enough to keep most of his body hidden from view. The guy regarded Dez with the narrowed eyes of someone used to working alone at night, where everyone who came in was a potential threat to life and limb.

And, sure enough, there was a security camera mounted high behind the desk, leaving Dez recorded here for posterity, should Forbes ever come calling. Dez couldn't imagine Lachlan was too fond of being recorded each time he came and went—Dez sure wasn't happy about it, particularly given he and Eva were potentially obstructing a police investigation—but you took what you got with a twenty-four-hour business.

"I help you?" the clerk asked, voice low and questioning, a hint of a Slavic accent mixed in.

"I need to access a storage container," Dez said. One of Lachlan's other numbers clicked into place. "Number 63."

"You're not the usual guy," the man behind the desk said. His hands weren't in view, and Dez imagined he was fingering a firearm or some other potentially devastating weapon. Anyone worth their salt these days kept some sort of weapon while working a night job.

Dez didn't provide Lachlan's name, certain there was no way in hell the ex-cop had purchased a container under his true identity.

"He's a friend. He's been hurt, and he asked me to get something from his container."

"You have a key?"

Dez held up the item, receiving a hint of a nod from the clerk.

"And the code to access the compound?"

This was a test, it seemed. Thankfully, Lachlan had provided crib notes.

"5901," Dez said.

This time the clerk smiled. It was barely there, but it counted as a win for Dez nonetheless.

"Second row to your left, about halfway down," man said.

"Keypad is to the left of the gate. Drive through, and it will close behind you."

Dez nodded at the man and left the office. He hadn't noticed the keypad in the dark, and he kicked himself mentally for providing the unneeded footage of himself in the office. Sure, that camera mounted above the gate would record his comings and goings just the same, but he could have put his hood up to make recognition more difficult.

Then again, there weren't exactly a lot of people with his size and build in KR. Add in vehicle recognition and Forbes's job wouldn't exactly be a tough one.

Dez opened Eva's door. "Slide over. The camera over there is on the driver's side. I don't want it picking you up."

"What about you?"

"I was probably screwed a while ago."

Eva did as asked, nimbly shifting herself over the centre console and into the passenger side while Dez moved the seat back and took up her vacated position. He steered toward the gate and reached out to key in Lachlan's code, pleased when he got the right response. As he watched the tall steel gate slide open, it occurred to him this was entirely more befitting Lockwood.

He turned left and followed the clerk's directions to the second row, the two of them watching for cameras en route and thankfully finding none.

Having located the right container, Dez got out. He turned the key on a lockbox next to the big, blue roll-up door and located a button inside to work it. The inside of the container, as made clear by the light of the car's headlights, provided room to park, and Eva climbed back over and drove in. Meanwhile, Dez searched for and found a light switch.

A second button for the door was inside, this one unguarded, and Dez hit that one next, closing them in and granting them extra privacy should the clerk or anyone else come snooping.

Hoping Pax wouldn't take a leak on any of Lachlan's personal possessions, Dez let the dog out of the vehicle, and turned around for a better look at Lachlan's hidden world.

A few pieces of old furniture, covered in reams of heavy plastic, were hard to make out beyond their shapes. A handful of paintings—prints of famous artwork Dez couldn't identify but remembered seeing somewhere—were propped against various surfaces while a large area rug gave that portion of floor a surprisingly luxuriant feel. On top of the rug was a plush armchair, the kind Eva liked to curl up in to read. And it looked like it would be getting plenty of use as the most obvious features in the unit were several tall stacks of bankers' boxes and a long row of metal filing cabinets lining the back wall.

Eva's eyes, ordinarily more almond-shaped, made a significant move toward round. "I don't suppose he gave you any clue where to start looking?"

Dez shook his head slowly as he mentally calculated the number of boxes and drawers in front of them. "I wish."

SULLY HADN'T INTENDED to fall asleep, didn't realize he had until a nightmare woke him.

He was unnerved to see her standing next to the mattress, watching him with those large, pained eyes, blood ever-present on the front of her white nightgown and turning her purple hair black on one side.

Sully sat up, sliding himself back to sit against the wall facing her. She wasn't fully solid like she so often appeared, but filmy, enabling him to see the edge of the door through her body.

Ordinarily, the sight of her unsettled him, even scared him in those instances where he hadn't been expecting her. But here, in this place, locked in this small cell with nothing but a spider for company, he greeted her as a friend.

"I wish you could talk," he said. "I could use the conversation."

As expected, she didn't respond, instead holding him in that wide-eyed stare he was trying very hard to ignore despite his unbroken track record of failure. It occurred to him he'd never looked for other ways to converse, never really wanting to go too far down that path. Today—or tonight, if that's what it was—felt different. Today, he needed her in a way he'd never felt before.

"If I ask you questions, can you nod or shake your head? Or can you respond some other way?"

Her answer came in the form of a slow nod and, for the first time since he'd been brought to this place, Sully smiled. It might not be a traditional conversation, but right now anything was better than nothing—even if that anything was talking to a dead girl.

"I know you can't tell me your name, and I can't even begin to guess it. If I go through the alphabet, can you nod when I get to the right letter?"

Her head moved slowly side to side this time.

"You don't want me to know your name?"

Another slow shake, no.

"Okay. How about your age? Can I ask that?"

Another no. Sully moved on.

"Do you know how long you've been dead?"

Again, she shook motioned the negative. Sully believed he'd been about four or five when he first saw her—or at least when he first remembered seeing her, and it seemed to him she'd be impossible to forget. That meant she'd been in this form for at least twenty years. How time passed for a ghost was something he'd never got his head around. Did they feel time like everyone else, or did it pass in some other way? Did twenty years drag on or did it blink past like the bat of an eye? In those moments when they weren't seen, heard or felt, did they still exist somewhere, or did time and space in that other world bend and unfold somehow, pulling them from one location to the next? If so, did they control it, or did it control them?

He'd given those ideas a lot of thought over the years, but now wasn't the time to ask. He had bigger fish to fry.

"Am I in danger here?"

This time a nod, up and down.

"Bad?"

He regretted the question immediately, the reply a yes.

"There are just two of them?"

She shook her head, no. The answer surprised Sully, only two people having attacked him in the park. It was possible, of course, someone had been waiting in the van, or even back here, wherever this was. Or it could be the people who grabbed him had done so under orders from someone else. Were that the case, he was left with even more questions, since Brennan was not—at least from what Sully could tell—capable of orchestrating anything like this on his own. But if someone else was in charge, where were they? What did they want from him?

That brought him to the question he'd been dreading asking.

"Is one of them Gerhardt?"

He blew out a breath as she shook her head.

"Hackman?"

Another no.

That was something at least, an indication his darkest fear hadn't been realized. He wasn't back at Lockwood and, if things were to go seriously sideways in the course of this, at least it wouldn't happen while he was subject to a drug that forced him to relive someone else's brutal end.

What he didn't have were further answers as to what he was doing here and, without a better idea, he didn't have the right questions either.

With nowhere else to go on this particular fact-finding mission, he set off on another, taking advantage of this newfound form of communication to learn more about the girl who had repeatedly popped up in his life.

"You've been trying to protect me, haven't you?"

She watched him a moment, then nodded slowly.

"I know you were trying to help me earlier. I'm sorry I didn't listen. I was worried about my brother. I know I need to stay out of Gerhardt's path, but it's this other person I'm worried about, the one in the mask from the blue room. Do you know who it is?"

Another slow nod. Unlike the other physical responses, which had at least provided some form of answer, this one left Sully reeling under the weight of everything he didn't know and couldn't uncover. She knew. She had the answers he needed, and he had no easy means of pulling them from her. And, in a way, that was worse than learning she was just as ignorant to the truth as he was.

"This other person, the one in the mask. Is he responsible for what's happening to me now, for me being here?"

This time, she shook her head, no.

"And this isn't all about Brennan, is it?"

Another head shake, another negative.

Sully gave it a moment, deciding whether he wanted to ask the next question, whether he could live with the answer. He decided it would be worse to live without one.

"Is it Lowell Braddock? Does he know I'm alive?"

He'd asked two questions, but a response to one would do for both. The head shake dispelling that thought came as relief while bringing with it even more confusion, and he cast his eyes down to his hands, as if looking away from her might help steady him. It didn't, his thoughts still roiling within his brain as he searched for something further he might do, something he could ask. Anything to get to the answers she held. But there was nothing, and he found himself studying a scar on the palm of his hand, on the meaty section between wrist and thumb. It was one of several on his body, but this one meant something, had come at a turning point in his young life, taking him from darkness into the light. Received at age seven, the injury was a lasting, physical reminder of the discovery of his own courage and strength. He'd been left scraped, bruised and bloodied trying to pull Dez from the river. A part of him had been healed even as he'd bled over himself and his new foster brother. Since that day, Dez had returned the favour again and again.

Sully didn't know if or how his brother would manage it this time, but he knew Dez would move heaven and earth to find him. The truth of it was so deeply embedded within him he'd never question it.

But, for now, he was on his own. Just him and this murdered kid consisting of little more than loosely packed energy, consciousness and a swiftly fading light. She was almost gone from his view again, taking with her any hope for additional answers. At least for now.

He asked the next question, needing the answer, but wary of her response just the same.

"If none of them are the reason I'm here, then who is?"

Staring up into her face, he watched her eyes until they faded away into the shadow.

Sully let his head fall back against the wall with a light thud, closing his eyes and searching for calm through the heavy weight of anxiety he'd carried since regaining consciousness. He took a few deep breaths, trying to quiet his mind, give it a temporary break from dark thoughts and predictions. Failing at mental escape failed, he opened his eyes, and spotted something that could help.

A subtle light—not from the dim bulb—had fallen on a deep crack in the corner opposite, running from near the ceiling midway to the floor. Sully watched for a moment, long enough to see the light fade from the spot just as the Purple Girl had disappeared from his view not two minutes before.

Ordinarily, a crack in cement wouldn't have been enough to draw his attention but he needed a distraction, particularly one that appeared to have been shown to him deliberately. He approached it and ran his fingertips along its length.

Thinner near the top and bottom, it widened in the middle, allowing him to slide his fingertips inside. There, they brushed against something solid and smooth. Maneuvering carefully, he was able to secure the object between his index and middle fingers and draw it from the crevice.

It was a pen, one of those cheap ones, the kind you could pick up at any dollar store. It appeared to have been well-used, the clear plastic tubing revealing most of the ink had been depleted.

The find had him returning to search the wall with more urgency, trying to be careful as he dug back within the crack created by time, settling and perhaps some human intervention. His fingers touched on something else, something like a thick folder or notebook. Once again he eased his fingers around the object, one on each side, until he had a firm grip. Wedged in as it was, his fingers slipped several times before he was able to withdraw it.

It was a ruled notebook, similar to those he remembered from his grade school days. The dull cover might have lost some of its original colouring with the wear of time, but the shade was all but lost behind drawings, which covered both front and back. They were eyes. All of them. Just eyes, of varying shapes and sizes, staring unnervingly from the cover. They were different, some round, some almond-shaped; some youthful, some lined with age; some calm, some narrowed in the heat of rage, and some expanded in terror.

Perhaps worst of all, they were lifelike, as if the artist had been putting them to paper while studying a subject right in front of them.

The effect was unsettling and had Sully quickly turning his attention to the notebook's insides. As he flipped through the pages, he could see tiny writing filling it, not sticking to the wide lines favoured by school teachers with students learning to print. Rather, the writer had created rule of his or her own, fitting two or three lines of minuscule print to every one ruled space, as if expecting this to be the only paper they'd ever see.

He hoped to find one answer immediately, and he closed the book and searched within the eyes for the name and subject lines usually included on the front covers of students' notebooks. This one didn't disappoint. While the subject line had been left blank, filled in only by several glaring eyes, something was written next to "Name" in big, looping letters.

Lucienne Dule.

19

LACHLAN LIKELY HAD a hidden method to his madness, to this mess that was his collection of files and various other information.

But what it was, Dez had yet to uncover.

File folders appeared to collect pieces of paper relevant to each other—one, as an example, containing names of people believed to be members or associates of the Red Jacks motorcycle gang, along with any and all other information Lachlan was able to obtain on them. And there were folders for other criminal organizations, whether affiliated by ancestry or race or by common interest, and even one for loose groupings of individuals brought together by nothing more than a desire to make big money in drug and weapons trafficking.

One of the boxes was dedicated solely to the Co-ed Killer case Lachlan had been key in cracking, while another contained all the information he was able to gather on six-year-old Michael Kilbarton, one of the city's most heartbreaking missing persons files.

Eva stood next to a filing cabinet, flipping through the contents of its drawers, while Dez sat crosslegged on the rug, digging through box after box in a search for anything with Sully or Lucienne's name on it.

"This is incredible," Eva said.

Dez's head shot up, his neck cracking with the sudden move-ment. "You find something?"

She met his eye and winced slightly, telling Dez he must look as hopeful as he'd sounded. "No, sorry. Just thinking of the amount of work Lachlan sunk into this. I mean, back at HQ, we've got access to a pile of information on the police central informa-tion system, but Lachlan has everything short of fingerprints and DNA. He's got birth dates, family and friend relationships, crim-inal connections, last known addresses and phone numbers, crim-inal records, even drugs of choice and what restaurants and bars these people frequent. This stuff would be invaluable down at headquarters."

"Lachlan was invaluable down at headquarters," Dez said. "And no one knew it better than he did."

Eva chuckled and went back to work. "I wish I could figure out how he's got this organized. I mean, it's Lachlan. He's got this in some sort of order, don't you think?"

"He's not going to come in here and waste three hours digging for one document, if that's what you're asking. He's got this sorted the way he wants it, no doubt and, knowing him, it's arranged in a way that makes sense to no one but him. Let me know if you crack his code, huh? You've always been the smart one."

"Sucks for you. That means I got the brains and the looks."

Dez was about to open another box when his eyes wandered to a dresser covered by plastic wrapping. Lachlan had advised him to play his cards close to his chest on this one, suggesting the man was plenty aware he'd landed in something sticky. He wouldn't have left the files in with the others; he'd have added a layer of protection. While potential intruders wasted their time digging through boxes and filing cabinets, the subject of their search would be just feet away, waiting them out. Lachlan would anticipate the moment where patience ran out, and the search was abandoned.

Staying on the rug, Dez slid himself over to the piece of furniture, taking some satisfaction in what was looking to become a correct read as he noted the plastic wrapping was simply tucked under in front. At some point, the makeshift cover had been sliced through at the bottom, a detail visible only to those who specifically went looking for it.

He lifted the plastic in front, exposing the dresser's drawers and allowing him to pull them open. There, in the middle one, tucked beneath a pile of folded sweaters, old T-shirts and a thin piece of plywood meant to appear as the drawer's base, were two folders.

"Eva," he said, heart thumping against his chest wall as he read the names on the pop-up tabs. "I found them."

LACHLAN HADN'T USED both given and last names on the folders themselves, restricting himself to just the former—his way, no doubt, of further protecting the subjects from those who might happen upon his files.

Not that it mattered much, the folders' innards containing plenty more information than just full names.

Dez was sitting now in Lachlan's armchair, Eva settled next to him on one of the plush armrests while Pax sprawled at their feet. Neither Dez nor Eva wanting to miss the information contained in either file, they'd settled for flipping through both together. Anyway, two sets of eyes were far more likely to spot important details and find the significance in them.

They went through the file on Sully first, Lachlan having written a short biography of sorts as a title page, outlining details like approximate birth date, known family—both birth and foster —and life history as it was known. Lachlan had never come to Dez with questions about Sully, but the information was all here nonetheless, right from his discovery on that doorstep to his supposed death in the cave collapse. There was mention of the abuse he'd endured in his pre-Braddock years, the suicide attempts that led to his committal to Lockwood, even his little-known ability to see the dead.

The contents beyond those first handwritten pages appeared to be, more or less, in chronological order, starting with a copy of the social services file launched at the time of his abandonment.

"How do you think Lachlan got a copy of the file?" Eva asked.

Dez flipped a page and found the answer, tapping at it with his forefinger. "It helps when you're the first officer on the scene."

Eva leaned in closer, and Dez felt her breath on his cheek as she spoke. He tried to ignore the resulting pleasant shiver, but wasn't surprised when he failed. "Seriously? God, that must have killed him, not getting to the bottom of that one back then."

"No wonder he clued in so fast when Lucienne came to him to find her son," Dez said. "He didn't need to go digging for a pile of info or do a whole lot of adding up of what he found. He already had everything right at his fingertips."

"You don't think there's any chance he worked to make the pieces fit on this, do you? I mean, the man was probably driven half mad by the idea of leaving a major case like this unsolved, not figuring out the baby's identity or finding his mother."

Eva's answer was on the front page of Lucienne's file.

"She told him Sullivan was a family name, and he put together a tree that confirms it," Dez said. "I can't imagine there were a whole lot of babies named Sullivan left on doorsteps that year, can you?"

"Let's not lose track of something. The case made the news for weeks; Lachlan has all the clippings right here. Everyone in KR—hell, everyone in the country—knew the name Sullivan back then. Are you one hundred per cent sure the woman you met is who she says she is?"

"I get what you're saying, and I'd be suspicious if it wasn't for the fact she knows what Sully can see. Barely anyone knows about that. I'm not sure I trust her. Come right down to it, I really don't. But that's nothing to do with her identity and everything to do with her intentions. It's weird, her turning up right at the moment

Sully comes back from the dead and then disappears again, don't you think? I mean, it could be coincidence, but I'm thinking it's more likely Lachlan started asking questions and someone besides him—someone he talked to—put two and two together and acted on it. Maybe someone's trying to keep Sully and Lucienne apart."

"Plenty of maybes there," Eva said. "Hopefully Lachlan's got some answers buried in here somewhere."

It had been some time since Dez had had opportunity to check out Sully's file and, at that earlier opportunity, he hadn't had longer than ten minutes with it. Sully always had questions about his birth family and, more specifically, his identity, and Dez had entertained the notion maybe he could use his then-job with the police to help.

The file in the police records room hadn't been as thick as the one Lachlan had, restricted to the immediate investigation surrounding the abandonment. Some of the same items were present in both instances, leading Dez to believe Lachlan didn't just have copies; he had the real deal in his possession. The giveaway came early on in Dez and Eva's scan, the note stating, "Please call me Sullivan" visible through the plastic evidence bag that protected it. Fingerprint dusting powder was still visible along the edges, although it had turned up nothing helpful, the only discernible prints belonging to the social worker who made the startling find upon going to collect her morning paper. There were witness statements from that worker, Denise Wilson, as well as the paperboy who'd seen nothing as he'd dropped the paper at the edge of the driveway and pedalled on.

The first major stops for investigators were the maternity wards within KR and other hospitals within the province. But all the babies born within hospital walls could be accounted for and, as it turned out, so could all those brought into the world with the help of a midwife.

Someone had given birth without anyone knowing, and had promptly given the child up. Blood was taken from Sully and compared against samples within the national criminal DNA databank, but it became apparent upon receipt of the results Sully did not come from anyone with a serious history of crime. Lachlan noted while the databank had grown and improved since, no further attempts at a match had been made.

Sully had been placed with one foster family at the start, but he wasn't an easy kid, so was moved from place to place until, at age seven, he ended up with the Braddocks. Dez could only guess, but it was an educated one, that Sully's frequent crying and screaming as an infant and toddler had far less to do with bad temperament and everything to do with fear, his then-lack of understanding and acceptance of what he could see and feel around him.

Dez didn't dig too far into Sully's past as it appeared on the page. He skimmed enough to know he'd heard the stories, and there were many things about Sully's distant past he wished he could simply forget. And everything else, everything that had come since, Dez had been a part of.

"Is there a chance any of his previous foster families might have held a grudge over something?" Eva asked.

"One of his foster fathers was criminally charged with assaulting him, but he never did time for it," Dez said. "I think the guy and his wife were just removed from the foster system. Sully was moved afterward, so I doubt there would be any lasting grudges there. Anyway, that was two decades ago."

"Yeah, that seems like a stretch. How about the fire? What were their names?"

"The Blakes."

"Right. Did they have any other family, someone who might have held onto something since then?"

"From what I understand, they didn't have much for family, and those they did have were focused on the girl who did set the fire. Sully and the other foster boy living there had nothing to do with it. And, again ...."

"Long time ago. I know," Eva said. "What about you? Have

you thought about whether you know of anyone who might want to hurt him?"

"Sully was always pretty shy and kept to himself," Dez said. "But the people who did know him liked him. I can't think of anyone he could have rubbed the wrong way. He isn't that kind of guy."

"He provided information to your dad over the years about the people he saw, didn't he? Police were able to use his info to make arrests and lay charges in otherwise-unsolved homicides."

"No one ever knew it was Sully. Dad didn't tell anyone where he got the info, just said it was from a confidential source. Major Crimes ran with it, and Sully didn't have much to do with it afterward. There would be no reason anyone would know he was involved in those arrests."

"Maybe we should start looking at Lucienne's file."

"In a second." Dez flipped to the end of Sully's file. Lachlan hadn't added to it, so Dez figured anything new would have been placed in the file he'd started on Lucienne. It made sense. At some point, Lachlan would have to return Sully's file to whomever had pulled it for him down at headquarters—unless, of course, he'd removed it himself just before his retirement. Either way, if anyone found out he had it, there would be hell to pay and, quite possibly, more people out there looking for work. Lachlan's additions to the file seemed to be the social services records from Sully's childhood as well as the handwritten cover page and several pages of notes on Sully's life—easy enough to remove when the time came.

On the other hand, the entirety of Lucienne's file seemed to consist of handwritten notes and photocopied documents, along with a number of old family photographs depicting whom Dez assumed was the Lucienne Dule of the 1970s. A brief family history had been compiled during an interview with Lucienne, her heavy participation evidenced by Lachlan's frequent use of quotes.

She had two siblings, Artie and Rhona, but Artie—the baby of the family—had died young, drowned in the tub at just three years of age. His sisters were supposed to have been watching him and both were punished, locked up in their rooms for most of that summer, allowing their mother to grieve in relative privacy. Their father left shortly after Artie's death, perhaps unable to cope, perhaps simply recognizing the incident as the excuse he'd been waiting for. At any rate, Lachlan seemed to have concluded the girls' parents were far from close and shared little, including parenting styles.

Lorinda Dule was a hard woman, made harder by the life she'd been handed. Her estranged husband Robert Forrester went unwaveringly by the name Bobby, the choice of name suggestive of his attitude to life. Bobby's youthful energy and lust for fun countered Lorinda's near-puritanical existence, and while Lorinda was often too hard on the kids, their father was too lenient. It was Bobby who'd left his daughters in charge of their brother that weekend. His wife away on a religious retreat, Bobby had taken advantage of what he'd hoped to turn into a bachelor weekend and left the girls so he could head out on a bender with his pals. Unlike many Dez had known, Bobby sounded to be a happy drunk, but he was a drunk nonetheless, and his lack of responsibility led to tragedy on the Sunday his wife was to return.

Lorinda had come back to a dead child, a husband shattered in both emotion and sobriety and two daughters whom—in Lucienne's words to Lachlan—she had to keep from sending to the same place they'd sent Artie. She'd vented her anger initially on Bobby, who took that as his cue to exit stage left. According to Lucienne, none of them saw him again and, for all they knew, he'd died in a gutter somewhere.

If the parents' reactions to the death were very different, so were the girls'. Rhona fell silent and, in fact, didn't speak for a full six weeks; Lucienne fell into a state of constant dread, unable to sleep as she was visited night after night by the ghost of her brother, accusing her of abandoning him to his death.

Lucienne recalled this as her first experience with a ghost, a phenomenon that repeated itself throughout the course of her life.

Rhona, older by two years, had just moved out by the time Lucienne got pregnant. Their mother had remarried by then, to a man more in line with her own personality. While Rhona hated Wayne Usher's intrusion in their lives—even a full decade after he'd come into the picture—Lucienne had taken him more or less as her father. Wayne wasn't an easy man, but he was responsible and present, which was a lot more than any of them could say about Bobby.

Unfortunately, Lucienne's faith in the man would prove ill-founded, as he provided no port in the storm that broke upon her issuing the news of her pregnancy. Wayne had, in fact, led the initial charge that the baby be aborted. When Lucienne refused—thankfully backed by her ultra-religious mother—the decision followed that the baby would be given up. In the meantime, every effort was made to conceal the pregnancy, Lucienne forced to wear baggy clothes until, when that no longer worked, she was kept at the house. She ultimately delivered there, with only her mother and stepfather to guide her through the agonizing process.

That was Lucienne's story, as told by Lucienne.

In true Lachlan style, he'd sensed some bullshit afoot and went looking for the truth.

The cover pages in Lucienne's file consisted of handwritten notes beneath two headings. The first—containing the details Dez and Eva had just read—was titled "Lucienne." The second underlined heading, beneath which precious little had yet been written, read "Other."

Beneath that second heading, Lachlan had written the word "Lockwood," underlining it twice for good measure. He'd also written the name Rhona, followed by a question mark.

They flipped through the file, locating copies of birth certificates, little Artie's death certificate and a copy of his autopsy report, as well as references to the mother's work with her local church. There were also, Dez noted, certificates stating both Rhona and Lucienne had successfully completed their home schooling and earned their high school diplomas.

"Huh," Dez said.

"What?"

"Just something Lucienne said. She told me people used to say she'd slept through the entire male half of the school population."

The answering expression on Eva's face suggested she, too, found that strange. "Maybe she still hung around those people, though. Nothing says you need to go to school together to have sex, right?"

"Yeah, I guess."

He wasn't convinced. Come right down to it, he was becoming less and less convinced about everything to do with Lucienne Dule. The only thing he was now satisfied about was that she was who she said she was. The photos Lachlan had gathered were plenty clear in substance and content. Lucienne Dule, the child and the teen—pictured in most of the photos standing next to Rhona—was without a doubt the Lucienne Dule, adult, currently sleeping in Dez's bed back at the apartment.

"What are you thinking?" Eva asked.

"She's holding something back. Something big. I just can't get a handle on what."

"Maybe Lachlan did," Eva said. "And that could be why he's in the hospital right now."

"Maybe."

"I think you need to wait and talk to him when he's more lucid, when he can give you some proper answers. Something's not right here."

"Damn straight something's not right," Dez said. "Sully's missing. I haven't got the luxury of sitting around, waiting for Lachlan. He sent me here for a reason, and I think it's that he needs me to get to the bottom of this. He solved the abandoned baby mystery when Lucienne turned up on his doorstep, but he's landed himself another one in the process."

"One that might be behind him almost getting killed today," Eva said. "We don't know who he talked to or what he found, just that he had questions and suspicions. If this case is the reason for what happened to him …."

She trailed off, leaving Dez to finish the thought his own way. "Then it might be he was closing in on something that could lead us to finding Sully."

Eva smiled at him, but there was no humour there. Only sadness and defeat. "If this case is the reason Lachlan almost died, then who's to say the same won't happen to you?"

20

Dez ARRIVED home to find Lucienne asleep on the pullout in much the same spot as Sully had spent last night.

While Pax found a comfortable spot on the rug to sleep, Dez took a moment to study his visitor in the light of the lamps she'd left on, as if he could spot the truths she was concealing if he watched long enough. When that venture proved as fruitless as anticipated, he allowed simple curiosity to take the place of suspicion, searching her features for similarities to her son's. He supposed he could see something there, the two sharing what his wife called "fine bone structure." He recalled her eyes were a similar shade as Sully's, somewhere between grey and blue, and that Sully's hair, as blond as hers until age had darkened it, still took on a golden cast in the summer months.

But all in all, Dez didn't see a whole lot of his brother in this woman, this relative stranger who had shared nothing with Sully in his twenty-four years but blood, eye colour and high cheekbones. Then again, it was possible there were other similarities escaping Dez's immediate notice; he wasn't exactly skilled at this sort of thing. Eva had made apologies for him once when he'd inadvertently angered a friend of theirs, a new mother who he later learned had been fishing for remarks on how much her new baby's features mirrored hers. Dez thought he'd been offering the woman a compliment by telling her the two looked nothing alike; the mother didn't resemble a prune in the slightest.

Dez checked his watch. A little past two in the morning, the sun long past set. And it occurred to him his energy levels had sunk as well.

Not bothering to change, Dez slumped into his living room chair and covered himself with an afghan his mom had crocheted during the brief period she'd taken it up. It had been helpful in this at least, Dez often having to look long and hard for quilts and blankets that fully covered him when lying out flat. He turned slightly in the chair, enough to enable him to rest his cheek on the cushioned backrest, and closed his eyes. Sleep, in his current state, was only moments away.

"Where were you?"

Dez's eyes shot open. Lucienne was sitting up on his pullout, eyes accusing as she regarded him.

Dez tried to decide how much to tell her, how much to leave out. "I wasn't tired so I went to see Lachlan."

"All this time?"

Not "How is he," Dez noticed. Lucienne's first thought wasn't of Lachlan's condition, but rather her own. Then again, the way she'd been raised, self-preservation had become the rule rather than the exception. Dez had seen plenty of that during his years in policing, still saw it in many of the street people whose company he'd been keeping.

"No," Dez said. "He sent me to check out a lead."

"I thought we agreed you would involve me in this."

"You are involved," Dez said. "Far too involved, if this investigation is the reason Lachlan was attacked. He had some information he'd gathered on Sully and he wanted me to see it. He sent me expressly on my own. Lachlan took a pretty good shot to the head, by the way. He's in and out of consciousness and is likely to be recovering from this for some time."

Recognition settled across Lucienne's face, the realization

she'd made something of a social blunder. "I'm sorry. You're right. It was thoughtless of me not to ask. Is he in much pain?"

"Whatever painkiller they're pumping into him helps, but he's not a happy camper. And I'd imagine that's not likely to improve once they start weaning him off the drugs."

"I'm sorry to hear that. Is there anything I can do?"

"Just don't try to visit him right now," Dez said. "They've got him under guard until they can get to the bottom of this."

"Do they know about me?"

"They know of your existence, to some degree anyway. Lachlan hasn't told anyone much, and he's essentially sworn me to secrecy, too."

Her eyes closed briefly as she released tension in one heavy exhale.

Dez hadn't intended to get into these questions tonight, but patience had never been his strong suit—particularly given the current situation. "Lachlan had some questions, didn't he? Questions about your family. So do I."

Whatever stress she'd just exhaled, she drew right back in. "What do you want to know?"

"Tell me about Artie."

"I can't talk about that."

"Why not?"

"It's too hard."

Dez took a deep breath of his own, sensing some quid pro quo might be needed to get the ball rolling. "I think I understand better than you think I do. When I was a kid …."

"You lost your brother. Aiden. I know."

Dez felt the blood drain from his face. "How did you know that?"

"The same way I know a lot of things. He's around you, you know. I've seen him a couple of times. He doesn't always come right out, mind you. He likes to hide."

Hide and seek. Aiden's favourite game.

The last game he played.

"Dez? Are you all right?"

"Yeah. Fine."

"You don't look fine."

He drew in several long, deep breaths, quelling the desire to walk out and leave everything behind, just go find the guys in the park and drown all his sorrows for another night.

Drown. Like Aiden had drowned.

Because of him.

"I understand, you know," Lucienne said. "What it's like to feel responsible for a sibling's death. Artie was the best of us. He was tiny and gentle and loving. He had this wild blond hair and these chubby little cheeks that made him look like an angel. And he was an angel. But Rhona and I were just kids ourselves, and I've tried to remind myself of that when I get lost in the guilt."

Dez could still see Aiden, strawberry blond and freckled, dashing off joyfully at the prospect of playing the game with his big brother. Dez had rarely seen Aiden's smile brighter than it was that afternoon ....

"Dez?"

"Yeah. I'm fine."

"I know it's hard. It's impossible to not feel responsible. They're so small and helpless at that age, so reliant on everyone around them. Rhona and I, we were having an argument as usual, and Artie started to cry. We left him for just a few minutes. It was all over something stupid, so stupid I can't even remember anymore. I just remember my mom had this set of encyclopedias, and we knew we could settle the matter easily enough by looking it up. When we got back upstairs, Artie was floating facedown in the tub."

The horror was clear on Lucienne's face, mouth contorted, eyes wide as if she were witnessing the scene all over again. "We pulled him out. I tried to give him mouth to mouth, like we saw on TV. But it didn't work. He just wouldn't breathe."

"You didn't call for an ambulance?"

"That's what makes it so much worse. We didn't call anyone.

We thought we'd get into even worse trouble, that we'd go to jail. So we just wrapped him up in his bath towel and left him on the bathroom floor. I know how it sounds, believe me. And what we did—what we didn't do—is every bit as awful, and more. But we were so young. Rhona was the oldest of us, and she was only eight. How many eight-year-olds have you heard of being left in charge of children for longer than a few minutes? Our father was away for hours, our mother for even longer. And Mother put full blame on our shoulders, as if they deserved none between the two of them for leaving us all alone."

Dez thought back to the file, to the question mark behind Rhona's name. "Where's Rhona now?"

"I don't know. I haven't seen her in years. Didn't Lachlan tell you?"

"We didn't have time to get into every detail of the case," Dez said. "When and where did you last see her?"

"Longer ago than I care to think. It was around the time Sullivan was born. She moved out as soon as she turned eighteen and got her high school diploma. She never looked back. I can't say I blame her. I just wish she'd stayed in touch with me, at least."

"And about that whole education thing. You made it sound like you went to a regular school, but you didn't. Your mother homeschooled you and your sister."

"Not the whole time," Lucienne said. "We got to go to school for a while. Mostly we had to study at home, but one or two years, when money was tight, Mother would have to go to work, so there was no one to teach us. At least that gave us a chance to make some friends."

"I thought you more or less said you didn't really make any friends."

Lucienne smiled. "I made plenty of friends. It was keeping them that was the problem. Look, why do I feel like this is an interrogation?"

Dez leaned a little farther forward in the chair. "Maybe it is, kind of. I can't help feeling like you've been holding out on me about something."

"I was, I guess. I didn't want you to know about Artie."

"Why not?"

Lucienne's expression registered disbelief. "Come on. When kids were feeling particularly mean—and, let's face it, they often do—they called us the Baby Killers. I needed your help, and it was bad enough having to admit to you that I abandoned Sullivan to what turned out to be a pretty bleak childhood. The last thing I wanted was to further risk poisoning you against me by telling you I was also partially responsible for my baby brother's death. Anyway, that has nothing to do with any of this."

"Are you sure about that? Where are your parents now?"

"I have no idea where my birth father is. Probably dead, given the life he led. And my mother is in a care home. She developed an early form of dementia. Dr. Gerhardt—"

"Dr. Roman Gerhardt? From Lockwood? Is that where she is?"

"I said she was in a care home, not a psych hospital. But love him or hate him, when it comes to mental illness, he's the best. Anyway, my mother swore by him since he supposedly cured me of my so-called hallucinations. She refused to see anyone else, and he was plenty happy to oblige her. He'd developed something of a soft spot for me and, by the look of things, my mother, too. He says the heavy amount of depression and stress she had to endure likely took a long-term toll on her mind. She's not a vegetable or anything, and there are days where she's perfectly lucid. But sometimes I don't know who she is."

"So you still go to see her?"

"Rarely, but yes. In many ways, she ruined my life. But I also have her to thank for all the good I've accomplished. And, after all, whatever I may think of her when she's at her worst, she's still my mother."

"Listen, this might sound strange, and you might not like it, but I think I need to talk to your mother. Which care home is she in?"

A shade drew across Lucienne's features, her doubt clear in the way she turned her head to look at him out of the corner of her eye. "Why do you need to talk to her?"

"Because I think I need to find Rhona."

"I've tried repeatedly to find Rhona, never to any success. I don't think she wants to be found, and I don't blame her. We both wanted to put our childhoods behind us, never look back. Only somehow, I think she's managed it."

"Do you think she changed her name?"

"I'm certain of it. Look, I work in IT. I know computers, the web, various systems. I know how to find people. I have never been able to find her. It's like she just disappeared."

Like Sully disappeared. Dez kept the thought to himself, but it was sitting there heavily now at the front of his brain, at the tip of his tongue, in the pit of his stomach. He had nothing to base it on, nothing at all. But he knew, as clearly as he knew his own name.

Find Rhona and he'd find Sully.

21

FOR SEVERAL HOURS, no one had come, as near as Sully could determine in the unending dim of the room, leaving him to suspect it might be nighttime.

He would have liked to rest as he suspected his captors were, but sleep would leave him vulnerable. He was hungry, parched and well past tired, the added psychological strain pushing him into exhaustion. But sleep built on fatigue gave no guarantee he would awaken in time to recognize and fight whatever danger might next come at him.

Lucienne Dule's journal proved a godsend, the slightly tattered find acting like a jolt of caffeine as he read through it.

It was undated, and Sully quickly realized why that was. Like him, she'd been a captive here. Like him, she'd had no awareness of night or day—or of any passage of time save that which her guards might share.

I thought things couldn't get any worse than Lockwood. Now I'm not so sure. Mother and Wayne say I have to stay in this room. They say it's for my own protection. But now I'm afraid Gerhardt is going to come through that door and tell me I have to go back. I can't go back. Not ever. I'll die first.

The journal went on from there.

Wayne brought me this notebook to pass the time. Time for what? I don't understand. I still haven't seen Mother since they brought me to this room. Wayne says seeing me is too hard for her. He's nice, at least. Funny how sometimes the people who share your blood are the people in the world you know the least. I wish Wayne would stay and talk. It's lonely down here. At least until THEY come. And they always come. Walls and locked doors can't stop them. And I have nowhere to run ....

I have no idea how long I've been down here. A few days for sure. I think Wayne said it was Tuesday when he gave me the notebook and pen. It was a Sunday when I came home and they brought me to this basement room. Tuesday feels like forever ago ....

I asked Wayne today if he'd heard anything about Gerhardt. He said no. I don't know what that means, but I'm afraid to ask any more questions. I don't know what Mother and Wayne would think if they knew the truth. Maybe Gerhardt will come back for me. Maybe he will come back in a way only I can see ....

I wonder about him all the time, that beautiful baby boy. With nothing much else to do down here, I think about him all the time. Where is he now? Is he okay? Will I ever see him again? If I don't, will he ever know about me? How will he ever know how much I loved him, that I loved him enough to let him go, to give him hope for a better life than he could have with me? It was amazing, seeing him for the first time after all those months. His tiny face, those little fingers and toes. I only wish I could have looked into his eyes before I had to give him away. I know they will be beautiful too. It's terrible and amazing at the same time: how could something so perfect come from something so ugly? ....

I'm beginning to think I'm never going to leave here. Today, Wayne told me it's Tuesday, so it's been at least a week. Wayne was quiet, just brought me my breakfast and answered that one question and then he was gone. He seemed sad. Like really sad. I don't know why, and I can't hear anything from down here. The walls are concrete and the house is so big. If they're fighting again, I would probably never hear from down here. Rhona used to say Mother is a hard woman. I used to think Rhona meant Mother's figure. But I understand now. It's not Mother's body Rhona meant. It's her soul ....

Artie came again today and looked at me with those eyes. They're dead eyes, not really seeing, but it's like he can see through me anyway. "Bad Lucky," he said to me. "Bad Lucky." I know I am, and I told him that. I told him I was so sorry I left him there with Rhona. Artie was my responsibility, and I let that stupid fight get in the way. I know it sounds weird because I'm just so terrified every time I see Artie or the others, but I wanted him to stay with me. I just want someone. Sometimes I'm selfish, and I just want my little baby Sullivan ....

The blood rushed from Sully's head along with all sense, his vision swimming and his breath catching. Had he not already been sitting, he would have fallen.

Lucienne Dule—or Lucky as she called herself—wasn't just some girl who had been trapped down here like he was now.

She was his mother.

He tried to think through what that meant for him now, why he was here, who was responsible, but it was like something had short-circuited in his brain. Thoughts roamed free, none connecting, few making sense. Questions formed but disappeared before he grasped them. Answers were non-existent in his current state.

He'd spent his whole life wondering. He knew he'd been given up, left on a doorstep, but nothing else. He'd always assumed he'd been so despised, so unwanted that his own mother figured leaving him with a stranger, abandoning him to the outdoor dangers until he was noticed, was preferable to a proper adoption. Her way of letting him know he didn't deserve that dignity or comfort.

And yet, he'd never hated her for it. It was impossible to know where his life would have led had it gone down another path. He knew it never would have led him to the Braddocks. How could he hold a grudge over that?

The journal hadn't answered everything—not by any stretch— but it did provide a few basic truths. One was her youth. Her writing was small but bubbly, and her style and language spoke of someone too young to have endured what she had and, as a result, too old for her years. And, most importantly, she had loved him. She had not thought him a curse but a blessing, one she believed she did not deserve.

He wondered what kind of mother she would have been to him had their situation been different, had her family supported her as the Braddocks had supported him.

His heart broke for her, and he didn't even know her.

Or maybe he did. They were bonded, after all, in a way neither time nor distance could sever.

"I always know when Dez is in trouble," Mara Braddock had once said when her then-teenaged son was getting his first taste of freedom, out past curfew and causing no end of worry to his parents. "A mother knows these things."

Sully wondered if his own mother had known, had felt something was wrong all those times he'd been frightened or in pain. Was she aware on some level? If she was, had she ever tried to find him?

Had she ever even had the chance?

He thought back to his time at Lockwood, to the faces of the other patients. Was one of those women his mother? If Lucienne Dule had him as a teenager, she would be close to forty by now. There were plenty of women around there that fit that age frame. She had known Gerhardt, seemed to hate him as much as Sully himself, and he wondered whether she too had been exposed to his experiments.

The idea that she might have been there, so close, the comfort of family within reach in those moments when the Braddocks weren't there—that was almost as hard as the thought he might have been some comfort to her and hadn't been given the chance.

His head stopped spinning, leaving him with the exhaustion that was becoming his constant companion.

It was a risk, and a big one. But lack of sleep wouldn't help him either, so he finally gave in and laid back on the mattress, allowing his eyes to close only after he'd tucked the rolled note-book and pen within an inside pocket of his outer jacket.

He tried to find some comfort in the proximity in space to his mother, that she'd once been right where he was now, that she'd once breathed this air and touched these walls. He tried, but ulti-mately found nothing but sadness there.

And then, as a dead sleep closed over him, all thought bless-edly faded.

DEZ AWOKE to the smell of maple bacon and the feel of a tongue on his cheek that definitely did not belong to Eva.

He cracked an eye open to see Pax sitting next to him, tongue hanging out as the full morning sun began warming his apart-ment to the point of serious discomfort. The place had come with a small box unit air conditioner mounted in the wall. Naturally, on the hottest days, the fan was not always content to spin at higher speeds. He could hear it wasn't running now.

Dez lifted his head from the back of the chair and gave Pax's ears a good morning scratch as he massaged the kink out of his own neck. His upper spine responded with a satisfying crack as he turned his head to look at the pullout.

It was empty, and he spotted Lucienne in the kitchen, standing at the stove as she monitored a couple of frying pans.

Pax seemed to have noticed, too, his dislike of Lucienne all but forgotten as he trotted to the stove to supervise her progress.

Lucienne at last turned to look in Dez's direction, and she smiled a greeting. "Good morning. I was wondering when you would wake up. I hope you don't mind, but I noticed your fridge and cupboards were almost bare, so I went out and bought some groceries."

Dez stood, his hip cracking. "You didn't have to do that."

"It's the least I can do, given everything you're doing for me and my son."

"Well, thanks. I appreciate it. I haven't managed to make it to the store recently."

Lucienne smiled. "You don't say. Oh, and I couldn't find any dog food here, so I picked up a small bag. I'm guessing he'll likely go through it within a day, though. He's a hungry guy."

"So he ate?"

"Yeah, and it looks like he's still plenty interested. He only left the stove long enough to go check in on you."

"Yeah, I'm noticing he's kind of a pig in wolf's clothing. Is the air conditioner on the fritz?"

"No, I turned it off. I was a little chilly."

If there was one blessing to being on his own—and one blessing was just about all he could come up with—it was that he could have it as cold as he wanted, when it worked, and not worry about offending shivering females. "Are you still cold? I mean, it heats up in here pretty fast when it's hot out."

Thankfully, Lucienne gave him the go-ahead to turn the unit on, and he was doubly blessed when the thing actually kicked in on high. He thought better of it, splitting the difference and lowering it to medium before taking the few steps to the kitchen to check out breakfast in the making. Lucienne had bought a loaf of bread; he dropped a couple slices into his toaster as he considered how best to broach the necessary topic of conversation.

Then he decided there really was no best way, or even a good one.

"Sorry to bring this up again, but I really need to talk to your mother. I'm thinking I might need your help with that."

Lucienne stiffened, hand stilling over the frying pan containing the scrambled eggs she had been in the course of flipping. "I don't think that's a good idea."

"Why not?"

"She's not well, like I told you. She upsets easily."

"Look, I'm not a jerk. I'll be sensitive about it, and I won't push her hard."

Lucienne gave up the eggs for the moment, turning to face Dez head-on. "Why is it so important you talk to her?"

Dez crossed his arms, forming his own immovable wall—because one way or another, he was not giving an inch on this. If he was going to find Rhona, what better way than to go through her mother, presumably the person who had been in a position to know her the best, even if just for a while?

"I was a police officer long enough to know the answers to most questions can be found with the people surrounding the subject of an investigation, whether that's a suspect or a victim," Dez said. "Nine times out of ten, that's family or close friends. Now, as far as Sully goes, I'm family and a close friend, and I know all of his secrets involving the life he knew. What I don't know is what he didn't know, and that's his birth family. Now, Lachlan was piecing something together, and he ended up being attacked. Sure, there's a chance it was about some other case, but I seriously doubt it. If Sully really is out there and needs our help, I am going to turn over every stone until I get what I need. What he needs. Right now, your mother is one of those stones. You have to help me, Lucienne. For Sully."

Studying him, she didn't answer immediately. Dez held both his position and his ground. He'd meant every word and if she wasn't going to help him, he would find another way.

With Dez remaining firm, it was only a matter of time before Lucienne broke, a sigh escaping as she first looked away and then returned to the frying pans. It was likely the eggs had partially burned in that weighty pause, but if she provided him with what he was after, he'd happily eat a barely edible breakfast.

Lucienne's voice was barely above a whisper. "She's at Lockwood."

"I thought you said she was at a care home."

"It is a care home, in a way. They have a building on the grounds for seniors suffering from dementia and Alzheimer's. She's nowhere near old enough to be there, not really, but Dr.

Gerhardt insisted she be somewhere he could work directly with her each day."

"Do you visit her?"

Lucienne shook her head. "I would never willingly set foot inside that gate. Not for anything."

"Or anyone? Even Sully?"

Lucienne spared him a glance before going back to her cooking. "If you find anything to suggest Sullivan is there, then I'll go back. But not for anyone else. No one else in my life is worth it."

THE GATES WERE OPEN, the treelined gravel road setting a straight course toward the massive Victorian-era structure at its end.

The last time Dez had passed through these gates, he'd been leaving with Sully, who had been silent but vibrating with tension beside him. Dez and Sully shared a love of camping and the outdoors, instilled in both of them by their deceased father, and so, after Flynn's memorial service, Dez had taken Sully to the quiet of the nearby Winteredge National Park. There, next to the campsite they used to frequent with their dad, Dez had the first real conversation with his brother since he'd been committed to Lockwood.

The result was horrifying and left Dez both sickened and enraged. Had it not been for the obvious need to keep Sully as far from that place as was humanly possible, Dez would have driven back there and put Gerhardt and Hackman through the window of the head psychiatrist's office.

Instead, he'd focused his energy on something more productive and less likely to land him in prison for the better part of a decade. In concealing Sully, he knew he was committing an offence that could easily put him out of work and saddle him with some sort of criminal charge for obstructing a police investigation. But there was no debating the issue for Dez, no way he would have been able to live with himself if he took Sully back, not after everything he'd learned.

Dez hated Lockwood, and he hated Gerhardt and Hackman. And as he closed the distance between the gates and the main building—that building that might even now hold his brother—he said a silent prayer to his father to keep him steady.

There was too much on the line. And it was one he realized he was dangerously close to crossing.

22

Dez knew his stature made him memorably imposing, but he suspected there was more to the glances exchanged in the reception area than could be blamed solely on his appearance.

The question was whether those looks meant people remembered him as the guy who had secured a patient's escape, or whether they knew him to be the brother of a patient who, only recently, had been recaptured and secreted somewhere inside the facility.

He'd left Pax with Miss Crichton, the woman having turned into a dog lover overnight despite her typical adherence to rules and building code. Lucienne had offered to watch him, but Dez wasn't sure how willing Pax would be to keep up the niceties around her once the food supply ran out. Better safe than sorry.

That expression applied to himself at the moment as well, and he reminded himself to keep his mouth shut about Sully at all costs. He had yet to find any proof his brother was here or that anyone from Lockwood even knew he was alive. The last thing Dez wanted was to blow Sully's carefully constructed cover by laying out cards that weren't his to play. He'd have to stay cool, assemble this bit by bit like a jigsaw puzzle. The piece he currently needed was named Lorinda Usher, and he asked for her at the desk.

"You're Desmond Braddock, aren't you?" the bespectacled receptionist asked.

It took him a moment, but he put a name to the familiar face. "Hi, Peggy. It's been a while."

Her smile wavered with uncertainty. "I'm not sure if …."

She was a polite one, Peggy. Too polite to say what had to be on her mind.

Dez made it easier on her. "You're not sure I'm supposed to be here. Look, that was two years ago. I'm hoping to talk to someone else, a Lorinda Usher. I'm told she's in the building where they look after people with dementia and other age-related problems."

Dez watched Peggy for reaction. The way he'd thought this through, his request would probably relax her a bit once she knew he wasn't here to bust heads over Sully. Additional or continual discomfort, though, might suggest she knew something she didn't want him to catch wind of. Either that, or inadvertently reveal she shared Dez's knowledge about the connection between Lorinda and Sully.

There was no pause between his statement and the slight but clear release of tension in her face and the increased uplift at the corners of her mouth. If Sully was here, or if anyone knew Lorinda was Sully's grandmother, they hadn't bothered to tell Peggy.

"Are you family?"

"No," he said. "I'm actually just checking into something for an associate of mine. He might have been here to see her recently? Older guy, bit paunchy around the middle—"

"Lachlan Fields," Peggy supplied. "He was here yesterday morning."

Now Dez was paying extra attention to his own facial muscles, trying hard to keep them from giving away his excitement. "Yes, that's right. Here's the thing. He was assaulted yesterday, and is in serious condition in the hospital. We're trying to figure out who was involved."

Behind her trendy cat's-eye glasses, Peggy's eyes had grown a size or two larger. "Oh, that's awful! Such a nice man too."

Clearly, Lachlan had put his best foot forward yesterday.

"Mrs. Usher might well have been the last person Lachlan spoke with," Dez said. "I need to find out if there was anything said that might shed some light on who attacked him."

"Certainly, I understand. I'll just call Dr. Gerhardt."

"I'm sure I can find the way myself, if you'll just point me in the right direction."

"Sorry, facility rules," Peggy said with a small shrug, her ever-present smile now apologetic. "Visitors all need to be cleared with him."

"Just a second." Dez paused a moment to think through a strategy. If he came face to face with Gerhardt, there were two likely outcomes, with neither ending in an actual visit to Lorinda Usher. The first scenario involved Dez beating the psychopath to within an inch of his life and being removed in handcuffs by attending members of the KRPD; the second would see him thrown off the premises, once again quite possibly in the escort of his former colleagues. He needed to appeal to Peggy's sympathy, and fast. "Listen, Peggy—"

"Kimotan Rapids PD," came a voice from near his left shoulder. Dez turned to see Eva approaching, badge and ID card flashing. "Is there a problem with us talking to the lady?"

Dez wasn't sure whether he should be grateful or terrified by Eva's unexpected presence. "Peggy says she has to clear it with Dr. Gerhardt."

Eva stared Peggy down as only she could. "I hardly think that will be necessary. We'll be just a few minutes."

"I'm required to clear all unknown visitors with the doctor—"

"I'm a police officer," Eva said. "Dez is working with Lachlan Fields. Did he tell you what happened to Lachlan?"

Peggy nodded. She seemed to have given up trying to form

words. When Eva was all-business like this, she could have that effect. Dez tried to keep his pride from poking through whatever he had going of a poker face.

Eva continued. "So I don't need to tell you time is of the essence. You've heard about the forty eight-hour rule?"

Peggy nodded and then decided an answer was called for. "You mean that crimes not solved within forty eight hours are harder to solve?"

"You got it. You know what happens when you call the doctor. He'll take a while to get down here, then there will be questions and paperwork to fill out. And that's all going to be made far more complicated by the presence of my former colleague here. Obviously, Dr. Gerhardt will not want him anywhere near here, given past events. Now I'm not excusing Desmond's behaviour in the past, but that was the past. This is now, and we need to move on this immediately. There's a real concern Lachlan's assailant is preparing to flee the jurisdiction, and that's going to make it really, really hard to bring him to justice. Do you want to be charged with obstructing justice?"

Peggy shook her head, no.

"So, please, point us in the right direction."

Peggy raised an arm and pointed back toward the entrance, before deciding words were necessary as well. "Building on the left. I'll call through and tell them to let you speak with her."

"Thank you," Eva said, leading the way out the door so fast even Dez had trouble catching up.

"Where did you come from?" he asked once they were outside and out of earshot.

"Later," she said. "The way I see it, we've got all of five minutes with the woman before Gerhardt comes flapping in to break up the party. We need to get what we can and get the hell out."

"Okay, but quick, then. How'd you know?"

"You didn't answer your damn phone this morning, so I stopped by to check on you. There was a woman there, and I took a shot in the dark and guessed Lucienne. Once I convinced her who I was, she told me where I could find you. Then I drove like a bat out of hell to get here before you ran into someone you were likely to kill and bury."

"Thanks, Eva. You have no idea."

"I have every idea. Now let's just get this done and leave, all right? This place gives me the creeps."

Dez had never been inside the building they entered now, a slightly newer construction as compared to the main institution. Seniors' Care, as it was now called according to the nameplate, looked to be a converted two-storey mansion that might once have housed the head psychiatrist and whatever family and staff he'd brought with him. Since those early days, economic woes had encroached on many a lavish lifestyle in KR, and Lockwood was no different.

Mental health had not been the highest priority in most recent government budgets, despite the increasing need. Not that everyone got that care at Lockwood, in Dez's opinion, but the programs and staff here had somehow or other continued to win accolades for what they did for those in need. Once fully run on the taxpayers' dime, Lockwood had since been forced to supplement its dwindling budgetary income through privately paid care. Dez guessed the doctor's former residence was one of the first buildings on the site to go, refurbished and divvied up into individual units for dementia sufferers whose families were willing to pay for the best care. And, for some reason Dez couldn't fathom, Dr. Roman Gerhardt was considered the best.

The entry hall of Seniors' Care boasted a large oak desk that made efforts to blend in with the panelling on the walls and the banisters of the wide staircase that led to the second floor. Paintings adorned the walls, many likely original to the house or at least the last doctor to call this structure home. They appeared classical to Dez's untrained eye, ships on calm seas, bowls of fruit and dour women in high-necked dresses.

If the desk and wall art were doing their part to fit into the surroundings, so was the receptionist. She was an older woman, though not old enough to expect a place here just yet, and she was every bit as colourless as many of the women in the portraits.

"I understand you want to see Mrs. Usher," she said, voice a train of monotone syllables.

"We would, thank you," Eva said.

The woman looked disapprovingly at Eva, and Dez bristled. Since he'd started dating Eva years ago, he'd gotten almost as good at picking out racists as she was. Eva knew it, and she stepped slightly in front of him so she could touch his hand without anyone taking notice.

"She's in the sunroom, back of the house. But don't expect much. She's having more bad days than good lately."

"Thank you," Eva said and led the way to the back through an archway past the stairs. Dez, bringing up the rear, took advantage by levelling a glare at the older woman.

Boasting pristine white walls and windows that rose to the high ceiling, the sunroom must once have held wicker lounge furniture, thriving potted plants and decorative indoor trees, and coffee tables filled with the latest reading material. The wicker had given way to chairs only a step above those Dez recalled from the main building, rickety looking card tables and bookshelves featuring rumpled romance novels and jigsaw puzzles that, by now, were likely missing several pieces.

Some seniors looked happy enough, playing away at card games with friends and visiting family while others sat chatting. But a handful sat alone, facing the large window, and Dez felt a cold chill as he considered that, for some of them, this might be as close to the outdoors as they'd ever get in what little time they had left. It might be that staff here took them outside once in a while, but given his experience with Sully in the next building, he wasn't about to lay any money on it.

"I'm guessing she's one of the ones by the windows," Eva whispered. "Probably the skinny, grumpy one in the wheelchair who looks like the American Gothic painting."

Dez had no idea what painting Eva was talking about, but he went with it. There didn't seem to be anyone around to ask.

They approached the woman from the side, Eva taking the lead.

"Lorinda Usher?"

The woman didn't move, didn't speak. Just continued to glare out the window.

Eva tried again. "Mrs. Usher?"

"Oh, that's me!" exclaimed a voice from nearby. Dez turned to see a second seated, window-watching woman who, at first glance anyway, looked too old to be Lorinda Usher. But then, he guessed a life like hers aged a person, perhaps significantly. This woman, unlike the one they'd first approached, looked bubbly and welcoming, and he was plenty happy to sit down with her instead.

Eva didn't sound quite as sure. "You're Lorinda Usher?"

"Ye-es," the woman said, ending the one-word statement with a giggle. "What can I do for you dears?"

Dez met Eva's eye for a moment, found her giving him a little head shake, no. Dez shrugged. With no other takers, what choice did they have?

"I'm going to go look for a staff member," Eva said. "Have a chat until I get back."

As Eva left the room, Dez pulled up a plastic chair and, hoping it would support someone his size, eased himself onto the seat. It held, and he celebrated with the smile he gave the senior in front of him.

"You're sure you're Lorinda Usher?"

"Of course, I'm sure, dear. You think I don't know my own name?" He would have thought her insulted but that she ended the statement with another light laugh.

"All right, then," Dez said. He'd quickly become as skeptical as Eva but forged on anyway. They didn't have the luxury of time and hopefully his questions would draw a response from the real Lorinda. "I need to speak to you about Rhona."

The bubbly lady continued to grin. "Oh, Rhona. Such a dear. Such a dear."

"Bitch," said the other.

Dez's gaze snapped back to the younger woman. She had not looked at him, had given no sign she'd said anything, yet he was certain the curse had come from her. "Did you say something, ma'am?"

Silence.

He turned back to Bubbles. "I'm working with a private investigator, and I'm trying to find Rhona. I'm wondering if you can help me."

"That nice young man who was here the other day?"

Dez didn't think he'd ever in his life heard Lachlan Fields described as a nice young man, and it merited assurances they were talking about the same guy. "Do you remember his name?"

"Lachlan, I believe I heard. I only remember because that was the name of my oldest brother, God rest."

She took a breath and Dez could tell she was about to launch into a story not likely to relate to the topic he'd come here to discuss. Once started, there would be no stopping her. "I'm sorry to hear that, ma'am. Did he ask you about Rhona too?"

"He did, asked about how to find her. I wanted to help him, poor man, but I had no idea."

Dez leaned in and smiled, hoping she'd get the hint. "Might anybody *else* here know how to find her?"

The older woman smiled sheepishly. "Well …."

"You aren't Lorinda Usher, are you?" He leaned closer to her. "Lorinda is the woman in the wheelchair on my other side, isn't she?"

Bubbles didn't get the chance to answer before Eva returned with a nurse. And not just any nurse, the sight of her drawing his eyebrows up his forehead. "Greta? You work here?"

"I'm a volunteer, and I really need to insist you not speak with our patients without first checking with Dr. Gerhardt," she said.

Dez stood and looked Greta up and down without thinking,

hoping in retrospect no one had misconstrued anything. This Greta looked vastly different from the one he'd seen the other night at the bar, that woman having been strung out on something or other and sporting a spaghetti strap top and short shorts. In uniform with minimal makeup and her blonde hair pulled back into a sleek bun, this Greta was like the Dr. Jekyll to the other night's Ms. Hyde.

"Are you all right?" he asked her. "The other night—"

Greta instantly looked uncomfortable. "Can we not talk about that here?"

"Not that I care what Forbes is dealing with ordinarily, but he's worried about you. I told him about the night at the bar."

"What about it?"

"Someone followed you. Didn't you see him?"

Greta shook her head in the negative. "No one followed me."

"I know someone followed you. I saw him. I kept an eye on him for some time, at least until he headed into the cemetery. Someone attacked me at that point, and I never knew what happened to you after. I just wanted to make sure—"

"I appreciate you looking out for me, but it wasn't necessary. Like I said, no one followed me. As for Forbes, he needs to mind his own business. We're not together anymore."

"That doesn't mean he automatically stops worrying about you."

Eva cleared her throat, and Dez looked over at her. She was smiling and doing one of those little headshakes that suggested strongly he shut up. Eva, as usual, had clued in faster to Dez's meaning than even he did. He hadn't been talking about Forbes, after all, but himself.

"I just wanted to make sure you were okay, and to check you didn't see anyone," Dez said. "I was hoping you might have some sort of description to provide."

"You're the one who followed. You should be the one with a description."

Dez shrugged a shoulder. "I was behind him initially but lost him in the cemetery. He had a hat on besides, so I didn't get a good look. All I know is he was a bigger guy, solidly built. Ring a bell?"

"No, sorry."

Eva cut in, returning them to the issue that had brought them here in the first place. "Look, we really need a few minutes with Mrs. Usher."

"No. It's not possible. Now I'm really going to have to ask you to leave. Dr. Gerhardt is on his way over, and I hear he's not happy Dez is back on the property."

Eva plucked at Dez's sleeve. "Let's go."

Dez looked back to the younger woman by the window. She was no longer facing the grounds outside the sunroom. She was watching them.

There was a smile on her face but, unlike the one her neighbour Bubbles had worn, hers was cold enough to set the hairs on Dez's arms and the back of his neck on end.

It took every ounce of willpower Dez possessed to hold her eye. The hateful smile didn't waver until her lips parted to speak, her words as black as her expression.

"They will burn," she said. "They will all burn."

23

WHILE PART of Dez wanted to stay and question the woman further, he didn't fight Eva or Greta as much as he might have as they pushed and pulled him from the sunroom. That unnatural grin and the words that had come from it had been like something out of a horror movie.

"What do you think she meant by that?" Dez asked once he and Eva were alone outside.

"They will all burn?"

"Jesus, don't repeat that."

Eva chuckled. "Seriously? You're scared of her? She's so frail she makes some of the folks in there look like Olympians, and most of them are twenty to thirty years older. And, God, Dez. The woman's out of her mind. Surely, you can see that."

"She knows something, Eva. I'm telling you, the woman knows something."

"I'll tell you what *I* know. If Raynor or anyone else finds out I've been here, I'll be lucky to keep my job."

"I'm sorry. I hadn't planned on you being here. But I really do appreciate it."

"Forget it," Eva said. "I did it for Kayleigh, anyway. Last thing

I want is her having to visit her father in prison because he beat a psychiatrist to death. Speaking of, let's get out of here before he sees us, okay? And, Dez? Promise me you won't come back here. Please?"

She deserved an answer, but he couldn't provide the one she wanted to hear and so kept his mouth shut.

"Dez."

"You know I can't promise that, Eva. If she knows something that could help Sully, I need to figure out a way to get it out of her. You know that."

They had reached the vehicles, but not quite in time, as Dez heard his name shouted from the direction of the main building. He turned to see the lean, older man making his way slowly but purposefully down the steps toward them.

Eva shoved Dez toward his SUV. "Go. Please, Dez. Go."

There was no point. The main entrance and the reception area were covered by surveillance. Eva had flashed a badge, so if there was any question as to who she was, the video would be circulated to the KRPD. She'd face questions, quite likely sanctions over this. There wasn't much option but to stay and try to smooth things over with Gerhardt. As the man limped over, Dez reminded himself if he assaulted him in Eva's presence, it would only be worse for her.

Gerhardt closed the last few steps, barking out the question as he approached. "Just what in God's name are you doing here?"

He had changed little in the past couple of years, although his permanent limp had worsened significantly, making the man appear shorter than his six-foot frame. Cane in one hand, Gerhardt used the other to prop himself against the hood of Dez's SUV as he peered at them above the low-riding rims of his half-moon spectacles. Dez had never been convinced the man needed glasses, rather suspecting he used them to make himself appear more scholarly. He had a little less hair than before, but what remained had maintained its ash blond shade. His face showed the remains of what were once handsome features, but they had been twisted with the rest of him. It was funny how dark thoughts and emotions did that over time, made a person look the way they felt.

"An associate of mine was attacked last night," Dez said. "I was asking some questions on his behalf."

"What associate is this?"

"Lachlan Fields." Dez watched the man for a response. There was none, but then Gerhardt probably would have been a shark at poker. Had he been born a little earlier in time, he could easily have been one of those itinerant gamblers who went from town to town raking in the dough and putting slugs from his six-gun between the eyes of anyone who crossed him.

"I don't know what Lorinda Usher could possibly have to do with Lachlan Fields."

"So you're aware what happened to him."

"Of course I'm aware," Gerhardt said. "It's been all over the news. Now, what does it have to do with Mrs. Usher?"

"Her name came up in the investigation, and he was here to speak with her shortly before he was assaulted," Dez said. "I'm not at liberty to discuss anything further."

"That's my patient you're harassing."

"We barely spoke to her," Dez said. "I don't see how that counts as harassment."

That argument failed, Gerhardt moved onto one that was indisputable. "I thought I said you were never to come here again."

"And I was quite happy to oblige but, as they say, needs must."

His tone was edging toward threatening, and Eva stepped in quickly. "I apologize, doctor. We were just leaving."

"You're his wife, aren't you? You're not wearing a ring."

"We're separated."

"Smart woman."

Dez started to take a step forward, but Eva's hand on his chest prevented him.

Gerhardt still had Eva fixed in his stare, seemingly unperturbed by any threat Dez might present. "I'm well aware Desmond is no longer with the police department, but I believe you still are, are you not, miss?"

"Constable. And, yes, I am."

"So why are you here? Is this official business?"

"No, it isn't. I'm off duty, here strictly for personal reasons. I learned Dez was on his way here, and I came to see to it he didn't do anything he'd regret."

Gerhardt smiled, the expression only a shade warmer than Lorinda Usher's. "If it's personal business, why did you present your badge to our receptionist?"

"I never go anywhere without it," Eva said. "It's become force of habit to pull it out when I sense a situation that looks a little tense. I shouldn't have used it."

"Peggy said you threatened her with an obstruction charge."

Eva smiled back at Gerhardt. "I'm afraid Peggy is mistaken. I was speaking to my estranged husband here."

It was bullshit, but Eva was far smoother than Dez, and Gerhardt looked like he didn't know quite what to do with it. "I will be speaking with everyone here about this situation. If I find out about anything inappropriate, you'll be hearing from me. You are both to stay away from here from now on, do I make myself clear?"

"Perfectly," Eva said. "And, rest assured, I'll be speaking to my supervisor about the situation as well."

"Good," Gerhardt said. "Because if you don't, I will."

He lifted his hand from the hood of the SUV and paused as if assuring himself he'd remain upright before turning to head back to the building.

The question was out of Dez's mouth before he could stop himself. "Do you remember Lucienne Dule?"

Dez could no longer see the man's face, but his head and

shoulders visibly stiffened, and his gait faltered. Gerhardt stood still. Only for a heartbeat.

Then, he returned to the building.

A KEY in the lock awoke Sully from a dreamless sleep.

He started to stand, but then remembered how furious Brennan had become the last time he'd taken that posture. Instead, he pushed himself farther forward on the mattress so he wasn't right up against the wall, leaving him in a better position for a fight should it come to that.

He recalled the notebook and looked around quickly before remembering he'd tucked it safely within his jacket. It was all he had of his birth mother, with enough inside those scrawled words to allow him the chance to get to know her a little.

Brennan entered the room carefully as he had the last time, ensuring Sully wasn't about to spring a trap.

This time, the larger man had brought something with him, a bag from a fast food chain. The smell of warm bacon and potato not only let Sully know it was morning, it reminded him he was hungry.

"I got us something to eat. Hope you're not a vegetarian or anything."

"I'm basically homeless," Sully said. "I can't afford to be choosy about my diet."

Brennan nodded what looked to be some sort of approval before closing the door most of the way and sliding down to the floor so he was sitting with his back next to the only escape route. That done, he dug into the bag and pulled out a couple of wrapped items, throwing one to Sully. He then drew out some deep fried potatoes before tossing the bag and the rest of its contents to his prisoner. Inside was another order of the potatoes, and Sully next caught a plastic bottle of orange juice Brennan produced from an inside pocket.

"Thanks, Brennan." He unwrapped what ended up being an English muffin sandwich and took a bite.

"Sorry, I meant to get you something last night. Things … kinda didn't go so good. I shouldn't'a gone off on you like that."

Sully shrugged, deciding downplaying was the safest route. "Forget it."

The two ate in silence for a few minutes, Sully debating how much to ask Brennan, or whether he should question him at all. There was a reason that notebook had found its way into the wall, after all. That said, Brennan was too close to the edge, and Sully didn't want to risk pushing him over. Last time, things had resolved before Sully had gotten seriously hurt. The next time he might not be so lucky—especially since Brennan's mood swings were getting more extreme.

The safest route was to stay quiet, at least on all but one subject. If he could get Brennan onside, maybe he could find a way out of this.

"Can I ask you something?"

Brennan looked at him from the corner of an eye, suspicion colouring his features. "What?"

"When did you first start seeing them?"

Relief appeared but passed quickly from Brennan's expression, leaving behind a different kind of tension. "My whole life."

"Me too, I think. I mean, it's as far back as my memory goes, anyway. Have you ever figured out what they want?"

Brennan shook his head. "You?"

"Mine are a little easier in a way, I guess. I only see the ones that need some sort of justice. I figure the reason I can see them is because I'm supposed to help them. Problem is, I don't always know how."

Brennan thought that through a moment before breaking into a wry laugh. "And you can't even help yourself right now."

Sully wasn't sure how he was supposed to take that. He decided to match Brennan's laugh with one of his own and hoped for the best. "Yeah, you're right there."

Brennan didn't react either way, which Sully counted as a win.

"Not sure what I'm supposed to do with mine, either," Brennan said. "They're everywhere."

"Have you ever talked to them, asked what they need?"

Unfortunately, that proved Brennan's tipping point, his eyes narrowing as he shouted his response. "I don't give a shit what they need! No one ever cared what I need!"

Brennan drew a few shaky breaths in through his nose, sounding more like rage than regular strain, and Sully gave him time to collect himself, returning to his food as he studied Brennan for signs of an escalating threat.

But the moment seemed to be over. "I'm sorry. Sometimes I get angry."

"It happens."

"I just want them to leave me alone. I can't even handle my own shit most days. How can anyone expect me to handle theirs?"

"You're right. It isn't fair. I wasn't judging or anything. I'm just trying to help."

"Yeah. I know." Brennan had been focused on his food, at least visually, but now met Sully's eye. "You're a good guy, man. I'm sorry this is happening to you. If it was up to me …."

"But it's not."

"No."

The obvious next question was right on the tip of Sully's tongue, but he suspected all it would do was get Brennan's hackles back up.

The trick, he figured, was to continue the conversation in a way that had some benefit to Brennan. He was thinking through his next conversational move when he heard a phone buzzing. Brennan removed a flip-up handset from a pocket and pressed it to his ear. Likely a burner, Sully decided; everyone had smartphones these days.

"Yeah? … What? … Jesus Christ …. Yeah, okay …. Yeah, I

said!" He closed the phone, stuffing it back into his pocket. The rage had returned, simmering quietly just below the surface.

Sully treaded quietly. "Is everything okay?"

Brennan jumped to his feet and it took everything Sully had not to do the same. "No, everything is not okay. Your fucking, goddamned brother."

Sully felt a bubble of hope, his heart thudding against his chest wall at the mention of Dez. "What about him?"

"He's trying to find you. And I wouldn't get too excited if I were you, 'cuz now I've gotta go and deal with him."

The bubble popped as Sully's stomach dropped. "What do you mean, deal with him?"

Brennan didn't answer, turning for the door. This time, Sully wasn't prepared to leave well enough alone.

He climbed to his feet. "Brennan, what are you going to do?"

Brennan was about to leave the room, and Sully knew if he didn't act, the next ghost he could be meeting was Dez.

The Purple Girl was a presence in the corner of his eye, a warning to hold back. But it wouldn't do any good. Not now. What it did was provide a reminder, and Sully reached into his pocket, retrieving his mother's pen as he rushed Brennan from behind. Sully wasn't as large or as strong as Brennan, but he was quick, and he managed to secure an arm around Brennan's throat with his left arm. Brennan made a choked sound and reached up to grab the arm, working to pry it off. Sully wasn't letting go, not for anything.

But the room was small, and the nearest wall just inches away. The problem with fighting Brennan was he'd lived with the pain and fear of abuse and torture far longer than Sully had. There was nothing Sully could do that Brennan hadn't already survived. Except one thing. And while Sully might have ordinarily dreaded the idea of killing a man, he feared far worse letting his brother die without doing everything in his power to stop it.

Sully lifted the pen, plunged it as hard as he could into the soft spot between Brennan's shoulder and neck.

Brennan howled but didn't fall. Instead, as Sully struggled to pull the makeshift shank free, Brennan took two steps backward, and Sully felt his spine and skull collide hard with the wall. Once. Twice. Three times.

The fourth slam knocked Sully loose, his head swimming under the impact and his back screaming abuse at him.

Whatever fury Brennan had managed to squelch moments ago was unleashed; he turned and rained punches down on his captive. With little left to do, no easy way to move now that he was pinned here against the wall, the pen out of his reach and still buried within Brennan's shoulder, Sully curled in on himself to shield head and face within his arms.

He lost track of the number of blows, his focus shifting entirely to how long it was going to take Brennan to kill him. Because there was no longer any question about that. Brennan wasn't slowing or easing up and, whether or not he had any intention of ending Sully's life, that's exactly what he was in the process of doing.

But, just as suddenly as it started, it stopped. A choked sort of sound came from Brennan's throat, and he took a large step back from his target as an icy chill settled in Sully's chest.

Sully shifted an arm enough to look and saw the Purple Girl standing not in front of him, but *in* him, her legs appearing from somewhere within his torso. Brennan's eyes were fixed on her, a grimace twisting his face as he took another step toward what would be his escape.

Sully tried to move, but icy pain seized his chest, and he fell back against the floor as Brennan rushed from the room and slammed the door behind him.

Sully had been holding back his emotion in favour of rational thought, focused on figuring a way out of here, finding and following a strategy with Brennan that would earn his trust and gain his loyalty. Now, nothing mattered. He'd failed, and Dez would die because of it.

As the key turned in the lock, Sully gave up, the scream

rending its way from his lungs and throat and reverberating off the walls.

Footsteps in the concrete hallway beyond his cell stopped. Waited in silence.

Then they set off again, growing distant as Brennan walked away.

24

EVA FOLLOWED Dez back to his place, but stayed only long enough to give him hell.

"If you ever make a move like that without letting me know first, I will kick your ass from here straight across the river."

Dez grinned but quickly realized he'd do better to look regretful. "I know it was stupid. I'm sorry."

"No, you're not."

"I didn't really have a choice, Eva."

"So you keep saying. Tell me something. What did you get out of today's little visit other than a pissed-off wife and a serious case of the heebie-jeebies?"

Dez was so pleased to hear Eva use the word "wife" rather than "ex-wife" that he almost forgot about the heebie-jeebies. Almost.

"Lorinda Usher knows something."

"She's crackers, Dez."

"Maybe, but that doesn't mean she's not involved."

"How exactly would she be involved? I can't imagine she can leave the place at will, let alone get up out of that wheelchair for more than a few minutes at a time—if she can get up at all. We don't really know, do we?"

"No, we don't. Come right down to it, there's a hell of a lot we don't know. That's the problem."

Eva put her hands on her hips, appeared to reconsider, and slid her fingers into the pockets of her jeans. "Dez, think about it. You're saying someone took Sully, right? Do you really believe a middle-aged woman in her condition is capable of overpowering and making off with an able-bodied twenty-four-year-old man?"

"She wouldn't have had to if she had someone who could do it for her."

"So it's a conspiracy, now?"

"Eva, come on. Stay with me, here. I was attacked and left in a situation that ended up drawing Sully out. Pax was tranqued and Sully went missing, leaving what looked to be physical signs of a struggle. Lachlan, who was investigating Sully and his mother, was attacked and almost killed. This was planned, Eva. From what I can tell, it was planned to the teeth. Now someone knows something, and they've essentially committed the perfect crime, because no one but me and you and Lachlan and Lucienne knows Sully is alive. You can't launch a kidnapping investigation when the victim doesn't exist, can you?"

"Maybe it's time we tried. I'm not trying to be difficult here, but I think it's far past time we thought about coming forward with all this, let the police handle it."

"We can't do that, not until we know something for sure, anyway. There are still people Sully needs to stay hidden from. If we go public with this, we blow his cover. You know what kind of fodder this will be for the news media, a supposedly dead guy now alive but possibly not for long. Add in the fact he's the same guy who made headlines over his abandonment as a baby, and the whole world will know his name by the time everything's said and done."

"You're worried he'll end up back at Lockwood."

"Damn right, I'm worried. Aren't you?"

Eva scanned the ground, and Dez saw the fight leave her. "Okay. But we need to be ready, just in case."

"Just in case, what?"

"In case the two of us aren't enough to save him."

Eva didn't come upstairs, needing to pick up Kayleigh from Dez's mom.

Dez trudged to his apartment, and was trying to figure out his next move when the next move came to him.

He had just stepped inside his apartment when he caught sight of movement from the corner of his eye. He wheeled in time to spot the business end of a baseball bat coming at his head.

He didn't have time to do much but sidestep before it caught him a glancing blow on the shoulder. Given the quick dodge, it hadn't been hard enough to break anything, but it still hurt like a bitch. Dez tried his best to ignore the pain as he squared off against a masked assailant.

Within the eyeholes of the balaclava, the man's eyes looked huge and terrified, and Dez's first thought was that he was about to go toe-to-toe with a meth addict. If so, it was quite possible he had a real fight on his hands. The guy was a few inches shorter than Dez, but he was no small fry, and there had been power behind that swing. And people high on meth were unpredictable, paranoid and delusional and, quite often, didn't feel pain the same way they would sober. Not only that, but he wasn't likely to listen to reason.

Dez's study of the man lasted only a few seconds, but it was long enough to find further proof for his theory as he saw the man's eyes darting around the room before once again landing on Dez.

"I don't know what you're after, but I don't have anything of value," Dez said. "I need you to put down the bat."

The man didn't answer. Not in words anyway. His eyes did it for him, the fear giving way to focus as they narrowed, gloved hands tightening around the bat.

It was go time.

Were this a simple hand-to-hand fight, Dez would have let the man come to him, would have waited out his opponent's first move and countered with something intended to put the man on the ground and out of commission. But with a weapon involved, he didn't have that luxury. He lunged toward the intruder, hands reaching to grasp the bat.

He got his hands on it just as the masked man raised it up and to the side as if preparing for a home run swing. Instead, the man released the weapon, the move coming so suddenly and unexpectedly, Dez was thrown off balance. That was the moment he realized he wasn't dealing with a meth junkie. Nor was he up against some typical street hoodlum whose version of a punch-up involved throwing shots like a five-year-old in a snowball fight.

This guy knew what he was doing, and Dez—out of condition after all this time off the job—wasn't prepared.

Dez's forward momentum had propelled him into the wall, and the intruder landed a solid punch to the side of his head that left him seeing stars. The blow pushed Dez sideways, and his fingers brushed the wall as he fell, finding nothing there to grab onto. He landed on the bat hard enough to bruise the back of his right thigh, but there was no time to wallow in the pain. The intruder was fast, already at Dez's side and landing two kicks to his mid-section. Curling in on himself, Dez protected his belly, leaving his knee to absorb the next kick. He yelled in pain and reached out, seizing his assailant's stationary leg. The man shifted his weight to his free foot and lunged in a move to strike, but Dez was ready, getting one leg up in a kick directed at the side of the man's knee.

The intruder buckled, hitting the ground with a howl, and Dez followed up with a punch he was forced to deliver with his weaker left hand, his right busy bracing himself against the floor. They were grappling now, no time to think, Dez's brain fully locked into survival mode as his body reacted with as much muscle memory as he had left from his defensive tactics training. He drove a knee up, trying to strike his opponent's abdomen, but the other man's movement blocked him. The intruder was closer now, taking this from fistfight to wrestling match. Stuck between his assailant and the wall, Dez wasn't in a good spot, and he knew it.

The man seemed to be trying to get on top of him, and Dez got his hands up, attempting to push him back. He didn't see it in time, the sucker punch to his throat that left him gagging and unable to draw breath. Panic set in at the possibility his throat had collapsed, and he didn't notice the man had retrieved the bat until, now wheezing on his hands and knees, he felt a blow to his back that laid him back out. A second followed, then a third.

And he knew instinctively the next one would be to his head.

"Drop your weapon, or I'll shoot!" came a voice from somewhere above. The command—which was female but didn't sound at all like Eva—was followed by the growl and bark of a large dog on the attack, then the sound of a man shrieking in pain.

Dez was on the verge of passing out, only vaguely aware of the sound of the man's continued screams. He battled unconsciousness, dragged a few breaths into his spasming throat until he managed a good coughing fit that felt surprisingly refreshing.

His vision swam, but he could make out enough now to see Miss Crichton leaning over him, checking him for injuries. He opened his mouth to order her back to the safety of her apartment but managed nothing but a croak followed by another coughing attack.

"Take it easy, Desmond. Just try to breathe. You're going to be fine."

He managed the word, "Where?" which proved enough to get him an answer.

"He's unconscious and is bleeding quite badly. I'm afraid Pax did quite a number on him. I should go check on him."

Dez snagged the woman's arm. "No."

For some reason, that drew a chuckle from her. "Oh, now, don't you worry about me. I've got my little Smith & Wesson right here. I don't expect our friend here will give me much trouble."

She held up the snub-nosed, nickel-plated revolver for him to see before making her way over to the unconscious man. Gun or no gun, Dez wasn't about to leave little Miss Crichton to deal with that lunatic alone, so dragged himself to his knees and crawled over to her side.

The man was indeed bleeding badly, a wound in his arm spurting blood despite Miss Crichton's attempts to stem the flow. For his part, Pax was sitting next to the man looking, in Dez's view, rather pleased with himself.

"Atta boy, Paxie," Dez said.

"Oh my," Miss Crichton said. "I didn't intend for Pax to go after him. I sure hope he doesn't die."

"Did you call 9-1-1?" Dez asked, dragging in one more solid breath before taking over First Aid duties from his neighbour.

"I did, as soon as I heard all the commotion. I'd imagine they should be here any minute."

As if on cue, Dez heard sirens approaching from several blocks away. Taking advantage of what time he had, Dez pulled off the intruder's mask, revealing the face of a man in his late twenties or early thirties, his skin scarred by a handful of old injuries. There were fresh-looking bruises around his throat and a bleeding puncture wound to the crook of his neck that Dez was certain neither he nor Pax had caused. Dez studied the face, trying to fit it to a name or at least to someone he might have encountered in the past. The mental search came up empty.

As they waited for the emergency vehicles, something else occurred to Dez.

"There was a woman here, Miss Crichton."

"Emily, please."

"Did you see her?"

"If you mean Victoria Ward, then, yes, I did. She left not long after you did. I'm afraid I didn't get a chance to say hello."

"Listen, the police are going to ask you some questions. I need you to forget you saw her, all right?"

Miss Crichton smiled coyly. "Are you having a fling?"

"Uh … no. She's someone who came to me for help finding someone."

"I thought she said she was an old colleague of yours."

"She wasn't exactly on the level with you. I'm sorry."

"I see. And you say no one can know about her?"

"She's in some trouble."

Miss Crichton was smiling again. "If she has anything to do with all this nonsense, I'd say it's more likely she *is* trouble."

"Fair enough. You're probably right. Listen, I don't think I need to tell you that you saved my life here. Thank you."

"Think nothing of it. You would have done the same for me."

Dez smiled. "You know it, Miss Crichton."

"Emily."

"Right. Emily."

THE ER WAS BUSY, even for the General, with countless people in and out of hospital garb bustling past the curtained entrance to the cubicle in which Dez sat waiting for the all-clear.

He'd already provided a couple of statements about the attack —a brief one to a patrol member at the scene and a second, full statement once he had been examined in the ER. At this point, he just needed the outcome of various tests, the doctor having noticed his goose egg from the other night.

He was hoping he'd be discharged before Forbes Raynor showed up, as he no doubt would, given the similarity between this attack and what had happened to Lachlan. Then again, it was more than likely Forbes was with the attacker, trying to crack him as the man lay there shy of blood and too lightheaded to know to shut up.

When the curtain moved, Dez braced himself for whatever

news he was about to receive. Instead of chart notes, Miss Crichton appeared, peeking through the crack between curtain and wall.

"Are you decent?"

Dez checked his hospital gown and pulled the sheet a little further around his hips. "All clear."

The woman came in, toting a repurposed plastic grocery bag, and perched on the cubicle's sole chair—one of those bright orange padded, metal-framed affairs all hospitals seemed to have gotten at a discount in the mid-eighties.

"I brought you a change of clothes. I thought the ones you'd been wearing might be in a bit of a state."

"Thanks, Emily. As it happens, the police seized the ones I had on."

"Well, glad I thought of it, then. How are you feeling?"

"Like I've been beaten with a baseball bat." Dez tempered the statement with a smile he hoped she'd read as cool and collected.

"Did you call your family?"

"No. I don't want to worry them. Anyway, my wife's been through enough on my account lately, and I don't want my daughter to see me like this." While he'd been assured his face had been spared, he had a painful spot on the side of his head that was likely turning some interesting colours to match the bruises he was now displaying on his arms. He didn't even want to think about his back, which hurt like hell.

"Is anything broken?"

"Still waiting on X-rays, but the doctor suspects a cracked rib or two."

"Oh, dear. I wish I'd been there sooner. It took me a moment to call 9-1-1 and retrieve my gun."

"The police didn't seize it on you, did they?"

"No. It's registered, I'm licensed, and I was using it in self-defence. I can't imagine they're about to bust a little old lady who was standing up to an armed hoodlum."

"You're pretty awesome, you know that?"

Miss Crichton giggled. "Oh, go on with you."

"Where's Pax?"

"I left him at my place so I could come check on you. You had me worried."

"Well, I appreciate that, but I'm fine. By the way, you didn't see the woman come back, did you?"

"Not before I left. You're quite concerned about her, I gather."

"Given what just happened, I guess I am."

Miss Crichton looked to be considering her next words. "Now, granted, I spend a little too much time watching television these days, but are you certain you can trust her? I mean, it seems odd she left, and then this man turns up, don't you think?"

"The thought had crossed my mind," Dez said. "Thing is, I don't trust her exactly, but I've got nothing at this point to suggest Lucienne is responsible for this."

Dez realized his error as soon as the name was out of his mouth. Miss Crichton was having issues of her own, her jaw slackening as she stared at her neighbour.

"Lucienne, did you say? I thought she told me her name was—"

"You didn't hear me say that, okay?"

"But that's her name? Lucienne?"

"Why? Does that name mean something to you?"

Miss Crichton appeared to be thinking, but from where Dez was sitting, it looked less like she was figuring out what to say and more like she was considering whether to say anything at all.

When she at last responded, the answer didn't get Dez very far. "Just a name I hadn't heard in a long time."

"Emily—"

"I'm very glad you're okay, dear, but I'd best get back to Pax. He didn't look all too keen to stay behind, and he's big enough to turn my apartment inside out if he sets his mind to it."

She leaned forward and gave Dez's hand a pat. "You phone me if you need anything, you hear?"

Dez called out to her as she turned, but she simply replied

with a wave of a hand and a parting smile before slipping back through the curtain. He listened to the sound of her feet shuffling away down the corridor.

25

No TRIP to the hospital was complete without at least a little pain and, this time, Dez received extra in the form of Forbes Raynor.

Dez was officially cleared of having a severe head injury although, as he could have predicted, the doctor suspected some form of concussion. He also had a cracked rib, which explained why his back in particular was screaming at him like a toddler being refused ice cream before dinner.

But Dez had a high pain threshold, and the sharp throbbing had blessedly receded to manageable levels once the doctor had wrapped his ribs, offering a few instructions before discharging him. Dez had suffered a range of other injuries—bruises and scrapes mainly—and none of the affected body parts were too pleased with him as he struggled into the change of clothes Miss Crichton had brought.

He was grappling with his jeans, the bent position doing nothing to help his back, when the curtain parting had him drawing up to standing. He'd expected the doctor with some final instructions but instead found Forbes appearing at the gap in the curtain.

"Sorry," Forbes said, backing out upon finding Dez in a partial state of undress.

"See anything you like?" Dez asked through his smirk as the curtain snapped shut.

The predictable response sounded from the other side. "Piss off."

Dez finished with his jeans and drew the curtain back, finding Forbes with his back to the wall separating examination rooms, arms crossed. Slap on a suit and a pair of dark wraparound sunglasses, and he'd look like he was guarding the prime minister.

"I provided a full statement to patrol," Dez said.

"I read it. I've still got some questions."

"You're asking the wrong guy. I'm as much in the dark as you are. Didn't you talk to the asshole who attacked me? I mean, he's in the ER, too, right?"

"Yeah, he's here. But that's the thing right there, Braddock. He says he won't talk to anyone but you."

"What? Why?"

"How the hell should I know? He wouldn't talk to patrol and all he said to me, in terms I won't repeat in full, was that you were the only one he'd speak with. So, now I'm wondering. First Lachlan Fields, now this guy, and neither will deal with anyone but you."

"So you're asking yourself how to replicate my obvious charm so people will talk to you too?"

Forbes's eyes narrowed. "What I'm asking myself is what you've got to do with all of this. After all, you're the one who found Fields. And now this guy, this Brennan Wakeman. Something smells here, Braddock, and I think you know more than you're letting on."

What smelled to Dez was the way Forbes had enunciated the word "found." "If you're suggesting I had anything to do with the attack on Lachlan, you can go to hell. And as far as this other guy, this Brennan Wakeman ...." Dez trailed off, his oral repeat of the name triggering something inside him, recognition of a memory he couldn't quite put a finger on. Not yet, anyway.

"What?"

Dez thought fast, putting out a hand as if to steady himself. "Dizzy."

To Forbes's credit, he guided Dez back to the bed despite his muttering the word, "Bullshit," while en route.

Dez hunched over, lowering his face into a hand as he sat there, head spinning around that name, trying to slot it into the correct place in his brain. It had been somewhere in the files he'd read back in Lachlan's storage container, he was sure of that.

He asked the question as much for himself as Forbes, hoping the spoken repetition would snap the puzzle piece into the overall picture. "Who's Brennan Wakeman?"

"It's the ID matching to the fingerprints patrol used when he wouldn't provide a name," Forbes said. "Interesting thing is, he doesn't have much of a record for violence—certainly nothing to suggest he'd be capable of the assaults on Fields or you. One common assault as a youth, but otherwise what he's got of a record is all drug and property offences and breaches of court orders. After that, he pretty much disappears, for a whole decade in fact. Does the name mean anything to you?"

That was a really good question. "Not off the top of my head, no. Maybe if I talk to him."

"So you can have something else you can hold back," Forbes said. "I don't know what's going on here, Braddock, but I do know you're obstructing this investigation. And when I put this together—and you can bet your ass I will—you can count on it that I won't rest until you get what's coming."

If Dez could only piece this together himself so he could see Sully alive and safe, he would gladly accept whatever sanctions Forbes or anyone else thought he'd earned. If all he had to do to find and save his brother was obstruct a police investigation, that was small potatoes. After all, should the situation force his hand, there was far worse he was willing to do.

Forbes grudgingly led the way through the halls in the expansive ER until they were in the section furthest from the one where

Dez had been—the distance not unusual given the recent violent exchange between Dez and Brennan. A hard-done-by young patrol officer sat on guard at the drawn curtain, looking plenty bored as he leaned back in his chair and checked his smartphone. When he saw the two men approaching, he jammed the device inside a pocket, cheeks reddening just enough to tell Dez unnecessary use of personal phones while on duty was still frowned upon.

"Constable," Forbes said, the word coming out more warning than greeting. "How's the patient?"

"All quiet, Sergeant. A nurse was just in to check on him a few minutes ago. She told me she gave him something to help him rest. He was pretty worked up."

Great, Dez thought. So much for getting any immediate answers out of Brennan Wakeman.

Of course, there was a chance whatever sedative he'd been given hadn't yet taken full effect or that it might leave him partially aware.

"Mind if I pop in and take a look?" Dez asked.

The patrol officer looked to Forbes for the all-clear.

"He's fine, Constable. Used to be one of us. Go take a break. I'll keep an eye on our suspect here."

As the constable took advantage of his good fortune, Dez tried to ignore the way Forbes had leaned on the words "used to be," turning what should have been a simple explanation to the departing officer into a jibe. Dez bit his tongue as he pulled the curtain aside and entered the enclosure.

He recognized the guy from the apartment as he stood over him, the man looking no more alert than he had in the moments that followed his run-in with Pax. A heavy bandage had been wrapped around his wounded arm, but a spot of blood showed through the white. A blood pressure cuff encased the opposite arm while an oxygen mask covered his face.

Dez placed a hand on the man's uninjured shoulder, giving it a tentative squeeze. There was no response, so Dez pressed a little harder and followed up with a light shake.

The man's eyes eased open and he looked to be struggling to fix Dez in his shaky gaze.

"You wanted to talk to me?" Dez said.

A sound midway between a moan and a mumble sounded from behind the mask and Dez risked moving it aside for a moment, hoping the guy wasn't too far gone to make some sense.

"Wanna repeat that for me, buddy?" Dez asked.

"Desmond Braddock?" The words were whispered, the last name ending in an outtake of breath.

"Yeah, that's me."

"Sully's brother?"

Dez stared at the man as one of many scattered pieces clicked into place. He leaned forward, close enough to whisper, close enough his words wouldn't be heard by anyone besides the two of them. "Where is he?"

"Don't … don't want him haunting me."

The words sent a chill through Dez, the possibility that the worst had already occurred making it next to impossible to keep himself from adding murder to his lifetime's list of transgressions.

His words, choked as they were with a threatening rage, were almost enough to make him fear himself. "Did you hurt him, you son of a bitch? Is he dead?"

"Not dead yet."

"What the hell's that supposed to mean? Where is he?"

"Sorry." The word was a hissed sigh, providing no real reply and yet enough of an answer to get Dez's heart pounding.

"Sorry about what?"

"Graveyard. Burying you. And Sully. Sorry."

The truth and the possibilities it stirred up hit Dez as hard as the baseball bat Brennan had wielded not so long ago.

"Jesus Christ, no. Did you fucking bury him?"

There was a slight headshake in response, but it wasn't

enough to satisfy Dez, not with so much at stake. It was damn near impossible to keep talking in a whisper, and Dez had to check himself and his mounting terror as he repeated his question in the hopes of a clearer reply.

"Did you bury him? Answer me, damn it."

"No. Wouldn't do that. Not to him."

The wave of relief was almost enough to knock Dez on his ass, but he kept his feet and his senses. The danger, after all, was far from over.

"But you took him somewhere. Against his will."

The man managed a slight nod, up and down. Dez resisted the urge to add more bruises to Brennan's throat. And suddenly, the bruises and the puncture wound made sense. *Atta boy, Sull.* "Where did you take him?"

"Dark … dark …." Brennan's eyes were slipping shut, his words weak and breathy, as if it was taking everything he had to stick around and provide this single meaningless word.

"Give me an address, Brennan, a location. Where did you take him?"

"D … dark …."

Brennan's eyes closed and remained that way, the final word a long exhale. Dez shook the shoulder again, but this time received no response.

Replacing the oxygen mask, Dez followed the rubberized line from the cuff to what he only now noticed to be a blank monitor. Granted, he didn't know much about the world of medicine, but he had spent enough time in hospitals to know machines like that one should be making some sort of noise, should be revealing something on the screen.

His eyes snapped back to Brennan, from his still face to his equally still chest. Realization hit hard as Dez snapped into action, calling for Forbes as he checked for a pulse at Brennan's neck.

"Get help," Dez shouted as, finding no pulse, he began chest compressions. "I think his heart stopped."

As Forbes ran off, yelling loud enough to bring the entire hospital running, Dez pushed out a solid, rib-cracking rhythm on the man's chest, fighting to save a life that might well be responsible for ending Sully's.

He puffed out commands to Brennan as he did what he could to save him, urging him to live as death closed in. He was so focused on his task he didn't notice the appearance of medical staff until he was being yanked aside by Forbes and a pair of nurses intent on replacing Dez with a crash cart.

"What the hell did you do?" Forbes asked, his horrified tone suggesting he was fixing either Brennan or Dez in a wide-eyed stare. "What the hell did you do?"

Dez said nothing, attention rooted to the still body on that bed, remaining focused there until the curtain was drawn shut, blocking Brennan and the medical team from view.

DEZ AND FORBES were sitting side by side in the ER hallway when they received the news neither, for his own reasons, wanted to hear.

Brennan was dead.

Neither man spoke, creating one of those shocked silences that felt immeasurable, the kind that didn't seem to fit the confines of time. It could have been seconds, minutes or hours they remained there, staring down the hall to where Brennan's lifeless body lay behind a curtain on an ER bed.

"I need to call this in," Forbes said.

Dez wasn't sure the words were meant for him, but responded anyway. "Yeah. You do."

Out of the corner of his eye, Dez watched as Forbes fumbled in his pocket for his phone. But though he managed to locate it, Forbes made no immediate effort to dial, the hand holding the device dropping like a leaden weight into his lap.

"What did you do, Braddock?"

The reason for Forbes's shock, his reluctance to call this in, swam into focus, chasing away all other thoughts for the moment. Forbes had allowed Dez to speak to a suspect, and now that suspect was dead. Forbes's career would be in the toilet if it turned out he'd allowed it to happen, if Dez had—

"Fucking hell, Raynor, you can't think …. I didn't do anything to him, you moron!"

"So you didn't …?" Raynor didn't finish the question. Didn't have to.

"No! What the hell, man? Come on."

It proved enough to break the spell, to convince Raynor of the truth, because he was up and on his phone immediately, calling in the troops to begin the sudden death investigation.

And Dez knew how this would go, knew he'd be stuck in some interview room, likely for hours, then would spend days as a potential suspect until they determined a cause of death that would exonerate him. There would have to be an autopsy, which might not take place until two or three days had passed. And there would be tests to determine whether Brennan had any pre-existing illnesses or chemicals in his body that could have caused death by non-homicidal means.

More than likely, Dez would be questioned and released pending the outcome of that investigation. But it was impossible to say how long he would be questioned. And right now, given what Brennan had supplied in the moments before he drew his last breath, Dez knew time was not something he and Sully had on their side.

Brennan had tried to warn him, to right a wrong. Of that much Dez was certain. But it didn't leave Dez a whole lot closer to finding Sully, not unless he could find a way to retrace Brennan's steps, and fast.

And he couldn't do that from an interview room in police headquarters. Nor could he find a way to explain that final conversation between him and Brennan without revealing more than he was prepared to share.

"Where the hell are you going?" Forbes called out as Dez started off down the hallway.

"Bathroom," Dez said.

He turned the corner. Passed the bathroom.

And kept going.

26

Dez thought about heading home and picking up Pax from Miss Crichton, a stop that would have the added benefit of allowing him to question her further on whatever it was she was concealing.

But Forbes—and quite possibly others—would be looking for him now, and home was the first place they'd check.

Instead, he went hunting for answers to his other pressing question. His path took him once more past the drive to Lockwood as he sped along the north bank of the Kimotan to the storage compound holding Lachlan's secret stash of information.

Thanks to last night's work, Dez knew exactly where to find the necessary files, and he pulled them both out as he searched for a reference to Brennan Wakeman.

He flipped through the file on Sully first and found his hunch had been correct, a small thrill of excitement thrumming through his chest as he located a photocopy of the police report on the fatal fire at the Blakes'. Brennan Wakeman had been the second foster child and had, like Sully, been questioned about his possible role. Unlike Sully, suspicion hadn't fallen away from Brennan quite so fast, and he'd remained a suspect until police had received a complete and verifiable confession from Margaret Parsons, a troubled fifteen-year-old girl who'd endured abuse at the Blakes' hands not long before. Brennan—fourteen years old and therefore chargeable under the law—had stayed in custody in the meantime and endured a handful of increasingly tense interviews.

Notes from various police officers had been appended to the file, including those tasked with watching him in cells. On two occasions, a child psychologist had been called in to talk to the boy amid concerns he was approaching a mental breakdown. He'd been found huddled in the corner, knees drawn to his chest as his wide, terrified eyes focused intently on a blank section of wall. And, as the psychologist took her leave on the second occasion, Brennan had begged her not to "leave me alone in here with him." There had been no one else in the cell at the time, and all thoughts turned to the likelihood the boy was slipping into a state of psychosis. They'd brought in the big guns. Dr. Roman Gerhardt was called in to speak to Brennan and administer something to settle the boy's hallucinations.

But Dez knew something they didn't, had memories of similar reactions from another boy who could see things others couldn't. Though Sully's sightings had supposedly stopped for a time— while at Lockwood and in those handful of days that followed his escape—Dez knew there was no medication, no treatment in existence to stop hallucinations that were anything but.

Dez's mind flipped back to Brennan's words to him in those moments before he'd taken his final breath: *Don't want him haunting me.* It made sense now, that statement, although it did nothing to quiet Dez's anxieties. A haunting required death and, while Brennan had been clear Sully was not dead yet, it was the "yet" that worried Dez. That "yet" left him focused with nausea-inducing intensity on questions about time and location. Snowballed into how he would cope, could he not answer those questions before they all melded into the one conclusion Dez couldn't bear. Not again. Not so soon after getting Sully back.

He'd been so close. So close to finding his brother. Brennan would have talked; Dez knew he had intended to. But it was too late, the darkness of his final words closing in before Dez could glean the information he'd needed.

He resisted the frustrated urge to fling the files across the room, and instead pounded them down against the arm of the chair on which Eva had been perched not so long ago. What he'd give right now for just one more minute with Brennan.

Instead, what he had was the silence of a storage container and files containing everything but the answers he required.

He pinched at the bridge of his nose, stemming the rise of desperate tears as he guided his rational brain through the storm of emotion. Though functional, it took longer than he cared to admit to think his way to a next step. He would have to take a page out of Lachlan's book, piece together what he could find of Brennan's life, hoping there would be some clue in that history leading to Sully's location. The question was where to start, given he didn't know the first thing about the man and no longer, as a fired cop, had information at his fingertips.

He opted for a social media search, and was tapping Brennan's name into his internet browser's search bar when his phone rang, obscuring the web search page with the call display showing Miss Crichton's name.

"Hi, Emily."

"I called in to check on you and was told you had been discharged. Are you all right?"

"Yeah, more or less. Couple cracked ribs, but nothing awful, all things considered. Brennan's dead, by the way."

"Brennan?"

"Right, sorry. The guy who attacked me. His name was Brennan Wakeman."

"I'm sorry to hear that."

Dez smiled into his phone. "You don't sound sorry."

But Miss Crichton wasn't in the mood, it seemed, for idle chat, an event Dez wasn't sure he'd ever witnessed. "Desmond, I need to speak with you. Immediately."

It occurred to him the police might have got to Miss Crichton, might have directed her to call and arrange a meeting so they could be there and pull him in for questioning. If Dez had felt himself pressed earlier, he'd now come to a point in which extra time was non-existent.

"I'd like to, but there's something really important I'm in the middle of," he said.

"This is very important too. Please, I really must speak with you. It's about Lucienne."

At this moment, with sand passing rapidly through the hour-glass, only a handful of magic words could stop time.

She'd just spoken one of them.

"Meet me at Benny J's," Dez said. "I can be there in half an hour."

THANKFULLY, Miss Crichton hadn't been expecting a meal at the Riverview diner as, Dez noted, she'd brought Pax along.

Dez hadn't bothered to go inside, opting to hold down the seat in his SUV next to an expired meter while he waited for his neighbour to show. He rolled down the window as she approached, waving her over.

Miss Crichton opened the rear door to let Pax in, and Dez was immediately treated to a slobbery greeting. Meanwhile, Miss Crichton climbed into the passenger seat.

"Well, this is rather cloak and dagger, isn't it?" she said, a thrill in her voice and a light in her eyes that likely hadn't been there in decades.

"Something like that. Mind if I drive for a bit? I don't want to sit in one place for too long."

"Of course. But may I ask why you seem so reticent about drawing attention to yourself?"

"I was with Brennan when he died, and some people want to ask me questions. And, no, I had nothing to do with his death."

"Of course you didn't, dear. Anyone who knows you would

know that. Anyway, as it happens, I'm rather glad you've seen fit to meet in private as there's something rather delicate I need to tell you about."

"Concerning Lucienne?"

"Yes. At least, I believe so. Perhaps we can find somewhere quiet to talk?"

Dez opted for the multilevel parking lot at the Riverview L-train. During weekdays, it provided a place for area commuters to leave their cars while they went to work downtown, thus preventing them from paying the exorbitant rates in the lots around their shiny new places of business. That meant an abundance of vehicles on hand and plenty of opportunity for Dez to hide in plain sight should police be actively searching for him. He had to circle to the sixth floor before he found a spot, and he backed in, keeping his plate obscured while allowing him to keep an eye on the area.

"Very wise," Miss Crichton said, tapping the side of her nose with an index finger.

Dez replied with a brief smile before getting down to business. "So what was it you wanted to tell me?"

"It occurred to me after I left you that I was rather too quick to leave the situation. But I wonder if I might ask you for a little more information before I divulge something I might otherwise live to regret."

Dez had his own reservations on that point, but hoped a little quid pro quo would benefit him in the long run. In any case, Miss Crichton had proved herself ten times over today. "What do you want to ask me?"

"This Lucienne you mentioned. She's the woman who's staying with you?"

"Not staying, exactly. She was just there overnight, maybe will be a bit longer. Like I said, I'm helping her with something."

"And you can't tell me what you're helping her with?"

"Sorry, Emily. That's not really my information to share, and she's sworn me to secrecy on that point."

"I understand. May I at least ask you this much? Can you tell me her last name?"

"Why do you want to know?"

"Because she looks very much like someone I once knew. And once you said the name …. Anyway, I saw her come back, and I tried to speak with her, but she just ran off."

"What? When?"

"Shortly before I called you. In fact, it was seeing her that spurred me into calling you about her."

"And you think knowing her last name will help?"

"I think it will, yes."

Dez thought about it a moment before deciding he had far more to lose by not cooperating—namely Sully if he couldn't find a way to get to the bottom of this.

"It's Dule. Lucienne Dule."

This time it seemed it was Dez who'd spoken the magic words —only, in this case, Miss Crichton wasn't as pleased as he had been when he'd heard the same first name emerge from the older woman's lips.

"Emily? Are you all right?"

"I'm fine, Desmond …. It can't be …. It can't be."

"Emily?"

As quickly as the moment had hit, it passed, and Miss Crichton turned to him with a story in her eyes. He'd seen that look before and, when it happened in the confines of her apartment, it typically meant his chances of escape were next to nil until he finished his coffee and cake and grasped the moral of the story.

"Did I ever tell you what I did for a living prior to my retirement?"

Dez resisted the impatient sigh standing ready on the tip of his tongue. "You told me you were a nurse."

Miss Crichton nodded. "Yes. A psychiatric nurse. I worked at Lockwood. For thirty-five years, in fact."

Dez was no longer hoping for a way to end the story early. "And you knew Lucienne Dule while you worked there."

"She was a patient. Very young at the time, just a slip of a girl, really. And very sweet."

Miss Crichton paused—or at least it looked like a pause to Dez, rather than an end to the conversation. She was thinking, likely through what she could share and what she needed to hold back. If no one else could appreciate that, Dez certainly could. But when the pause continued to a point that had Dez worrying Miss Crichton might not emerge with the full truth, he decided he needed to meet her midway.

At any rate, the way she struggled told Dez his neighbour was solid when it came to keeping secrets. If he shared one of his own, it was a safe bet she'd keep it.

"I don't know if this will help you out," he said. "But you remember the brother I told you about, the one I'm looking for?"

Miss Crichton appeared relieved for the lifeline, and nodded.

Dez took a quick breath and forged on. "Lucienne Dule is his biological mother."

The smile Miss Crichton had been wearing fell away. "And what did you say his name was?"

"Sully. Well, actually, it's Sullivan, but pretty much everyone who knows him calls him—Are you all right?"

Miss Crichton had turned now, back toward the windshield, horrified shock in her expression. Words passed her lips, a whispered mumble that sounded to Dez like, "That's impossible."

"Emily? Are you okay?"

She nodded slowly, the nod of a trauma victim unable to locate the line between reality and nightmare.

Dez gave Miss Crichton a moment, but when that didn't get them anywhere, he laid a hand on her shoulder. That broke the spell, had her looking over to him.

"I'm sorry, Desmond. You must think I've lost my marbles."

"No, but you've definitely got me a little worried over here."

"Have you found him yet? Sullivan, I mean?"

Dez shook his head in the negative. "I'm trying. I've been working my ass off. But it turns out Brennan took him somewhere against his will and now Brennan's dead. I'm working against time here, and I'm hitting roadblocks all over the place. I can't explain why, but I keep thinking if I can unravel the Dules, I'll find Sully."

"You think they know more than they're letting on?"

"One of them does, anyway. Lucienne's mother."

"Lorinda." Miss Crichton said the name like she was rolling vinegar over her tongue.

"Clearly you've met her."

"She's an awful woman. Now, I'm not usually one to judge, especially someone who's lost a child. But Lucienne didn't belong in that place. She wasn't mentally unwell, you see. She had a gift. One that scared her."

"She could see the dead," Dez said. "She told me. So can Sully."

"Lorinda was a very religious woman, and she turned more fully to her faith after her baby boy was taken from her. I spoke to her once about Lucky, and—"

"Lucky?"

"That's what Lucienne liked to be called. She hated her given name. Thought is was too old-fashioned. Anyway, Lorinda told me even if Lucky wasn't insane, she needed to be there, if for no other reason than to be purified over her brother's death. 'Purified.' That was the word she used."

"Did Lucienne ever talk to you about her little brother?"

"The baby was named Artie, and he drowned in the tub, I understand. The girls had been left in charge of him, but they were just children themselves. Lucky was five or six and the other one …."

"Rhona."

"Yes, that's right. She was a couple years older. The father, I heard, was a drinker, and he'd been off somewhere on a bender at the time. Anyway, Lucky started seeing her brother's ghost and, eventually, she was seeing spirits everywhere. It terrified her. She looked to her family for help, but Lockwood was what she got, instead. And for people like Lucky, people who don't truly belong in an institution, Lockwood can be a terrifying place."

Dez was well aware. "How long was she there?"

"Two years, give or take a couple of months. Back then, a parent could commit a child of fourteen, and that's exactly what happened."

"What about Rhona? Did you ever see her?"

"Only once, after Lucky left Lockwood. She turned out very like her mother, that one. I suppose I can't blame her. There were only two ways to deal with Lorinda. One was to agree with her on all matters; the other was to leave."

Given that, it seemed strange Rhona should have dropped off the face of the earth. "So Rhona was close to her mother?"

"As close as anyone could ever get to Lorinda, I guess. My understanding is Rhona agreed to be 'saved' after Artie's death, so she started going to church with her mother, soaking in everything she could learn about the faith. Lucky rebelled, and she ended up where she did because of it."

"Must have thrilled Lorinda when Lucky got out and ended up getting pregnant," Dez said.

"What?" The way Miss Crichton had asked it made it clear she wasn't looking for a repeat; the surprise was written all over her.

"But you knew the name Sullivan," Dez said. "You must have known about his birth."

"I did. In fact, I was one of the few who did."

Another long pause had Dez cutting in with another question. "What do you mean?"

"She didn't get out and get pregnant, Desmond. She gave birth inside the institution. Sullivan was born inside Lockwood."

Now it was Dez's turn to utter the "What?" that begged no repetition. "But she said …. She said she got pregnant in high school. She said she slept with a lot of different boys and didn't know the father."

"No. If that's what she's told you, she lied. There were no boys, certainly none her own age with whom she had any contact in that manner. There was only one, a man."

Miss Crichton drew in a breath as if preparing to dive head first into a deep pool with no immediate expectation of resurfacing.

"Desmond, Sullivan's father is Dr. Roman Gerhardt."

27

Dez dropped Miss Crichton and Pax a block from home, not wanting to get too close lest his fears be correct about the police watching for him. He travelled a few blocks before deciding he'd better pull over, realizing he wasn't paying adequate attention to his driving when a protracted horn honk told him he'd inadvertently blown a red.

He'd put his phone onto silent earlier, wanting to enable an undisturbed conversation with Miss Crichton. Now he discovered Forbes had tried him seven times in the past hour, leaving him to debate calling him back.

But not now. He had too much else on his mind; he'd never be able to keep his head fully in the game with Forbes, leaving him open to any tricks the guy might have up his sleeve.

Then there was the fact Dez and Miss Crichton had sworn each other to secrecy on what they'd each shared, about Lucienne, about Sully, about Dr. Gerhardt.

Gerhardt, it seemed, had been conducting his little experiments far longer than Dez had realized—more than two decades, in fact—having discovered the same thing about Lucky Dule he'd later learned about Sully. Lucky didn't suffer from psychosis or any other mental disorder; the things she could see were real. And something about that fascinated the doctor, made him want to learn more about it.

Only it hadn't stopped there with Lucky.

Miss Crichton said the girl would be taken once a week for her "treatments" with the doctor, with those dates eventually coming closer and closer together until the two were meeting sometimes once per day. Lucky had become quiet, withdrawn, refused to speak to anybody. Eventually, she'd simply refused to speak at all.

Miss Crichton had tried, coming each day to the girl in an attempt to figure out what was happening. To someone with a backlog of experience with psychiatric patients, it was clear something was very wrong, and it was just as obvious Lucky didn't feel free to speak about it.

Then one day, she found the girl, then fifteen, in her bathroom, vomiting violently. That time, she did speak. The outcome was more unsettling than her silences.

"I sometimes wonder what it's like," she'd said once Miss Crichton had settled herself on the floor next to the girl.

"What's that, dear?"

Lucky's reply had been devoid of emotion, as if she were already halfway to the state she referenced with her unsettling words.

"To be dead."

In the end, Miss Crichton had learned Lucky was of no mind to commit suicide, was far too terrified of the spirit world she witnessed. She'd been taught "suicides" went to Hell and she'd since decided, based on her own observations, that people could remain in this world too—trapped between worlds while they searched for the answers that would provide them with the same peace as those who had crossed over quickly.

But, like Sully, Lucky didn't see those who had already found peace. Just those tortured souls growing increasingly desperate as their confinement on earth went on and on without the help they needed.

And Lucky, at that point, needing help of her own, was in no position to lend a hand to anyone who came calling. At just fifteen, she was pregnant, and it took Miss Crichton little time to learn the awful truth. The institution's new chief psychiatrist—at that time, as now, the only psychiatrist—had become obsessed with the teenager.

Lucky had refused his advances, but one didn't deny the man who held all the cards in that place. And, through threats and promises and increasingly intimate touches to which she'd in time grown accustomed, he'd eventually worn her down until, one day, he took her fully. And while Lucky hated Gerhardt for what he was doing, she hated herself too—perhaps more, for her own helplessness and inability to fight back, for what she believed were the allowances she'd granted this man with her own body.

Nothing Miss Crichton said could change the girl's mind, could convince her this was as much rape as if he'd violently forced himself on her. Lucky had been unwilling to let go of the guilt, wearing it just as intently as that involving little Artie.

Miss Crichton had made some quiet inquiries, heard whispers of other wrongs committed by the doctor. But no one would come forward. Even in those days, times were tough in Kimotan Rapids, few jobs to be had, particularly for those with their training. So Miss Crichton learned to wear her own guilt for a couple of months as she continued to question but ultimately did nothing to help Lucky, whose sessions with Gerhardt continued.

Then, one day, Lucky didn't come back.

After two days with no sign of her, word went around that Lucky had died, had committed suicide, hanged herself in her room using her own nightdress. It was said a young orderly, Larson Hackman, had found her, had removed the body quietly in the middle of the night so as not to upset the other patients.

It wasn't good enough, not for Miss Crichton, and she dared to do what she should have done before and went to Gerhardt. She was startled to see genuine signs of distress in the man's countenance as she expressed her doubts about Lucky's death, demanding to see the body.

She was told it was too late. They'd contacted the family who had asked she be buried on site. That, he said, had already been done. Miss Crichton asked if police had been notified. Gerhardt's expression soured as he warned her about job loss and worse, should she seek to involve the authorities in their business. They were, he insisted, entitled to deal with their own here, and he would see to it Miss Crichton herself was "dealt with" if she pushed the issue.

That night, as Miss Crichton crossed the street with her shopping, she was hit by a car. The vehicle fled the scene. Of the few witnesses, no one could provide an accurate description.

Miss Crichton spent a month in hospital with numerous broken bones and a severe concussion as well as internal bleeding, thankfully mended through surgery.

Her first visitor had been Gerhardt and, through the haze of pain and the medication meant to take it away, she'd been aware of him peering down at her.

"You really must be careful, Emily," he'd said. "I'd hate to see something like this happen again."

Once she'd been released and sent home, she bought her first handgun.

But the worry for Lucky proved heavier than for herself and, after a couple of months of physiotherapy, Miss Crichton was able to return to work. There, she began to suspect Lucky was not, in fact, dead, but had been confined somewhere by Gerhardt once her pregnancy could no longer be concealed or explained away as simple bloating or weight gain.

Miss Crichton had searched. First in the now-disused wing of the facility, blighted as it was by black mould, crumbling walls and bad memories of hideous Victorian-age procedures. Then she'd turned her attention to rumours of a passage that ran between that wing and the doctor's residence on the hill behind.

She'd enlisted the help of the building's retired caretaker, a man named Nate Waterston who had once taken quite a shine to Nurse Crichton. He was old enough to remember the tunnel, was one of few people still at Lockwood who, having lived through the threat of the Cold War, had known the tunnel as an emergency bunker should the need arise.

One night, they entered the old wing, flashlights in hand, and went in search of the entrance.

They'd entered the darkest section of the wing and descended a flight of stairs, the blanketing dust interrupted only occasionally by largely covered-over footprints and the trails of rats. It was clear the doctor, and anyone else who might be using the tunnel, were entering from the house.

At the bottom, a solid wooden door blocked their path. This proved a simple challenge to Nate, who drew out a set of keys and flipped through them until he found the right one.

"I doubt they figured on me still having keys to the place," he'd said with the sort of smile that had Miss Crichton wondering what else he'd surreptitiously held onto over his lifetime.

The passage lay before them, pitch black with a coating of dust disturbed only by the tracks of the men's work boots Nate had suggested they wear. As long as the two of them weren't seen, it would keep the heat off the nurses when the doctor tried to discover who had been down here. If they were seen, well, not much would matter then, would it, Nate had reasoned.

Thankfully, Nate wasn't a large man; his boots fit Miss Crichton's feet. She moved along quietly enough as the flashlight beam bounced over the floor, exposing dust and insects and crumbled pieces of wall.

Then they heard a girl scream.

The sound stalled them temporarily in their tracks, thoughts of ghosts left unspoken but clearly at the top of mind with both of them. It was likely a full minute before the fear—both of inhuman and human things—allowed Miss Crichton to forge ahead once again.

"I think that was Lucky," she whispered to Nate, who looked to be working hard to nod in reply, his frightened face just visible in the castoff light from the beam currently shaking against the floor.

Rooms lined the way, and it was at the door to one of these where they found a busy track of shoe prints, showing movement to and fro numerous times along the hall. As Miss Crichton had suspected, they set a course from the direction of the doctor's residence and back again.

The door to the room was closed, no doubt locked, and Miss Crichton took a moment to listen with her ear to the wood. She could hear heavy breaths from inside, the sound of a girl sobbing, and she realized with no small amount of relief that not only was Lucky alive, she was alone.

Nate was fumbling through his keys, trying them one at a time as they rattled against the old lock, leaving Miss Crichton a moment to speak quietly to Lucky behind the door.

"It's Emily, my dear. I'm with a good friend. Just hold on. We're finding the right key."

The weeping changed in tone, at least in Miss Crichton's mind, some of the desperation replaced by relief.

At last, Nate succeeded in finding a key, a long, chunky thing that looked like it predated the institution itself.

"I never knew what this one was for," he said, his trembling hand struggling to work it in the lock. "It didn't fit anything, thought it must be there by mistake."

As the door swung open and the beam from the flashlight located the girl in the dark, Miss Crichton felt their luck had run out.

The wide-eyed girl was lying on the cold, white-tiled floor, clothed in a filthy nightdress, blonde hair sweat-drenched and dishevelled. In the dark as she was, she appeared feral, a wild animal in a cage. The smell wasn't much better, the stench of human waste mixing with vomit, blood, sweat and something else Miss Crichton couldn't put a finger on.

Nate dry heaved but managed to hold onto his stomach contents, while Miss Crichton pushed through, crossing the floor in quick strides and kneeling next to the girl. Hands latched onto the nurse, cold and clammy and small but strong. The flashlight beam wavered, lowering to a spot nearby on the ground as if Nate felt he was intruding by revealing too much. But there was enough lingering light for Miss Crichton to confirm this was indeed Lucky, no question needing asked once she saw those eyes.

She swept the girl's hair back from her face as she looked once again at her positioning on the floor. "Don't worry, my dear. We'll have you out of here in no time."

And then Lucky screamed. Her little hands squeezed Miss Crichton's arm hard enough to bruise, as if they were trying to pass straight through bone. The older woman winced but didn't pull away as Nate stated the obvious.

"I don't think we're going nowhere, Em. The girl's in full labour."

While there was no denying that fact, Miss Crichton had hoped they could at least get her out of here, even as far as the car before the baby came. But, as she looked more closely at Lucky— needing to beg the shy Nate to bring the light in—Miss Crichton could see just how right the retired caretaker was.

"The baby's crowned," she said. The nurse, experienced in psychiatry rather than medicine, positioned herself between Lucky's legs. "Nate, put the light down and hold Lucky's hand."

"What if the doctor comes, Em?"

Having found the girl a prisoner, alone in the dark and about to give birth to Gerhardt's baby in a dark, dusty, filthy room, Miss Crichton was left in no doubt of her answer. "Then you leave him to me, Nate. I'll kill him with nothing more than my bare hands."

She ordered Lucky to bear down, thanking God the girl had at least been fed well enough to maintain her strength as she obeyed the nurse through the remainder of the agonizing process.

There was no telling how long it went on, Lucky already exhausted by the time they'd arrived. But, at last, the baby's head appeared in full and, within moments, was wailing through his first breaths.

With nothing to properly clean him, Miss Crichton wiped him off as well as she could with her shirt, then bundled him in the jacket Nate removed.

Lucky—who had yet to say a word—wept as Miss Crichton handed her the baby. While the girl's tears had never stopped, not in full anyway, they now changed, coming through a wide grin and an occasional joyous laugh.

Nate's voice in Miss Crichton's ear was whispered urgency. "Em, if we're going to get her out of here, we have to leave now. He could come back at any time."

Miss Crichton nodded her understanding, then turned back to the girl. "Lucky? Lucky, we need to leave. Do you think you can walk?"

But Lucky was in another world, enraptured by the face of her now-gently crying baby. She said something, but her first word was whispered, heard by no one beyond herself and her infant.

"Lucky?"

The girl spoke again, this time loudly enough to be heard by the others. "Sullivan. His name is Sullivan."

Miss Crichton smiled. "Why Sullivan, dear?"

"My grandpa. His name was Sullivan. He was the only person I ever knew who really loved me. The way I love my baby." She looked up into Miss Crichton's eyes, and the older woman felt her own smile growing as she recognized the joy in the girl's face—quite possibly the first time it had ever found its way there in all of Lucky's sixteen years on this earth. "He's perfect, isn't he?"

Miss Crichton looked into the baby's face. While newborns often looked the same to her, this one was different. And she was pleased to see very little of Dr. Gerhardt in the tiny features, reminiscent as they were of Lucky's fine bone structure and petite form.

"He's beautiful, Lucky. He really is."

"Em?" Nate was no longer whispering, urgency giving way to near-desperation.

Miss Crichton took another run at getting them away. "Lucky, dear, we really need to go. Let me take the baby, and Nate will give you a hand so we can—"

"No."

"Lucky—"

"No one's taking him from me. He's all I have. No one's taking my baby."

"No one's going to take him from you, dear. We just need to get away from here quickly and quietly, and you're not going to be able to do that if you're carrying a baby."

Lucky tried anyway, but blood continued to flow from her, and she nearly dropped the baby as she doubled over in pain. She made it only as far as the hall before she admitted defeat and handed Sullivan to Miss Crichton. She then accepted Nate's offered arm for support as they continued to make their way back down the hall, following the lonely trail of bootprints illuminated in the flashlight's glow.

But progress was slow and so it happened that, as they approached the stairs leading from the basement level, they were interrupted by a wild shout from somewhere behind and the sound of thundering footsteps echoing off bare walls and floor.

"Run," Nate said as he placed Lucky next to the stairway's railing. "I'll hold them off."

Miss Crichton opened her mouth to protest but was cut off by one last urgent command. "Go! Get out of here!"

The sound of approaching men grew louder now, and Miss Crichton had a baby and a teenage girl to consider, so she did as Nate had asked and made for the stairs.

Lucky managed the stairs but, by the time she reached the top, any strength she'd had left had waned, leaving her sinking to the floor against the wall.

From below came the sounds of a struggle, and Miss Crichton fought every urge to return when she heard Nate cry out in pain.

But Sullivan was snuggled against her bosom now, and Lucky had collapsed, leaving the nurse with far too much to handle as it was.

"Lucky, I know it's a lot, but I need you to fight through and come with me. It's not much further. You can make it."

"No, I can't."

"Lucky, please."

"I'm so tired, Emily. I can't do it."

The sounds of fighting continued, and this time the yelp of pain belonged to someone other than Nate. Even so, the former caretaker wasn't as young as he once was; he wouldn't hold them off for long.

Miss Crichton looked from Lucky to Sullivan and back again. It felt like something of a low blow, but if she had to play on the mother-child bond, she would. "Think of your baby. Think of Sullivan."

The tears were back in Lucky's eyes, only this time they didn't signify pain or fear; they were tears of defeat.

"Take him."

"No, Lucky. I told you—"

"Take him, Emily. I'll find somewhere to hide, and I'll sneak out while they're looking for me. I'll find you later."

"I'm not leaving without you. Now—"

"No. I mean it. I won't make it. Please, take my baby. Protect him. Please, Emily. Please don't let Lockwood or my family get my baby. Hide him for me, please. It's the only way to save him. Please don't let anyone get Sullivan."

And so Miss Crichton made the hardest decision of her entire life.

It would haunt her forever.

⸻

NATE TURNED up after daybreak the next morning, bloodied and beaten and bringing with him a tale that both amazed and sickened Miss Crichton.

Nate had found himself up against the doctor and the young orderly Larson Hackman, had managed to hold his own for some time. The slight doctor provided little challenge and Hackman, though bigger and stronger, had no real experience in a fight—at least not one that didn't involve backup from fellow orderlies.

But Hackman was stubborn, refusing to stay down, and Gerhardt wasn't opposed to fighting dirty. And Nate had to admit he wasn't getting any younger, and a battle that might once have been his to take now belonged to his opponents.

At least until Lucky had stepped in.

Where she'd come from, Nate didn't know. But she'd landed a solid kick to the side of Gerhardt's knee, dropping him howling to the floor just before he could blindside Nate.

Nate and Hackman stood a moment, startled into a temporary ceasefire as they stared down at the wild-eyed girl, and Nate recounted a chill running down his spine as he took in the expression on her face, the look in her eyes.

"She wasn't a scared little girl anymore, Em," he'd said that morning. "She was a woman hell-bent on revenge."

Miss Crichton corrected him. "Not revenge," she said. "She was protecting her child."

The fight had not ended there, Nate breaking the spell first and lunging at Hackman. But the orderly hadn't been far behind. The two struggled, but Nate managed to get in one last solid punch, spinning the younger man around. Hackman reeled into the wall, dropped to the floor and stayed there. Nate ushered the girl toward the stairs.

But Gerhardt, it seemed, had one last trick up his sleeve. The doctor's hand grabbed Nate's ankle in a vicelike grip and Nate, not expecting the move, toppled forward and banged his head, knocking himself out on the stairs.

The next thing he remembered was coming to in the woods

surrounding Lockwood, head and body so pained he could barely move.

And Lucky, the young girl he credited with saving his life, was nowhere to be found. Nor, to Miss Crichton's knowledge, was she ever seen again.

At least, not until now.

THE STORY HAD BEEN ENOUGH to change Dez's view of Lucienne. Anyone who had risked her life to save her child—especially given that child was Sully—deserved some serious credit in his books.

After dropping off Miss Crichton, Dez tried the number Lucienne had called him from earlier, but got nothing but a message reporting the phone was out of the service area. Burner phone was Dez's first thought, which made perfect sense given Lucienne's need to keep her presence here under the radar.

Once again, Dez was left with more questions than answers. Was the reason for her lack of an online presence because she lived under an assumed name? If so, what was it and what would it reveal about her? And, more importantly, why had she lied about Sully's birth? Not only had she said nothing about Gerhardt being the father, or that Sully had taken his first breaths inside Lockwood, but Lucienne hadn't been honest about how Sully had come to be left on the doorstep.

Lucienne had said she'd left her baby there. But Miss Crichton provided a wholly different version of events, telling Dez she'd kept Sully for a full month while she and Nate—the latter in hiding after the events of that night—searched for Lucky. But the girl had disappeared, no indication she was anywhere near Lockwood and no sign of her anywhere else. Eventually, they'd run out of places to look and avenues to explore and, as Miss Crichton's name and address were readily available in the phonebook, she and Nate eventually accepted Lucky's continued absence meant one of two things.

Either she was on the run and had decided her son needed a more stable life than she could provide. Or she was dead.

Either way, Lucky wasn't coming back for Sullivan.

Miss Crichton, deciding the baby was better off—and far better protected—starting over free of the stigma of his conception and birth, left Sully on the doorstep of a social worker she knew well, a lovely woman who would ensure the baby was looked after. But she'd left one clue before finding a spot to surreptitiously keep watch until Denise found the child: the note that gave his name as Sullivan. It had been a way to honour the girl who had risked her life to save her child, and a means for her to one day find him should she decide she was at last free to do so. But it also gave the baby the opportunity to carry with him a little piece of his mother, the only piece he might ever have.

Dez realized, while most of the questions remaining would require answers from Lucienne, Sully's current location was not one of them.

Nor was the problem of how much he should reveal to his brother once he found him.

28

SULLY PACED in the small room, time ticking by with no sign of Brennan and therefore no answers on what had happened to Dez.

His body ached from the assault, and he rubbed at a sore spot where ribs met abdomen, worry for his brother minimizing the physical pain he might otherwise be suffering now.

The fact Brennan hadn't returned could mean Dez had killed or hospitalized the guy, which wouldn't trouble Sully so long as Dez hadn't gotten himself killed in the process. Or, if Sully's worst nightmare had come true, it might mean that Brennan just hadn't made it back yet. If that were the case, if Brennan eventually walked back into this room, Sully had made up his mind he would kill the man or die trying. The alternative—continued life in captivity with the knowledge his brother was dead because of him—was not an option he was prepared to accept.

The wait with its accompanying dark thoughts was driving him to the edge of madness, and Sully sought a temporary out by returning to his mother's journal, lowering himself back onto the mattress and pulling the notebook from his inside pocket.

He'd stopped reading when he'd first seen his own name, written in the teenager's bubbly handwriting. She'd used strokes that appeared neater and more careful than the surrounding words. As if his name itself was sacred text to the young writer.

Needing to settle his mind, Sully forced himself to focus on the battered pages resting in his lap.

He read further entries speaking of Sullivan, of Lucienne's fears of Gerhardt, of her anger at her mother and stepfather, of her guilt over Artie's death and of questions about where her birth father had ended up or why Rhona never came to see her.

Then came a passage in which Lucienne mentioned a woman named Emily.

I will never see my son again, at least not through living eyes. My mother and Wayne aren't going to let me leave here and, anyway, I'm sure by now Sullivan is being cared for by someone else. Maybe Emily kept him, but I kind of hope not. What if Gerhardt finds him? I would die before I'd allow what happened to me to happen to my baby boy. And if Gerhardt finds out Emily came for me, her life, and Sullivan's, would be as good as over.

I hope he finds a family somewhere who loves him the way I do, the way I wish I could. If things go better than I think, I will find him one day. And if they don't, if I don't leave here alive, then I'll find a way to watch over my boy. And I'll make sure he's never alone, not even when he feels like he is, when he feels the way I do now.

The entry ended there and, when Sully flipped the page, he discovered the journal concluded there too.

Which left him wondering what had happened after Lucienne had penned those last words. Had she ever made it out? If so, had she ever sought him out in the hopes of reforming that bond they'd had only moments to forge? Or had her life ended instead, perhaps here in this room?

He received his answer as he had so many in his life, an unexpected find setting his world on its head.

There, tucked deeply into the crease between the pages, was a single strand of long, purple hair. And while the puzzle that was his life still needed assembling, it was like finding a box containing not only a number of previously missing pieces, but a picture of what the puzzle was supposed to look like once complete.

He felt her presence so strongly then, it was like a current of electricity had passed between them. Slowly he raised his eyes, his pulse galloping through his veins, yet his heart catching in his throat. She stared down at him through eyes filled with cautious hope tempered with the fear he had so frequently seen there.

"Mom?"

Sully's voice cracked as he said the word, his emotion as unanticipated as his reality.

And, as the corners of her mouth turned up, slowly at first, and then a little more, it occurred to him he had never before seen the Purple Girl smile.

29

Dez had hit a roadblock and it pushed him directly into Riverview Park.

He found Bulldog on his way up from the bank, grinning one of those ear-to-ear smiles that helped him keep friends despite his occasional sour turns.

His voice boomed across the park when he saw Dez. "Copper! Anything?"

"Keep it down, man."

Bulldog kept quiet until they met at a park bench. "Hey, I wasn't going to say anything about our mutual friend. So, anything on that?"

Dez frowned. "I actually came to ask you the same thing."

Bulldog scrubbed his jawline. "Our boy is still just like one of his ghosts. Far as the world's concerned, he's dead and no one's seen or heard anything about him. One thing came up, though. Some old guy in one of the buildings across the way saw a couple people dragging some dude to a van early yesterday morning. Figure it had to be around the time you and me were chatting, 'cuz he remembers seeing you. You're kinda hard to miss."

"Hang on, Bulldog, back up. This 'dude' you're talking about."

"Yeah, the old guy thought he was three sheets to the wind,

way he looked. Some young homeless scruff, he figured. Problem is, my source on this didn't bother getting a better description, and the guy's left town now for holidays with his kids. I checked. Said he thought he saw one of the two people pull off some kinda mask. Both people appeared to be in their twenties. One was a man, one a woman."

"A woman? You're sure?"

"Yeah, what he said."

"And you're sure he said she was young too?"

"Yep, apparently. He was a little more descriptive about her. Said she was a looker. On the small side, but seemed to be pretty strong, the way she was helping to hold the guy up between them. White woman, blonde hair, nice rack. Wasn't a whole lot else he had to say."

Dez had no doubt they were talking about Sully's kidnapping here, meaning the man mentioned was Brennan. It was the woman troubling Dez, the description doing little to provide a decent clue to her identity. Prior to learning what he had of Lucienne today, it had occurred to him she might have had some role to play in this and was simply keeping close to Dez to ensure he wasn't getting too near the truth. But he'd thought better of his earlier suspicions, and now this description proved it. Sure, Lucienne looked younger than her forty years. But he was willing to bet whoever had been in this park yesterday was not the woman who had slept on his pullout bed that night.

One other question occurred to Dez, but Bulldog didn't have much insight on that, either. The vehicle involved had been a delivery van, nondescript and white. An older model, bare of markings with no discernible licence plate. The only item of note was the tires, which appeared to be missing rims, at least on the passenger side visible to the witness.

It wasn't enough to go on, particularly since the man wasn't around for further questioning. Even so, Dez took his leave from Bulldog, intent on heading to the witness's building to check for any neighbours who might know a way to reach him. If Dez was lucky, he'd leave with a phone number, but he wouldn't complain if all he came away with was a name. If there was one thing he was good at, it was finding people. People who hadn't faked their own deaths and gone off the grid before ending up imprisoned somewhere else, anyway.

His course was interrupted by Eva's ringtone sounding in his pocket.

"Dez, where are you? Are you okay?"

"Fine. Why?"

"Don't even try it, you jerk. I know all about it. Raynor's been going nuts trying to find you. He came to me asking if I could reach you, and he filled me in on everything you hadn't bothered to share. Had you been planning on telling me you spent the morning in the ER?"

"I had nothing to do with the man's death, Eva."

"I know that, dummy. I'm talking about you getting beaten up. Forbes said you have broken ribs."

Dez dropped his head into a hand, rubbing at his temples. He was going to kill Raynor. "One rib, and it's just a crack."

"Like that's different somehow. Why didn't you call me?"

"Because I didn't want to get you worried over nothing."

"In what imaginary world does this pass as nothing? Someone tried to kill you."

"He didn't. I'm a little banged up, but I'll be fine. Listen, Evie, I knew you'd come. That's why I didn't call. I knew I'd be stuck there into the noon hour and you'd be left trying to figure out what to do with Kayleigh or what to tell her. Neither of us would have wanted her to see me like that. It just seemed a better option to wait on it and tell you later."

"And were you going to tell me later?"

Unfortunately, the question wasn't one Dez could answer both honestly and in a way that would avoid frustrating her further. "Evie …."

"Damn it, Dez. It's a damn good thing I'm not there in front of you right now, or I'd put you back in the hospital."

Dez grinned into his phone. "I love it when you play rough."

"Shut up. Now listen, Forbes really needs to talk to you. And before you freak out, you're in the clear on the guy's death. The coroner spotted a track mark from a needle in the crook of the guy's arm, and they sent a blood sample for a quick tox screen. They found a lethal dose of some sort of tranquilizer."

Dez guessed azaperon or zolazepam, the drugs the kidnappers had used to down Pax and quite likely Sully. He thought back to when he entered the guy's hospital room. "The constable said a nurse went in to see the guy shortly before he died. I didn't see her, but the officer should have a description."

"Forbes is all over that. I really think you need to give him a call."

"Not now, Eva. I've got too much on my plate. I've got a lead I need to follow up. Can I give you a call later?"

"Don't you dare hang up on me. I've got something else for you here. I've been doing some digging based on what we read about Lucienne Dule. I found Artie's file. It was buried pretty deep back in records, but it was there."

"Anything new?"

"I don't know. I mean, nothing jumping out at me exactly, but I haven't been down as deep in this as you have. I've signed the file out and I'm thinking you should have a look, see if anything clicks."

"You're beautiful, you know that?"

"Crap."

"Hey, I'm serious."

"No, I mean Forbes is coming this way," Eva said. "Listen, I'll call you later, okay? Make sure you pick up."

"For you, always."

He wasn't sure if she heard his last statement as the call was dropped immediately after. Now he had only to sit here and wait.

And worry.

Eva's next phone call, coming within five minutes of her ending the previous one, didn't bring Dez much relief.

"Don't hate me," she said.

"What did you do?"

"Forbes took the file."

"What? Why? You weren't breaking any rules signing out a closed file."

"No, but I was breaking the rules signing it out for someone who isn't authorized to see it."

"You didn't tell him that, did you?"

"I didn't have to," Eva said. "Forbes is investigating what happened to Lachlan. It's obvious you know more about that case than Forbes does, and it's just as obvious you know more about Lachlan's most recent client than you've let on. Forbes scanned the file and he saw the name Lucienne. Things went downhill pretty fast after that."

"Define downhill."

"If you look it up online, you'll see a picture of me on the unemployment line."

"Christ, he's not reporting you for this, is he?"

"He said he'll keep it to himself as long as you meet with him. Right now."

Forbes had played his ace, leaving Dez with no choice but to fold.

"I'm sorry, Snowman."

"It's all right, Evie. Thanks for trying. Just tell me where and when."

Dez wasn't surprised to learn Forbes wanted to be picked up. It was a lot harder to get in a good punch from within the confines of a vehicle, particularly while driving.

Dez had expected smug from his new passenger. What he got instead was a good dose of paranoid.

"Jesus, what the hell's wrong with you?" Dez asked, taking in Forbes's paler-than-usual face and the shoulders hunched so near his ears it was a wonder they didn't impair the guy's hearing.

"Just drive."

"Where to?"

"Doesn't matter."

Forbes had a battered file in hand and was working on adding a few dog ears of his own as he bent it and toyed with its edges. Dez tried to read the name on it, hoping it was indeed the file he needed, but Forbes was playing around with it too much to allow more than a second to scan the writing on the front.

Dez drove a few blocks with no further conversation passing between them. While he normally believed silence was golden as far as the two of them were concerned, right now it was downright nerve-wracking.

"Is there something you want to discuss or would you rather I hum the theme song to *Driving Miss Daisy*?" he asked.

Forbes looked up, eyes a little large as if he'd momentarily forgotten Dez was there. Dez figured there a smart-ass comment would be coming his way, but it turned out his passenger wasn't playing.

"Riverview Cemetery," Forbes said. "It's quiet there. Anyway, it's where everything started, isn't it?"

"Usually cemeteries are places things end, not start." Dez's attempt at a joke sounded hollow even to his own ears, his anxiety taking a couple more steps up that internal ladder toward full-blown panic. What did Forbes need quiet for, anyway? The way things had been playing out lately, Dez was all for large crowds full of potential witnesses, which was exactly what he wouldn't get where they were headed. Then there was the matter of Forbes's use of the term "where everything started." It was unclear what he'd meant by that, but Dez was banking on its meaning nothing good for him.

"Wouldn't you rather head to, I don't know, maybe the park or something?"

That at least put a smile on Forbes's face. "Scared, Braddock?"

There was no backing down from that challenge, so Dez responded with a "Piss off" and a flick of his signal, turning his vehicle in the direction of the graveyard.

As suspected, the place was all but deserted, and it didn't do Dez's nerves any favours as Forbes directed him to drive them further in. It wasn't until they were near the few rows of standing tombs near the back of the cemetery's east side that Forbes told him to stop.

Dez pushed the stick into park and turned to face the other man. "So what do you want to see me about?"

Forbes didn't answer immediately, and Dez could physically see the thoughts passing across Forbes's face as he considered how best to answer. He settled for tapping hard at the file folder in his lap. "What do you want with this?"

That answered the question about the file's subject. "I can't discuss it with you. Not yet."

"Then you're not going to see it."

"Come on, man—"

"No, you come on," Forbes said. "You've been turning up left, right and centre lately, and it's never in a good way. Now I've got stuff I need to work out, and I think—no, I *know*—you've got answers I need. You can cooperate or you can risk an obstruction charge and the lifelong guilt of putting your wife out of work beside you."

"You fucking asshole."

Dez guessed he looked every bit as pissed off as he felt when he saw Forbes flinch, so he went with it. "You do what you want where I'm concerned, but you mess with my wife, we've got a problem. You hear me, Raynor?"

Forbes's response was to distance himself from the threat, getting out of the SUV. Unfortunately, he took the folder with him, leaving Dez to follow his lead.

Forbes was pretending to read the writing on one of the old family tombs, the bodies it held locked behind a wrought iron gate. It was clear he was trying to get his game face back in place, but the man's gaze wasn't focused on anything in front of him like he was making out. He had turned inward and, judging by what Dez could make out on the cop's face, he didn't like what he saw there.

"Look, I came out here with you," Dez said. "Now, what do you want?"

Forbes didn't turn his head. "We both have wives we love, even if they don't love us back. At least not the way we need them to." The answer was as cryptic as it was frustrating to someone who just needed this meeting over and done.

"What the hell are you talking about? Did you seriously drag me out here to have a chinwag about our love lives?"

Forbes gave a barely there headshake. "I need you to tell me what you're up to and why."

"Look, Lachlan was working on something when he was assaulted. He asked me for help but needs his client protected. Problem is, I'm trying to piece it together but he didn't give me much to go on."

Forbes's eyes snapped from the tomb onto Dez's face. "Bullshit. You know exactly what you're working on. Why else would you need this?" Again, Forbes indicated the file, holding it up between them. Dez was tempted to grab it and run, but there was too much on the line that stood to impact the people he loved.

"I don't know what you're talking about, Raynor."

"You're crap at lying, Braddock. But just in case any part of you is on the fence here, let me help you out. I haven't had much time with this file, but I've scanned the lead investigator's final report. It's interesting because the name Lucienne pops out pretty damn quick. So, tell me. Would this be the same Lucienne as the one you mentioned as Lachlan's last client? The same Lucienne you're apparently trying to help now?"

"I need to see that file."

"What you need is to tell me the truth."

"It's not mine to tell," Dez said. "If you want answers, go to

Lachlan. Or track down Lucienne. But I can't say anything. I promised."

"Promises don't mean anything where you're going."

Dez barked out a quick laugh. "What, seriously? You're going to haul me in over this?"

But Forbes, it turned out, wasn't interested in hauling him anywhere. He pulled a gun—not his service sidearm, but an old revolver—and aimed it at Dez's heart.

Dez struggled to drag his eyes from the barrel of the weapon back to Forbes's face. He couldn't fully get there. "Put that away, man."

"I can't do that."

"That gun's so old, it's just as likely to backfire or explode in your hand as it is to kill me. Put it away."

"I can't." And, this time, Dez could hear desperation in the words, enough that he was finally able to pull his gaze up to Forbes's. The man's face was twisted, not in rage but in some sort of undefinable pain as his eyes blinked back the first signs of unshed tears.

"What are you doing, Forbes?" But the question had become unnecessary, just a way to fill the silence. Because it was clear what Forbes was doing, or at least what he intended to do.

Dez knew if he turned his head, he'd be able to look to the spot where his family was buried. If Forbes followed through on his reason for being here, Dez was about to join them.

30

Forbes didn't have the look of a killer but, in Dez's experience, that didn't mean much.

Murder wasn't like it was on television. Many gangsters of Dez's acquaintance now serving life sentences had relied on the haze of alcohol and peer pressure from their bros to take a life—at least the first time. And Dez had read that abusive men who killed a spouse were unlikely to do so again.

Murder was a messy business, and people didn't die quick and quiet. As a Major Crimes investigator, Forbes knew what he was in for and, while he didn't particularly like Dez, he was a fellow human being at the end of the day. A shot to the heart would kill, but not immediately. It could take as long as thirty seconds to a minute, and they both knew that was plenty long enough to give Forbes some lifelong PTSD issues to wrestle with.

"You don't want to do this," Dez said, the statement more observational than an attempt to convince. Because, right now anyway, it didn't look like Forbes needed a whole lot of convincing.

Then again .... "I don't have a choice."

"Yes, you do. You can tell me why you're doing this."

Forbes shook his head, the movement more reminiscent of chasing away a fly or a bad thought than an indication of a "no."

"Come on, Forbes. You know what will happen if you kill me."

"No one will know it was me. This gun is untraceable."

Dez caught himself before he could say Eva would know. If he didn't find a way out of this, she would make a logical next target.

"There's always a way. You know that better than I do, given the section you work in."

Forbes didn't say anything, but he didn't lower the gun either. Dez checked the distance, figured he was within reach of the revolver if he took a quick step forward. Of course, bullets moved a lot faster.

The best approach seemed to be continuing the conversation, and Dez took a moment to gauge Forbes's mind. If he could grasp his reasoning, he could try to deconstruct it, pull it out from under Forbes before this got to the point where there were no take-backs. It wasn't enough that Forbes disliked him, hated him even. Dez thought he found a clue in what Forbes had said a few minutes ago about his wife, about loving her when she didn't love him back.

And then Dez saw it. The woman who'd helped Brennan kidnap Sully had been described as blonde and attractive with a large bust—all apt descriptors for Greta Raynor.

"Is she putting you up to this?" Dez asked. "Because this isn't you."

"How the hell would you know what I am? You don't even know me."

"I know you're a cop. A good one, right?"

"Don't try it, Braddock. We both know what you think of me as an investigator. Anyway, I'm a husband first."

"I've only ever tried to help her."

"Yeah? Well, she tells me you're the one who's been stalking her."

"But you don't believe her," Dez said. "If you did, I'd be dead already. Face it, she's got some pretty significant problems, Forbes."

"Her problems are none of your goddamn business."

"Really? 'Cuz I'm being held at gunpoint right now by her estranged husband, apparently under her say-so. I'd say her problems have pretty much become mine."

Forbes appeared even more uncertain than before, and that was saying something. Dez dared to take a step forward, but stopped when Forbes looked up and solidified his stance, turning it into an unwavering two-handed grip as the file dropped unheeded to the grass.

"Back the fuck up, Braddock!" But Forbes followed up the command by taking a backward step of his own.

Dez stopped walking but not talking. The conversation, he realized, might be the only thing saving him right now.

"There's a reason she sent you to kill me, and it's not that I've done anything wrong, is it? It's that I've done too much right. I'm too close to something she doesn't want revealed."

Someone she doesn't want revealed.

Forbes's already fragile surface cracked further, china on display in a shop Dez's bull was trying to bust into. "I need you to tell me what you know, Braddock. I need to know what's going on with her, and I need to find out where she is, if she's safe. So who is this Lucienne Dule, and what does she have to do with Greta?"

Dez had a decision to make. Keeping quiet about Sully, Lucienne and the whole business might protect his brother, but only until Forbes dug deeper into Greta's activities—and he would, no question. Then there was Brennan's warning that Sully was running out of time.

The alternative was to tell Forbes the truth and expose Sully to a man Dez didn't trust to shine his shoes. But, at least in that version of reality, Dez had a chance of getting his brother out alive if they played their cards right.

Dez decided on option two, with a catch. "I don't know everything, all right? Not by any stretch. But what I've come to believe is that Greta and Brennan Wakeman were involved in the kidnapping of a man yesterday, and it has something to do with Lucienne Dule. I think the man is family to Lucienne, but I honestly have no idea why they would have taken him, or where. I'm hoping that file will tell me something I haven't been able to figure out yet."

"So the attack on Lachlan and then on you, those were both Brennan trying to keep this thing quiet?"

"Yeah, I think so. Only problem was, Brennan was getting cold feet. He wanted out. But he was in too deep, and someone took him out before he could say anything useful."

Dez expected Forbes to say something about Greta, about how she might well have found herself in the same terrible predicament as her accomplice. But no such statement followed, and the reason became clear as Dez stood there, watching for emotions on Forbes's face that never appeared.

"Does Greta work at a vet clinic?"

There was emotion there now. Not fear or worry, but shame.

"Forbes?"

"She volunteers at a few places in the community. One of them's a vet clinic. She can't really hold down a proper job right now, but she loves being busy. Takes her mind off things, she says."

"She also volunteers at Lockwood."

"With the seniors, yeah."

"How long?"

"A few years," Forbes said. "Why?"

"Did she ever mention a resident by the name of Lorinda?"

"No. Who's that?"

"Lucienne's mother."

"And why should that matter? Who are either of them to Greta?"

"Search me," Dez said. And he meant it, although he was hoping to have an answer shortly. "I need to see that file."

"Why? It's ancient. It can't have anything in it that's going to help us."

"Look, just trust me on this, okay?"

"I don't trust you on anything." But Forbes took a few steps back nonetheless, enough to allow Dez a free run at the file.

Taking the chance Forbes wouldn't shoot him in the head, Dez knelt to pick up the folder and its contents, which had partially spilled out from between their cardboard cover. Standing with file in hand, he flipped through the papers inside.

There were the usual scene and autopsy photos, which Dez did his best to ignore, the image of a drowned child the last thing he needed to add to the already horrific contents of his brain. There were a coroner's report, notes and reports from the officers who'd handled the case at various points and in various ways, and the final report from the lead investigator Forbes had already mentioned.

There was a lot to read, a task not made easier by the gun hovering within Dez's peripheral vision.

"You know, I'd really appreciate it if you'd put that thing away if you're not going to use it," Dez said.

"I haven't made up my mind yet."

Dez met Forbes's eye and managed a smile. "Bullshit. You made up your mind before you walked in here. You just didn't know it."

Forbes had returned to an uncommitted one-handed grip, which wavered as he considered. "Don't try anything."

"I've got bigger fish to fry."

At last the gun dropped completely, and Forbes tucked it safely back into the back of his pants.

"I'd put the safety back on if I were you," Dez said. "One wrong move, you'll blow a second hole in your ass."

Forbes's reply was mumbled but Dez made it out easily enough, anyway. "I never took the safety off in the first place."

Threat subsided, Dez's focus shifted entirely to his task of reading through the lead investigator's report. It quickly became clear that, while this report contained a few additional details, there wasn't much Dez hadn't already known thanks to Lachlan's own accumulation of material.

"Damn it."

"What?" Forbes asked.

"Nothing. I mean, there's nothing else here."

"Let me see."

Dez handed over the file, and moved in next to the older man, scanning the pages as Forbes turned them. Once again, Dez averted his gaze for the photos.

But Forbes didn't. And, finally, he stopped flipping the pages altogether.

Dez's need to see what had caught Forbes's attention outweighed his fear of catching a glimpse of the little boy in the bathroom. He was grateful all he saw was a photo of the front of the large house, its numbered address of 752 displayed on a flowered arch that stood where two sides of a front yard picket fence met.

There wasn't much else to see, no people within the photo, so Dez found himself repeating Forbes's earlier query. "What?"

Forbes looked to be shaking himself out of memory as he lifted his face toward Dez. "Huh?"

"This house. You know it."

Forbes returned his gaze to the photo and nodded slowly. "Greta took me there once, back when we were still dating. It was deserted by then. Said she'd spent some time there as a child."

There was a connection there somewhere—had to be—between Greta and the Dule family, but this wasn't the time to figure it out. Right now, Greta's connection to the house, however tenuous, was enough to merit a drive there to check, particularly given it was empty. It could make the perfect place, after all, to keep a captive.

"What's the address?" Dez asked, leaning in and reaching to flip back through the file.

Forbes spoke before Dez could get his hands on the file, speaking from memory. "752 Dark Ridge Lane."

The words—or one of them anyway—hit Dez's brain like a slap. His mind caught on the word "Dark"—only it was no longer Forbes's voice he heard speaking it. It was Brennan's.

Brennan had been trying to give him a location, after all.

"Come on," Dez said. "We need to get there. Now."

But Forbes wasn't looking as gung-ho about the idea. "Hang on, Braddock. You do know that Dark Ridge Lane is in The Forks, right?"

The Forks. Once the site of many of the city's most genteel homes and businesses, now the perfect setting for a zombie flick—provided you could round up and safely pen all the criminals that had moved in since the flood had left the place deserted.

"You don't just walk into The Forks," Forbes said. "We'd be robbed, beaten and left for dead as soon as we crossed that bridge."

A fair point. And yet not one Dez was prepared to concede.

"I know we'd be taking a chance. A big one."

"Damn straight, it's a big one. The KRPD and every other emergency service has sworn the place off. It's no man's land. We go in there, we're going without backup."

"You love Greta, right? Well, I think she's closing in on doing something bad. Really bad. Something that will land her in prison for the rest of her life. Now, I'm going in there to stop her. Are you coming or not?"

Put like that, Forbes didn't waste time giving it much thought. "Let's go."

The two of them ran back to the SUV. Dust billowed from behind the tires as Dez accelerated away.

31

SULLY HADN'T HEARD the key in the lock, or the door open.

But as he awoke from a fitful sleep, he discovered he wasn't alone.

A sharp intake of breath passed his lips as he focused on Brennan's face, hovering just above his in the dim room.

Sully's first thought was that his worst fears had become reality, that Dez was dead. But as his exhaustion-addled mind cleared, Sully looked at Brennan. Really looked. He was there. And yet he wasn't. And as Sully stared up at him, he realized he could see the edge of the lightbulb through Brennan's right shoulder.

"Who did this to you?" Sully asked. Then, hopefully, "Dez?"

Brennan shook his head. He tried to speak but Sully couldn't make anything out.

"I can't hear you, Brennan."

The other man once more opened his mouth, trying again to form the words. The image of him wasn't clear enough for Sully to make out; Brennan's lips and the message they struggled to convey were impossible to read. But his eyes and his expression said plenty where his voice could not, and there was no question what Brennan meant to say. *I'm sorry.*

Sully's thoughts dove into the blackest pit they could find.

"Dez? Please tell me he's okay, man."

This time, Brennan nodded yes.

Sully closed his eyes and let the tension out in one long exhale. Relief proved short-lived. Now awake, he heard the lock turning and, given Brennan was already with him—and dead—he worried who was about to come through that door.

He'd been expecting another male, so was surprised to see a woman. She was blonde and attractive, probably in her late thirties or early forties; slim and shorter than Sully's six feet. And there was something else about her. Something familiar.

Something that had him focusing on her face despite the gun in her hand. "Who are you?"

The woman's answering smile supplied the appearance of warmth, belying the fact he was still here, confined in this small cell as she positioned herself in front of the door.

He supposed he should have been more surprised by her reply. "I'm your Aunt Rhona. I can't imagine you've heard of me."

Lucky's journal had told him about Rhona, revealing just enough about her and the Dule family tree that Sully wished the Braddocks were his blood.

But the journal and its contents—once his mother's secret—were now his, so he shook his head and waited for whatever explanation she planned on offering.

"I hope you weren't hurt too badly," she said. "I know Brennan could be a little rough, and I'm sorry about that. There really wasn't any other way."

"Any other way for what?"

"To ensure you were kept safe here until we could be certain about you," she said. "Now we're out of time. Dez is a lovely guy; he cares a lot about you. But he's looking for you, and he's getting too close."

"So you sent Brennan after him."

"We didn't have a choice."

"There's always a choice."

"Not this time. This is too important. You're too important."

"What does that mean?"

"I know you have questions. So do we. I'd hoped the investigator I hired might answer some of them, but there are some things only you can tell us. Maybe we can give you some answers in return."

Sully had been about to ask who she meant by "we" when Rhona turned and stepped back into the hall. Sully thought about rushing her before sober second thought held him back. She was armed, after all, and there was the added threat of the unknown, the fact he had no idea who else might be standing on the other side of that door.

And there was no denying the other reason keeping him rooted here: curiosity. He'd spent his life questioning who he was, where he'd come from, why he was born with this ability. Now, for the first time, he was on the verge of receiving answers and, even if they did nothing to help him, they might be enough to allow him to help Lucky.

Rhona reappeared, pushing before her a stick-thin figure in a wheelchair with a stare as cold as death.

"This is your grandmother, Lorinda Usher," Rhona said.

"Hold your tongue, girl." The woman leaned forward in her chair, eyes narrowing as they fixed Sully in a glare that dared him to look away. "Step into the light, boy."

Sully fought for a defiant sneer he wasn't sure he had the immediate strength to back. "What light?"

His jibe drew no verbal reply, so he provided the response she'd sought in the first place, taking one step forward to stand below the low-watt bulb.

"Pull your hair back."

Rhona's gun was fixed as firmly on him as Lorinda's dissecting gaze, so Sully obeyed, raking fingers through knotted strands of hair and drawing it behind his ears.

Rhona's eyes shifted from Sully to the top of the older woman's head, as if looking for confirmation. From her angle, there would be no way to see what Sully did: the shine of recognition upon the older woman's face, the lift of a brow, the upturn of one corner of a tight-lipped mouth.

"Oh, yes," Lorinda said. "That's him, all right. I would know those eyes anywhere. Those are Lucienne's eyes." She sat forward another few inches, might have toppled but for her white-knuckled grip on the chair's armrests. "And her lips, I believe. Hard to tell under the beard. But your nose, boy. That's my father's nose." She tapped her own as an offering of proof, and Sully recognized a bump along the bridge that matched the one he saw when he looked in a mirror.

"She named you Sullivan," Lorinda said. "That was my father's name, you know."

Sully said nothing, and the woman read the silence.

"You did know. How? You couldn't have known any more about us than we knew of you." She was awaiting a reply. Sully held his tongue. Lucky's journal was rolled within an inside pocket where, were it a living creature, it would feel the staccato rhythm of his heart.

Once again, his silence had formed a response, revealing more than he'd hoped.

The other side of Lorinda's mouth turned up, a self-satisfied and knowing leer. "Of course. You see them too. You've probably seen *her*, haven't you? Tell me, is she here now?"

Lorinda had unwittingly provided some quid pro quo: Sully's ability to see the dead was not shared by his biological grandmother.

Mara Braddock had taught her foster son chess. Sully wasn't about to enter any competitions, but the lessons had instilled in him an ability to think a few moves ahead. In holding his tongue, there was a chance he could draw out the answers he needed without revealing more of himself than necessary.

"I don't know what you're talking about."

Lorinda's sneer told him she was playing her queen. "There's no need to hide from us, boy. We know. *I* know. The male line in the Dule family is cursed with evil. Once we learned of your existence, we knew you had to be dealt with. I don't need you to admit anything to me. The very fact I know you are Lucienne's son is all the proof I need. We managed to gather plenty of evidence, but this is what I needed, a chance to see you for myself. So I'm going to ask again. Can you see her?"

"What do you mean, I need to be 'dealt with'?"

"I think you know. There's a reason, after all, Lucienne concealed your birth from us. Is she here?"

"You said the male line is cursed. How?"

Lorinda Usher looked frail, but the voice that boomed from her chest told him there was plenty enough fight left in her. "Tell me the truth, boy, or suffer the consequences! Do you see her?"

The reasons for holding onto his secret were fading as quickly as Sully's remaining life seemed to be. There was no point denying it anymore, not when it seemed they already had most of the answers they claimed to be seeking.

"I can't see her, but she's here."

"If you can't see her, how do you know?"

"I've been seeing her my whole life. I know how it feels when she's around."

Lorinda raised an eyebrow. "And what has she told you about us?"

"Nothing. I've never heard her speak. I can't hear them."

Lorinda's eyebrows both lifted, this time. "My father had the same limitation. Lucienne, I believe, saw and heard. I didn't know about her at first. Not until after Artie. I thought Artie was the only one."

"Artie saw them too?"

"He would come to me at night in tears, talking about the bleeding man. It took me a while to understand he wasn't scared. It was that he could feel the man's pain. And I knew the man he was seeing was my father."

There was movement in a corner, a shifting in the shadows, and Sully saw the image of a man slouched there, holding the hand of a sodden blond toddler who Sully could only assume was

Artie. The child was otherwise unmarked, but the older ghost's skin was blackened and charred, blood pouring from a gash in his head. One shoulder was out of joint, the arm badly twisted from a break. And he was stooped, not from age or disease, but from what Sully suspected was a broken back.

Sully followed the ghost's sightline to Rhona. "He was pushed."

Rhona squinted from what, to her, was likely empty space back to Sully. And he could see the fear there. "He fell."

"I only see them if someone killed them." The broken man continued to stare, the agony in his eyes going beyond that of simple physical pain. Sully continued, speaking for him. "Why did you do it? He was your grandfather. And he was a good man. If he wasn't, my mother wouldn't have named me after him."

"Because he was a man," Lorinda said. "Because we had no choice. Once the door is unlocked, there is no stopping the darkness. The women of this family have a duty to keep that door sealed."

Rhona provided the explanations her mother was circling. "We always knew there were unnatural abilities in our family, people who saw and heard things that weren't part of our world. Until I dug back through our family tree, we just thought insanity ran in the family. As I learned more about the Dule line, we came to realize it was far worse. There are stories of ancestors who, in cold blood, killed family and friends. My own great-grandfather fled Scotland after being implicated in the murder of a minister and two altar boys at his village church. He claimed he had no recollection of it and believed he'd been possessed by the Devil.

"I learned the Dule men are born to kill, that they each claimed to have been possessed when they murdered their victims. At first, we didn't believe it. It was far easier to think they'd all suffered from some form of psychosis. But then my grandfather—an otherwise kind, rational and God-fearing man—began to claim he was being plagued by a demon."

"Until then, my father had kept the family stories to himself,"

Lorinda said. "When this entity came for him, he confessed every-thing to us. He'd hidden it because he knew what his father and his grandfather had become, and he broke his silence for that reason. He told us he felt he was being pulled down the same path, and he feared for his family. In the end, he accepted his fate where others had not."

Sully doubted his biological great-grandfather had accepted it in the manner Lorinda claimed. He was here, after all, broken in both form and psyche, eyes never leaving the image of his grand-daughter as she hovered behind Lorinda's chair, clutching a handgun Sully felt certain she was prepared to use.

"How old were you when you killed him?" he asked her.

"Seven," she said.

Her answer would have shocked him, had he not begun to doubt the existence of her soul. Some people were like that, he'd noticed. There were those who did terrible things because terrible things had been done to them. But there were those for whom the line between right and wrong was non-existent, their choice between the two dependent upon nothing more than a whim or an ill-conceived desire to protect themselves or the world from which they drew comfort.

"It wasn't hard, in the end. I knew it was the only way to save his soul. I tripped him as he led the way to the basement. Then I set fire to his house as Mother suggested. They say fire is purify-ing, that it rids body and soul of evil. It's how they used to save witches' souls from Hell."

"And no one suspected you?"

"I was a seven-year-old girl, and my tears were genuine, although not for the reason police believed. I didn't want to do it. But in the end, there was no choice. Three times, I did what my mother couldn't."

Three. Her grandfather, Sullivan Dule. Artie. And Lucky.

"I almost failed with Artie. I adored him. We all did. It was so easy to look at him and see nothing but good. But the night after Grandfather's death, Artie saw him, described his injuries in detail, and we knew. He had the curse. The ability to see and hear the dead has been passed to both males and females in our family, but only the women are strong enough to control it. I knew Artie would succumb just like the others. In time, Mother came to accept it too.

"I waited until the weekend Mother was away, once Bobby left us alone. I knew I couldn't set fire to the house, but I'd read dunking had been used to expose witches and to purify their souls. So I gave Artie a bath and I held him down. I held him until he stopped struggling."

A sob escaped Lorinda's lips, but she allowed nothing else, no other sign of emotion, her face hardening back into stone.

What anger Lorinda had suppressed, Sully let fly in his accusation. "He was just a little kid. How could you do that to him?"

"He was a child in body only. His soul was rotten."

A wave of nausea washed over Sully, and he fought it back along with all the things he wanted to say. There were other questions that needed answering first. "What about Lucky? If the women in the family aren't cursed, why kill her?"

This time, Lorinda answered. "Just because our women don't fall to possession doesn't mean they can't be touched by evil. After Artie died, I struggled to accept it, that his death was necessary to protect others. There are times Rhona has been more capable than I have been. I punished the girls after Artie's death, kept them locked in their rooms. Rhona came back to me quickly, as she always has. But not Lucienne. I could hear her, late at night, talking to her brother, begging his forgiveness that she hadn't been able to protect him. It wasn't until then I realized she had the sight.

"My church refused to help as our minister didn't believe in such things. Lucienne became more and more disturbed until, at fourteen, she tried to commit suicide. I sought the advice of a psychiatrist. Dr. Gerhardt said he would be pleased to help her, so I had her committed to Lockwood. If the doctor could keep her from seeing and hearing evil things, that was good enough for me. But then, two years later, she escaped and returned home. And she was unchanged, just as wild, her hair bright purple, lies spilling from her lips."

"She told you Gerhardt hurt her," Sully said.

"Lies," the woman said. "Lies intended to make me do as she wanted. I wanted to send her back immediately, but my husband, her stepfather, argued against it. I thought he pitied her. He didn't. My husband had been drawn in by the evil inside her, falling victim to it just as surely as any blood-born Dule male. I learned he brought her gifts—makeup, clothes, magazines—and provided her company when she was supposed to be left alone to repent. In time, I found out she'd tricked him into having her. I might never have known her true evil had I not walked in on them. He told me he'd been under a spell she'd cast."

The nausea returned full-force, threatening to expel whatever was left in Sully's stomach as the image of his biological mother's rape passed through his mind—along with it, the possibility he had been born of that act. "And you actually believed that? She was just a kid."

"He wasn't the first she opened her legs for. You're here, after all."

Sully allowed himself a moment of relief, but there wasn't much to be found. Not anymore. "Who is my father?"

"We don't know," Rhona said. "She never told us about you. We only learned about you after her death."

The older woman picked up the explanation. "Lucienne abandoned you after your birth. She meant to hide you from us. Then we received information through a boy named Brennan. Like you, like your mother, he saw evil things. He described a ghost with purple hair and a child named Sullivan staying with him at the foster home. We could think of no reason Lucienne would be there, would be hovering around a child of that name and age, save one. Lucienne had a child. And we knew you would need to be dealt with."

Sully thought back to the Blakes, to the blaze that had killed them. Would have killed him and Brennan but for Lucky. "The fire wasn't meant for the Blakes at all, was it? It was for me."

"Fire purifies the soul," Lorinda said. "You were just a child. You deserved to be saved. You still do."

"But the fire was set by a teenage girl."

"Margaret."

"Mother, no."

"It can't hurt to speak about her now." The older woman returned attention to Sully and to her explanation. "Rhona was very young when she gave birth. Much too young for us to keep the baby."

Rhona's head drooped as if it weighed too much for her neck. The gun, still in her hand and aimed in Sully's direction, had been brought to rest on the wheelchair's handle near Lorinda's shoulder. "The father was a boy from down the street. I was only thirteen. I thought I loved him."

"I put the child up for adoption," Lorinda said. "Rhona wasn't happy about it, but she learned in time it was for the best. More than a decade passed before she thought about finding the child, and she hired a private investigator. We learned the girl had turned out wild as well, had run from her adoptive parents until they were at wit's end. Margaret Parsons eventually ended up a ward of the state."

"I decided I would give her a home," Rhona said. "Margaret was just eleven, and was searching for her identity. When we met that day, it was like we'd known each other forever. It was like God had guided us to each other."

"We worked with the girl for some time," Lorinda said. "We were relieved to discover she was not touched as Lucienne and Artie had been, as my father was. As you are. In time, she found her place in the world. So we turned our attention to you."

The connection clicked. "Margaret stayed at the Blakes and met Brennan there," Sully said.

"He was smitten with her," Lorinda said. "He shared all his secrets with her, even about the things he saw. They stayed in touch after she left, would meet secretly without our knowledge. We eventually found her out and she confessed, told us about Brennan, about the things he saw. That's how we learned about Lucienne's ghost and you."

"But you couldn't have known then about the things I saw. No one knew, not even Brennan. And you still tried to kill me."

"The curse has touched every male born within the Dule line. There was no possibility you had escaped it."

"But the Blakes, and Brennan. Didn't you care about killing people who had nothing to do with this curse?"

"The Blakes might have had nothing to do with the curse, but they were no less evil," Rhona said. "We knew about the terrible things they had done to Margaret and others. If she hadn't been so pleased with the idea of starting the fire, I would have happily done it myself. And it was never our wish for Brennan to die. He didn't welcome the evil inside him. I'm still convinced we could have saved him, given more time."

"But you didn't help him, and now he's dead. He did everything you asked and you still killed him."

"You were turning him against us," Lorinda said. "His loyalties were shifting. You spoke to the darkness inside him and he was starting to pull away from us. We had no choice."

"You keep saying you had no choice, but you did. You murdered Brennan. All of you. And he wasn't evil. He recognized what he was doing, what you were asking him to do, was wrong. You realized he wanted to right the wrong, and that would ruin your plans for me and expose you and all the horrible things you've done. You didn't kill him to save him or to rid the world of this 'evil' you keep talking about. You did it to save your own asses."

The older woman leaned forward in her chair, fixing Sully in her glare. "Don't think for a moment Rhona or I have enjoyed what we've had to do. I will carry the weight of my grief to my grave. But we are fighting on the side of angels, and sometimes terrible things must be done in the name of all that is good and holy in this world. You are my blood, and I do care for you. And that is why I have to save you. Please understand this." She looked to her daughter. "Rhona, we have our answers. It's time."

The women were blocking the sole escape route, a revolver held steady in the hands of Sully's biological aunt acting as an inducement to keep him from trying to push past them. But his grandmother and his aunt had made it clear he would die here, one way or another, and it was possible death by gun would be preferable to whatever alternative they'd planned for him. Sully took a breath, preparing himself for both a rush for freedom and the feel of a bullet that would, no doubt, result.

He hadn't expected a second gun, emerging in Lorinda's hand from next to her leg. He pushed forward as a high-pitched pop sounded, followed by the sharp impact of a dart embedding itself into the flesh of his abdomen. Sully yanked it out, forcing his brain to continue its focus on escape rather than the inevitability of succumbing to the effects of what he knew to be a tranquilizer.

He fell back on years of roughhousing with his brother as he shoved past Lorinda and shouldered Rhona into the wall, the revolver clattering to the cement floor as Sully pushed through the gap into the hall. A set of stairs was visible at the end of a hall and he ran toward it. But it was as if he was in a dream, his feet moving too slowly, never reaching the stairs that appeared to be getting further and further away at the end of a long, dark tunnel. He searched for something solid, found what felt like a wall, and he tried to locate a connection to consciousness there. But the line was breaking, the tunnel growing longer and darker, the stairs becoming smaller and smaller until they disappeared in front of him entirely.

He was dimly aware of his knee colliding with something hard, and then the cool press of what had to be the floor beneath his cheek.

A voice sounded, as if calling out from the topside of a well. "Just like Lucienne. She failed, too."

"No, girl," said a second. "We all failed."

32

THREE BRIDGES HAD ONCE CONNECTED The Forks to the rest of KR. Now there was just one, the others destroyed by a combination of flood waters and, later, dynamite.

While Forks Bridge still stood, the maintenance of it left something to be desired. Since dubbed Hell's Gate, it was a crumbling ruin, passable only by truck or SUV, and then only by navigating a careful path around the potholes and cracks in the pavement.

Guarded by signs to use at one's own risk, the bridge was thankfully only a few city blocks long. It tended to feel a lot further—giving travellers a good long while to think about what it was they were about to drive into.

It was early evening, the summer sun dropping but still hanging in there as Dez's vehicle bounced across Hell's Gate.

Dez and Forbes remained silent, each locked inside his own thoughts as their apocalyptic destination loomed. Dez had come here only once since the flood, searching for a missing friend. During the brief time he'd been in The Forks, he'd had to fight through a throng of would-be robbers and narrowly avoided a carjacking.

Little had changed in The Forks since, and the few differences only made the place worse. Nature grew unchecked out of every crevice; grass and weeds filled cracks and potholes on the streets; trees obscured what the groundcover could not reach: street signs, broken power and phone lines and abandoned homes and businesses. Here and there, wildflowers had been naïve enough to spring up, as if believing they might still have the power to deliver beauty and hope to a place long since abandoned by both.

If the scenery was eerie, the faces peering from it were terrifying. Junkies were everywhere, meth use having turned many into walking zombies. Occasionally, Dez would catch sight of a person coming into view from behind a tree or the edge of a building, leaving him to wonder whether a larger group lay in wait behind, ever-prepared to surround the vehicles of the few unwary fools who dared to trespass into this world.

Dez drove past a large melee of men in bandannas, some red and some blue, the colours of men in the midst of a full-out battle for territory or whatever it was rival gangs were warring over out here. Knives glinted pink in the slowly dying sun and long metal bars swung as the two sides clashed. Dez saw more than one man on the ground, the entrails of one flopped out next to him on the pavement.

"Keep driving," Forbes said. "Just keep driving."

Dez sped past, and no one broke off to come after him, the fight for survival outweighing any desire for an operating vehicle or the property of those within. He glanced at his passenger once they were clear, finding Forbes's eyes wide and his lips parted as he drew in shallow, audible breaths.

"You all right?" Dez asked.

"Just don't stop this vehicle, you hear me?"

Dez didn't need the direction. Only the crazy or suicidal would pull a fool move like that. "I'm going to need you to direct me, here. You're still checking the map, right?"

It was clear Forbes hadn't been, as his eyes snapped back down to the screen of his smartphone. "Shit, you're going to want to turn left. We were supposed to turn two blocks back."

"Mind on the task, man," Dez said. "Leave the rest to me."

As they drove farther in, the signs of disaster were less obvious, the flood not having ravaged this part of the large island quite as badly. But the area remained just as dangerous, if not more so, given the homes were more habitable.

Ahead, a man appeared in the roadway and, as Dez continued forward, several more flanked him, fanning out across the street. Several, Dez noted, had guns.

"Shit," Forbes said. "Just go through them."

"I might hit someone."

"So you hit someone."

"Are you serious?"

"Hey, you stop or try to turn, we're dead. Just floor it. They'll move."

"Bloody hell," Dez said. The damnable thing was Forbes was right. If bullets started flying, he stood a better chance of avoiding them if he was speeding past. That said, would-be killers or not, Dez would have a hard time sleeping if he ran over someone. Saying a silent prayer, he stepped on the gas. "Get your head down and hold on."

Blaring the horn, Dez sped toward the group. The sound of three gunshots spurred him on, and he held one eye shut and squinted through the other as he neared potential impact. The group cleared a path for him at the last moment, throwing themselves onto the pavement as Dez blew past. A hail of gunfire sounded behind them but it didn't sound or feel like anything impacted.

A wild laugh erupted from his throat as the rush of narrow escape hit him. Forbes didn't sound quite so excited.

"Fucking hell. Fucking hell."

"You all right?"

Forbes stared at him. "Ask me that when we get out of this hellhole."

But the fear had left Dez, at least for the moment; he could only hope his courage would hold out once they reached their destination.

FORBES WAS STILL PROVIDING DIRECTIONS, but Dez now knew their destination without being told.

The smoke, rising from behind a row of overgrown trees and neglected homes up ahead, was all he needed. He would not easily forget the words spoken from within the frozen sneer on Lorinda's face.

They will burn. They will all burn.

"It should be just up ahead and to the right," Forbes said. "Must be one of these estates." He finally looked up from his screen. "Holy hell, it's got to be where that smoke's coming from."

Dez would have made a smart comment had his pounding pulse not been threatening to choke him, had he not known instinctively Sully would be in the middle of that.

Dez turned through an open gate and flew down the treed drive, the branches of the untrimmed elms bowing low enough to scrape at the top of the vehicle until, on the far side, they parted to reveal a large house in flames. Nearby, close enough to be clear it was meant to catch fire, was a white delivery van.

"No," Dez said. "Jesus Christ, no."

"What?" Forbes said. "You think she's in there? You think Greta's in there?"

Dez threw the van into park and jumped out, shouting directions. "Move the van! If it goes up, it'll explode!"

Fire was visible through the house's windows, the open doorway encircled by tongues of it. It was only a matter of minutes before the house was fully engulfed.

A small pond lay just to the left of the driveway, and Dez sprinted over and belly flopped in, soaking himself head to toe before racing back to the house.

Forbes's voice came from behind him. "There's no key!"

"Hotwire the damn thing!" Dez yelled back, not stopping as he ran headlong through the doorway. He thought he heard Forbes yelling at him, but he didn't care. Only one thing mattered, and he knew without a doubt it was somewhere inside this house.

The smoke wasn't heavy yet, but it was bad enough, the worst of it pillowing against the high ceilings as flames ate their way up a set of curtains in the sitting room and chewed away at the edge of an area rug.

Dez screamed his brother's name and ended in a cough, keeping low as he moved through the house.

The smoke grew heavier and the heat higher as Dez kept low. Not for not the first time in his adult life, he cursed his six and a half feet.

He called out again for Sully, this time managing just the first syllable before choking on the name. A coughing fit followed, and he moved lower still, dropping into a full crouch as he continued into a kitchen. The smoke was even worse here, black and poisonous, and the tears that formed amid coughing grew thick enough to obscure vision.

There was no sense trying to call out, no way he'd manage anything other than a squeak. He dropped to his hands and knees, pressing forward, holding his breath as he prayed for a break in this somewhere.

His eyes burned, and he gave them what relief he could, clamping them shut as he felt his way forward. He had yet to attempt another breath, and he knew without seeing there would be no oxygen left to allow it.

What was left of his logic suggested he could go back the way he came—if he could figure out which way that was—but he knew that wasn't an option. Not really. He'd come here for Sully, and he wasn't going anywhere without him. They were leaving here together, one way or another.

He was still in what he believed was the kitchen, and that was where he'd be staying, unable to find a way forward as he butted against a wall in one direction and something metallic—fridge? stove?—in another. His head swam, starved of oxygen and sense, his body acting on instinct as he drew in a partial breath that left him gasping and choking. Each cough drew in more smoke-poisoned air, and he collapsed onto his belly as unconsciousness lurked just inches away, preparing to take him down.

And then he heard a voice.

Quiet at first. Then louder. His name repeated over and over, coaxing and then ordering him forward.

"Dez. Dez! Open your eyes. Open your eyes, Dez!"

He obeyed, hot tears partially blinding him as he cracked one eyelid open. He was amazed to see the blackness had abated, a small clear bubble around him, enabling him to take in a ragged breath, to see the edge of a fridge on one side and a wall on the other. Just in front was an opening, an entrance to what looked to be a rear porch or a mud room.

And there, standing in that gap, a gentle smile on his freckled face, strawberry blond hair made darker by the water dripping from the ends, was Aiden.

33

SHE WAS THERE, hovering nearby, watching, waiting.

At some point—Sully had no memory of how or when—he had made it to his feet, and she was now standing in front of him, large, kohl-rimmed eyes staring up into his.

And for the first time, when she opened her mouth, he heard her.

Her voice was what he'd imagined it to be, soft and feminine with the ring of youth. "You're giving up, Sullivan. You need to fight. You have to live."

"Why didn't you tell me? All these years and you never told me you were my mother. Why didn't you want me to know?"

"You were afraid of me."

"Only at first. I was afraid of everything back then. If I'd known—"

"You deserved better than me, than this family."

"What are you talking about?"

"I should have gone back for you. If I had, I wouldn't have ended up here, with them. I might have lived. But I wanted you to escape the fate of my grandpa and my brother. And I wanted you to have something better than I had to give. Instead, what I gave you was pain."

"That's not true. I found a family."

"And that's why you need to hold on. Dez is coming for you. He's close."

"I want to stay with you."

"I will always be nearby, Sullivan, and I won't cross until you're beside me. But that time isn't now. You have so much more to do."

"I'm tired, Mom. I don't know how much longer I can do this."

"What about Dez? He's already broken. Losing you again would kill him."

"He'll get through it." But the words rang untrue even as he uttered them. Just a few years shy of thirty, Dez had already dealt with far too much heartbreak.

"The danger's not passed for him. Rhona's daughter is back, and she's waiting. She'll kill him. Now, listen. You need to fight. The drugs are slowing your heart but it won't stop unless you allow it. You need to wake up, Sullivan."

"You mean this is a dream?"

"It's an in-between. You need to go back. Please. I need you to live. I need you to live for me."

She was weeping, black eye makeup streaking her cheeks, and Sully realized he was seeing the Purple Girl free of blood.

He reached out for her, expecting to find nothing more substantive than the usual combination of energy, consciousness and air. What he found instead was a solid shoulder in his gentle grasp, the feel of flesh and bone beneath his touch. He choked on a sob as he folded the slight teen into an embrace that might have been too tight had she been fully alive to feel it. He felt her arms around him, squeezing back just as hard.

She pulled away first, that familiar urgency in her eyes. "Go, Sullivan. You need to go. Now."

"What about you? You can't stay on this side. If I find your mother and sister, if I can bring them to justice, then—"

"No. They can't know you're still alive. They'll come back for you. They won't stop, not ever. I will find them, and I'll watch them. If you see me again, you'll know they're close by, and you should take precautions."

"I need you to tell me how to help you."

"You've already helped me. I've found my peace in you."

Sully gave her one last hug, closing his eyes tight and committing the feeling to memory, praying it would still be there when he returned to the dark reality of full consciousness. "I love you, Mom."

"I love you, too. I always will."

———

SULLY OPENED HIS EYES. The image and the feel of Lucky was gone, replaced by darkness and the unsettling feeling of being upside down. There was a solid pressure against his abdomen and the jarring feeling of movement as awareness settled in more fully, and he became aware he was slung over someone's shoulder.

He drew in a partial breath and started coughing immediately as smoke invaded his throat.

"Hang on, Sull. We're almost out. Don't you give up on me, buddy, you hear me?"

The voice, low and gravelly with smoke inhalation and, quite possibly, emotion, was the sound of safety, and Sully nodded his agreement before realizing Dez wouldn't see it.

"I hear you," Sully managed before breaking into another coughing fit. In the midst of it, he heard what he recognized as one of Dez's ridiculous laughs of relief. The sound of his brother's broken tension eased Sully's as well and, by the time he felt the cool outside air against his face, he was no longer struggling to breathe.

Or maybe it had something to do with Aiden, standing as he was in the back doorway of the house, an aura-sized bubble around him untarnished by smoke and flame.

Sully had been in the dark so long, the low sun was to his

vision what the heat and smoke had been to his throat. He squeezed his eyes shut against it as he was first righted and then laid down in what felt like a layer of long grass. Beside him, he heard the heavy sound of Dez's body impacting against ground and a series of heaving, gasping breaths punctuated with periodic coughs.

Sully wrenched open one eye and blinked away the tears created by smoke, heat and the outside light. He turned his head, taking in the sight of Dez's smoke-smudged face next to him, face twisted in a grimace as he rubbed at his chest.

"You okay, D?"

Dez's response began as it so often did when they survived one of their mutual scrapes: with a wide grin and a chuckle. He turned his head, meeting Sully's gaze with red, watery eyes.

"Am now. You?"

Sully's smile was a natural response to his brother's. "Am now."

They rested back in the thigh-high, wild grass as they worked on drawing in fresh oxygen, breathing becoming less laboured and riddled with hacking coughs. Sully lifted himself just enough to look back to the door they'd left by. Aiden was gone, replaced by billows of black smoke and hungry flame shooting up the walls and through the roof. Any longer in there, Aiden's protection or not, and neither of them would be lying here breathing.

A moment of panic seized Sully and, lying back, he felt around inside his jacket until his fingers closed over what he'd sought: the notebook.

"Think you can walk?" Dez asked, voice no less croaky than it had been on the basement stairs. "We need to get out of here."

Sully wasn't sure, head still spinning under the influence of tranquilizer and smoke, but he was willing to give it a go, bearing in mind his mother's warning. Margaret was returning, and she'd go through Dez to get to Sully.

He was about to nod yes when he froze under the sound of an

approaching voice. It belonged to a man, not a woman, and he was addressing someone named Greta, not Margaret.

"Greta. Greta, wait. I need you to talk to me. Please."

"That's just Raynor and his wife," Dez said. "Stay down. I don't want them to see you if there's any way to avoid it."

By the time the warning bell sounded in Sully's brain, it was too late to stop Dez from climbing shakily to his feet. "Dez, wait. Her name's not Greta. It's—"

The woman's voice drowned out his whispered warning. And Dez had taken a few steps forward, distancing himself from his still-concealed brother.

"Dez," she said. "What are you doing here?" To Sully, she didn't sound overly surprised, which made perfect sense since, given her connection with Brennan, she'd no doubt aided in Dez's premature burial the other night.

"I was going to ask you the same thing."

There was a short pause in the conversation, ended by a stunned-sounding Forbes.

"Greta, what are you doing?"

The warmth from the house fire was stolen from Sully at Dez's words. "Put the gun down, Greta."

"Where is he?" she asked. "Where's Sullivan?"

"I don't know what you're talking about."

"Sullivan who?" Forbes asked. "Sullivan Gray? Greta, he died two years ago."

"No," she said. "He's here, and he's alive. Even in a place like The Forks, nothing stays hidden forever." She spoke more loudly, as if to ensure Sully would hear should he be on the opposite end of the property. "Come out, Sullivan. Come out or the next time you see Dez, he'll be one of your ghosts."

Dez spoke in a mumble through largely closed lips, quiet so only his brother would hear. "Sully, no."

But the time for concealment was over, Dez's life worth far more than any threat Sully would face by revealing himself. He forced himself to his feet as Dez, in front of him and just to the right, heaved a pained sigh.

"Damn it, Sull."

Forbes and Greta stood to the north side of the house, Rhona's revolver in Greta's hand levelled unwaveringly at Dez. And, unfortunately for him, his height and muscle made him a significant target.

Forbes, staring at Sully through saucer-round eyes, had yet to close his mouth. He fumbled through a few attempts at speech until he finally came up with something he could pronounce. "Jesus Christ."

Dez spoke through a forced grin, an effort at de-escalation. "I see the resemblance but, no, wrong guy."

Forbes looked to be fighting to turn his gaze to the other sight which probably seemed just as impossible as Sully's return from the dead: his estranged wife aiming a shaking gun at the brothers. While it was clear she was no gun expert, that probably made the situation worse given the unpredictable tremble of her finger on the trigger. Add to that the fact she looked to be tweaking out on one or more substances, and the situation was set to go from bad to worse at a moment's notice.

"Greta, come on, babe. Someone's going to get hurt."

She giggled, the sound wild rather than innocent. "Really, Forbes?"

"What are you on this time?"

"That's just your trouble, baby. You always want to explain me away. It was easier to say it was drugs or mental illness than to just accept me the way I am."

"But this isn't you. You're not a killer."

She laughed again, higher pitched this time and containing even less humour. "You think so? Look me up. You'll find out a few things about me you wouldn't believe."

"I have looked you up," Forbes said. "Your past is clean."

"You never wondered why there was no trace of me before I

was sixteen? That you never saw a birth certificate, anything with my name on it before then?"

Forbes stumbled over his words, so Greta helped out. Her voice was growing louder, her gun hand waving wildly between Dez and Sully as she vented her anger at her estranged husband. "It didn't bother you, did it? Because you'd rather I was the perfect little angel you fell in love with than have to face the truth about me. Let me tell it to you now. Or better yet, let Sullivan. Go on, Sullivan. Tell Forbes a story. Make it a good one."

Sully dragged his eyes from the gun and looked to Forbes. "Her real name is Margaret Dule, daughter of Rhona Dule." He risked a glance at Dez, whose eyes remained fixed on Greta. "Rhona's the one you've been dealing with, Dez. Not Lucky. Rhona was keeping an eye on you, making sure you weren't getting too close while they satisfied themselves I was Lucky's son and that I shared the one trait with her. Once they had their proof, their plan was to kill me."

"I was starting to come around to that," Dez said.

Sully returned his attention to Forbes, providing the history Rhona and Lorinda had shared. At the end, Greta provided her confirmation.

"I didn't get far after the fire at the Blakes. I was charged with three counts of murder and two of attempted murder, so I faked insanity. Any decent shrink probably would have seen right through me. But you know better than most, don't you, Sullivan? Dr. Gerhardt is no decent shrink. After two years in Lockwood, I wished I'd just pled to my charges in court and taken a youth custody sentence."

"He knew you were Lucky's niece, didn't he?" Sully asked.

"My legal last name was Parsons, due to the adoption. But I blabbed the truth to him eventually, about who I was. She was all that freak talked about. Lucky this, Lucky that. Lucky, Lucky, Lucky. He wanted to find her. Said she needed his help. If only he knew."

"Knew what?" Dez asked.

"Lucky was murdered shortly after she escaped Lockwood," Sully said. "I think Rhona did it in the end, but there's probably no way to know for sure. I guess it doesn't matter. They were all in it together, anyway." He focused back on Greta. "How did you get out?"

"Lockwood? Simple. I lied. Told him I could find Lucky for him. It was the one lie he was willing to believe."

"What did he want with her?"

"People said she was trying to help him find his kid. Everyone knew the story, how the little boy was kidnapped from his back-yard when he was five or six. But I think it was more than that. I think he convinced himself he loved Lucky. And it wasn't just her he wanted. It was her child. He wanted you." Greta's explanation stunned Sully into silence, providing her the opportunity for a quick giggle. "Funny, really. Because he had you. You were right there, under his nose a few years ago. And he didn't even know it."

"But you did," Dez said. "And you didn't tell him. Why?" But his brother's attention was on him, and he felt a pulse of fear in his gut.

"I know what my mother and grandmother think of him, what they believe about his supposed curse. But I think the whole thing's a crock of shit. Sullivan and me, we fought the same war. We survived the Blakes, other hellhole foster homes, group homes, Lockwood." She cocked her head toward him. "You're not my enemy, Sullivan. I've got nothing against you."

Dez snorted. "Which explains why you've tried to kill him twice."

"I didn't set the fire at the Blakes' because of him. All I wanted was to get back at the foster family from hell. My mom and grandma told me that's why I was going to do it, to right a wrong from my past. They told me they'd make sure no one but the Blakes were inside. The first time I heard any different was from the cops after I was picked up. As far as today, I thought Sullivan was already dead when I started the fire. My mom said she'd given him a lethal dose of azaperone. They asked me to destroy the evidence."

"Hold on," Dez said. "Sully was seven when you killed the Blakes under orders from your family. But no one came after him again until now? Why? Why now?"

"They talked about it. They lost track of him for a few years after the fire. When they found out where he was, they learned his new foster father was a high-ranking cop, and you became one later yourself. It was too risky, so they decided to bide their time, wait for an opportunity. Then your father died, and Sullivan turned up at Lockwood a couple years ago. The name Sullivan Gray meant nothing to Gerhardt. I didn't tell anyone about him— not Gerhardt and not my family. I knew they'd all want to know. But I'd already gotten what I needed out of life: I got my justice against the Blakes.

"When we heard he'd died following his escape, I let my mother and grandmother enjoy the relief. But Brennan and I, we learned the truth. We saw Sullivan one day when we were in The Forks, but lost sight of him before we could find out anything more. I planned to keep it to myself, but Brennan told my mother in exchange for cash for a fix. My mother figured he'd come if you were in danger or died. As usual, Brennan and I were supposed to do it, take Sullivan once he tried to dig you out of that grave. But he had a big dog with him, so we had to find another way."

"And Brennan?" Dez asked. "It was you, wasn't it? You put on scrubs and just walked in there, right past the constable on duty. And Brennan didn't say anything because he trusted you. By the time he realized you were giving him something other than what the two of you were hooked on, it was too late. Why'd you kill him?"

"I wasn't planning to. I wanted him to just walk away. But something had changed in him. He kept talking about Lucienne, saying she'd never leave him alone until he helped Sullivan. He was going to tell. If I left him like that, his next conversation would have been with that cop. I may not agree with everything my family thinks or does, but they're still my family. I needed to protect them, and I needed to protect myself. And Brennan was no angel. He was out of his mind half the time, damn near killed me not so long ago. But get one thing straight. I never wanted to kill him, and I never wanted to kill Sullivan. The Blakes, yes, and if I had the chance, I'd take Gerhardt too."

"So what are you doing volunteering there?" Dez asked. "If you changed your name to escape the place, why go back?"

"That's not why I changed it. You try living with that past hanging over your head. I wanted a fresh start, and my mother helped me get it. I still kept a part of my name, though. I wanted that much. As for volunteering, my grandmother was a patient there—and, yes, her illness is legitimate. She's always been a little crazy, but she's lost whatever was left of her mind. Anyway, what better way to learn about the enemy than to work alongside him? Gerhardt is next on my list, baby. I'm going to burn the place down, him inside."

Forbes had reached the end of his rope, pain and anger written all over him. "Greta, you stop this right now, you hear me?"

"There's a lot of stuff I gotta stop," she said. And without warning, she spun, redirecting her aim at him. "Maybe I should start with you."

Dez was already moving in, taking advantage of the situation to rush her. Sully was a step or two behind, wanting to back up his brother, but they both stopped short at a shouted command from somewhere nearby.

"Drop the gun! Now!"

Sully would know that voice anywhere; it would have put a smile on his face were it not for the lingering threat. Greta shifted her attention again, this time toward Eva who was standing, gun drawn, behind a curtain of smoke at the house's edge.

Dez was still a couple steps away when Forbes, taking advantage of the distraction, tackled his estranged spouse from the side. The impact—Sully hoped it was the impact—caused the gun to fire, the shot earsplittingly loud in this all-but-abandoned part of town.

Greta wasn't a large woman but, tweaking out as she was, she had the fight in her of three people. But Dez was there now, helping Forbes restrain the woman as Eva, uniformed and on-duty, rushed forward with a set of handcuffs from her duty belt.

Dez managed to wrest the revolver away from Greta, and he tossed it to the side before grinning widely at Eva. "You're a superhero, you know that?"

Eva graced him with a smile. "Blame Forbes. He called in a panic, said you'd just run into a burning house, and he could use a little backup. Asked me not to call it in. I'd more or less stopped listening at the part involving you and the burning house." She launched into the reading of Greta's rights as she finished cuffing the struggling and wailing woman. But even as she was finishing with that, Eva's eyes were darting repeatedly to Sully.

"We need to discuss this," Forbes said, his face reading desperation in a way rivalled only by Greta's.

"In a minute," Eva said. She circled the small group on the ground until she was standing in front of Sully. There, she unleashed the anticipated but flinch-inducing slap to his face.

"Eva, honey?" Dez said. "Violence isn't the answer, remember?"

"Shut up, Dez."

"It's okay," Sully said. "I had it coming."

"Damn right," Eva said. "Do you have any idea what you've put all of us through? Do you?"

Eva wasn't a crier, but there were tears rimming her lower lash line as she glared at him with a heat rivalled only by the fire raging behind her.

"I know. I'm so sorry. More than you realize. But you need to know it killed me too."

Eva shook her head, plenty of anger lingering in the set of her jaw and the narrowing of her eyes. But she hugged him anyway, arms encasing him like a vice.

Greta had quieted for the most part, sobbing having tapered into gentler sniffling and weeping, allowing Forbes a chance for his question to be heard.

"Does someone want to tell me what the hell is going on?"

Dez spoke through a grin. "Once I've got a handle on it myself, I'll fill you in. You hurt?"

"I'm fine," Forbes said. "But we need to discuss this. All of this. I mean, that is your brother, right? Your dead brother?"

"And as far as everyone beyond us knows, he needs to stay that way," Dez said. "As of now, Rhona and Lorinda believe Sully's dead, and so does Gerhardt. As long as Greta keeps quiet, Sully's safe."

"You know I can't do that," Forbes said. "I can't just pretend something like that."

"Come on, man—"

"Not unless you can do something for Greta. Look at her. She's a mess. Let me take her somewhere, get her off whatever it is she's on. Then let me help her disappear."

"She killed a man, Forbes," Eva said. "And what's more, it was premeditated."

"Carried out by a young woman messed up on drugs and brainwashed by her family. And let's not forget the motive. The second Major Crimes starts pulling the case apart, Sullivan's out in the open."

Dez raised an eyebrow. "So, what, you're saying we give you Greta and keep quiet about her, you'll keep your mouth shut about Sully?"

"That's what I'm saying."

"And Greta? How do we know she won't say anything?"

"I'm facing a life sentence, you moron," she said. "And I already told you, I don't give a damn about my family's issues with Sullivan. He's all yours."

Sully had known plenty of people with addictions, knew Greta wasn't agreeing to go with Forbes to get clean; all she wanted was the first opportunity to escape so she could go back to her old world, her old ways. Maybe that included her family, maybe it didn't. Right now, it didn't matter all that much. The alternative wasn't good for anyone.

Dez's next comment was directed at the person most likely to be the holdout, the idea of letting a killer walk free running contrary to everything Eva Braddock held dear. "If Sully's exposed, Gerhardt's going to want him back."

In the end, she was family first—just another piece of Sully's old life that hadn't changed in the two years he'd been away.

"Get her out of here, Forbes," Eva said. "And if I ever hear Sully's name so much as breathed by anyone, I'll know you or Greta reneged on this. And we'll all go down together. You get me?"

Forbes nodded, the relief clear. "You've got a deal."

"Don't use that word. Just go."

Forbes helped Greta to her feet and released her from the handcuffs, handing them back to Eva. Then, to Greta's evident chagrin, he slapped his own on her.

"Just until you're in the clear," he said.

Forbes gave Eva, Dez and Sully a final look as if assuring himself he was safe. Then he led Greta away.

34

Dᴇᴢ ᴀɴᴅ Sᴜʟʟʏ made it as far as the edge of the Riverview neighbourhood when Eva called from the police cruiser immediately in
front of Dez's SUV.

"Forbes just called from the van," she said. "Greta contacted
her mother. She told Rhona that Sully didn't make it out of the fire
and that you're coming after them, Dez. Rhona and Lorinda are
leaving town. Sounds like they'll be looking to lie low for a
while."

Dez looked to his passenger, wanting to pass along the good
news. But Sully was still asleep, having passed out within minutes
of finding himself safe within Dez's SUV.

"And Greta?"

"Forbes is taking a leave of absence from work. They're
heading somewhere so he can try to help her kick whatever she's
on. I guess Rhona asked her to join them, but Greta said she
wanted some space for a while. There wasn't much argument."

"Are we sure that's safe, leaving Greta with Forbes? There's
still the possibility he's the one who attacked her prior to all this
starting."

"Believe me, I asked about that. I could hear her scoffing in the
background. It was Brennan, not Forbes. Greta and Brennan

started using meth a few months back. They'd been on a binge and had been up four or five days straight. Forbes had been trying to find Greta, and Brennan—paranoid as he was—got jealous. You know what happened after that. He beat her up pretty bad, but she didn't want to get him in trouble, possibly land him back in Lockwood. She just disappeared from his life for a while, but returned as soon as she and her warped little family needed him."

"And you're sure Rhona and Lorinda left town? I want to get Sully back to my place, but I don't want to go there if they're still around somewhere, watching."

"Shouldn't he be in a hospital?"

Dez gave it a couple of seconds, long enough for Eva to realize the problem with that suggestion.

"Right," she said. "No hospitals for him anymore. You know, you could bring him back to our place."

Dez caught on the word "our," but then recognized Eva could simply be talking about herself and Kayleigh. "I don't think it's a good idea for Kayleigh to know about this just yet."

"I can't lie to her, Dez. Neither can you."

"We wouldn't be lying if she never asked."

"Well, I can't keep it from her. She adores Sully. She'd never forgive any of us if we didn't tell her."

"How can we be sure she won't tell anyone else?" Dez said. "Kids talk, most times without thinking."

"Well, you know our kid," Eva said. "She's no gossip. And despite the fact she takes after you, she's pretty mature for her age. If we tell her Sully will be in danger if anyone finds out about him, she won't tell. You know that as well as I do."

In all honesty, he didn't. The saddest part about the past couple of years was that his time with Kayleigh had become so limited. He'd missed so much. And while he knew his daughter, he wasn't sure sometimes if the Kayleigh he knew was the person she was now or the girl she had been when his life fell out from under him. The fact was, Eva knew their little girl now far better than Dez did. He didn't begrudge Eva that time or that joy, but he hated the fact he hadn't been there to share in it.

"Dez? You okay?"

"Yeah. Sorry. Just thinking. You're probably right. I'll bring him by sometime soon. But I need to keep him with me for now, all right? I don't think it's a good idea for him to be there, especially if I'm not nearby."

"Actually, I'd meant for you to come home too."

The offer had Dez grinning ear to ear, his brain on a high-speed train through a future he was suddenly envisioning in which this eggshell-thin reconciliation became rock solid. He saw poker nights with his buddies in the garage, while Eva had the girls over for wine and television, trick or treating with Kayleigh, lazy Sunday mornings with Eva in bed or on the back deck with a coffee as she chattered on about her plans for the yard.

Dez forced himself to apply the mental brakes. As much as he'd love to be back there, to work on convincing his wife he had his shit back together and that his stay should be permanent, now wasn't the time. There were questions about Sully Dez needed to address first, namely how big and widespread the danger to him was. Until he could ascertain that, Dez couldn't risk the rest of his family.

"I wish I could come home. There's nothing in the world I want more. But it's too risky, Eva. You and me, we can handle it. But until I've got a better grasp on what Sully's up against here, we can't risk exposing Kayleigh any more than she already is. I'll still bring Sully by to see her, but I need to take him back to my apartment with me after. Or else we'll find somewhere else to hole up for a bit. But I really think we need to play this safe for now."

He was met with silence on the other end, and Dez gave Eva the time she needed to recognize what he'd said as indisputable truth. And then, at last, she spoke one of her own.

"I miss you. I miss our little family."

"I do too. You know that."

"Promise me you'll be careful, that you'll keep your head on straight. And for God's sake, Dez, promise me you'll stop drinking with your park buddies."

"I can do that."

"Good. Take care of Sully, but let him take care of you too, okay?"

"I will, babe. Thanks."

"Don't call me babe, Snowman."

———

PAX WAS a large black streak of fur charging out of Miss Crichton's apartment, stopping only once he reached Sully. As the dog whined and danced around his human's legs, tail wagging hard enough to take out a small child, Dez approached his neighbour.

"Hope no one else is at home to catch that display," Dez said. "I wouldn't want to get you in trouble."

But Miss Crichton wasn't focused on the elated dog; her eyes were on Sully.

"Is that Sullivan?"

"He usually goes by Sully." Then to his brother, "Hey, Sull? You wanna come here a minute? There's someone you should meet."

Sully had been kneeling, letting Pax treat his face like an ice cream cone. Now he walked over, gracing the woman with a soft smile. "Sorry. Wish I could've cleaned up a bit first. My brother told me about you, about what you did for my mother and me. I don't know how to thank you."

Miss Crichton's age frequently set her eyes to watering, but Dez suspected there was more to the tears this time as she closed the distance and wrapped her arms around Sully. Her words were partially muffled by his jacket. "I'm so sorry I couldn't save her."

"Don't be sorry. If it wasn't for you, she would have died in that place."

Miss Crichton stepped away, sniffling and wiping her tears away with her fingers. "She died anyway."

"But not because of anything you did or didn't do," Sully said. "She thought she'd be safe going home, that no matter what they thought of her, they wouldn't turn her away when she really needed them. She was wrong."

"I'm so sorry for what she went through, for what you've been through. It's not fair."

"Dez told me about Nate, too, but he didn't know what happened to him."

"He passed away a number of years ago. Natural causes. Died in his sleep, lucky man."

"I wish I could have met him."

"He would have liked that. You know, I haven't felt at peace since that night. I've always wondered about you, hoped you'd ended up all right somewhere. I'm so glad you found Dez and his family."

"Me too," Sully said. "Listen, I hate to ask it like this, but there really isn't a good way. You worked at Lockwood when my mother was there. Do you have any idea who my father was?"

Dez's heart thudded against his chest wall as he stood slightly behind Sully, wide eyes seeking out Miss Crichton's as he shook his head from side to side. Thankfully, she looked over, caught the message and its meaning.

"I'm sorry," she said. "No, I don't. I wish I could help you."

Sully dipped his head, shoulders drooping. "Thanks anyway. And thank you for taking care of Pax."

"My pleasure. He's a joy."

That drew a laugh from Sully. "I don't think anyone's ever called him that before. He hasn't liked most people he's met."

"He likes us well enough," Miss Crichton said, shifting a pointed finger back and forth between herself and Dez.

"I guess that shouldn't surprise me," Sully said. "He likes good people. I guess it's just that I haven't had a lot of those in my life the past couple years."

"You've got them now," Dez said, thumping Sully on the back. He turned to Miss Crichton. "Listen, the danger's not passed, it's just in remission. We're gonna need you to keep this to yourself, okay?"

Miss Crichton smiled conspiratorially. "I'm as silent as the grave."

Sully shifted his gaze from her to Dez, a raised eyebrow and a grin lightening his features. "Then we're in real trouble."

DEZ AND SULLY took turns showering and changing, then spent a few minutes comparing injuries—another brotherly pastime Dez had missed.

Once he'd satisfied himself Sully wasn't seriously hurt and that he'd come through being drugged without any lingering or dangerous side effects, he left Sully and Pax at Miss Crichton's while he headed to the hospital.

Lachlan looked better than he had the night before and, although dopy, he was at least conscious.

"Braddock," he said. "They let you in, I see."

"I'm a likeable guy."

"As you know, I love to argue but, if you take after your old man, there's not much I can say to the contrary." He lowered his voice. "So, what happened? You find what you need?"

"I found everything I need." Dez pulled up a chair and spent the next ten minutes providing an explanation, and a complete one at that. There was no point holding back. Lachlan already suspected Sully was alive and, if Dez didn't confirm it, Lachlan would devote at least a few minutes of every hour of the rest of his life to proving this theory.

When the wrap-up was finished, Lachlan was so quiet Dez thought he'd passed out with his eyes open. Finally, he spoke.

"You're wondering how I let Luc … Rhona, I mean, get the best of me on this. How I let her pull the wool over my eyes."

Dez shrugged, not wanting to take the risk of confirming that out loud.

Lachlan didn't need prodding. "If you want to know the truth, I guess I was thinking with my downstairs brain where she was concerned. A divorced man misses certain things, and she was a beautiful, warm, interested body. After that first night, I probably would have believed her if she told me she was the heir to the Romanov dynasty. Interesting she didn't try the same thing with you."

"I guess she could tell it wouldn't have worked. I've pretty much accepted I wear my heart on my sleeve, and it only ever beats for one woman."

"You're a romantic fool, Braddock. But between the two of us, it turns out I was the bigger one. You did some good work here, especially since I kept things pretty cryptic and damn near buggered it up completely."

"Thanks. But Eva helped."

"Even so. Listen, they tell me I'm not going to be fully functional for a few months. I figure I can do it in two."

"Come on. If the doctors want you to—"

"Shut up. What I'm trying to say is that I'm going to need some help around the office for a while. I'm still just a one-man show there, and I don't want to risk losing my business if I'm laid up. If clients come calling, I want to be able to take them on. Now, I know you're unemployed—"

"How do you know …? Never mind."

"Yeah. I'm like God. I know everything. So, what do you say? You want the job or are you enjoying the company on the unemployment line?"

Dez grinned. "Do I have time to consider?"

"Screw you."

"Damn right, I want the job. When do I start?"

"How about now? You can start by sneaking me the hell out of here."

LACHLAN STAYED WHERE HE WAS, and Dez went home, finding Sully crashed out on the pullout, Pax next to him.

Dez guessed his brother hadn't gotten a lot of sleep—at least none that wasn't drug-induced—over the past couple of days, so he was inclined to let Sully rest.

Only it seemed he wasn't really sleeping.

"Something you're not telling me," Sully mumbled.

"What?" Dez's mind turned immediately to Gerhardt and his true relationship to Sully. Dez had wanted to hold onto that information, at least for now, until he had satisfied himself his brother was well enough to process it. Sully was strong, one of the strongest people Dez knew. But he was fragile too. And two years had passed, after all. Two years about which Dez knew nothing at all.

Sully didn't look at Dez but sighed out one word, a question called out into the semi-dark of the apartment. "Mom?"

Dez breathed out his own sigh. His brother talked in his sleep sometimes, and Dez had never been so relieved to hear it.

Sully had settled himself into his old spot next to the wall, leaving a space for Dez. Once he'd shooed Pax out of it, Dez settled in and pulled his grandmother's quilt over his legs. He closed his eyes, then thought better of it, turning to Pax on the area rug next to him.

"If this jerk so much as gets up to take a leak, you'd damn well better let me know."

Pax's mouth dropped open and his tongue protruded to the left as his tail gave two solid thumps against the floor.

"I'll try to take that as a yes." Dez turned back over and eyed Sully one last time before closing his eyes to await a sleep that didn't feel too far away. For the moment, his world was turning in the right direction, and that was a welcome and unexpected change.

He thought better of things, reached out and closed a hand over Sully's wrist. If his brother tried to get up in the night, Dez would know.

He was surprised by the quietly spoken reassurance from next to him. "I'm not going anywhere, Dez. I promise."

"I've heard that before."

"I mean it. You're going to need my help for Aiden."

The mention of his brother's name at the end of a long and emotionally draining day put a lump in Dez's throat, particularly since it had been spoken by his other brother, the one he'd succeeded in saving. And right now, in this moment anyway, that was enough.

"You okay, D?"

Dez smiled into the darkness, certain his brother would hear it in his voice. "Yeah, Sull. I am now."

AFTERWORD

Thanks so much for reading! I am continuing to work on the next Sullivan Gray books, and would be pleased to keep you updated on future projects and release dates if you would like to join my mailing list. As an adding bonus, a growing anthology of short stories, entitled *Haunted: The Ghosts of Sullivan Gray*, is available as a gift to subscribers. Visit my website at hpbayne.com to sign up.

The books in *The Sullivan Gray Series* can be read as stand-alones to some extent, each with a plot that wraps itself up by book's end. But there is a deeper plot that threads throughout the series so, for that reason, I always suggest the books are best read in the following order:

Black Candle

Harbinger

The Dule Tree

Crawl

Hollow Road

Second Son

Spirit Caller

As always, my deepest thanks to my family and friends for their undying support. You have not only made this possible for me, you have made it fun.

My editor Hannah Sullivan is a godsend, a wizard with words whose sharp eyes pick out both typos and plot holes. She consistently helps make my books all they can be (plus she's a lovely person).

Thanks, too, to my cover designer Fiona Jayde, who always manages to capture the essence of the book, turning it into something cool and eye-catching.

A huge thanks to my fantastic team of advance readers (including you, Mom!). You guys always manage to catch the typos I've missed in my edits, and you provide me with incredible feedback to boot. Your assistance is absolutely invaluable to me!

And to all of my readers and subscribers: your encouraging words have helped spur me on, and make me want to drag my butt out of bed every morning to keep writing—even on the days when I'd love to just sleep in! Without you and your support, I very much doubt I would have continued to publish this series, so know that it means the world to me.

ABOUT THE AUTHOR

Fascinated by ghost stories and crime fiction, H.P. has been writing both for well over two decades, drawing on more than fifteen years in a career in a criminal justice setting. Raised on a farm on the Canadian Prairies, H.P. enjoys reading, portrait drawing, travel and spending time with family and friends.

For more information, visit H.P.'s website at hpbayne.com.

Made in the USA
Monee, IL
01 July 2021